THE SYNNER

WEAVINGS OF FATE

BOOK ONE OF THE SYNNER SAGA

SECOND EDITION

NOOBURAI

PUBLISHED BY DRAFT2DIGITAL

ALSO BY NOOBURAI

Creating *The Synner* universe, writing it out, editing, and self-publishing it for the world to see was once a distant dream, but know that it's here, I know that I wouldn't have made it here without a few people:

First and foremost: Mom. At the time of writing this, it's been *three and a half* years since you left the Realm, and while I know that death is not the end of all things, I can only hope to hold my head up high, knowing I've done you proud.

Second: My siblings. If it weren't for their support, encouragement, and presence during my childhood, I don't think I would have been able to accurately portray a sense of *family* that these characters have.

So, thanks for that, assholes. I love you all.

Third: Everyone else who's either read it, supported it, commented, or given their honest feedback. This kind of stuff has certainly helped me grow as an author, and we all know that a good author doesn't evolve or grow when placed inside of a bubble. Thank you.

Finally: The haters. I feed off your tears, jealousy, and whatever else you decide to throw at me, and will continue to stand by what I've been saying from the start:

Git gud... *fuckers.*

PREFACE

The Synner Saga initially began as a passion project born from my deep love for immersive storytelling. With *heavy* inspiration from series such as *The Witcher, Lord of the Rings, The Beginning After the End*, and *The Name of the Wind*, it grew, evolved, and over time, became a world that's very near and dear to my heart.

With that said, I must note that this *is* the second edition of this book. When I first published it in 2024, I found that there were a lot of mistakes and formatting errors I'd made, and while I apologize for those, they've taught me valuable lessons about producing content and having an increasingly scrutinous eye for detail.

Keep in mind that there are a total of *six books* in this series that are *planned*. That doesn't mean that there isn't room for one or two more, but I'll let you do what you will with that information.

I hope you enjoy the world I've built here, and look forward to hearing from anyone who reads it.

Sincerely,

Nooburai

DISCLAIMER

Many of the topics, verbal descriptions, and uses of language are NOT appropriate for children. If you have to ask whether your child should read this, the answer is *no*. In all honesty, if you've made it this far in the series, I shouldn't even have to tell you that, but here I am, beating a dead horse for the sake of those who haven't gotten that through their heads yet.

Seriously, do NOT let your children read this, unless you're one of those parents who doesn't give the slightest turtle shit. Just saying. That said, any and all characters are merely created to serve a purpose, and are not intended to depict my personal views or feelings toward anything that could be (somehow, probably through *extreme* extrapolation) connected to the real world. Again, this is a *fantasy series,* meaning any similarities to real people, living or otherwise, is purely coincidental.

CONTENTS

PROLOGUE
THE FIRST SWING

"Gather around!" I heard the Master call out to us.

It was my first day of training at my new home in Codrean. It had only been a few days since I left my old home in Kinth behind. I couldn't tell which direction we had gone from there, as it took us the better part of a week to arrive at the fortress.

The sun had barely risen over the distant peaks of the Rhydian Mountains, and even though it had been raining the past few days, the warm, summer air felt more welcoming than I had originally expected it to.

I distinctly remember the awkwardness of the previous night; walking into a cold, stone room with two other boys, Batch and Edryd, already having settled in. I'd not said much that evening, since I was too shy and still getting used to my surroundings, but the following day, I was immediately paired up with them and found myself mimicking their pose as we lined up in front of the Master.

"Everyone, I'd like to introduce you to the latest addition to the New Bloods, Thoma Fayren from Kinth. It's his first day, so I expect you all to help him where he needs it, and make sure he doesn't hurt himself; is that understood?" he asked. "Yes, Master," our group of fourteen, me included, responded in unison.

"Good. Thoma, you will be training with Batch and Edryd today. They have been here a little longer than you have, but not so much to where the difference in skill will be too great. Right now, I just want you to keep up with them as best you can," he said plainly.

It sounded like there's more to it than just that, I thought.

"Yes, Master," I responded with a bow. I had noticed some of the others doing the same when we arrived the day prior, so I figured it was probably a custom they had. He smiled, and nodded his head. "Very well. Go line up with the others. We're going to start off with a short run today," he said, gesturing to a dirt trail that led off somewhere into the forest surrounding the Northern side of the fortress.

"Come on, we don't want to be late," Edryd said, pointing his upturned nose in the general direction of the trail. "A-alright," I said, still feeling a little nervous about having to interact with people on a much more regular basis. "It's not that bad, we promise. It just looks harder than it is," Batch said, patting me on the shoulder.

Both Ed and Batch, the former with dark brown hair and eyes, and the latter with blonde hair and blue eyes, couldn't have been more different in their personalities, as I found out over the course of the day. Batch was a little slow to learn new things, while Ed constantly over-thought them. Nevertheless, they were instrumental in my early days there at Codrean.

During the run that morning, I quickly discovered that I was *not* in good physical condition. Sure, I had played a lot outside when I was still in Kinth, but ever since my father had taken me to that old bastard in a cottage, my energy levels had simply not been the same.

"Come on, Thoma," Batch said, encouragingly. "Breathe in time with your steps, three counts in; three counts out," he said, briefly and promptly demonstrating what he meant. I followed his advice, and while it helped for a little while, it didn't change the fact that I was still struggling to keep pace.

"Hey, are you alright?" Ed asked, slowing his own pace to match mine. "Yeah, I'm fine. First day and all," I said dismissively through battered breath. I felt something aching in my chest, but it wasn't my lungs, that much I knew.

Not much else to do but try to keep up, I guess, I thought, watching their pace slowly pick back up.

I did what I could to keep up, but over the course of the league-long run, or so I was told the distance was, I had come in last place. As I ran through the large, wooden gate, I was greeted by my two training partners, who were already grabbing their training swords from the rack. As soon as I crossed the threshold of the gate, I doubled over and lost what little was in my stomach.

"Not bad for your first day," Batch said, patting me on the shoulder comfortingly. "I thought you were going to pass out for a second, there," Ed chimed in. Even though I knew these two for all of a night and that part of the morning, I already felt much more comfortable knowing they were going to treat me like an actual person. "Thanks, guys. I'll try to do better in the future," I said, wiping my mouth off.

"You'd better," I heard a familiar voice come from a short distance to my left. I looked up to see a familiar face. His raven-black hair was about as long as mine was at the time, and combed over to the side. His green eyes were a few shades lighter than my own, but in reality, he was just like a five-year-older version of me.

"Bernar!" I said, rushing over to him, and giving him a hug. "It's been a while, little brother. I heard you were coming, but I didn't expect to see you training so soon," he said, putting a hand on my shoulder. "I didn't either, and I definitely didn't realize you would be here, too!" I said excitedly. "The Master mentioned you to Father a few days ago, but I didn't think you'd *actually* be here," I said, pushing my fingers into my hair in astonishment.

"Well, I know it's been almost a year since my last visit, and I'm sorry about that, but there's just been so much going on lately," he said, ushering me over to the training rack. "But we'll talk later. You're here now, and that's all that matters," he said with a bright smile. "Thanks, big brother! I'm so happy I have family here," I said, not realizing just how deep that sentence alone actually went.

"So am I, little brother. But you've got to go. You don't want to be late for your first *real* lesson, do you?" he asked, gesturing over to where Ed and the others were lining up against a few sets of training dummies. "Here, a little tip before you go so you don't make a fool of yourself on your first day more than you already have," he said, grabbing my hand and my training sword.

He pushed my right hand up near the guard, and pulled my left hand down towards the pommel. "There, now you'll have to use the pommel to help rotate the angle of your sword, since your right hand is, effectively, going to act as a fulcrum for much of its movement, though your hips and arms will do most of the work," he said in a teacher-like voice. "What's a *fulcrum*?" I asked, genuinely confused.

I don't think it had dawned on him that I had never held a sword before, let alone the fact that it was *actually* my first day interacting with a weapon.

"*Ah*, right. Think of it like sticking a rock beneath a stick to help you move something heavy," he explained simply. "*Oh*, I see," I said, not fully understanding, but at least I had a mental image to go off of. "In any case, you need to get over there before you get yelled at and forced to run a lap around the training yard," he said with a wave of his hand.

"That's something you do here?" I asked, beginning to fear for my life. He quickly nodded a response. "You're right, I should go. Can we talk after dinner?" I asked, half-turned to him as I started moving towards my group. "Yes, of course. Go!" he said, shooing me with the backside of his hand flicking in the air.

I lined up behind Batch, who was next in line for a demonstration of a three-hit combo that we were watching Edryd perform; one from the top-right, then the bottom left, then straight across. A simple combo, sure, but for someone who had never swung a sword before, it felt like it was far more complex than it really was.

I can't make a fool of myself here, I have to pay close attention, I thought, noting Ed's positioning and how he held himself.

I shifted my body a little bit to slightly mimic his movements, but I didn't want to get called out for looking like an idiot.

"*One, two, three!*" I heard Edryd mutter in unison with his strikes. "Good hits! Excellent form! Again!" the Master called out. Apparently, it was normal for him to train the New Bloods, as he always wanted to instill *good habits* from the start.

Ed struck the dummy again, but staggered a little on his last hit, having lost a small portion of his footing. "Be mindful of how you're angling your feet when you strike, young Edryd. Keeping your balance could mean the difference between life and death out there; do you understand?" he asked in a warm tone.

"I understand, Master. I'll do better next time," Ed replied with a bow. "I'm sure you will. Now, go to the back of the line and wait for the next round. Think about how you're going to move your body and try it again here in a few moments, okay?" he replied with a light chuckle, tousling Ed's dark brown hair.

Batch was up next, and while his strikes weren't very graceful, he *did* have a lot of power behind them. "*One, two-three!*" he said, increasing the speed between the last two strikes. "Very good, Batch! I'm glad you're not only relying on your powerful strikes, but changing the tempo between strikes. It is a good way to throw off your opponent, but it can often leave you open to counter-attacks, as well. Try it again with a consistent tempo, this time," the Master said encouragingly. "*One, two, three!*" Batch said, having taken the Master's feedback into account. He had, apparently, successfully chained his movements together so well that everyone in our group *ooh-ed* in unison.

"Much better! If you can keep up that level of physical prowess, I'll waive some of your scores on the written tests," the Master said playfully.

Batch's eyes, of course, lit up at the thought of not having to study as hard.

Next was my turn.

After having seen my two companions' strikes, and hearing the feedback from the Master, it was clear to me what I needed to do; find a good middle ground between power and accuracy of movement when it came to performing the combo. I'd memorized the correct tempo from Batch, but I knew that imitating Ed's positioning would pose a challenge.

"I see you've already gotten a pointer from Bernar," the Master said, watching me approach and looking directly at my tightly clenched hands. I had been gripping my training sword the same way since my conversation with my brother. "Y-yes, Master. He told me how to hold it, but I've never swung a sword before," I said bashfully.

I want to look as good as they did when they were doing their combos, I thought.

The Master smiled as if he had read my thoughts.

"Well, why don't you at least try. You've already had a demonstration from your two roommates, and I saw that you were watching them closely. Try to imitate what they did, okay?" he said encouragingly. "I'll do my best, Master," I replied with a nod. He gestured for me to move forward, and I squared off with my training dummy.

Given our age group, it wasn't much taller than I was, but it was certainly wider than any of us present. The straw-stuffed dummy had a pole that ran through it to the ground, and a set of rounded red targets painted on all the vital spots of a humanoid body.

Ed struck the one at the neck, armpit and stomach. I should aim for those three, I thought as I recalled his performance.

"Begin," the Master called out.

I would love to say that I hit my targets accurately and efficiently on the first strike, but this was not the case. My sword ended up falling a little short of the target, and I quickly found myself falling forward, eating a mouthful of dirt in the process.

Naturally, there were a few scattered chuckles from the group behind me.

"It's alright, young Thoma. Like you said, that was your first swing, and honestly, mine wasn't much better when I first started. Try again," the Master said, glaring at the others behind me with his glowing, sun-like eyes.

I picked myself back up, wiped my mouth, and held my training sword in the same position I'd just had it in before my embarrassing demise. This time, however, I took a step closer, and pre-measured the length from the target to the upper quarter of my sword.

I'm not going to make the same mistake twice, I thought.

"Begin!" he called out again.

I felt what little muscles I had in my arms, hips, and legs tightening as I kept my eyes on the rounded target near the base of the dummy's neck, and heard the training sword slicing through the air as it met its first target with a dulled *thwack*. "*One,*" I said, feeling the vibrations sent up my arm that were like nothing I'd ever experienced. I could feel my hands beginning to sting a little from the impact, forcing me to wince from the pain.

I drew the sword back enough for the tip of it to slide off the dummy, and performed the next uppercut. "*Two,*" I grunted, the same *thwack* and stinging pain resounding from the strike, but I pushed through the pain and moved onto the next blow aimed for the dummy's midsection.

Thwack.

"*Three,*" I said, feeling the slight swelling in my fingers, wrists, and forearms from the strikes, but I'd done it. I'd completed my first-ever sword combo. It wasn't graceful, not when compared to Ed or even Batch, but I'd done it nevertheless.

"Well done, Thoma," I heard Ed and Batch say in unison, but the Master didn't seem as pleased as they were. Whatever he saw in me had clearly left a bitter taste in his mouth, because his expression soured a little. "Try it again, but a little faster this time," he said with the same warm tone that didn't match his expression. "Yes, Master," I said, adjusting my grip on my sword for another round.

I performed the combo again, and while it was a little smoother, it was still nothing to brag about. The Master's face, still soured by whatever he'd seen, had softened a little when he saw my brow furrowing as I struck.

"Again," he ordered. I followed his order, the burning sensation in my arms beginning to grow more and more intense with every strike. "Again," he said, his tone growing a little more harsh this time around as I winced through the pain. *One more,* he commanded, his tone much more forceful, almost as if I'd heard it in my own head rather than through my ears.

I bared my teeth and struck, mimicking a mixture of both Batch and Ed's movements to the best of my ability. "*One, two, three!*" I grunted, feeling my arms grow almost limp with the final blow. My hands were numbed to whatever vibrations were carried through them, and I could feel the muscles in them and in my forearms feeling taut like a bowstring.

I panted heavily as the tip of my training sword sunk into the ground in front of me, but I felt a warm sense of pride flush over and through me, vaguely reminding me of the tendrils of mana I'd seen coming off the Master just a few days prior.

"Well done, young Thoma," the Master said, his expression softening once more. I looked up at him from beneath my brow, not bothering to hide my exhaustion.

That run really took it out of me. I can barely stand as it is, I thought, wiping the sweat from my brow.

"Thank you, Master," I managed to say. "I know that must have been difficult for you, but it's essential that you practice just as hard, if not harder than the others to catch up," he said, taking a few steps forward. "There is a lot I wish I could tell you right now, but it's not my place to do so," he said in a hushed voice before taking a few steps back.

What is that supposed to mean? I asked myself.

"Now, get to the back of the line and get ready for another round here in a few minutes," he gestured in the line's general direction. I followed his orders, and continued my training throughout the remainder of the morning. After a quick lunch, and another training session for another three-hit combo that afternoon, I was absolutely exhausted.

Why does it feel like my bones are trying to leap out of my skin? I thought as I made my way down a cold stone corridor towards my brother's room.

I finally came to the wooden door, but just as I was about to knock, my brother's face took the place of the door, causing me to briefly wrap my knuckles on his nose. "*Ow*, you little shit," he said, rubbing the bridge of his nose. "I was just going to look for you, and this is how I'm greeted? *Sheesh*," he said jokingly.

"Sorry, my arms feel like that goop we had for lunch," I said, recalling the strange, lumpy pudding. "*Oh*, yeah. That stuff is nasty," he said in disgust. "Anyway, it's good to have you here, little brother, but we need to talk," he said, ushering me away from the door. "Where are we going?" I asked. "*Meh*, just getting away from unwanted eyes and ears," he said with a shrug.

We walked outside the fortress to the training yard we had spent most of the day in, and I could swear that I could still see my facial imprint in the dirt under the moonlight.

"It's good to see you again, little brother. I mean it," he began, putting a hand on my shoulder. "It's good to have you back. Gods above and below, I've missed your sorry ass, little shithead," he said. "When did you learn to swear like that?" I asked jokingly. "I've spent a lot of time training with the seniors the past few years," he said, scratching the back of his head awkwardly.

"*Oh*, so they *all* talk like that?" I asked, genuinely curious about how life outside of my little group was like. "S-sure," he said, a bead of sweat running down the side of his cheek. "I-in any case, that's not why I wanted to talk to you," he stammered, finally turning to face me.

"Well, what did you want to talk about?" I asked plaintively. "I... *uh*... I'm going to Caegwen soon," he said with a small amount of dejection in his voice. "*Caegwen*? Isn't that where the Elves live? Why do you need to go there?" I asked, not bothering to hide my confusion. "W-well, it's not something I can really talk about right now, but don't worry, it won't be for at least a year... I think," he said, clearly unsure of his own words.

"So, I only get a year with you before you're gone? How long are you going to be there?" I asked. "Dunno. The Master says that it depends on how well I do, apparently," he replied with a shrug. "*It depends on how well you do*? Are you going there to train or something?" I asked.

He let out a heavy sigh, and put a hand on my shoulder. "Look, there's only so much I can say right now, but the fact is that I *am* going there. I can't talk about why or what I'll be doing over there, but that's where I'll be going," he said, averting his gaze momentarily.

I was stunned. He and I never really held secrets, and I could tell, even at that young age, that whatever he wasn't telling me was probably hard for him to keep quiet about. I did the only thing I could think to do, and put a hand on his shoulder in return.

"It's okay, brother. You don't have to tell me, but I *am* going to ask a lot of questions when you get back," I said, trying my best to sound encouraging. He held a pained smile on his face for a few moments before he spoke. "I'm sorry I couldn't stay longer, but I'll do my best to help you get as far as you can in your training, okay?" he asked.

I nodded my head in agreement. "Good. So, tell me, how was life over there with dad? Did he treat you okay?" he asked, seemingly worried about my mental or emotional state. "Not really, but he did take me to see an old man not too far from our house. He apparently did something to me, or at least that's what the Master told me," I said with a shrug.

"That fucking bastard," Bernar spat. "I promise that when I get back, we'll do our best to figure out what happened, okay?" he said encouragingly. "Alright, then. I'll train as hard as I can until you get back," I said, balling my fists together near my chest.

"I know you will, little shit," he said, tousling my hair.

CHAPTER 26

DAWNING

What time is it? I thought as I opened my eyes.

I looked out the window only to find the bright, morning sun with its perfect aim shining between the peaks of the distant Rhydian mountains and beaming into my eyes. I was in a room that took me a few seconds to recognize, since the dream I had was still a little too fresh in my mind. I decided to get up and wash my face after having noticed that the sun was already bleeding its light over the distant peaks.

"Thoma, come back to bed already. It's too early, and I'm too cozy to follow you anywhere right now," I heard Meliss groan through a raspy voice. "I know you are, darling, but unfortunately for both of us, we have to get going," I said, knowing it would take her about as long as it takes to bring a kettle to a boil for her to get out of bed. The protesting groan that resounded from her lips forced mine to bend into a slight grin. "Come now, my love. We have to get up," I said, kissing her forehead gently after brushing her hair aside.

Just as I was pulling away, she grabbed the back of my nape, and pulled me in for a *good morning kiss*, as she liked to call them. The smell of the lavender-scented sheets nearly made me fall back into bed. "Okay, *now* I can get up," she said, her phthalo-green eyes darting to each of mine as a smile grew on her porcelain face. I smiled in return, stealing one or two more kisses before finally moving towards my gear. She reluctantly tore the covers off her body after a brief moment of what could only be described as a *mental fortitude enhancement exercise.*

A few little jumps to ensure my hose was on securely, and a few splashes of water to my still-puffy face later, I was ready to go and meet the others. Today, after about three solid weeks, was the day we were going home to Codrean. "Meliss, are you ready?" I asked, though I probably already knew the answer to that. Surprisingly, she jumped out from behind the changer in the corner of the room in a beautiful, blue dress. "Do you like it? Leona has one that's similar to this, but her figure is much less brutish than mine. She had to have one made for me," she said, a slight gleam growing in her eyes as she watched the excitement on my face begin to show.

"I think it looks *incredible* on you. Give us a twirl, will you?" I asked, not bothering to hide my genuine happiness at the sight of her smile. She twirled back and forth, and then completed one final spin, grabbing the sides of her dress and bending into a graceful curtsy. "Do you wanna know the best part about this dress?" she asked, a mischievous grin showing on her face. "Of course I do," I said matter-of-factly. "It should be obvious that I want to know what part of this *beautiful* dress makes you the happiest."

She pulled out two, dog-ear looking flaps of cloth near the height of her waist. "It has these things called *pockets,*" she said excitedly. "You didn't know what pockets are?" I asked, rather incredulously. "First off, I thought *you* wouldn't know what pockets are. Second, it's not common for dresses to have pockets, as it's considered *unladylike* to put your hands in them for any other reason than pulling something out of them," she retorted, a slight pouting attitude resonating from her. My eyes squinted, as I tried to figure out the reason for it to be *unladylike*. While I had never been formally trained for royal courts, I had at least *some* education in formalities.

"Well, either way, I'm really glad you enjoy the dress," I said, ending my effort to find the reason it would be unladylike. I looked around the room, and noticed she only had a small bag with her. "Are you sure you have everything you need?" I asked. I had always heard women needed more things than men do. Something to do with *looking pretty for other women rather than for men*, or at least that's what my older brother, Bernar, told me.

"I have everything I own in that bag," she said somewhat solemnly. Only then did I realize what she meant by that. She *has been* a slave most of her life, after all. I picked up her bag, smiled, and kissed her on the forehead. "Then we're all set to go. I also have everything I need," I said, patting the blackened, wire-wrapped hilt of my blade. She glanced down at it, but where her thoughts went, I could only imagine. Until a few weeks ago, she had never even considered what it would be like to kill a person, let alone a person *and* a monster within the span of roughly two weeks.

We eventually made our way downstairs to where the others were gathering their things and preparing to leave. I greeted Edryd who was looking a lot better with his dark brown hair still tied in its short ponytail and whiskers finally shaved off. "Ready to go home?" I asked, cautious of my words. Batch's death still took its toll on him, and while he seemed to finally be over it, I didn't want to accidentally trigger any sort of emotional response. Like walking on eggshells with an explosive mana-crystal strapped to your chest.

"Oh, yeah. I'm more than ready to go home and eat nothing but snot-like gruel and get my ass kicked by your brother again," Ed replied sarcastically. "It's not like I have an easy time with him, either," I retorted. "He's a fifth-stage mana manipulator, after all. I've only just broken through the second, so there's still a massive gap in our abilities," I continued. *"Massive gap?* I heard you speed-blitzed the absolute *fuck* out of Irun during your fight," Edryd said emphatically. "Is that jealousy I hear in your voice?" I asked, trying to sound as playful as I could.

Ed cast his eyes downward, and I realized where that jealousy stemmed from. *Egg shells,* I thought. "Listen, I'm sorry. I know it still hasn't been a long time since Batch's... well, you know," I began. Ed didn't look at me, but simply nodded. "I know you mean well, Thoma, and there is a slight bit of jealousy indeed. I wanted to beat the absolute *shit* out of Irun when I heard he was at the castle. I know it couldn't have been an easy fight, but I just wish I could have been there to help take him down," he said, dodging my gaze and focusing on securing his equipment.

"It's okay," I began. "I'm sure there are going to be other opportunities to kick his ass. Now that he's with the Masked One, it's not too unlikely that we'll never see him again," I said, trying to bring *some* positivity into the conversation. "Yeah, but if you end up getting to him first, make that fucker wish he had never been born," Ed said, his tone darkening to a depth I didn't know he had. *He'll be alright,* I thought. "Don't worry, I will," I replied, patting him on the shoulder. Meliss said nothing during the exchange, but gave him a warm smile, and a quick, friendly hug.

Making my way to Celer, the black stallion my older brother gave me for my birthday a few months prior, I tied my bag and Meliss' to the saddle. My brother noticed me from across the room, and began to make his way over to me. "There you are, shit-bird," he said in his usual, playful tone. "Ah, the leather donut himself," I retorted. He clasped my hand, and pulled me into a brief embrace. It *had* been at least two weeks since I last saw him.

Obviously, I knew where he had been the whole time.

"So, tell me, brother; how is Leo-..." I began, but he stopped me by putting his hand over my mouth. "*Shhhhhhhh,*" he hushed, his glowing, yellow eyes flaring as they stared into mine. "For the love all the breasts and buttcheeks you've ever wanted to grab, *shut the fuck up,*" he said quietly. His leather glove smelled of horse and old sweat from past battles and training, even after a few cleanings from the battle. I nodded my understanding as best I could, with a muffled sound from my mouth exiting the cracks between his glove and my skin. I pulled his hand off my face, and stared at him curiously.

"What the hell happened?" I asked, trying to figure out why he was asking for so much secrecy. "I know she's still technically the queen and all, but she up and murdered Truls not too long ago," I said quietly. "That was in self-defense, and you *really* should shut up, now," he said quickly and quietly. "Just tell me what's going on and I will," I said, trying to appease his better nature.

He pulled me aside and took a deep breath. "You know Leona is of royal blood, right?" he began in a hushed tone. "*Duh,* but what of it?" I asked, not fully understanding what he meant by that. He sighed in response. "Remind me to give you some court lessons when we get back. Listen, royal blood can *only* marry into other royal blood. It's how these families stay in power for so long," he said in a tone that reminded me of Taegin, the Master of Codrean, when he would give his lessons.

"Okay, and that means what? That she can't have some fun with you? She's the *queen*, for fuck's sake," I said, still incredulous at the ridiculousness of the situation. "That's the problem; she's the fucking *queen*. If people she doesn't trust or know well begin to find out about our relationship, how do you think it will end, eh?" he asked. I still didn't understand what he meant, but I could guess.

Many of the royals, at least from what I had read in books and learned from overhearing conversations in the castle, were capricious as hell; bowing only to their own whims and willing their desires into existence, even if it meant destroying someone's life.

"Alright, alright. I get it, but why couldn't she take you in as some sort of consort? Wouldn't that make your relationship more legitimate?" I asked. I watched his face pale for a moment at the thought of being married, but the pale aura was soon replaced by a massive flush of blood. "I-I-I g-guess it wouldn't be *so* bad to be a c-consort," he struggled to say the words. "I don't fucking believe it. My own brother is *scared* to get married?" I jested, poking his shoulder playfully as I accented my words. "You're dead when we get back," he said, grabbing my hand and trying to sound serious behind the beet-red face he held.

"Not as dead as you're about to be if you don't let go of him," a soft yet forceful voice said from behind him. "My lov-... I mean, *Queen* Leona," he stammered, scratching the back of his head as the smile grew on his face. "Your Majesty," I bowed, grinning from ear to ear as I pulled my own brother down to match my height. "You two really are something special, aren't you?" she asked through a stifled giggle. "Arise, my two, *brave and wise* synners," she accented, gesturing for us to raise our heads.

We lifted our heads to admire her beauty. The pale blue eyes, accented by her luscious black hair, pierced into our very cores. "Now, Thoma, if you would be so kind as to say what you just said again, please," she asked me. I would be lying if I said that her tone and use of the word *please* didn't immediately send a slight chill down my spine. "Your Majesty," I began but she held up a hand. "Remember what I said before? So long as there are no royals around, you don't have to address me like that, Thoma," she said, her tone lightening a little.

Bernar's face in response to her comment was priceless.

"Leona, as I was just telling my beloved older brother here, I clearly know of your relationship and was wondering why you couldn't take him as a consort. I mean, it seems like you two love each other, and I think it might do him some good in the long run. Before you say anything, no I'm not just saying that because you're a royal. I can tell you're genuinely good for him," I said as diplomatically as I could. *Shit, was that even good enough?* I thought.

Leona paused, and gave Bernar a warm look which he returned immediately. *I think I might be sick,* I thought. "Well, at your request, I will certainly consider it," she said cheerfully. The weight that sat on my chest seemed to disappear, as I breathed a deep, yet subtle, sigh of relief. "Well, given my brother's reaction to me having the balls to say what I just did, I think he would also very much like it if you took it into consideration," I poked.

Bernar, now unable to hide both his embarrassment and joy, put his hand around my shoulder with a broad smile showing on his face. "I guess I should consider myself lucky to have such a *doting* younger brother," he said, sarcasm dripping from every word. *I'm so fucked when we get back,* I thought as I felt his grip on my shoulder tighten. Leona saw my expression shift from happy to slightly concerned, so she shot my brother another glance as if ordering him to let me go.

Thankfully, he did.

"In any case, I just hope you find a way to be together. That's all I want, at the end of the day," I said, smiling at the two of them. "I'm sure she'll make him very happy. That way, you won't have to worry about him anymore," Meliss chimed in as she walked up to us. Apparently she had overheard the entire conversation that was meant to be private.

"Oh, Meliss! How nice of you to join us! Wait, what do you mean *you won't have to worry about him anymore*? He worries about me?" Bernar said with a shit-eating grin slapped across his mug. "I was just going to tell the queen how much you meant to me; but if I'm right in discerning where you're about to take this conversation, I'll rescind my comment," I said, putting my foot down.

Meliss chuckled lightly, and the sound of her encroaching laugh made me forget about all of the horrible things that have happened in my life. Even if it were for just a few seconds, her laugh made it impossible to feel anything other than pure bliss when hearing it, making the rest of us join in. "Ah, it feels good to be able to laugh like that," she said, wiping a tear from her eye. "It does indeed," Leona agreed, pulling Bernar close.

And here he was trying to be cautious, I thought.

"Before you leave, I would like to share a few words with Meliss, if you don't mind, Thoma," Leona began. I immediately understood what she meant. "Of course, Leona. Take your time. We will finish getting our things ready for the journey home," I said, bowing lightly. "This could *also* be *your* home, one day," Leona said suggestively. Meliss, like me, blushed harder than I think we ever have in our collective lives. "Ha! Payback's a bitch!" Bernar said more loudly than he meant to, pointing a finger at me.

I tried to compose myself and not act the fool in front of the trio. "I will *also* take that into consideration," I said, bowing one last time. "Find me when you're ready, Meliss," I said, dragging my brother by the collar behind me. "I won't keep her forever, reluctant as I am to let her go," Leona said in a motherly tone I hadn't expected. "Of course. We will take our leave," I replied.

After having finished packing our supplies, clothes, and weapons, we only stood by for a few minutes before Meliss came along. I helped her up onto the saddle on the horse provided to her directly by Leona. Meliss waved good-bye to her former master, and I could see a few tears welling in her eyes. I figured it would probably be best if I performed a simple hand gesture as a farewell. My brother, on the other hand, waved voraciously at the queen who observed our departure.

Surprisingly, Thorsen had said his farewells to Pyle, but I never quite heard what they said. I imagined they would talk about seeing each other again someday soon.

As for the rest of us heading to Codrean, The Master, Tacgin, was once again at the forefront of the formation. He was followed closely by Master Pyle Rumia, the Fangsdalr master synner, and

Master Garett, our master Archer and close friend of Taegin. My older brother, this time around, decided to ride beside Edryd and Roburn, allowing Meliss and I some time alone.

Over the hills and through the valleys we rode, keeping conversations low in volume due to potential stragglers that have wandered from the castle. While we were sure that the controlling crystals had been destroyed, we *also* knew that these creatures were going to go their own ways and infest the forests and bogs of the land around us.

"Oh, look! It's where I had my first battle," I said, pointing out the spot where the carriage had been stuck. "Yeah, it's also where you tried out that spell of yours and almost got me killed," Edryd said in as light-hearted of a tone as he could manage. "Ah, don't remind me. I still feel horrible about that," I said, recalling the events. "You saved my life, and suffice it to say that I'm very grateful, even if it did hurt a lot," Ed noted. Meliss could see the expression on my face turn a little sour, but I was still glad my best friend was still around.

"I wonder if I'll be able to use mana like you do," Meliss said quietly, though not enough for Pyle to not hear her. "It might take you a little while longer than the rest of them, since we're starting you so late," he said, pulling his horse up next to hers. "Master Pyle," she greeted him. "Don't worry about calling me *master* just yet. I still need to give you some of the Gwynnleaf before we begin training," he said.

"Wait, we brought some back?" I asked, genuinely confused. "Why do you think it took us three weeks to leave Coltend? Not only did we have to help restore the city, but we also had our own agenda for our own sakes," Pyle said, his final words a lot more grimly stated than

I had anticipated. "I see, and what does the Gwynnleaf even do?" Meliss asked, confused about my concern.

"While the connection created to the Ethereal realm, where we draw our power from, requires a certain process, this plant was gifted to us by the gods to facilitate the process. It also makes it a lot less... *risky*," Pyle said, the last word being uttered through a side-gap in his mouth and clenched teeth. "Risky? What do you mean by that?" she asked, concern beginning to show on her face.

"Ah, well, you see, through the process of connecting to the Ethereal, there is a *slight* possibility that your consciousness might not make it back. With the Gwynnleaf tincture, it makes it so that risk is no longer a possibility," he explained. Meliss pondered his words for a minute, certainly questioning her decision to come along with me. "I see... and will I get any of that *tincture?*" she asked, her thick accent from the Gramm Isles made pronouncing the word difficult. "Well, no one here would want you to turn into a vegetable, would we?" Pyle asked. "A *what?*" she asked.

"What he means is that if your consciousness doesn't make it back, your body will be left in a vegetative state. Your bodily functions will still go on, but you will have no conscious control over anything. Basically, turning you into a sort of undead or vegetative state," I said, knowing my words were *not* likely to help the situation. Surprisingly enough, Meliss remained composed. While she might not have known exactly what manipulating mana was like, I could tell her thoughts were trying to piece together just how dangerous it would be without the Gwynnleaf, and why the Masked One, Ardrin, wanted to take it all in the first place.

"Well, I just hope it doesn't taste bad," she said, snapping out her train of thought. I looked at Pyle, and the responsive shrug he gave me was a little less than reassuring to Meliss and her hopes of a decent flavor. "I wouldn't worry so much about that right now. However, with you, we're going to have to take a bit of a gamble," Pyle said, re-engaging the conversation. "What do you mean by *gamble*?" she asked.

"Normally, when we train synners to manipulate mana, we have to make sure they can do it without the Gwynnleaf first. That way, we know for sure that their connection will be on par with that of the others when the tincture is introduced into their system. Think of it as showing a predisposition for mana," Pyle explained. "I see. So, you are just making sure that the tincture you use isn't going to waste, is that it?" she asked. "That's correct," he nodded.

She was lost in thought. For a second I could've sworn I saw her mouth move, and say something akin to a prayer, but I couldn't quite make it out without enhancing my senses with mana. "I'd like to try it without the tincture first," she said, confidence lacking in her voice. "Are you sure? You know the risks are pretty high, right?" I asked, concerned about her decision. "Thoma, if I'm going to walk this path with you, I want to be able to keep up and not become a burden to you," she said.

Fucking hell, she's got a way with words that could melt the coldest ice in the Hjalfarian tundra, I thought.

"If that's what you want to do, then I won't be able to stop you. I just hope you understand the risks," I said, trying not to discourage her. "I do, and thank you for your concern," she said. I could tell, right then and there, that if she succeeded, she would be a formidable synner to be reckoned with.

Pyle, who had seen the whole exchange and heard her words, chuckled lightly. "Well, Meliss. If you turn out to be a monster like your future husband, I'll stop worrying about the future of the synners," he said playfully. I'd be lying if I said I didn't feel a tinge of excitement flare up in my belly when her face flushed with color. "I can't wait to spar with you, and see what you can do," I said as encouragingly as I could.

"Oh, fuck no. Nuh-uh. Not happening. You're sparring with me, fuckface," Bernar chimed in, pulling his horse up next to mine. Meliss flinched at the curse word he spat in my direction. "I think I still need to get used to the swearing. I know you use foul language and insults to avoid fighting each other, but it is a far cry from the language I'm used to hearing in Coltend," she said, rubbing her temple. "Yeah, sorry about that," I said, nervously scratching the back of my head.

"Also, brother, I want to spar with her at least once before we... well, you know," I said, not trying to bring up the fact that I would eventually be going to Caegwen to train. *Not ready to have* that *discussion again*, I thought. "Trust me, I know, but for most of your training, you'll be sparring with me," he said. "In any case, I look forward to training with both of you, and under Mast... I mean, *Pyle's* instruction, I'm sure I'll be alright," she said, building up her confidence a little.

The conversation with Bernar that followed us the rest of the way to Codrean was, for the most part, in regard to Leona. I think I lost count of how many questions he asked about her, her likes and dislikes, as well as her favorite foods. While Meliss had enough patience to answer most of his questions, there were some, I felt, that were a little too personal. It felt strange to see him so worked-up about a woman, as most of his life he was fairly nonchalant about anything and everything pertaining to them. I liked seeing this side of him.

Our eventual arrival at the fortress was heralded by a few of the synners the Master had sent on ahead to make sure everything was in order. Out of the original five hundred we stormed Coltend with, only a little over half survived against the horde. However, with Pyle's added forces, and some of Nenvalur's people agreeing to help train us, Codrean was back at full strength and then some.

As soon as we arrived, the stable hand from our journey North, who stayed behind during the assault, helped us to take care of our horses. The voyage from Codrean, to Hjalfar, and then to Coltend was the furthest he'd ever been from home, and he was always excited to see new things. "Hey, Thoma!" he rushed over and greeted me.

"Darren! How was the trip, buddy? I'm sorry I didn't get to talk much on the way here," I said, scuffing up his curly, red hair. His bright, hazel eyes accented by the freckles strewn across his cheeks responded to the smile that grew. "Oh, that's alright! I just wanted to let you know that I'll take good care of Celer as a thank you for your help back at the palace," he said cheerfully.

"Help? When did you have time for that?" Meliss asked. "It wasn't much. I just wrote out a few things for him to try out in a note, and told him to take it to Roburn. That way, he could get training from one of our certified instructors, who I'm sure had not much else better to do," I replied, making the last part sound a little more sarcastic than my usual tone. "I heard that," Roburn said from across the way, removing his saddle from his horse.

Darren chuckled. "Now that we're back, do you think you could also help me with my training?" he asked. "I'm not even sure of my own training schedule at this point," I sighed. "I'll still help you where I can, I promise. I know you're excited, but for now, let's just settle back into this place, yeah?" I invited him to reconsider.

"Okay. I guess I'll wait," he said, scrunching his left cheek up by pushing his mouth towards it. "Don't worry, it won't be too long before we can spar," I said, trying to cheer him up. The smile regrew on his face as he darted off to tend to the other horses.

He reminds me so much of Irun when he was younger, I thought.

"You have a way with children that I didn't expect," Meliss said, tugging my arm as we walked towards the fortress. "Well, I know he doesn't look to be the type to say anything philosophical, but my brother taught me something very important; that I should always be the person I wish I had there for me as a kid. I was lucky that my brother was there for me, so now, I want to do the same for others where I can," I replied. "A surprisingly mature outlook on life for someone who swears as much as you do," she said, pinching my arm. "Ow! What was that for?" I asked. "Just making sure you were still real, and not the perfect boy from my imagination," she replied playfully. I smiled and pinched her back for the same reason.

The sun was beginning to hide behind the distant hills, and we were nearly finished settling in. Meliss, unfortunately for me, was sent to another area of the dorms, while I set my old room back up. The charring on the wall from that night with the mana-flame was still present, and I could swear I still smelled the burnt bucket of piss-water. "It's good to be home, but damn does it feel empty," Edryd said, noting the two empty beds. "Yeah, a little," I said, realizing what he meant. "Hello there! Sorry to interrupt, but are these beds taken?" a voice came from the door.

I turned around to see who it was, but didn't recognize them. A pair of elves that didn't look much older than I was, stood in the doorway. The first, and taller of the pair, had shining, golden hair, pointed ears that stayed close to the sides of his head, and nearly gray eyes. The second had similar features, but blood-red eyes and tar-black hair instead. Both were wearing similar armor to that of Nenvalur when he first appeared at the portal stone, so I concluded they must have been some of the augmentees to our forces.

"I suppose they are now," I said welcomingly, outstretching my hand. "Thoma Fayren from Kinth," I introduced myself. The pair of elves looked at my hand, questioning the gesture. "Thorn Thuridan," the taller one said, slowly grasping my hand in a less than usual manner.

Gotta give him points for trying, I thought.

"And you? What's your name?" I asked the one with the red eyes. He muttered something I couldn't quite hear. I assumed he was just being shy, or perhaps he was just extremely soft spoken. "I'm sorry, I didn't catch that. What was your name, again?" I asked.

"His name is Rennyr Virie, but you can call him Ren for short," Thorn said in his place. "It's a pleasure to meet you," I said, bowing this time, instead of outstretching my hand. I figured it was the better of the two options after the previously awkward experience. Ren bowed in return, and it was only then that I remembered how elves were with physical touch.

Anwill would have a field day if he saw this majestic fuck up, I thought.

"I promise that it's nothing you've done. He's just a quiet person. Has been for the last two hundred years I've known him. Never bothered to ask why because I was always sure he'd never tell me. He's loyal, dependable, freakishly good with a sword, and trustworthy with any secret," Thorn said. "Well, that's good to hear," Ed chimed in. "I'm Edryd Baelis. It's nice to meet you both," he said with a bow, avoiding my earlier display of awkwardness. "Edryd? The one who slayed the addia with Nenvalur? We've heard a lot about you. It's an honor," Thorn said, initiating a bow with Ren following suit.

I knew it was still a sensitive subject for him, but I was very happy to see Ed's face crack a little smile at the sight of these two, much older than he was, paying him respect. "Oh, lighten up. You've more than earned their respect for what you've done," I said, patting him on the shoulder, hoping to carry the positive momentum forward and help bring my friend out of his depression. I missed Batch, too, but I knew that my sadness couldn't compare that of Ed's while watching him get ripped apart.

"Thank you for the kind words. My friends, Thoma and Roburn, have been helping me cope with what happened, but I'll get over it eventually," he said, lacking confidence in his own words. Thorn looked at him questioningly, and with a quick glance to Ren, the shorter one stepped forward. "Here," Ren said, putting his hand over Ed's core. "Wha-what are you doing?" he asked, nervous about the interaction. "Just trust him," Thorn said reassuringly.

I couldn't even see Ren's eyes change, but I knew he was channeling mana. I could feel its warmth resonating through the air, and with a subtle pulse, the mana left as quickly as it came. Ed's eyes were wide open, almost like he had seen an addia appear in front of him. "Wh-... what the *fuck* was that? H-how did...?" he stammered, grasping at his chest, though he didn't seem to be in any pain. "Ren has the extraordinary ability to mend cores," Thorn explained. "He can do *what*?" I asked, incredulous to the words I just heard.

"As everyone who deals with mana knows, a core is where the soul resides. If someone is emotionally damaged, that also means that their core is damaged, to varying degrees. Negative emotions not only affect our bodies, but our cores as well. While a core can mostly heal on its own, it will never be the same as it once was. What Ren did was simply speed up the recovery process," Thorn explained as if talking to a child.

How the fuck did he figure out how to do that? I wondered. *I guess living as long as they do means you have to try all sorts of interesting things.*

The color on Ed's face returned, and he breathed a sigh of relief. "Ah-ha.. *Hahaha!* I don't fucking believe it," he said, struggling to understand what he was feeling. "Feel better?" Ren asked in a gentle voice. For an elf of a few words, he was surprisingly caring of others. "Y-yes, but how did you...?" Ed began to ask, but Ren simply held up a hand. "I couldn't tell you how many times I've asked him that, but he's never once told me *how* he does it, only *what* he does," Thorn explained.

"I feel like there is going to be so much we can learn from each other here, and I look forward to working with both of you," I said, realizing just how much more I had to grow. "Indeed, and we look forward to learning from you, too," Thorn said with a slight bow. Ed and I helped them settle into their new quarters, with Thorn taking Irun's bed, and Ren taking Batch's.

The following morning we did our usual ritual of endurance training and breakfast in the morning. Meliss, entirely unaccustomed to this life, struggled to keep up during the run, but we had both seen that coming. She knew from the start that she would have a lot to keep up with and learn in a short period of time. Nevertheless, Rosie was there to help her keep an acceptable pace for the morning run.

We met again after breakfast in the training ground, where I could see her coming out of the female dorms with her own jerkin, boots, hose, and a training sword Pyle had provided for her. "You look amazing in black," I said playfully. She rolled her shoulder, briefly massaging the top of it. "It's just as heavy as the one I wore in the battle," she noted. "Sorry about that, they really don't get much lighter, at least not to my knowledge," I said, trying to soothe what ailed her. "It's alright. I'll just have to adapt to it like everything else," she said, shaking her head.

"Thoma! Meliss! Get over here already," my older brother shouted from behind a small group of other synners. Nenvalur and Pyle's additions to our forces rallied around him, Taegin, and Pyle. We scurried up to the group, working our way to the front. "I see a lot of new faces here, and I can honestly say that I'm grateful for those of us who have made it back here in one piece," the Master began. "While I understand that there are a lot of differing disciplines here, I believe it will benefit us as a whole to learn what we can from each other. With that said, I propose we have a few one on one duels to see where everyone stands with each other," he continued.

"Master Pyle, Bernar, and myself will be the judges of these duels, and while we won't allow for beat-downs entirely, we *will* be trying to pair senior synners and those of Nenvalur's former group with juniors to help us assess everyone's abilities. We do not know when the enemy will try to strike again, so we're going to do this as efficiently as possible," Taegin said, glancing at all the faces reacting to the news. I saw an opportunity to raise my hand, and immediately took it.

"What about Meliss, Master?" I asked. He smiled at her gently, and gestured for her to step beside them. "She will be learning the basics from Rosie, one of our seniors, under the instruction of Roburn and Thorn," he said as I watched the two of them step out of the small gathering and walk over to their side.

Oh shit! She's in for it, I thought.

"Good luck, and make sure to control your breathing when you're fighting," I whispered just before she walked off. "What's that supposed to mean?" she shot back. At that point, she was a little too far for me to continue speaking without interrupting the rest of the group during the remainder of the Master's speech.

Once the speech was over, we were split into multiple groups that were fairly balanced across the board. Many of Pyle's synners were to duel against our own, while Nevalur's augmentees dueled most of the seniors. "Looks like you two are stuck with me," Bernar said, pointing at both myself and Edryd. "Better the enemy you know than the one you don't, I guess," Ed replied, elbowing my side. I smiled, but I knew what was going to happen.

As the duels went on around us, I tried to focus on what Meliss was doing in her training. I could tell she was learning some basic forms and guards, while learning to use her body as best she could under

Thorn's watchful eye. Roburn was teaching her some sword-casting pointers for when she would eventually begin casting, while Rosie acted as the enemy due to their similar strength.

Meanwhile, Ed and Bernar's duel had already come to a close, and I'd be lying if I said that I caught more than a few seconds of it. "You move... way... too... fast," Ed said, completely out of breath with my brother's sword at his neck. "You're still at the first stage, so it's understandable why you think I'm so fast," Bernar said playfully. "You weren't that fast when we dueled last time," Edryd said, finally catching his breath as my brother helped him to his feet. "That's because like Thoma, you need to unlock the second stage. You're experienced enough for it to begin appearing on its own, though I don't know why it hasn't yet," Bernar said pensively.

"I just don't think I've ever been in a position to need a constant flow of mana like Thoma did," Ed replied. "But you fought the addia," I interjected. "I did, but whatever power I had back then came from anger more than anything else," he explained. "Speaking of which, are you...?" Bernar started to say, but Ed held up his hand. "No, I'm fine," he said plaintively, walking off at a faster pace than normal.

The hell was all that about, anyway? Didn't Ren fix his core? I thought.

"Focus!" I heard at the last second, realizing my brother had already begun the duel, and that his sword was right in front of my face. I could feel the mana seeping into my muscles and bones, pulling me backwards and downwards away from the blade. "What the actual fuck?" I shouted. My brother, as was his prerogative, wasn't going to give me an answer nor make this easy. He swung again, nearly missing my waist this time, barely allowing me to draw my own sword. I parried a few of his incoming blows, but his speed was phenomenal.

Since having reached the second stage, my mana manipulation has allowed me to augment my body through mana. Right now, however, I felt like I was a river of molasses flowing in winter by comparison to my older brother. Regardless, I tried my best to attack from overhead, hoping to catch him off guard. His reaction speed was incredulous, as he managed to whirl his blade over his head just in time to deflect my blow. He nearly caught me off balance, were it not for the stone my foot met before touching the dirt beneath it.

I felt a strange sort of connection to the rock, and immediately understood how strong I could push off it without it causing me to lose my footing. As I pushed off, it apparently caught my brother off guard, since he wasn't expecting me to do that. His speed ramped up to match mine, and we traded a flurry of rapid blows, causing a minor dust cloud to form around us. "Come on, you can do better than that!" he taunted. "If you say so," I said with malicious intent, opening the floodgates of my mana.

I dashed in behind him in the same way that I had caught Irun off guard just a few weeks prior, but somehow this bastard kept up with me. "You think you can get *me* with that trick?" he asked without turning to face me entirely. I could only see the corner of his glowing eye peeking out from behind his cheekbone.

Well, I'm fucked, I thought.

Sure enough, I felt the solid steel pommel of his sword bash right into my solar plexus, causing me to lose my breath and, ultimately, taste dirt. "*Hehe,* I knew you would try to pull that one on me," Bernar said, extending his hand to lift me up from my writhing on the ground. "H-how did you...?" I asked through gasps of air. "What? You thought I wasn't keeping an eye on you during your fight with Irun? I saw you speed blitz him the same way you just tried to do to me, dipshit," he said, dusting my back off. "Yeah, I probably should've thought of that," I said, understanding my mistake. *Note to self: Don't try that on him again,* I thought.

"It's all well and good to have a trick up your sleeve, but it's almost pointless if your opponent already knows it. You're going to have to do better than that," he added. I nodded my agreement, as his voice rang out for the next person to step up to the plate.

Meanwhile, both masters had observed our duel, and made inaudible notes to each other. *It sucks that I can't hear what they're saying,* I thought. Even if I had activated my second stage, I wouldn't have been able to hear them. Either way, I noticed Pyle's hand gesturing me over to them. I trotted over, one hand still on my injured solar plexus, and greeted them accordingly.

"Your second stage has gotten much more natural in its usage," Pyle noted. "I agree. That was a fairly impressive display just then, Thoma," Taegin added. While I wanted to be proud of the compliments, Ren had already shown me just how far I really was from their level. "Thank you, masters, but I still have a long way to go," I replied, showing my gratitude. "What did you do with the rock earlier?" Taegin asked. "Did you unlock the third stage and just didn't tell anyone?" he continued.

I didn't know how to reply to that question. "I'm not sure. I felt a connection to the rock, almost like I could *feel* it being a part of me. It was like I knew its strength and it knew mine," I tried to explain. "This *fucking* kid, I swear," Pyle muttered under his breath. Taegin heard it, but said nothing. Frankly, I couldn't say anything either, otherwise the smug, shit-eating grin I was hiding would've outgrown my ability to hide it. "Thoma, I know we're still sending you to Caegwen for third stage training, but I feel like you're almost ready to begin right now," Taegin said confidently. "Tomorrow, you'll be sparring with me," he continued, the most subtle grin on his face beginning to show.

Fuuuuuuuuuck, I thought.

"I understand, Master," I replied with a bow. "Good, now go to Meliss, *lover-boy*," Pyle said, jokingly. "I think you should see how she's doing," he continued. About as gracefully as a goose, I took my leave with a slighter bow than I had intended, and went over to where Meliss was conducting her drills.

"Again," I heard Rosie say, deflecting a short chain of basic attacks. Meliss' form looked decent for someone who had never trained with a sword before, let alone hold one for more than a minute. I remembered the first few swings she took with mine in the privacy of our room at the palace, but without any instruction, she was as clumsy as a newborn mountain cub. Since those first few days, I had given her *some* guidance, but what she was showing now was on a different level entirely.

She learns quickly, I thought.

"Again, but now at full speed," Thorn chimed in, hoping to test her limits. Breathing heavily, Meliss grunted forcefully, and swung her sword in as quick succession as she could manage. Rosie, for the first time that day, backpedaled about three steps, sparking curiosity visible by way of Thorn's raised eyebrow.

"Good enough," he said, holding up a hand. "What did you think, Roburn?" he asked my senior. "She's doing well for her first day, and she seems to pick up on complex movements quickly," he said. "Her physical fitness *is* a little lacking, but we can always fix that," he said, not meaning any malice, but I knew what he meant. Rigorous training exercises were some of his favorite things to do, particularly with large amounts of mana manipulation involved.

"Thoma, what do you think?" Meliss asked me directly. Stunned by her question, I wanted to be as fair as I could in regard to her training. "I think you did well enough for your first day, and that you're going to pick the basic forms up quickly. However, I do have to agree with Roburn on the physical fitness part," I said, not meaning anything by it.

"Did you mind your breathing when you were swinging?" I asked, genuinely curious. She pouted a little bit, as I think she expected more praise from me out of anyone. After a few seconds, she nodded her agreement. "I did, but I guess I'm still far and away from where I need to be," she said reluctantly. "I just want to get to a point where I'm not a burden to you, and be able to walk alongside you," she continued, a small glimmer of hope shining in her eyes.

"I know, my love," I said, making all but Thorn flinch at my show of affection. "And I will always do my best to support you however I can, even if that means being brutally honest or honestly brutal," I said, moving a loose strand of hair away from her face and tucking it behind her ear.

"Alright, lovebirds," Roburn said playfully. "We'll continue her training tomorrow. For now, Rosie, take her to the baths to clean up and get ready for supper," he continued. The pair nodded, and walked off together. Rosie seemed to carry a somewhat playful tone, even after being pushed back a little during training. My guess was that she was praising Meliss for being able to do that.

Thorn and I began walking back to our dorm, as the remaining duels behind us were wrapping up. "After you," I gestured to Thorn after I had pulled the door open for him. "Is that common human behavior?" he asked. "Well, it's polite to open the door for someone. At least that's what my mother taught me when I was younger," I added. "Normally, where I come from, following someone into a doorway either means that you're going to assault the building, or drag their lifeless body into the corner," he said plaintively without missing a beat.

"I promise I mean nothing so nefarious," I said, holding up a hand. "If you say so," he said. "I understand you and your people have spent centuries fighting against all manner of enemies, but is everything so black and white for you?" I asked, my curiosity peaked.

"Normally, we're very pragmatic about things, though I can already tell that humans are a lot *less* so. I'm not saying it's a bad thing, perhaps it's something even I will come to learn at some point," he said. I couldn't feel or detect any sort of dishonesty in his voice, and so I simply nodded my agreement, and gestured for him to go in once more. "After you," I said again.

Just as I was closing the door, I could see Edryd pulling Bernar aside to have a chat, but I couldn't make out what they were saying.

I'm sure he'll tell me later, I thought.

CHAPTER 27
LICKED WOUNDS

"You called for me, my lord?" Athar asked, hardly out of breath after having run down the dark, violet halls of Valdis, the citadel far in the northern regions of Hjalfar. His long, dark hair was resting gently on his well-sculpted shoulders. "I did, indeed, Athar," Ardrin, the Masked One, said.

He's got that glow in his eyes again, Athar thought. "It has only been a few weeks and you've already forgotten I can hear whatever you're thinking? Has Karak not been monitoring your training properly?" Ardrin asked.

"He has been, my lord. Although, I would be lying if I said I didn't miss the privacy of my own thoughts, since that daemon can't read them," Athar stated, his voice trailing off with the last few words. "I have my reasons for keeping tabs on your thoughts," Ardrin began. "Yes, my lord. I remember you telling me about the thing you could not unlock within my core. I know, I know," the young man said in a tone he hadn't meant to.

"Listen to me carefully, Athar. That thing that is in your core, not even *I* would want to mess around with. I had rather hoped your training would help you contain it, but it seems it's gotten worse," Ardrin said, gazing at his servant inquisitively.

"What's gotten worse, my lord?" Athar asked. "Your attitude, for starters," Ardrin said, his eyes flaring with a little more mana. Athar swallowed dryly. "I apologize for any behavior that might displease you, my lord," the man said, bowing even lower. "Don't worry, we'll fix it. Irun!" the Masked One commanded, his voice enhanced by the mana he pulsed through the halls.

His thunderous voice resounded throughout the halls, permeating everything it came into contact with. It eventually reached its intended target, subconsciously forcing him to the main hall of the citadel.

How the hell did I get here so fast? Irun thought. *I was just tending to the stump that Thoma gave me in my room when my mind darkened. How am I here?* he asked himself. "Glad you could join us," Ardrin said, grinning beneath his mask at Irun's more than visible confusion.

"How did you...?" Irun began to ask, but was immediately stopped by the glowing eyes piercing his core. *Ugh, why does it feel like there's a creature crawling around in my chest?* he thought, scrunching the linen shirt he was wearing at the height of his heart. Ardrin finally found what he was looking for and began to diffuse his mana.

"I see you still have a lot of reservations about your old comrades," the Masked One said, fully releasing his grip on Irun's core. "Are you insinuating I regret my choice to join you, my lord?" he asked. "Watch your tone, *child*," Ardrin snapped, sending a chill down Irun's spine. "I'm not insinuating anything. I don't like doing that if I don't have to. I'm just saying aloud what I see happening in your core. Also, do enlighten me as to how you've been here for about a month and have not yet introduced yourself to Athar?" he asked.

Irun was at a loss for words. "I apologize, my lord. I've been re- covering from the blow that bastard gave me just before we managed to escape. Even with the augmentation you've already given me, this wound festers and hasn't fully healed yet," he said, gesturing to his missing forearm.

Ardrin looked at it curiously, and smiled maliciously beneath his mask. "You could have just asked," he said, getting up from his throne borne of dark mana. He went down the small flight of steps before him, walking past the two young men.

His eyes were glowing more intensely as he *drew mana from the Underworld. The lifeless, gloom-ridden, and ashen realm. The ten- drils of dark mana from the sphere far above him voraciously swarmed towards his outstretched hand* as he condensed the mana in the Be- tween.

He muttered something just out of earshot of either of the two, young men present, and slammed the globe of dark mana into the floor. The resulting eruption of violet and red tendrils of mana was astounding, forcing both Athar and Irun to shield their faces.

A claw sprouted out of the ground, as the mana whirled around its increasingly growing body, crawling out of the teleportation hole in the ground. It snorted and growled as it grew to its full size which was a little taller than Irun. Without another word, the Masked One created the scarlet claw he had used on the ochelon with Athar.

You're using that again? Athar thought, knowing his master could hear it. *Yes, but this time I would take a few steps back if I were you,* Ardrin replied with a small hint of amusement in his voice.

The claw spawned from the Nethersong Mask lashed out before the newly-spawned daemon could react, latching onto its core, tearing it out of its enlarged body. The result was an explosion of blood and entrails being strewn about the room. Athar, who had seen this before, already had a small, protective barrier to shield him from the gore.

Irun, for whatever reason, hadn't budged.

"What the fuck was that?" he asked, wiping the blood from his face. He noticed a piece of intestine hanging from his pauldron with other unidentifiable bits and blood littering the rest of his body. "Stop whining like you haven't been covered in worse before," Ardrin said condescendingly, holding the freshly extracted core in front of him. Irun felt a tinge of embarrassment at his own reaction, and began to pull himself together. Athar, on the other hand, lowered his shield, chuckling quietly as he did so. The entrails and blood that would have reached him were now falling to the floor with a *splat*.

"What are you going to do with that core?" Irun asked, still picking unidentifiable bits out of the crevasses of his armor. "I'm making sure that this core will be suitable, and that there are no imperfections," Ardrin replied. "*Suitable*? Suitable for what?" Irun asked. "For this," the Masked One replied, his eyes glowing intensely as he rammed the claw into Irun's chest.

The merging of the daemonic core and Irun's let out another burst of mana, with the boy's screams echoing throughout the halls. Dark mana could be seen flowing through his bulging veins, as his body grew and transformed.

While their cores were merging, Ardrin used the claw and sliced off one of the daemon's arms, and fused it to Irun's. The daemonic arm responded to the dark mana, and began to merge itself with

Irun's, replacing it entirely. "Wh-what happened?" Irun asked, his body ceasing to wriggle out of his control.

"I fused your core with that of a daemon's. Not to mention I just replaced your arm," Ardrin replied. "*Replaced*?" Irun asked, looking down at where his own arm used to be. He stumbled backwards and looked at his new arm, seeing its daemonic form fully integrated into his body. "What the fuck?" he asked quietly. "Where the hell did *my* arm go?" he asked, still moving the new arm around.

"First of all, in order for you to gain more power, you need the daemon's core. Second, for a daemonic core to be compatible with your body, you must take a piece of it and fuse it to your own. Think of it as a binding contract to use their power; for each core merged with, you need a piece of them to stay with you. Theoretically speaking, you could replace your entire body with daemonic parts, with the exception of your head, heart, and spine, of course," the Masked One explained. "I didn't know that was possible," Athar said.

"Well, he was already missing a limb, so I figured this would be a much easier demonstration than watching the daemonic arm *devour* the part it was meant to fuse with. Nevertheless, there are many things I have yet to teach you, Athar," the Masked One said, walking towards the pair.

"Thank you for the arm, my lord," Irun said, acknowledging his new situation. "You've done me a great service by providing me timely and accurate information on your former comrades. Consider it a token of my thanks, *you little shit*," Ardrin said dismissively. *It's probably best if I shut up now*, Irun thought. "Probably," the Masked One said, answering his thoughts and not bothering to look at him.

Athar put a hand on the astonished Irun's shoulder. "Don't worry, it takes time to get used to the fact that he can always hear your thoughts," he said, mildly shaking his head. "Yeah, I suppose this will take some getting used to," Irun said, rubbing his new arm. "I'm Athar, by the way," the man said, outstretching his hand.

"Irun. Sorry I haven't been very social since coming here," he replied, shaking the man's hand. "Oh, I'm sure it couldn't have been easy to leave the synners," Athar said, trying to sympathize.

Irun didn't reply, but instead nodded his agreement. *This isn't the time to talk about that,* he thought. "How the hell did you survive here? Wait, how long *have you been here*?" Irun asked.

He's got to be around my age by the looks of it, but how did he get here? he thought.

"I was about seven years old when my mother was murdered. At the time, Coltend Castle was a very different place. It had become lawless, unruly, and unfair to any and all who had lived there. It was no real surprise to me when I found my mother dead in the street with a fancy-looking knife in her chest," Athar explained.

"I... I'm sorry to hear that. I also know what it's like to lose someone close to you like that," Irun said, remembering his father. "Oh, I'm over it now," Athar shrugged. "Besides, it's not like anything I could've done back then would've changed the outcome," he continued. "Right," Irun said, his eyes veering away.

"It's not all been bad, though," Athar said. "Recently, I've learned to use mana and cast a few spells. I've only been at it for a few weeks, but I'm very proud of my progress," he said, slight hints of excitement seeping through his voice. "Has he given you the Gwynnleaf?" Irun asked, his eyes opening wide. "Oh, you mean the plant? No, no.

I learned it from a book by someone named Farenger Efer. Not a clue who that is, but his writings *did* teach me a lot," Athar replied. "You learned mana manipulation from a book? The Masked One didn't teach you anything?" Irun asked.

"Not really. The only thing he taught me was that because I immediately used dark mana, and haven't managed to use Ethereal mana, I have to keep that connection up by drinking this foul-tasting deathmold concoction," Athar began to explain. "Karak, a daemon who is his second in command, drinks this stuff like an ant to honey. I don't know how he does it, but I guess it's because it reminds him of home," he continued.

"I see," Irun said pensively. "How did *you* learn mana manipulation?" Athar asked, genuine excitement on his face like that of a child. "I was a synner, remember?" Irun replied. "Ah, yeah. So you've had some of that Gwynnleaf stuff my master was talking about, then," Athar surmised. "I did, and I'm genuinely surprised to hear that you're able to manipulate mana without it," Irun said.

"I'm not a genius at it like you might be, by any means," Athar said, nudging his newfound friend. "Well, it's a little different when your livelihood depends on it," Irun said with a shrug. "You mean to tell me that *all* of you know *sword castering*? At least I think that's what it's called," Athar asked.

"Sword-*casting*, and yes, I do," Irun replied more coldly than he intended. "Gods above and below, can you teach me?" Athar asked, a hopeful grin on his face beginning to show. "I'll think about it," Irun thought. "Better than nothing!" Athar, now riddled with excitement at the prospect, pumped his fist.

How isolated has he been? He's acting like a child, Irun thought.

Seeing the look on Irun's face, Athar regained his composure. "I'm sorry. I just... I haven't really had the chance to talk to anyone my own age, let alone have someone teach me sword skills," he said, patting his clothes down.

"It's alright. I'm just curious about a few things," Irun began. "Curious about what? Oh, gods, I didn't know having a conversation could actually be this refreshing," Athar said, still trying to contain his excitement. "Well, for starters you said your mother was murdered. How the hell did you end up *here*?" Irun asked.

Hmm, how do I explain this? Athar thought, rubbing his chin.

"Well, *for starters* I'm a bastard, so it wasn't going to work out for me to stay in the city any longer. With my mother dead, there really wasn't anywhere for me *to* go. I narrowly escaped a few more people wearing armor that tried to capture me, but for what reason, I still don't know. The Masked One seems to know more than he lets off, but I have a hard time conversing with him sometimes," Athar began. "You said that people in *armor* tried to capture you?" Irun said, trying to get the excited man back on track.

"Oh, yes. Like I said, I'm a bastard. King Truls' bastard nonetheless," he said, playing it off like it was a common thing to say. "You're fucking *who's bastard*?" Irun asked, trying to see if he heard that correctly. "King Truls Wishert? Or should I say *former king*, now that he's chewing dirt, I suppose," Athar said pensively.

Holy shit. This is Truls' bastard? I remember Mourtis talking about something like this when I first started communicating with him and the Masked One, but I had no idea he'd fucking be here, Irun thought.

"So, basically, King Truls sent people to capture you after he found out your mother had been murdered?" Irun asked. "Well, it's probably not *exactly* how that happened, but yes. For all I know, *he* was the fucker who stabbed her in the first place. Guess I'll never get that answer now," Athar explained. "Gods above and below," Irun exhaled.

"What ended up bringing you this far North?" Irun asked, trying to move the conversation forward. "Well, after I'd gotten away from the armed guards, I didn't know where I was going. I spent the better part of two years wandering around the Continent, trying to both hide my identity and survive. Instinct is a weird concept to grasp, but I quickly learned to trust it when it came to the outside world. One day, however, I was grabbing an apple from a merchant's stall in hopes of having something to eat that day, when I was suddenly stopped by an odd-looking tendril," Athar said.

"A tendril? You mean one of mana?" Irun asked. "I didn't know it at the time, but yes. The tendril grabbed me and pulled me aside just in time for a guard not to see me taking the apple. Once the guard left, the tendril moved like it wanted me to follow it. I didn't know why, but I felt I could trust it to lead me to safety. Eventually, I found *him*, standing there with his dark cloak and mask, towering over me. I felt scared, of course, but because he was the one who had saved me from the guard, my instincts told me I could trust him. Over the years he's treated me like a slave, but I suppose it's better than being killed by an armed guard," Athar explained.

"And I thought my story was rough," Irun said pensively. "Oh? What's yours?" Athar asked. "Dad was a synner, mom was a trader. I, uh... I don't really want to talk about that right now," Irun said distantly as memories of his childhood flashed in his mind's eye.

"That's okay, I won't pry right now, but I will expect a decent story sometime. After all, we're kind of stuck here together now," Athar said, shrugging his shoulders.

Was his attitude always like this? Even with the Masked One? Or is this who he truly is, and not whatever that weird servant-master *deal is they've got going on?* Irun thought.

"Why the synners, though? Why not go for a guardsmen position or something along those lines?" Athar asked. "That's a bit... morbid to answer right now, but in short, it wasn't really my choice," Athar said, scratching the back of his head.

"Alright, alright. I said I won't pry, but I didn't realize the two things were that closely related. I'm sorry. I'll wait until you're ready to tell me," Athar said. "Thank you for understanding," Irun said, his tone much softer than intended. "Oh, you don't have to thank me," Athar shrugged.

"We all have different experiences in life, and I can't compare my trauma to yours. What yours did to you might feel like the equivalent of what mine did to me. I have to accept the fact that what happened to us is different, and that we have each responded to those things differently," he continued, putting a hand on Irun's shoulder which was now much higher than his.

"That was surprisingly insightful for someone so isolated from society," Irun noted. "Heh, you remind me of someone's brother I once knew," he said, thinking of Bernar. Athar looked at him, almost as if he could see the gears turning in Irun's head.

"I'm not sure what ultimately led you to betraying them, but I think I agree with the Masked One that you still have lingering feelings about that place," Athar noted. "Shut up," Irun snapped.

"Sorry. I guess it makes sense, knowing that you spent most of your life with those people," Athar concluded. "It's fine, I just..." Irun stopped himself.

Just as I thought, there's no way he was completely sure of his decision, Athar thought. Luckily for him, Ardrin was either far enough away to not hear his thoughts, or simply didn't care.

"Speaking of family, you don't have any brothers, do you? Blood brothers, I mean, not your old brothers-in-arms," Athar asked. Irun took a second to think about the question posed. "I'd be lying if I said I knew for sure whether I have a sibling. It's been years since I've been able to speak to my mother," Irun replied, scratching his head. "I see..." Athar said, trying to piece together what information he could.

"Well, now that we've gotten to know each other a little, how about it?" Athar asked sheepishly. "How about what?" Irun asked, lifting an eyebrow. Athar gave him a wry smile in response. "You want to learn sword-casting at your age?" Irun asked, looking the man up and down. Athar was taken aback at the comment, putting a hand to his chest. "At *my* age? Rude. I'm a lot more fit than I look with these clothes, I'd have you know," he said, exhaling sharply.

Irun watched his unlikely companion hold the pose like he had been stabbed through the heart and sighed. "Fine. I'll teach you some of what I can," he caved. Athar, now giddy with excitement, pumped his fist again.

"Mission successful!" he hissed through a grin.

CHAPTER 28
OLD STONES

Far in the North, just a few days' ride from Odensby, Anders slept soundly for the first time in what felt like an eternity, his wheat-blonde hair strewn across his face. Meanwhile, Unni sat at the edge of the bed, staring blankly at the wall as she went over memories of her past. Scenes of bloodshed, screaming, and terror flashed rapidly in her mind, causing her to flinch at the mental image of the last memory that presented itself to her.

Well, that's enough thinking of that. I should probably try to get back to sleep, she thought, turning around to tuck herself back into bed next to Anders.

It's been 10 years since then, how am I still affected by the memory of that child? she thought, tugging the heavy quilt up to the tip of her nose as tears welled in her eyes.

Was there really no other way? Was there nothing I could've done? Could I even talk to anyone about this? How do I explain it, or where should I even begin if I tried?

She closed her eyes tightly in an attempt to flush the memories from her mind, to no avail. The silent sobs and minor convulsions she allowed herself were of little comfort anymore, as the memories had begun returning more frequently since King Mads' death.

Fuck, fuck, fuck! she screamed silently into the cacophony of her own mind. Suddenly, she felt a warm hand placed on her shoulder, with its thumb gently rubbing the linen that covered it.

"You know you can always talk to me, right?" Anders said with a voice that could have easily been mistaken for a creature mumbling in a mud and rock language. "I do. I just *can't* get the words out," she said, wiping away a small stream of tears that now fled towards the top of her ear. "I'm not ungrateful for your offer, just so that's clear," she said, trying to not make it sound like it wasn't as big of a deal as it was to her.

"Unni, love, I've known you for a long time. You've followed me on raids that have rarely ever gone well, and it took you all the way until this last one to fully trust me again. I've seen your exceptional prowess in battle, and I've always respected you for it," he began, turning over to look at her. He was only met with a large amount of hair since her back was turned to him with the covers pulled up to her shoulders.

"But I also know it took you years to recover from that night all those years ago, and I can honestly say I'm proud of your progress," Anders said as gently as he could with such a rasp in his voice. He leaned up on his elbow, and kissed her exposed temple, just barely seeing the tears glimmering in the moonlight from the window.

"I promise, if there's anything you need to talk about, you can always talk to me. I'm not one to judge. I've seen and done plenty of fucked up things in life, so don't think I don't know where you're coming from," he said, trying his best to sympathize.

"But that's just it, Anders," she began, finally turning to face him as her blue irises were caressed by bloodshot scleras. "You can't know where I'm coming from. You don't know the things I've seen, heard, felt, tasted, had to do, had to avoid, not been able to say, had to keep quiet, lie about, witness, and ultimately allow to destroy my sense of self. The only thing keeping me sane the past few years has been you and your mission to kill him, regardless of the failed missions because *I* felt and relied on *your* purpose. Now? Now what? What the *fuck* am I supposed to do now that it's over? These memories haven't gone anywhere! It's like they were just repressed," she paused, trying to take a deep breath to appease the oncoming sobs.

"By the fucking gods above and below, what do I do now?" she asked, using both palms to wipe away a stream of tears from her cheeks. "What should I do? Relive the memories? Relive the taste of blood in my mouth, or the sweat in my eyes from those times that have long since scarred me? Try to sleep at night and pretend I've been fine all of this time?" she asked rapidly, almost as if a floodgate had been opened. Anders remained quiet.

Shit. There's a question I know I don't have an answer for, he thought, unfocusing his eyes while trying to find something to say.

"I asked you a question," she said, her tone growing darker. "I heard what you asked, I just... I don't know. I don't have an answer, and I'd be lying if I said I knew what to do here," he said, defeatedly. "I've fought in countless battles, and slain even more monsters. Through my years of that, I have always felt I've known what the correct answer was for *me*. With *other* people and their emotions it's just... *different*," he said, emphasizing the last word.

Unni sighed. "I'm sorry. I didn't mean to put all of that on you like that," she said, wiping away another tear. He combed his fingers through her messy hair, pushing more than a few strands back behind her ear.

"No, no. You're fine, love. I just... I'm sorry that I don't have the answers or a way to help you dig yourself out of the emotional hole you're in. Nevertheless, I don't want you to feel like you're alone in this, though. I want you to know that you're heard and that your darkest, innermost thoughts are safe with me. Even if you feel like the world would turn against you for saying them aloud, I'll be here to face it with you for as long as I can be. Is that okay, or is there anything more I can do for you?" he asked gently.

Tears welled in her eyes, as she buried her face deep into his shoulder. He could feel the tears running down his exposed chest, and the small jolts from her silent sobs shook the bed lightly. "You *are* my world," she said hoarsely.

A few hours passed and morning finally came, with the rays of sunlight gently kissing the rooftops of the small village. With those rays came the sounds of cheers outside the house they were staying in. "Come on, love. They're waiting for us," he said, shaking Unni gently. Her puffy eyes opened slowly, as she nodded her understanding. Within a few minutes, the pair was ready, and performing some final checks near the front door.

"Are you ready to do this?" Anders asked, checking the straps on her armor and cloak. "When I'm by your side, I'm ready for anything," she said, forcing a smile. He returned her smile warmly, opening the door to a full crowd of outcast synners.

I can't believe we've come this far in such a short time since the raid on Odensby, he thought.

He waved his hand at the crowd while Unni simply raised hers curtly with a thin-lipped smile. He halted his raised hand to signal for silence.

"My friends! Today we retake Odensby as its leaders, not its enemies," he began, a loud roar resounding from the crowd. "It has been ten long and arduous years since we were cast out unjustly, but today is a day for celebration! Since the death of King Mads, we have stepped up and made preparations for us to take over Odensby as its rightful rulers. Today those preparations have come to fruition, and as such we will *finally* have our true homes back!" he shouted. The crowd before him roared once more, as a growing smile began to show on his face. "We ride for Odensby, and to our long-lost homes!" he shouted as the roaring continued.

Within the few days that followed, all had made the journey from their small village to the gates of Odensby. Signs of their raid just a few weeks prior still showed along the ramparts of the high walls. "Heh, I remember climbing down that wall like a thief in the night," Unni said, her disposition a little more cheerful than a few nights prior. "I know you're an expert sword-caster, but I had no idea you could also climb that well," Anders said playfully.

"Of course I can! I grew up climbing the trees that neighbored my house all the time. Did you really think I *wouldn't* be able to climb like that after having grown up in the Darlig forest?" she asked, lightly punching his shoulder. "Oh, no. I knew that already, but climbing a tree is different than scaling a wall this high with hooks and ropes," Anders said, pointing upward. Just as he did, Mads' former banner was released from the front of the gate.

"Why did they release the banner like that?" Unni asked, genuinely puzzled. "It's customary here in Hjalfar to drop the banner of the old ruler to welcome the new one. It helps signify the transition of power. They'll raise our banner as soon as we pass under the gate," he said, watching the massive banner float towards the ground, gently carried by the morning breeze. "I see," she said, observing the banner as well.

"Open the gate!" a voice called out from the rampart. The sound of the massive gears turning could be heard from behind the massive, oaken gate. "Welcome back to Odensby, *lord*," a woman's voice shouted over the sound of the gears clunking into place. "It's good to be back behind these old stones and not as their enemy, Commander Lande," Anders replied.

She's still the same Trina I know, and she's just as terrifying as before, he thought, looking back on his time in Odensby.

They had fought together on many occasions, and while they were on par with each other in terms of strength, she was always a bit quicker on her feet than he was.

"Won't you follow us?" he asked, barely needing to look down at her from atop his horse. "I'll be there after I've made sure all of your people have made it inside," she said, gesturing towards the carriages behind him. "We won't begin without you, then," he said, giving her a warm smile. "I know you won't because you know I'll kill you if you do," she said, returning a menacing smile.

Yep, still just as terrifying, he thought.

Unni, who had watched the whole exchange, eyed the giant woman. Her broad shoulders and shoulder-length, auburn hair peeking out from under her steel helmet made her a formidable entity. "Don't be late," Unni managed to say, trying to be friendly. Trina had other ideas, as the malicious smile turned to ever-so-slight disgust when faced with her radiant, green eyes peering deeply into Unni's soul. "I wouldn't miss it for the world," Trina replied.

Her presence is undeniably palpable, Unni thought as she passed by. *I can still feel her eyes locked onto me like a hawk to a rabbit. Who does she think she is?* her thoughts trailed as she slowly rode away from the gate.

Once everyone had entered, the gate was closed and Trina, soon after, worked her way up to the main palace, lost in thought.

Where the hell have I seen that woman before? she asked herself, trying desperately to put a face to a place.

"Commander Lande!" a voice called out, shattering her concentration. "What is it, sergeant?" she asked, already recognizing the voice. She turned around to find a young man in his mid-twenties, with the Odensby crest on his chest plate and his armor well polished, rendering a perfect salute accented by his pale blue eyes sternly looking ahead. "Your presence is requested at the front of the palace for the Change of Rule ceremony," the sergeant said, still holding the salute which she returned promptly.

"I was already on my way there, Sergeant Wien," she said plaintively. "Walk with me, will you? I want to pick your brain for a minute," she asked. "O-of course, ma'am," Wien replied, scurrying up beside her. "I'm not sure if you remember him, as it's been about ten years since his exile, but do you remember Anders?" she asked directly. "I remember him well, ma'am. He always treated me well as a child. Why do you ask?" he replied, intrigue ringing in his voice.

"Well, it feels like he's *changed*, and I don't know if it's for the better. That woman he's with... I feel like I know her from somewhere," she began, losing herself in thought once more. "You do? But, what about her? She seemed nice enough," Wien replied, scratching the back of his head. "You're only saying that because you're attracted to her," she remarked.

Wien blushed. "W-well, ma'am, she *is* quite beautiful," he stammered. "Yes, but beauty beguiles one's senses. You should've learned that by now after the *incident* with that prostitute," she mocked, jabbing him with her elbow. "How was I supposed to know she had the *leaky clam*? You think I wanted to put my *tool* through that?" he asked, spreading his arms wide.

She stopped and looked at him for a moment. Without a word, he was reminded of his position. "Ma'am...?" he added. She snickered briefly, proceeding towards the palace once more. "You could've smelled her *yeasty fish* all the way from Caegwen, if the wind were just right, but I digress. I want you to keep an eye on Unni, and *not* in that way, understood?" she asked.

"I do, ma'am, but why me? Why not do it yourself?" Wien nodded, trying to understand her reasoning for picking him. "I could tell from that first meeting that she's already wary of me. I'm not sure if she knows just *what* I am to Anders, but I don't trust her. Not. One. Bit," she said, emphasizing each word heavily.

I've never seen her this angry outside of training before, Wien gulped a ball of spit akin to cotton.

"I-it will be done, ma'am. How often do you want reports on her?" he asked. "Daily and without falter. If anything happens, if she wipes her ass back-to-front instead of front-to-back, I want to know about it. Is that understood?" she asked, still looking ahead toward where the ceremony was to take place. "I understand. It will be done, Commander," he replied, rendering an unseen salute before veering down an alleyway.

"Let's see what you're hiding," she muttered to no one in particular. Within the hour, the Change of Rule's set up had been completed. Bouquets and shields now riddled the courtyard before the entrance to the main palace. The ever-growing crowd began to cheer and *whoop* at the prospect of a new leader, even if his takeover was a little more sudden than most would have liked.

Anders changed out of his riding attire, and stepped into clothes that helped display his status. A thick bear coat draped atop his shoulders, with armor that could've made a warlord jealous hiding underneath it. Unni had also changed into a slim, white dress, though her battle-hardened figure was only enhanced by the tightness of the dress. "This is so fucking uncomfortable. I can't breathe," she murmured, testing the limits of the seams. "I didn't choose that dress," Anders said, turning to look at her.

"I think it suits you," he said after a few seconds of observation. Her eyes turned into little more than a pair of thin lines. "Wh-what? I'm no longer allowed to think you look nice in a dress as a *woman* and not as a *warrior*?" he asked, lifting his hands up slightly. She blushed mildly, taking in his words like an ant to honey. "Well, when you put it *that* way," she said, cracking a bashful smile. "Still, this dress is far too tight for me, beautiful as it may be. I'm changing into armor as well," she said, finally releasing her taut muscles, tearing the seams in the process.

Anders could only shake his head. "I should've guessed that would happen," he sighed.

After a wardrobe change, Unni and Anders walked out into the vast hall of the palace. Numerous skulls of fallen, legendary beasts hung overhead, witnessing all those who have ruled since the dawn of Odensby itself. While there were no stained-glass windows like in Coltend, there was no shortage of natural light beaming through the expertly crafted windows that riddled the walls. Unni gawked at all of these, but Anders held his gaze forward as they went.

"I've never seen *this* many skulls before," she noted, staring at one of the ancient wyrm skulls that hung a few meters above her head. "I tend to forget you didn't spend much time here at Odensby," he noted. "Well, I was always at Grundsvollr, and never got to live here like you did," she said, gently nudging his arm. "Grundsvollr wasn't a bad place to be, either. After all, I spent many of my formative years training there," he said as memories flooded his mind.

"The palace had its own issues, though, and none of them were ever fully addressed by the ruling family. They swept countless issues under the rug, pretending like everything was fine. In reality, like King Truls' reign, it was a nightmare," he explained.

"You don't talk about your time here often," she said, her eyes beginning to squint with the bright sunlight bouncing off the polished, stone floor. "There are memories I'd rather not keep of this place. Right now, however, I'd prefer to make newer and better ones than stay stuck in the past," he said without looking at her.

"That's... fair," she noted, lowering her gaze a little. "Come, love. Let's bring about a new era for this country together," he said, facing her with a warm smile. She met his gaze, kissing him before the pair stepped into the sunlight.

The gathered crowd cheered with their appearance, waving and jumping to try and be seen by the two, new, rulers. Both waved their hands as they walked towards their thrones that were placed on an elevated stage in front of the crowd. Trina watched from afar, as Wien moved into his position near the foot of the stage, nodding subtly at each other.

The new rulers were met by a druid in traditional garb. He stood atop the stage with an oversized cloak, painted face, and antlers atop his head. His outfit was accented by beads and other such trinkets of stone and bone, while he mumbled in some ancient language of mud and rock only he understood.

He raised his staff which was adorned with a deer's skull, antlers still attached, and mana seeping from its eyes. "Odensby! Hear me now!" he shouted, enhancing his voice with mana. The crowd immediately quieted down, listening attentively. "As the former king, Mads Oden, has fallen at the hand of Anders Ulvensson in battle, we anoint him Ruler of Odensby. May he rule justly and fairly, bringing peace and prosperity to our lands for as long as his line remains intact!" the druid shouted, raising his staff high into the air.

The crowd responded to this by cheering more loudly than before, as they watched the druid place the crowns atop Anders and Unni's heads. They arose from their kneeling positions, and greeted the crowd once more. Trina tilted her head at the sight of Unni, but merely clicked her tongue in disgust. The druid raised his staff once more, silencing the crowd. "We will now hear a few words from King Anders before he takes the throne," he stated.

"People of Odensby," he began, stepping toward the edge of the stage as he did. "I will make this brief, since no one likes long-winded speeches," he said, getting a small chuckle out of the crowd. "Many of you have known me, or at least of me before my exile. Since then, much has changed, as Mads' rule grew increasingly more devastating to the population. I took it upon myself to bring his madness to an end, as he exiled those closest to him after the loss of his wife and child due to unforeseen circumstances. The years he stole from those once loyal to him will never again be regained, but I will do what I can, where I can for those who were affected. I will begin remedying that which he has hurt, and rebuilding that which he has destroyed. Together, we will rebuild our great country once and for all!" he shouted, raising his arms as the last few words left his mouth, receiving cheers from the crowd once more.

First promise to keep his speech short has already been kept, I see, Trina thought, watching the crowd closely for any signs of danger.

The pair sat in their thrones, shifting subtly as the crowd burst into much louder cheers than before.

This is how it's supposed to be, Anders thought, gripping Unni's hand a little more firmly as the smile grew on his face.

She, too, couldn't help but allow for her smile to show, as the pair continued waving to the crowd. Within a few moments, the stage began to roll back into the palace, disappearing from the crowd. "Welcome to your new home, your majesties," the druid said with a bow, creating a root from pure mana to lift him off the stage. The two watched in amazement, as he appeared to float to the ground like a feather. "It's been ages since I've seen anyone do that with mana," Unni said, her eyes still trying to comprehend what she was seeing. "A third stage druid is nothing to sneeze at for sure," Anders agreed.

The stage stopped near the back of the large hall, lowering the thrones gently into position. The pair sat patiently as a few of their new advisors poured in to greet them, as Wien joined the ranks of the inner guardsmen for the remainder of the ceremony.

Meanwhile in the Harutian royal palace, Zari, Bashaa's widow, paced back and forth along her balcony. Her wavy, walnut hair flowed down to her waist, as her pale green eyes contrasted against an olive complexion hidden beneath a turquoise kaftan. "Your Majesty, are you alright?" a voice called out from inside the large bedroom.

The thin, fabric curtains that flowed gently in the afternoon breeze faded her in and out of view of the servant calling for her. "I'm fine, I swear," Zari replied. "But you haven't eaten much of anything in the past few weeks. I'm beginning to worry for your health, Your Majesty," the servant retorted, genuine concern ringing in his voice.

"How can I eat knowing that *whore* that got my son killed is still alive?" she asked angrily. While it had only been a short while since the incident, her rage still boiled like an unattended pot of hatred soup. "I can't say that I understand your loss because I don't, Your Majesty," the servant began.

"I did swear to King Bashaa, may Yarathea bless his name, that I would take care of you while he was gone. To what extent, exactly, would be entirely up to you, as I'm sure he told you," the servant continued.

Her eyes became downcast, as she breathed a heavy sigh. "You're right," she said "My love would only have wanted the best for me," she acknowledged, reaching for the plate. "And I think that the best for me right now, is making sure that *bitch* gets what's coming to her," she said, angrily taking a bite of her food, staring in the direction of Coltend castle. "Your Majesty, I'm not sure I'm following. What are you saying?" the servant asked.

"You likely don't know this, but the old stones of the palace walls hold many secrets. Some of which have been hidden from the Continent as a whole to ensure they were kept safe. Harut is an old country, and in times past, many would come to us for more... *nefarious* tasks," Zari explained, still chewing on a small bite of food.

"You will see, Fazel. By the time your beard grows back out for its next shave, I will have my pieces ready to move," she said, her mood improving a little at the thought of Leona dying.

"By *pieces* you mean the hashishin?" Fazel asked, his hazel eyes opening widely, raising his eyebrows. "So you *do* know more than you let off. My husband was right to make sure he left me in your care," Zari said with a wry smirk on her face.

CHAPTER 29
BLOOD DEBT

Thorsen briskly walked up the steps that lead to the re-built ravenry of Coltend Castle. His long, blonde hair and well-above average height made him tower over many of the guardsmen as he passed them. "Oh, shit. He's back!" he heard one of them say excitedly from a distance, breaking his usually fierce countenance into a wry smile.

"Aside from my little trip to the North with the queen and Meliss, I never *really* left," he said in his thick accent, walking up to the pair just ahead of him. "Well, you haven't been around here as much since just after the battle, so he's got a point," a female voice said.

Marte, one of the newest recruits said, polishing her sword with her chestnut hair and honey colored eyes aimed in the same direction as the sword on her lap. "I've been busy, and you know that," Thorsen retorted. "Well, hopefully the acting Commander of the Warrior's Guild isn't too busy to train us new recruits," she said playfully, glancing up at the giant.

"Hey, cut him some slack. There's been so much work to do since then, it's a wonder he's helped us train at all," another voice cut in. "Neko, I don't think he needs you to stand up for him. The top of your head hardly reaches his chest, so you wouldn't make much of a difference," Marte shot jokingly.

Neko pouted briefly, looking away from Marte like a toddler would when throwing a fit. His hair was cut close enough to his scalp to reflect the small amounts of sunlight from the window off his pale, olive skin and gently pointed ears. "Oh, I'm sorry, *Giantess*, I didn't know my half-elf ass was competing with your oversized one," he said.

Marte finally stood up, setting her sword down and proceeding to look over the top of his head. "When have we ever *not* competed? We've competed since we were kids, and you've yet to beat me *once* at anything," she said, moving her flattened hand from the top of his head to the base of her chin. "Hey, I've beaten you at that one, wooden puzzle the fish vendor gave us!" he exclaimed, smacking her hand away, forcing a giggle out of the tall woman.

"That's because I *physically* couldn't solve it. My..." she began to say. "Your *what*?" Neko asked with an expectant smile. "My hands are *too fucking big*. There, I said it. Can you wipe that shit-eating grin off your face, now?" she asked, turning an ever-so-slight shade of bright pink.

"Children," Thorsen sighed, shaking his head and lightly pinching the bridge of his nose. "In any case, I was told there was a message for me here," he said with a suggestive tone. "Oh, right. There's been an influx of ravens since we finished rebuilding the ravenry. Apparently not having anywhere to land was sending them back to their points of origin," Neko said, opening the door to it.

After a few minutes of searching, he returned with a piece of parchment. "It's from someone named Ahkmed, but we don't know who this person is. All we can tell from the handwriting is that it's addressed to you," he said, handing it to the large man. "I don't know anyone by this name," Thorsen said, eyeing the handwriting carefully. He broke the unmarked seal on it, and unfolded the parchment.

His eyes opened widely. "Gods above and below, how long has this been sitting here?" he asked. "I-I'm not sure. A few days, maybe a week now?" Neko replied. "Well, Commander Gorm is alive, and he's been recovering in a small village just off the Rhydian Pass. I have to tell the queen," Thorsen said with an air of urgency he rarely showed.

Neko and Marte glanced at each other briefly, nodding their silent agreement. "We're coming with you," Marte said. "What? Why would you *need* to come with me if I'm just going to report to the queen?" Thorsen asked. "Well, you see, it's because we have a few things to ask you while you're on your way there," she said matter-of-factly. "Fine, but when we get there, you're to stay *exactly* where I tell you to stay, understood?" the giant requested, peering inquisitively into their souls.

"Y-you don't have to say it like that," Neko replied, beginning to fear for his life. Thorsen allowed a small grin to cross his face. "Good. Let's move," he said.

The trio walked briskly towards where Leona was last seen. Along the way, some final repairs were being made to the shattered windows of the main hall, forcing them to detour. "How are there still so few workers for the castle?" Marte asked, a tinge of remorse swaying her words. "While many apparently managed to escape the Church of Mideia's uprising, or rather, *Mourtis'* uprising, a lot of people who worked in the castle were viciously slaughtered. Someone once told me it had to do with what the queen did, but I don't think that was the *only* reason," Neko replied.

"What did the queen have to do with their slaughter?" Marte asked. "According to a few witnesses who survived, apparently it had something to do with the queen having an affair wi-..." he stopped, noticing the giant in front of him standing like an obelisk. "I normally don't threaten people, because I don't have to, but watch your *tone*, boy," he said, his register lower than his usual, cheerful tone.

With a presence like that, it's not hard to see why he's the queen's primary bodyguard and acting Commander, Neko thought.

"I-I didn't mean anything by it," he said, putting his hands up in surrender. "I know you didn't, but *others* might take that a little differently, don't you think?" Thorsen retorted, giving a brief and suggestive glance at their surroundings. "I'm sorry," Neko said dejectedly. "Be mindful of your surroundings next time. More often than not, the last people you would want to be close to you will be the ones right next to you. Do you understand what I mean?" Thorsen asked, putting an oversized hand on the small man's shoulder.

"I do understand," Neko replied, nodding his head. "Good, then you won't make the same mistake twice, will you?" Marte asked, trying to lighten the mood, putting her arm around her friend as Thorsen removed his hand. "After the shit I've been meaning to take for the last two days nearly decided to present itself to my prospective judge, jury, and executioner, yes," Neko said, scratching the back of his head.

"I didn't need the mental image of that, but thanks," she spat sarcastically, awkwardly removing her arm from around her friend's shoulder.

"Regardless of who or *what* was at fault, a lot of people died during the attack. I'm just glad we were able to get out when we did," Neko said, recalling the vivid horrors of seeing people being ripped in half by countless glicks and other such creatures.

In broad daylight, nonetheless, he thought.

"He's right, though. We owe it to those who weren't lucky enough to make it out alive to *not* make similar mistakes. Even if it wasn't their fault, we *can't* let that happen again," Marte said, her eyes showing confidence in her words.

"You know, for as much shit as you talk, seeing you so determined has given *me* a sense of it as well," Neko said, an ever-so-slight blush appearing on his face. Marte couldn't help but blush as well, turning her face away from the much shorter man. Thorsen felt a small sense of pride in their words.

Even these new recruits feel they owe a blood debt to those who have fallen. I just wish I had more time to train them, he thought, observing the two awkwardly exchanging glances.

They eventually made their way to the queen's room, just as Claire was exiting. "Oh, Thorsen!" she said, blushing when she saw him. The color change to her face was minimal, however, as she was well known for constantly being pickled with eel vodka. "G-good morning, Claire," Thorsen said, holding as much of his breath as he could.

Fucking hell, she's sauced again, he thought.

"What's the head of the Warrior's Guild doing here? Has he come to make sure Her Majesty isn't oversleeping? Because I've already done that," she said, pridefully puffing out her, arguably oversized, chest.

"Not quite, though I'm sure she's already *very much* awake as it is," he said, desperately holding his hand back from pinching his nose. "Ah, well, then what brings you here?" she asked. "I have a message for her regarding Gorm," he said, taking a serious tone. "Gorm? That *handsome* man? He's still alive?" she asked excitedly.

There's no way she thinks he's handsome. Desperate times, I guess, he thought.

"If the letter is to be believed, then yes," he said, nodding his head. Claire squirmed excitedly, clenching her fists and shaking them near her chest. "I'm so glad to hear he's alive!" she said in as hushed of a tone as she could. "Go on and tell Her Majesty. I'll take my leave," she said, setting off at a rapid pace down the stairs, barrelling past the two recruits.

She's an absolute piece of work, but she's got a good heart. I'm glad she made it out in time, he thought, smiling gently as he watched her happily skip down the stairs.

He turned and faced the two who remained, and held up a hand. "Wait here while I go and brief Her Majesty. It shouldn't be long, but I don't want anyone else eavesdropping on the conversation, understood?" he asked, staring into the pair's eyes. "Yes, sir!" the two saluted. He returned the salute, and knocked on the door. A gentle voice beckoned him in, as he unlatched the bolt to the cedarwood door.

The morning sun shone brightly into the room from the large window, as golden rays pierced through the folds of the curtain. Leona, with her midnight hair, porcelain skin, and pale blue eyes twirled her brand-new dress in front of the mirror. The corset-like midsection held firm as the larger folds of the lower half flowed gently through the air. "What do you think, Thorsen? How does it look?" she asked, glancing at him briefly through the mirror.

"If I were a woman, I would wish that I could be even a fraction as *grossly incandescent* as you are," he said, putting a hand on his chest and bowing. "By the Graces, I never took you for a womanizer," she said, pleasantly surprised, turning to face him. "I might have picked up a thing or two from Bernar," he shrugged. Leona chuckled, her voice light and playful as the rays reflecting off her hair.

Bernar truly is a lucky man, he thought.

"It is good to see you, my friend," she said, walking towards him. "It is good to see you, too, my queen," he replied with a bow. "Oh, come now! You know how I feel about pleasantries when there aren't any nobles around. You *did* save mine and Meliss' life not too long ago, so I would be loath to treat you like a mere soldier," she said, flicking the back of her hand off his breastplate. "Ouch," she said quietly, rubbing her knuckles gently.

Thorsen chuckled lightly, his booming voice emanating a low, rhythmic baritone. "Be careful. Bernar would probably kill me if he ever saw a bruise on you," he said playfully. "Could he match you in battle?" she asked, genuinely curious. "My lady, I am, at best, in the second stage of mana manipulation. Bernar is well into the fifth. I am, ultimately, no match for him, regardless of my speed and size," Thorsen said humbly.

"Impossible," Leona said, her eyes opening wide. "It's true. Even Thoma would be on equal footing with me, which makes his older brother that much more terrifying," he continued. Leona was stunned. "I had no idea the difference in stages was that vast," she said pensively. "The difference between stage one and two is like night and day. Stage three would be the equivalent of throwing an eclipse into the mix. Stage four could be equated to having a second sun and moon spawn in, while stage five is *almost* otherworldly, mixing all of those elements together," he said as simplistically as he could.

"A difficult concept to wrap my head around, but if you say so, then it must be like that. I don't know much about mana, but I'm hoping Meliss will be able to tell me a bit about it when I see her again after her training," she said, glancing out the window towards Codrean. "Speaking of which, how are the new recruits?" she asked, changing the subject. "They're a little more eccentric than I'm used to, but they will make fine additions to the force," Thorsen replied in a low voice. "Why so quiet?" she asked, noting his tonal switch.

Thorsen fiddled with the message from the ravenry between his fingers, and handed it to her. "They gave me this. Apparently it had been there for a few weeks before reaching us," he said, watching her read through the letter. "He's still alive?" she asked, surprise reigning her voice. "He is, but he's in critical condition. Since the one taking care of him doesn't have mana capabilities, his recovery has been slower than it would be if he were here," he replied solemnly.

"I see," she said, thinking about his answer. "Since you're the new Commander of the Guild, do you think he would be fit to return to duty?" she asked. Thorsen thought about her question for a moment, but shook his head. "We don't fully know his current condition, but if he was on the Rhydian Pass when that horde was coming through, I doubt he would be fit for duty," he said, defeatedly. "I wouldn't mind him coming back to help train new recruits, but that might not be possible," he continued.

"Will you train them, then?" she asked after a brief, pensive pause. "I can put someone else in charge of administrative duties while you train them," she continued. "The only way I can think to train them is in the ways of a synner," he said, considering her offer. "I'd hope you would be able to train them in the ways of mana manipulation as well, to whatever extent you are able to," she said, a tinge of hope floating in her voice. "I can *try* to train them in mana, but it's not entirely up to me whether they'd be successful with it," he replied.

"What do you mean? Why wouldn't they be successful?" she asked with peaking curiosity. "Mana manipulation requires one to separate their consciousness from the real world, also known as the Between. When that happens, there is a chance that their concentration breaks, and their consciousness is lost to the Ethereal realm, leaving their body in a vegetative state," he began to explain. "By the Graces!" she exclaimed, her hand moving to her mouth.

"There is, however, a remedy for it, which is the Gwynnleaf plant's tincture, simplifying the process. I'm sure Bernar told you a little bit about it when we spent time with them on the way to Fangsdalr," he said, hoping she'd remember. "Yes, that part I *do* remember, among other things," she said, looking away and biting the corner of her lip.

Nope, stop it. Not right now, she thought, clearing her throat.

"In any case, we have the Gwynnleaf here, but is there anything else that needs to be done to it for it to be... *ingestible?*" she asked with a confused look on her face. "*Drinkable,* and yes, there are a few things that need to be done to it. Right now, however, we have other matters to discuss," he said, pulling out the letter and handing it to her.

She took it from his large hands, and unfolded the creases in the small parchment, struggling to make out the words that were written on it. Suddenly, her squinted eyes opened widely, as she realized what it said. "He's alive?" she asked excitedly. "He is, but he's been in critical condition since the horde came down the Rhydian Pass," he replied solemnly. "Without healers there to do their work, he'll be hard pressed to heal as quickly as he would if he were here. Whether he can make the journey to *get* here is another story entirely," he continued.

Leona looked pensively at Thorsen, flicking her eyes back and forth between him and the paper in her hand. "I think I understand what you mean," she began. "It's not that I don't want him back, but I don't think he will be able to lead the Warrior's Guild with his injuries even after they've healed. Perhaps being the head trainer for the new recruits, but even that he might end up struggling with," she explained. Thorsen nodded his head in agreement.

"I will do what I can in the meantime. However, there is one thing I would like to request of you, if I may," Thorsen said, his tone dropping a little. "And what could I possibly give to mine and Meliss' savior?" she asked inquisitively. "There are two outside that I would like to take directly under my wing. They've told me before that they owe a sort of blood-debt to those who lost their lives defending the castle. I would like to make sure that they are trained as well as I can possibly train them," he explained.

"You? Taking on two apprentices?" she asked, astounded at his request. "Is there something wrong if I do?" he asked, wondering if he had accidentally struck a nerve. "No, no! I just... I almost wish *you* had been the one to take up the mantle of training Meliss instead of Master Pyle," she said dejectedly.

By the Graces, I didn't know I'd miss her that much to the point where I would subject her to harsh training just to keep her around, she thought.

"Well, I would have, but Marte and Neko are at much different stages in their combat experience than she is. It wouldn't be fair to her if I were to have her join them," he suggested. "And you think her being trained by synners is any *less* gruesome?" she asked, raising an eyebrow.

"It..." he paused, gathering his thoughts. "It has nothing to do with it being gruesome or not. Both types of training would be difficult regardless of who it is; but their motivations are different," he began to explain. "Meliss longs for the strength to defend herself and her loved ones, yourself included," he began.

She considers me a loved one? Isn't she just the cutest? she thought, feeling the blood rush to her face.

"Neko and Marte however are out for blood, so I will teach them mana manipulation and sword skills that could make even the finest knight question his skills," Thorsen said confidently.

"You will?" the pair in question asked, bursting through the door. Thorsen didn't look at them, closing his eyes and sighing heavily. "Are these two the ones you were talking about?" Leona asked, chortling softly. "They are," he said, pinching the bridge of his nose, finally turning towards them. "While I'm disappointed, I'm not surprised you two were eavesdropping," he said, observing the two still sprawled on the floor. They got up quickly, dusted themselves off, and presented a salute to him, when Leona stepped out from behind him.

Shit, it's the queen, Marte thought, dropping her salute and elbowing Neko in the stomach in the time it took to blink.

As he doubled over, she moved with lightning speed to grab his nape and slam his head down into the ground. "Apologies, Your

Majesty," she said, bowing her head. Leona, still stifling a laugh, composed herself, walking towards the pair. Her majestic air radiated from her, as she held out her hand to the two. "I think I like you two already," she said with a warm smile. Marte took her hand, gazing into her sky colored eyes.

It's not much of a help to get me back on my feet, but it's a nice gesture. I should probably watch how much force I put into this, she thought as she gently pushed down on Leona's hand, getting to her feet.

Leona extended a hand towards the folded elf, and without even thinking, he took it, pulling much more heavily than he intended to, getting back onto his feet. Leona struggled, but managed to maintain her composure through it all. "Thank you, Your Majesty," he said, wincing slightly at the pain raging in his gut. "It's my pleasure," she replied with a warm smile.

She could melt a glacier with her smile, he thought as what could've been mistaken for a streak of light shone in his eyes.

He blushed, and backed away as quickly as he could. "Y-Your Majesty, w-we meant no disrespect by eavesdropping, but once we heard he was going to train us, we couldn't contain our excitement," Neko replied. "I see. But with that excitement, are you prepared to be rigorously trained and settle your... uh... what was it called again?" Leona asked Thorsen. *"Blood debt,* Your Majesty," he replied.

"Yes! Your blood debt!" she said, radiating more excitement than the pair in front of her. "We're ready, Your Majesty," Marte said, standing well beyond a head taller than Leona who strained her neck to look up at her. "Well, I'm sure that after Thorsen trains you, and you've settled your blood debt, you'll make *fine* bodyguards for me," she said, playfully hinting at their potential futures. "We... *what?*" Neko asked incredulously.

"However," Leona interrupted, "that is contingent on whether you can complete his training," she continued, gesturing at the giant behind her. "We'll do our best, Your Majesty," the pair said in unison, bowing as low as they could, though Neko winced through the pain. Leona smiled once again and put her hands on both of their shoulders. "Oh, I'm certain that you will! I look forward to watching your training," she said with a playful tone that immediately sent chills down their spines.

"You... *what?*" the pair asked.

"You heard me," she said playfully. "I'm going to observe your training for as long as you are here. By the Graces, I might even join in for a few lessons," she continued. Thorsen, on the other hand, was anything but amused. "Your Majesty, I can't allow you to join in on their training," he said with a heavy sigh.

"And why not? It's not like I'm going to learn mana manipulation like Meliss is doing... or am I?" she asked in jest, shrugging when she couldn't find the answer herself. "Then... what would you want to train in?" He asked, fearing the answer he was about to hear.

"Well, Meliss said that she wanted to grow stronger to protect herself, and while she is far younger than I am, I would also like a few lessons," she stated. "Besides, it's not like I can't surprise *you-know-who* with something to help ease his mind while we're apart," she winked.

The pressure to teach new recruits is one thing. Making sure I can teach her how to survive in a dangerous situation so that Bernar doesn't kill me is another kind of pressure. Gods above, was she serious about wanting to learn mana manipulation? Thorsen considered, digesting her request.

"Very well, then, Your Majesty," he caved. Leona brought her balled fists up to her chest and shook them rapidly, a high-pitched squeak resounding from her excited expression.

She took it from his large hands, and unfolded the creases in the small parchment, struggling to make out the words that were written on it. Suddenly, her squinted eyes opened widely, as she realized what it said. "He's alive?" she asked excitedly. "He is, but he's been in critical condition since the horde came down the Rhydian Pass," he replied solemnly. "Without healers there to do their work, he'll be hard pressed to heal as quickly as he would if he were here. Whether he can make the journey to *get* here is another story entirely," he continued.

Leona looked pensively at Thorsen, flicking her eyes back and forth between him and the paper in her hand. "I think I understand what you mean," she began. "It's not that I don't want him back, but I don't think he will be able to lead the Warrior's Guild with his injuries even after they've healed. Perhaps being the head trainer for the new recruits, but even that he might end up struggling with," she explained. Thorsen nodded his head in agreement.

"I will do what I can in the meantime. However, there is one thing I would like to request of you, if I may," Thorsen said, his tone dropping a little. "And what could I possibly give to mine and Meliss' savior?" she asked inquisitively. "There are two outside that I would like to take directly under my wing. They've told me before that they owe a sort of blood-debt to those who lost their lives defending the castle. I would like to make sure that they are trained as well as I can possibly train them," he explained.

"You? Taking on two apprentices?" she asked, astounded at his request. "Is there something wrong if I do?" he asked, wondering if he had accidentally struck a nerve. "No, no! I just... I almost wish *you* had been the one to take up the mantle of training Meliss instead of Master Pyle," she said dejectedly.

By the Graces, I didn't know I'd miss her that much to the point where I would subject her to harsh training just to keep her around, she thought.

"Well, I would have, but Marte and Neko are at much different stages in their combat experience than she is. It wouldn't be fair to her if I were to have her join them," he suggested. "And you think her being trained by synners is any *less* gruesome?" she asked, raising an eyebrow.

"It..." he paused, gathering his thoughts. "It has nothing to do with it being gruesome or not. Both types of training would be difficult regardless of who it is; but their motivations are different," he began to explain. "Meliss longs for the strength to defend herself and her loved ones, yourself included," he began.

She considers me a loved one? Isn't she just the cutest? she thought, feeling the blood rush to her face.

"Neko and Marte however are out for blood, so I will teach them mana manipulation and sword skills that could make even the finest knight question his skills," Thorsen said confidently.

"You will?" the pair in question asked, bursting through the door. Thorsen didn't look at them, closing his eyes and sighing heavily. "Are these two the ones you were talking about?" Leona asked, chortling softly. "They are," he said, pinching the bridge of his nose, finally turning towards them. "While I'm disappointed, I'm not surprised you two were eavesdropping," he said, observing the two still sprawled on the floor. They got up quickly, dusted themselves off, and presented a salute to him, when Leona stepped out from behind him.

Shit, it's the queen, Marte thought, dropping her salute and elbowing Neko in the stomach in the time it took to blink.

As he doubled over, she moved with lightning speed to grab his nape and slam his head down into the ground. "Apologies, Your Majesty," she said, bowing her head. Leona, still stifling a laugh, composed herself, walking towards the pair. Her majestic air radiated from her, as she held out her hand to the two. "I think I like you two already," she said with a warm smile. Marte took her hand, gazing into her sky colored eyes.

It's not much of a help to get me back on my feet, but it's a nice gesture. I should probably watch how much force I put into this, she thought as she gently pushed down on Leona's hand, getting to her feet.

Leona extended a hand towards the folded elf, and without even thinking, he took it, pulling much more heavily than he intended to, getting back onto his feet. Leona struggled, but managed to maintain her composure through it all. "Thank you, Your Majesty," he said, wincing slightly at the pain raging in his gut. "It's my pleasure," she replied with a warm smile.

She could melt a glacier with her smile, he thought as what could've been mistaken for a streak of light shone in his eyes.

He blushed, and backed away as quickly as he could. "Y-Your Majesty, w-we meant no disrespect by eavesdropping, but once we heard he was going to train us, we couldn't contain our excitement," Neko replied. "I see. But with that excitement, are you prepared to be rigorously trained and settle your... uh... what was it called again?" Leona asked Thorsen. "*Blood debt*, Your Majesty," he replied.

"Yes! Your blood debt!" she said, radiating more excitement than the pair in front of her. "We're ready, Your Majesty," Marte said, standing well beyond a head taller than Leona who strained her neck to look up at her. "Well, I'm sure that after Thorsen trains you, and you've settled your blood debt, you'll make *fine* bodyguards for me," she said, playfully hinting at their potential futures. "We... *what?*" Neko asked incredulously.

"However," Leona interrupted, "that is contingent on whether you can complete his training," she continued, gesturing at the giant behind her. "We'll do our best, Your Majesty," the pair said in unison, bowing as low as they could, though Neko winced through the pain. Leona smiled once again and put her hands on both of their shoulders. "Oh, I'm certain that you will! I look forward to watching your training," she said with a playful tone that immediately sent chills down their spines.

"You... *what?*" the pair asked.

"You heard me," she said playfully. "I'm going to observe your training for as long as you are here. By the Graces, I might even join in for a few lessons," she continued. Thorsen, on the other hand, was anything but amused. "Your Majesty, I can't allow you to join in on their training," he said with a heavy sigh.

"And why not? It's not like I'm going to learn mana manipulation like Meliss is doing... or am I?" she asked in jest, shrugging when she couldn't find the answer herself. "Then... what would you want to train in?" He asked, fearing the answer he was about to hear.

"Well, Meliss said that she wanted to grow stronger to protect herself, and while she is far younger than I am, I would also like a few lessons," she stated. "Besides, it's not like I can't surprise *you-know-who* with something to help ease his mind while we're apart," she winked.

The pressure to teach new recruits is one thing. Making sure I can teach her how to survive in a dangerous situation so that Bernar doesn't kill me is another kind of pressure. Gods above, was she serious about wanting to learn mana manipulation? Thorsen considered, digesting her request.

"Very well, then, Your Majesty," he caved. Leona brought her balled fists up to her chest and shook them rapidly, a high-pitched squeak resounding from her excited expression.

CHAPTER 30
A ROCK AND A HARD PLACE

I swung, and I missed.

No matter what I seemed to do, Taegin was just too fast for me. Over the course of the past few weeks, I'd been alternating between battling him and my brother whenever there was training to be had.

I know that while today might not be the day I finally land a blow on him, I'd still try my best to get close, I thought.

"Again, Thoma," Taegin said, having not even broken a sweat. Meanwhile, even with second stage mana manipulation having become second nature to me, I was still out of breath.

Just how large is this gap between us? I thought.

"You keep trying to hit me, but you're not making any progress. Do you know why?" he asked. I was dumbfounded by his question. "If I can't hit you, that means I'm just not going fast enough, right?" I asked, not entirely sure of the answer I wanted to hear. He sighed. It'd been a few days since I'd made any breakthroughs, but I couldn't understand what I was missing. "Attack me again, but this time, instead of paying attention to my body, pay attention to my mana," he said.

His mana? But his whole body is basically glowing with it when I'm in second stage, I thought. Not fully understanding his words, I got into my guard.

I lunged at him, but a side-step and a swift punch to the gut were all I got in return. "Read my mana," he said again. I swung an uppercut, hoping to catch him off guard, but my sword clashed with his. I twirled my blade out of the deadlock, and began a barrage of strikes that he adeptly deflected. "My turn," he said with a sly grin, as he bolted forward to strike at my weak spots. I was able to deflect a few of the blows, while being forced to dodge some others.

Read his mana, the words repeating in my head. Even in the second stage, there was little I could do to stand against him.

Fuck, he's fast. I can hardly keep up. No matter what I do, I feel like I'm stuck between a rock and a hard place, I thought.

A blow from above came, to which I countered with an overhead deflection, redirecting his sword away from my body. Suddenly, with little to no warning, I *felt* it. A pulse, ever so slight as it was, but it was a pulse I could identify.

Where is that coming from? I thought, trying to figure out the origin of it.

As another blow aimed for my liver was approaching, I felt the pulse again. This time, however, I felt it coming from roughly where his sword was about to meet my body.

I swung with everything I had to redirect the momentum of my own blade down towards the one that came for me. The resulting *pwang* was enough to tell me I had done it. "Holy shit," I said aloud, my mana-leaking eyes opening much more widely now. A small grin began to show on his face. "So, you felt that one, huh?" he asked slyly. "Yes, but how did you know?" I asked. "That's because I *let* you feel that one," he said. "What do you mean *you let me*?" I asked, taking a step back and rolling my shoulder out of its tense position.

"I sent out a little bit more mana than I normally would for that attack, seeing as how the mana I was already releasing was too little for you to detect," he replied with a shrug. I digested his words for a few seconds. "So, you're saying that when I reach the third stage, I'll be able to see it better?" I asked.

"Technically, you can already *see* mana, both ambient and personal, but the refinement isn't there. Think of it like a painting with only the base colors and blocky shapes put onto the canvas. The third stage adds more details and refinement to that painting, but it's not fully there yet," Taegin replied. "But how am I supposed to read something I can only feel?" I asked, genuinely confused. "Try it again, but now that you know the sensation of it, do your best to hone in on everything I'm about to do," he said, readying his weapon once more.

I got into my guard, and *drew some extra mana from the Ethereal. As much as my body can take,* I thought.

"Begin!" Bernar called out, noticing I had pumped more mana into my system. I dashed forward, but this time with the intent of trying to *feel* my target rather than *see* it. *There it is again,* I thought, feeling another pulse like a waft of warm air. This time, instead of swinging for where I *saw* Taegin, I swung towards where I felt his *mana was.*

While he was still a little bit faster than my strike, I could have sworn I saw him push off with his back foot to get out of the way in time. Or, at least I thought that's what I saw, but I later came to realize that it was what I *felt* him do. My sword struck the ground, but I used my newfound ability to try and predict where his counter-strike would come from. Sure enough, he aimed to trip me and knock me on my back.

I used the remainder of my kinetic energy that hadn't yet been carried into the ground to spin me around, extending my leg in hopes of reaching my target. Instead, however, I was met with what felt like an immovable object that my shin had graciously decided to introduce itself to. "Fuck," I cursed aloud, feeling the pain radiate up my leg and into my stomach as I writhed momentarily on the ground. "Not done yet," he said, aiming the point of his sword down at my chest.

Without realizing it, I instinctively rolled out of the way of his sword, getting to my feet quickly. This time, however, I began to notice something was different.

He's leaking more mana so I can read it, I thought. "Again," I said, realizing what he was doing.

It's a strange feeling. Almost as if there are these small tendrils of fire coming off him. I can feel it. It feels like a warm feather gently brushing against my body, but I can't quite see it yet. I'll have to rely on my other senses to help me pass this portion of my training, I thought.

Taegin, as it turns out, seemed to love countering more than attacking. Or, at least that's what I thought because in the time it took me to blink, he was nowhere to be seen. I *felt* his mana surging beside me, forcing me to infuse more mana into the muscles I would need to swing to my left. "Good, you're getting the hang of it," he said, deflecting my blow. "Still not fast enough, though," he said with an air of sarcasm I'd never seen him use.

Again, I felt a pulse come from the right though, this time, I was the one being forced to deflect. He repeated this back and forth process, changing his avenues of approach and forcing me to read and react to his mana accordingly.

I wonder what it will be like when I break through the third stage, I thought.

However, I quickly found that being distracted and training do not go hand in hand, as I received a swift kick to the crotch for my inattentiveness.

"Fuuuuuck," I coughed as I doubled over, feeling the pain radiate throughout my body; nearly forcing my breakfast and my soul to have an out-of-body experience. Taegin chuckled, but visually inspected my state to make sure I was okay after watching the mana leakage from my eyes dissipate. "What did I do to deserve that?" I asked through a pained groan. "You were distracted, and I figured this was one of the better ways to teach you not to be," he said matter-of-factly. I clicked my tongue, but said nothing in return because I knew he was right.

After dusting myself off, and making sure itchy and scratchy were still whole, Taegin beckoned me to follow him. "You're getting more stable with your second stage, and with today's progress, I can tell you're nearing the basis for third stage mana manipulation," he said, patting me on the shoulder, his scarred cheek wrinkling slightly. Since his reveal to me that he was my grandfather, it felt like a veil on his whole persona had been lifted.

"Thank you," I replied. "I just don't know how I'm going to cross over from the second to the third stage, but I'll do my best," I said, feeling the overwhelming difference in our abilities sinking in. He looked at me with a slight concern in his eye, probably understanding where my thoughts had gone.

"I don't blame you for feeling that way. After all, it took me over a hundred years to even reach the third stage," he began. "A hundred years?" I asked, incredulous to what I'd just heard. "You have to remember that we were still considered the pioneers of mana manipulation," he said. "Ah, yeah. I forgot how old you *actually* are," I muttered under my breath.

Obviously, he heard it, proceeding to give me a brief kick to sweep me off my feet.

"I heard that," he said, smirking like a pompous child. "Yeah, I suppose I deserved *that* one," I said, grunting as I got back on my feet. "We're done for the day, Thoma. You've learned a decent amount about how the third stage is going to feel, but your training in Caegwen will be *much* more difficult than anything I've been putting you through," he said.

The severity in his voice makes it sound like I'm in for it this time, I mentally sighed. "I understand, Master," I replied.

"Don't worry, little brother. I'll be there, too!" Bernar said cheerfully. "You're just looking for more opportunities to show off, huh?" I asked playfully. "Who would I be showing off to? Leona won't be there to see it, so I wouldn't be showing off to anyone, really," he said, a slight air of dejection reigning his tone. "Aw, ish shomewone shad dat his giwrlfwen won't be dere?" I mocked. "Aw, ish shomewone shtill a piesh of shit who doeshn't know when to *shut the fuck up*?" he returned in the same, mocking tone as he ruffled my hair.

"Meliss is going to miss you, too, you know," he said after a brief pause. We both looked over to where she was being trained by Rosie, Roburn, and Thorn. "I'm going to miss her, too," I said, feeling reality finally kick in. "Oh, I'm sure. Gods above and below, I miss

Leona every day," Bernar said, gazing off into the distance. "Never thought I'd see the day where you would actually consider settling down," I said smugly. He raised an eyebrow as he looked at me, not saying a word. "I also never said that she would be a bad person to do that with, you lucky chuckle-fuck," I nudged him with my elbow. "Shut up," he said, a wry smile growing on his face.

"She seems to be doing well. Her movement is decent, with little wasted energy," I noted, observing Meliss' movements as she practiced an intermediate-level sword drill. "She also has a four-hundred and something year-old teacher helping her fix her mistakes," Bernar said, though I could hear a tinge of jealousy in his voice. "I mean, she does have a lot to catch up to in terms of sword skills, but she's been doing very well. I'm extremely proud of her progress so far, but..." I stopped.

"You're worried about her, aren't you?" Bernar said, as if reading my mind. I nodded. "Of course I am. Why wouldn't I be? Just because she's learning the ways of a synner, doesn't mean her past trauma isn't still there," I said, recalling the events that happened in the castle.

I know those kinds of memories don't really go anywhere, I thought.

"But what is there to be worried about?" Bernar asked genuinely. "She's taking her experiences and turning them into something she can use to drive her forward instead of letting them drag her down. Hell, I think *you* could learn a thing or two about that from her," he said, nudging me. "I hate it when you're right," I sighed. "I'm your older brother. I'm *always* right," he said, puffing out his chest and tilting his chin upward.

Just as he did so, a *thud* came from where Meliss was training. We turned to see what happened, but all we saw was Rosie flat on her ass, with Meliss standing over her. Bernar and I looked at each other, raising our eyebrows and dropping our jaws without opening our mouths. "I... I did it!" Meliss exclaimed, panting heavily. Rosie got back on her feet, rubbing her backside as she did so.

"Congratulations! You're officially a pain in my ass in more ways than one!" Rosie said sarcastically, but holding a warm smile. "Thanks...?" Meliss said, unsure whether Rosie was being genuine. "Ah, that's right. I forgot you're still new to all of this. I actually meant it when I congratulated you just now," Rosie said, putting a hand on Meliss' shoulder.

"What happened?" I asked with an expectant smile. "I finally knocked her down!" Meliss said excitedly.

She sounds a little too *proud of that fact,* I thought, putting one hand to my nape.

"I'm impressed you could knock her down like that. Not many people here can," I said playfully. Rosie, on the other hand, took a light amount of offense to it, furrowing her brow. *Is she still mad about what happened with the portal stone guardians?* I thought.

"Well, I had a lot of solid tips and tricks from Thorn and Roburn, so I don't think it was entirely a fair fight," Meliss said, blushing lightly. I turned to Thorn, who held the same warm expression as the first day I met him. "Diolch, Thorn," I said with a bow. "No need to thank me for... wait, you speak Elvish?" he asked excitedly, as his gray eyes widened.

"Sorry to disappoint, but not enough to hold a conversation. I figured if you and the others from Nenvalur's group are going to be around, I might as well learn a little," I replied nonchalantly. Thorn's excitement fell from his face, but he was still visibly satisfied with me thanking him in his own language.

"Nevertheless, this isn't about me. Meliss, how *did* you knock Rosie off her feet?" I asked, trying to redirect the conversation back to her. "I just looked for a flaw in her movements and exploited it," she said without thinking.

Just how much have Thorn and Roburn put her through? I thought.

"A *flaw* in my movements?" Rosie asked. "Where was the flaw? I did everything the exact way that it's supposed to be done," she said. She wasn't angry, but I could tell she genuinely wanted to know where her mistake was.

"It was in your right foot's position; it was too close to your center of mass," Meliss said, pointing it out with her finger. "Rosie, don't move," Master Pyle said, walking up to us. "What? Why not?" she asked. "Because Meliss is right. Look at the direction your foot is pointing," he gestured for her to glance down.

"Son of a bitch, she was right. My foot is pointed too close to my center of mass. But how the fuck did she notice that mid-combat?" Rosie thought aloud, adjusting her footing.

"I-I apologize if I came off as being rude, Meliss," she blushed. "Oh, nonsense! You've also taught me a lot about how a female's weight distribution varies from that of a man's, so our footing *has* to be a little different," Meliss replied, waving the apology aside.

"I will say, that was still quite the impressive catch," Pyle began, looking at her inquisitively. "If I recall correctly, you said that you're originally from the Gramm Isles, correct?" he asked. "Yes, that's correct," she said, nodding her head in agreement. "And your parents?"

he asked. Meliss shrugged, bringing her hands up to shoulder height. "Pa died when I was very young, so I don't really know much about his side of the family. My mother, or *Ma* as I like to call her, never really talked about it either," she replied.

Pyle considered this for a moment, scratching the back of his head. "Ah, don't mind me," he said, noticing Meliss' eyes staring into him. "I would like to ask you about your father, however," Pyle stated. "Of course, ask away," she replied with a cheerful grin. I raised an eyebrow at her response. It had never really occurred to me to ask her about her father. I figured it was a sore subject, not unlike my situation, and so I simply avoided the topic altogether.

"Even though I was very young, I do remember my Pa being a swordsman. I don't know exactly what his position was, or if he just trained it as a hobby, but I recall sitting on the porch of our small house watching him train," she began.

I figured he might have been something like that, I thought.

"Every evening after he would come home from work, he would train. Sometimes late into the night, but he would always be happy if I sat there watching him. Occasionally, he would try to teach me something, but the body of a child doesn't have that much coordination. Instead, I learned to observe everything he was doing, even if I couldn't fully understand why he was doing things that way. Eventually, he passed away. I never really caught how he died, and Ma never talked about it either. The only thing I can remember is an old friend of his giving me these earrings, saying that they were a present from my father to keep me safe," she pointed at the small jewels embedded in her ear lobes.

Pyle's eyes widened. "D-do you mind if I take a closer look at those?" he asked. Meliss shrugged, and turned her face so he could see them better. "Have you ever taken them off?" he asked. "Pa's friend told me to never take them off, as they were a form of protection for me," she replied. "What kind of protection is he talking about, though? I don't sense any mana coming from them," I asked, finally stepping into the conversation as a whole.

"I'm not sure, he never specified," she replied. Pyle's mouth twisted into a wry grin. "I think I get what he meant," he said, nodding his head. Meliss looked at him curiously. "What do you mean, master?" she asked, touching the earring as if it were growing warm. "I need you to take them off. I have a hunch and I'm hoping I'm right," he said in a tone that conveyed safety and security to her. "Are you sure Master Pyle?" I asked, nearly whispering. "We don't know what's going to happen. If there *is* a spell, we don't know what releasing its seal will do," I continued.

Looking back, if there were ever a place to do it, it would have been there. Not only did we have Taegin and Pyle nearby, but we also had the Thorn, whose powers were not yet fully known, on standby.

"It'll be fine," Pyle said. Meliss gave him a curious look, but ultimately conceded. She began taking off the earrings, pulling the backstop off the thin rod that ran through the flesh of her ear. "Anything different yet?" she asked, holding the small, jeweled earring in her hand. "Both have to be removed, it would seem," Pyle said, gesturing for her to take off the second.

As she did so, I began to feel a small pulse of mana like a curtain of warm air passing over my face. As I blinked through the odd sensation her ears began to glow. After a few moments, the glow died down, leaving everyone around her curious as to what happened.

"Gods above and below, I don't believe it," Pyle said. "Is it bad?" she asked, touching her ears. As soon as she reached the apex of the top curve of her ear, she stopped. "W-what happened?" she asked. I walked up to her, and examined the changed shape. Her ear was still very much human in its general shape, but they eventually came to a rounded point like one of the dwarven folk's did. However, seeing as how they didn't stick out as much or as far, what came into my head next made the most sense.

"I think you're a half-dwarf, Meliss," I said softly, a smile growing on my face. "I'm a *what?*" she asked, touching her ears again quickly. "Dwarves were once prominent figures in the world, being masters of crafting and weapons alike. They were often known to develop fighting techniques on the fly, after noticing their opponents' weaknesses, allowing them a bit of an advantage, since their height was usually an issue," Thorn explained, his gray eyes turned into little more than slits on his pristine complexion, as a bright smile showed on his face. "What do you mean by they *were...*" she stopped. "O-oh... oh, gods above. But my Pa never had pointed ears, at least not that I could remember," she said, scouring her memories of him.

"Do you remember him ever wearing any kind of jewelry on his ears?" Pyle asked. Meliss pondered this question for a moment, then nodded her head. "He had small, golden hoops hanging off his ears, but I always thought that it was just a dress-code thing for his job," she said, shrugging her shoulders. "Apparently, your father didn't want it to be known that he was a dwarf. I don't know the reasoning for it, but it seems to me he was hiding from something," Pyle continued.

I watched as Meliss' expression dropped slightly, trying to piece together the information she just received. "I don't know the reasoning either, but I'm not afraid to show off my newfound heritage. In fact, I would like to ask Thorn to teach me a little bit more about this culture while we train," she said, her pleading eyes shifting over towards him. "I'd be more than happy to train you and teach you what I know of dwarven culture, though my information *may* be a little outdated, just so you know," he replied warmly.

I would be lying if I said I didn't feel a tinge of jealousy.

"In any case, your combat prowess finally makes at least some sense now," Pyle said, almost as if he noticed my reaction and tried to change the subject. "There is still much I would like to ask about your father, but I suppose that can wait for another time," he continued. "I'd be glad to share any knowledge I have of him," Meliss responded with a nod. "Good to know. I'll be looking forward to hearing about it," he replied, turning away from us and pulling Thorn aside.

I walked up to Meliss, that slight tingle of jealousy still floating in my stomach, though I couldn't exactly pin-point why I was feeling that way.

Am I just being insecure? I asked myself.

Meliss must have noticed a twist on my expression, and immediately put a hand on my shoulder. "I'm deafened by the sound of the gears turning in your head," she began, a worried look strewn across her porcelain face.

"Yeah, sorry. I'm just... overthinking things. Probably..." I said, trying to sound less perturbed than I actually was. "Is it because I would be spending more time with someone who is *far* more handsome than you are and talking about my past with him?" she asked with a sarcastically blunt tone as she elbowed my side. I was stunned by her question, but I recalled she had a lot more experience in these matters than I did. "I... yes. Was I really that easy to read?" I asked, feeling the blood rush to my face. "Like reading a children's book plastered on a castle wall," she replied with a wry grin.

"I'm sorry. I guess my inexperience is getting the better of me," I said, admitting my own weakness. "Oh, don't worry about it," she said playfully. "I know how it feels. Trust me," she said, her tone a little more serious than before. I could feel there was more to her words than she was letting off, but again, I recalled the fact that she had much more experience in these matters than I did. "You know I do," I said, feeling the wall I had apparently put up crumbling to the ground.

Let those thoughts go, Thoma, I thought in an attempt to calm myself down.

Thorn must have heard my thoughts from Pyle, because within a few seconds of me thinking those words, he walked up to us. "Thoma, I would like to extend my previous invitation to Meliss to you as well," he said plainly. "Wh-why?" I asked, mildly confused. "Well, now that you've mastered the second stage, you'll be going off to Caegwen to train with Anwill soon, won't you? It would be good to know some of the basic customs and courtesies before your arrival in the next few weeks," he said suggestively.

Are all elves socially inept? Ahhh, shit. I'm not ready for that conversation just yet, I thought, wondering how Meliss would feel.

Sure as shit, her face contorted into a frown at the thought of me leaving for an unknown period of time. "Ah, yeah. It would be good for me to know some stuff before I make another mistake like I did with you," I smiled nervously, rubbing the back of my neck. Thorn nodded, and also picked up on Meliss' emotional state. "Anyway, I'll be waiting to instruct you both. I have some other matters to attend to right now," he said, giving us both a short bow and walking speedily away like a child who has accidentally lit something on fire.

"Meliss, I-..." I began. "Don't worry about me," she cut me off. "I'll be fine, I'm just... still wrapping my head around having to lose you for a few months, maybe even a year? How long do you think it will take? You mastered the second stage pretty quickly, right? You should be able to get the third now that you have better insight into mana manipulation," she began to rattle off.

Even my inexperienced ass can see what's going on, I thought.

"Oh, shush," I cupped my hands around her face, and pulled her in for a kiss. I could feel the tension in her body leave a little bit. "I'll learn it as fast as I can and come right back to you, okay?" I said as confidently as I could. "Damned gnomes cutting onions," she said, wiping away a tear. "I'll send the best knights to get them," I said, my hands still cupped around her face as I stared into her eyes. "Fuck, I'm going to miss you," she said, hugging me tightly. "That's the first time I've heard you curse," I said more proudly than I had intended. "Shut up, dummy," she retorted, her voice muffled by my shoulder.

After a few moments like that, and not without more than a few pairs of eyes and ears witnessing the exchange, we pulled apart, heading to the showers to clean up. I opened the door for her, and just as I was about to follow behind her, I once again heard footsteps behind me. "Thoma," Ed's voice came from somewhere behind me.

"Hey, Ed. What's up? Is something the matter?" I asked.

I don't know what crawled into his soup, but something has been eating at him since even before the counter attack on Coltend, I thought.

He shuffled his feet briefly, and I could see his hand twitching from nervousness. "Can... can we talk for a minute?" he asked.

Yeah, someone's shit the bed and it stinks, I thought. "Of course. You're my best friend, Ed. Come on, let's take a walk," I said invitingly.

After a few minutes of silently walking to make sure that we were far away from prying eyes and sensitive ears, we finally stopped at a small clearing in the woods just beside the fortress wall. "So, what is it you wanted to talk about?" I asked, breaking the silence. You could cut the tension with a knife, I felt. I could see his hands fiddling and twitching behind his back by the movements of his forearms, and the nervous look on his face.

"Do you remember the collapse of the cave right after we pulled Nenvalur and his army from the Portal Stone?" he asked. "Of course... we lost a lot of people that day," I said, solemnly remembering the situation. "I remembered we had all wondered if Irun had died, but I..." he cut himself off. "You already knew he was the traitor, didn't you?" I said, piecing it together. He could only nod tersely.

"Before we left Coltend the first time, apparently Father Mourtis, that grumpy, old fuck had gotten a hold of him somewhere inside the castle. He was influenced into joining the Masked One, and became an official spy for him since then. The day he was supposed to leave earlier than the rest of us with Master Garret, I found evidence under his bed that he had received some kind of artifact that disabled a charm of some sort, but I couldn't figure out what it was for," he explained.

My eyes widened. "So *he* undid the charm on the ochelons in the cave," I said quietly. Ed nodded. "But if you knew all of this, why didn't you say something? Anything? A massive chunk of our problem could've been avoided," I asked, trying to figure out what his reasoning was. His face, once riddled with guilt, was stricken immediately by a quivering bottom lip and tears flushing from his eyes.

"He threatened our families," Ed said, coming clean. "What do you mean?" I asked. "He saw me trying to ask Batch if he knew what it was. Batch said he didn't know, but that we should confront the two of you about it. Apparently, he saw the pair of us holding the charm breaker in our hands," Edryd said, his voice beginning to tremble. "Batch was the first one to ask him about it, but as soon as the words left his mouth, Irun used some sort of spell I'd never seen before to pin both of us to the ground. I felt like... like I was going to die," Ed said, wrapping his arms around himself.

I only nodded in response, allowing him to fight through whatever was going through his head and continue to tell his side of the story.

"I was scared, Thoma. You can't begin to imagine what that felt like," he said, the tears streaming down his face. "The spell communicated what would happen if either of us said anything. It felt like all the joy in the world had died, and I was the cause of it, somehow chained to an eternal wheel of suffering and torment, as thoughts of my remaining family dying began to flow through my mind. It was horrible, a-and I..." he quivered, turning away.

I put a hand on his shoulder, feeling his entire body quiver and shake. "And... and now Batch is gone. He didn't even get the chance to apologize for keeping so quiet after we'd both found out. He told me, when we'd noticed Irun was missing in the tunnel, that he was angry at himself for not telling you he knew, too. I'm lucky enough to have had that chance, but now that I've said something about it, I don't know what's going to happen," he continued, his body trembling like a dog coming out of an icy pond.

"It's been fucking me up since we got back from Coltend that first time. When Ren repaired my core, it felt like the spell had finally broken off of me, so I talked to your brother about it before coming to you," he explained. It finally made sense. The weirdness during the journey north, the sadness and anger after Batch died, his emotional state the past few weeks.

Gods above and below, I'm going to turn that bastard from an is *into a* was *the next time I see him,* I thought.

"I'm sorry you had to go through that, Ed," I said, trying my best to be understanding of what he'd suffered. "I don't blame you for hiding it, and I never will. I can't. I wasn't in that situation, and I know you were only doing the best you could with the knowledge you had at the time," I said, trying to instill a sense of atonement for him to latch onto. "Coming clean about something like that isn't easy, and I think it took a lot of courage for you to come and tell me about it, especially after seeing how much it affected you," I continued.

Ed's entire body looked like a weight had been dropped from it, as he sobbed uncontrollably. "I'm sorry," he bubbled through a string of drool. "I'm sorry I d-didn't have the strength to say something earlier. I just didn't know how to handle all the a-anger and regret I've held until now," he continued.

"It's alright, Ed. I don't blame you for it, because I don't know how *I* would have reacted in your situation," I said comfortingly. "Again, you did what you could with the knowledge you had, and I respect you for coming to me with this," I said, trying my best to comfort him, as I put an arm around his shoulder.

"F-f-fank you," he bubbled again.

The following weeks went by in a blur, as Thorn instructed Meliss and I about dwarven and elvish culture. Alongside our training, each one of us was exhausted by the end of those few weeks. Staying up late and studying became a norm for Meliss and I, and it honestly helped me fall asleep a little easier, as my mind constantly raced with questions. Taegin allowed me to use his library from time to time, where I studied different aspects of mana manipulation on my own, as well as the first steps of stage three depicted in a dusty, old book I found.

Hmm, that's an interesting concept, I thought.

CHAPTER 31

FROM THE START

A spear of dark mana soared through the air.

Athar and Irun were in the depths of Valdis, the dark citadel to the north. Under the violet light that refracted throughout the fortress, their training session was in full swing, occasionally sending ripples of mana through the halls around them.

The spear continued to soar through the air, as it made its way to its target, Irun, who adeptly dodged the initial hit with a butterfly twist, grabbing it in midair, and returning it to the sender. Athar, who hadn't expected him to pull this kind of move, put up a shield of mana in front of him. The panel-like structure absorbed much of the initial impact, but began cracking as Irun poured more and more mana into his attack.

How the fuck is he doing that? I was the one who conjured the spear, and yet his counter attack is putting me on my back foot, Athar thought to himself, observing the panel straining and cracking before him.

"You'd better pour more mana into it," Irun said as if reading his thoughts. "Don't let your shield break, because if it does, it's going to hurt," he said, mildly increasing the force applied to the attack. Athar's eyes darkened *as he drew more mana from the Undergod's realm. The smokey tendrils raced towards him, gathering quickly in his* palm when he slammed it into the back of the shield, reinforcing his creation.

"Not a bad trick," Irun said, a smirk growing on his face.

He's gotten better the past few months. Seems to be thinking on his feet more, which is good, but it often comes a little too late, he thought as he countered the amount of mana Athar had just pushed out.

Furrowing his brow and gritting his teeth, Irun *pushed*. The added force behind the mana grew exponentially, eventually spreading throughout Athar's defensive wall. Cracks began to form, as the mana Athar had just condensed began to glow and dissipate.

Shit, he's going to bre-... he thought.

Crash.

Shards of the once-protective panel flew out in all directions like a wine glass hitting the floor. Athar was propelled backwards by the force of the exchange, slamming into the wall behind him and having the air stolen from his lungs. Irun, now panting more heavily than he originally was, regained his composure.

I didn't think it would take that much out of me, he thought, eyeing the man he had made airborne.

Athar coughed violently, his long, dark hair brushing the ground as he wrestled against his screaming body. "That one... hurt," he groaned, pressing his hands to his chest. "Yeah, I bet it did," Irun said, walking up to his fallen training partner and extending his hand.

Is it really worth the pain I'm about to feel to get up right now? Athar asked himself, eyeing the extended hand.

With his body protesting, he grabbed Irun's hand and allow himself to be lifted back onto his feet. "You're getting better at mana manipulation," Irun said, dusting his training partner's shoulder off.

The black tunic Athar was wearing had a gentle, velvet accent sewn in subtle details along the lengths of the arms and collar. "Thanks, but I'm not quite there yet," Athar replied, stifling another cough.

"Well, your quick thinking reminded me of someone back where I'm from," Irun began. "You've never really mentioned where you're from before, so why now?" Athar asked bluntly.

Straight to the point, eh? Irun thought.

"I just... I don't know. I don't really have much to say about it," he replied, his tone dropping a little. Athar observed his expression carefully. While most of his emotions were hidden by the disfigurement and changes due to the Masked One's influence during the attack on Coltend, there were still just enough features that allowed for emotion to show through.

"Well, we have nothing but time here," Athar began. "Even if the Masked One constantly says that *time is on no one's side*, we have a bit while we take a break," he said, using a suggestive tone to try and get his training partner to open up.

Irun sighed and turned away. "It's not exactly a fun story," he said matter-of-factly. "Neither is mine, but we all have our shit to deal with. Come on, open up," Athar said in a sing-song voice.

Should I actually tell him, or should I just glaze over the story? Would he judge me like the others did? No, he doesn't seem to think I'm a blundering idiot. *I actually think he's just happy to have someone to talk to for once,* Irun pondered momentarily.

"Fine, I guess it couldn't hurt to talk a little," he sighed, giving into Athar's invitation. "Fuck yes! Story time," Athar hissed, pumping his fist tightly by his chest. "Go on, then," he said, lowering his head and moving his hand in an ushering motion as a smile grew on his face. "Where do I start?" Irun asked.

"Like all stories do: From the start," Athar replied, walking over to grab the water skin, the deathmold concoction, and some food he had set aside before beginning their training.

Irun ran his fingers through his fiery, ginger hair, his once hazel eyes now red scattered their gaze across the floor. "I'll... try," he said, uncertainty ruling his tone. Athar groaned as he sat cross legged in front of him, offering a piece of bread and some deathmold concoction to his pensive training partner. Irun took it absent-mindedly, still visibly lost in thought. The cross-legged man in front of him munched on his meal, anxiously awaiting the start of the story.

"I'm not originally from Coltend," Irun began, his eyes still drifting around the training area. "My mother was Harutian, but fell in love with my Hjalfarian father. I spent up until my seventh birthday in Harut, though it was a bit of a challenge for me," he trailed off, thinking about his past. Athar silently munched on his food, a few crumbs of bread falling from his mouth.

"I... didn't really have friends there. While I have - rather, *had* - my mother's Hazel eyes, my red hair stuck out against the others who all had much darker hair. Eyes were always on me, watching everything I did, so I didn't really have much in the way of socializing opportunities just because I was *different* than the rest of them," he said.

"They were being racist towards you, then? I don't really know much of the outside world, but I've read about Harut in books," Athar began. "I know they value their family over just about anything else, and will go to extreme measures to make sure that their bloodlines are continued. They also don't really like intermingling with outsiders, so maybe that explains why they treated you like that," he said, trying to help.

"Maybe, but at the end of the day, I was a social outcast. I figured that if I couldn't socialize properly, I would just stick to being book smart, since that's all I really had," Irun replied. "In any case, one day my mother went out on a mission to kill a wyvern," he started. "Your mother... she was a synner?" Athar interrupted, his eyes widening in excitement. "Y-yes. Yes, she was," Irun said distantly.

"S-sorry, I didn't mean to..." Athar trailed off. "It's fine," Irun said, waving his hand. "She just... she didn't come back from it, at least not in one piece. She was severely injured, and by the time she had returned home to my father and I, her mental state was broken. Her wounds weren't severe enough to be life threatening, after all, she'd only lost an arm, but whatever had happened over there scarred her for the rest of her life," Irun said.

"I can't even imagine what that must have been like for him," Athar said, trying to sound empathetic. "Neither could my father, because he kept trying to use his connections as a trader to get him the help he needed," Irun added, his tone even. "Did his connections work? Did he get the help she needed?" Athar asked, genuinely invested.

"He did and he didn't. On the one hand, he had multiple healers come through and try to figure out what was wrong with her, but aside from the missing arm, nothing was physically wrong with her. Her mental state, however, was... broken. Even when she spoke to my father and I, it was like she was an empty shell. A vessel for a broken core. Nothing my father and I could do would help her, it seemed,"

Irun said, his dejected tone hung over the words like a chandelier in a castle. "I-I'm sorry…" Athar said, offering another piece of bread.

That's probably his way of consoling me, Irun thought, taking a bite out of the bread.

"The year I turned seven, my mother's situation had only gotten worse. It had been about three years since the incident at that point, and my father had all but given up on our family, as he had expended his resources and money to help her," Irun started again, still chewing on the bread. "The day before my birthday, and the same day my mother died, a man came to the door and took me away," he said, flinching at the thought.

"By all the gods, I'm so sorry, Irun," Athar said, putting a hand to his chest. Irun merely responded with a grunt. "Who was he?" Athar finally asked after a few moments' pause. "A synner. I don't remember his name now, it's been over ten years, but he pulled me away from the house, and stuck me in the back of a wagon for what felt like an eternity. Eventually, I ended up on the doorstep of Codrean; the place that would be my home until just a few months ago," Irun said, his eyes downcast.

Is that… sadness? Athar thought, reading Irun's expression.

"What was life like there at Codrean? If you don't want to answer that, I completely understand," Athar said, holding his hands up to shoulder height with his palms facing outward. "It was… good," Irun said after a few moment's pause. "That's it? Just *good*?" Athar asked, cocking his head to the side.

"It's difficult to speak well about people you've betrayed," Irun said dejectedly. "But yes, I would dare say it was simply *good*. Again, I didn't really have what one might consider *friends*, but I had people that I knew wouldn't stab me in the back," he continued. "And then you turned around and did it right to them," Athar said, clicking his tongue and shaking his head.

Irun scoffed. "You'd have done the same thing if you realized your potential was being nerfed into the ground," he said. "I don't think I would've chosen to be deformed by some dark power over people I could count on, even if I was never very close to them in the first place," Athar responded, putting a fingertip to his chin. "But hey, who am I to judge? I'm just a bastard who was cast away as a child, so what do I know, right?" he said, his self-deprecating tone heavily subdued with sarcasm.

What would *you know?* Irun thought.

"In any case, what were they like? Your old... uhm, *acquaintances*, I mean," Athar asked, trying not to use the word *friend* too lightly. Irun paused at this, considering and weighing his words carefully. "They were like brothers," he said almost painfully. Athar cocked his head. "*Brothers?* You betrayed your own family, so to speak?" he asked. "*Sheesh*, I thought my life was fucked, but you just took the whole concept of *blood being thicker than water* and lobbed it out the window into a burning pile of shit," Athar said, a heavy sigh fleeing his lungs as he pinched the bridge of his nose.

The fuck is he talking about? Irun thought, scrunching his features in an attempt to figure it out.

"Wait, have you not heard of that saying before?" Athar asked, finally reopening his eyes to stare at a confused Irun. "N-no? Should I have?" Irun answered, lifting an eyebrow. "*The blood of the pact is thicker than the water of a mother's womb*. Families fight all the time, the reasons thereof are often difficult to gauge. As the Masked One put it, you can much more easily become estranged by your own family members than someone you've *chosen* to have in your life, or so I'm told," Athar explained.

"I... I've never heard of that before," Irun said, digesting the new information provided to him. "How did the battle for Coltend turn out? You're missing an arm, replaced by a daemon's, so I'm assuming not well?" Athar asked. "Get to the point," Irun said, his irritation beginning to show at the mention of his missing arm. "Who did that to you?" Athar asked.

"Thoma Fayren. He's one of the synners of Codrean, and my old roommate alongside Edryd Baelis, and Batch. *Heh*, even years of knowing him, I never got Batch's last name," Irun answered, a tinge of nostalgia hinted in his voice.

He thinks kindly of them, even if he won't admit it to himself, Athar thought, reading the expression on Irun's face.

"How did he take your arm, might I ask?" Athar asked, staring at the daemonic and human arm fused together like a mangled scar. "He hit me with a spell of his own creation. A whip of pure mana that he caused to explode and wrench my arm off in the process," Irun replied.

Athar paused for a moment, imagining the scene and whistling critically. "Don't you think that if he really wanted to kill you, deep down, I mean, that he wouldn't have aimed for your head or torso?" he asked, genuinely wanting to hear the answer.

"I suppose he would have, but it doesn't matter now," Irun battered the question aside, not wanting to think about the implications laying just beneath the surface. "*Blood - water,*" Athar gestured a scale with both of his hands and a mocking scowl on his face. "You're saying that he chose *not* to unalive me there?" Irun asked. Athar shrugged. "What the hell would I know? I'm just an abandoned bastard," he said in jest.

A few moments of silence allowed the words just spoken to sink in. "Hey, I have an idea," Athar said, breaking the momentary silence of the training hall. "And that is *what*, exactly?" Irun asked, raising an eyebrow. "Why don't *we* create a pact of our own, and you *become my brother*," Athar said, a wry smile growing on his face. "Blood - water," Irun said, understanding what his training partner meant.

"Fine, but I think we need to establish some sort of hierarchy," Irun said, scratching the side of his face, visibly lost in thought. "Hierarchy? Wait, how old are you?" Athar asked, moving in closer to observe Irun's features. "It's a little hard to tell with *all of this* going on," he said, gesturing to Irun's entirety. "I'm nineteen," Irun answered.

Athar giggled uncontrollably.

"Aha! I've always wanted a younger brother! Oh, this is great! I can't believe it, I'm actually going to be an older brother!" Athar said, raising his hands to his face. Irun, unwittingly blushing at this point, cracked a slight smile. "*Ugh*, just please don't think you can bully me and we'll be fine. I'm tired of being at the ass-end of jokes and other such bullshit," Irun said, succumbing to Athar's infectious laugh.

"I couldn't bully you if I tried," Athar said, clasping one hand on Irun's shoulder. "Don't we need a drink of some kind? For this *momentous* occasion to not go uncelebrated," Athar said, glancing around the training room. "All I have is this deathmold concoction, though," he continued, disdainfully eyeing the vial.

"I don't think the Masked One even drinks, does he? Have you ever drunk before?" he asked. "I've been here a few months, and have seen him all of maybe four times. How the *fuck* would I know that?" Irun asked, spreading his arms wide.

"True," Athar said, scrunching his face. "Well, I guess that can't be helped. Deathmold it is, then," he shrugged, removing the small cork from the vial. The soupy, gray water sloshed lazily around inside as he shook it gently. "Shivers. Pure shivers. Every time," Athar said, grossed out at the sight of the concoction shifting around. Irun pulled out a flask of his own, and undid the cork as well.

"To blood being thicker than water, and to bonds we *choose* to make. Let us not beguile, bely, or betray one another, brother," Athar said, holding the vial in the air. "To blood being thicker than water," Irun returned, clinking his vial to Athar's.

They both imbibed the contents therein as quickly as they could. "It helps if you don't breathe in immediately after," Athar said, his eyes squinting like he had just bitten into a rotten lemon. "Yeah," Irun replied, stifling a mild choke.

"Well, I'm glad to have at least some semblance of a family now," Athar said cheerfully. "Ready to get back to training, little brother?" he asked. "How much older are you, anyway? And yeah, I'm ready," Irun replied. "I'm twenty-two, or at least that's how old I think I am, anyway. Can't really confirm it. You know, just *bastard* things," Athar replied.

That's... actually fair, Irun thought.

"Well, you'd better draw that training sword of yours. You still have a long way to go if you want to be at the level of even the junior synners, *big brother,*" Irun said, drawing his own. Athar nodded, drawing his guard and putting it into his guard immediately. "Begin," Irun said, immediately dashing in for a downward slash aimed at Athar's face.

Athar, just barely able to deflect the blow off to his right, used the momentum carried through his own blade to whirl it around and bring the tip to the front once more, lunging at his opponent. Irun saw it coming, and gripped the training sword's faux blade and quickly brought it into a position to fend off the lunge. Desperately pushing with both hands and having to turn his head, Irun twisted his elbow downward, aiming a pommel strike at Athar's face.

With a grunt, Athar bore the brunt of the blow on his cheekbone, but remained focused on the task at hand. With a swift push of his own pommel, he managed to get the blow into a downward slash position. Irun countered this move by pushing an Exar spell straight into Athar's midsection, forcing his downward strike to hit nothing but folded air.

Cheater, Athar thought, regaining his footing and shooting Irun a wry smile.

Let's see if he can handle this, he thought, pushing dark mana into his training sword.

Even though it's a dull blade, that spell is still going to sting. I've gotta be careful, Irun thought, observing the channeled mana form into a similar spell to that which was taught at Codrean.

With his sword emanating dark mana, Athar dashed forward, preparing a wide slash. Irun parried the first, and was immediately forced to deflect a rapid succession of slices aimed for his center of mass. "You're getting faster, but it's still not enough," he said, grinning lightly. He furrowed his brow in concentration, and began reacting to Athar's blows before they could even fully manifest. He allowed one of the blows to slip by him, catching Athar off guard, and grabbed him by the collar of his black tunic, throwing him off balance. Athar's eyes opened wide, as he realized what was happening.

I can't regain my balance in time, he thought, instantly regretting making that last swing.

With a quick jolt of force, he was knocked to the ground with such a force, it caused the stone floor to crack slightly. Air fled Athar's lungs, as the shockwave of the hit reverberated through his bones. A small spurt of blood flew from his mouth, as he gazed up at his opponent.

The dust kicked up from their quick bout began to settle, as Athar struggled for air. "You're... too... fast," he said between wheezes and gasps for air. "And you're not using your mana to your advantage. Try reinforcing your movements with a little bit of mana at the joints. You'll move much more quickly, and maybe even be able to keep up," Irun replied, extending a hand out.

Athar took the hand, and was brought to his feet, dusting himself off once more. "You're not bad for someone who only started swinging a sword a few months ago," Irun admitted. "I'm just doing exactly what you're telling me to do," Athar replied. "I've spent so long in the Masked One's service, I've gotten pretty good at following orders," he continued, rubbing the back of his head.

"One day, I hope to be good enough to beat you," Athar said, pursing his lips and firmly nodding his head. "That will be my goal while we train," he continued. "It's a good goal to have, but there are plenty of people more powerful than me you might have to face one day," Irun replied.

I don't want to discourage him, and I hope he notices that, he thought.

Athar, after a moment's consideration, understood his brother's words. "I'll keep that in mind," he replied. "One more round?" Irun asked, a wry grin showing on his face. "Yeah, just uh... don't slam me so hard next time," Athar said, a nervous smile showing on his face, still rubbing the back of his head.

Drip.

Karak, who had been observing them this entire time, snorted softly.

It would seem these two have made a pact, but how will the Masked One take this information? Did he foresee this happening? Is this all a part of his plans? I should let him know, regardless, the daemon thought.

He turned his misshapen body with more speed than his physical form suggested he had, and moved back towards the summoning hall where the Masked One held a meeting with Volzuk, the Undergod.

CHAPTER 32
UPGRADES

Meanwhile in the forested training area near Myrdin, the capitol of Caegwen, the trees shook with the sensation of mana reverberating the spaces between them. Leaves shuddered in response, as the rain drops had their trajectories mildly altered before reaching the floor.

Anwill cast multiple fireballs, forcing them to change their paths in midair to strike the target from different locations. His long blonde hair and fair features appeared tattered and coated with a sheen of sweat, rain, and mud, as did his training attire. His golden eyes focused on the blue, humanoid target ahead of him; a construct of mana that allowed him to gauge just how strong each spell that managed to reach it was.

The spheres floated momentarily, surrounding him like a halo, then suddenly shot out at a speed that would've been difficult for any normal human to follow in all directions. Through the will imbued in his spell, he forced the spheres to converge on the target, pomelling it from all directions, leaving no room for escape. The construct glowed a bright yellow, not quite the vibrant red he had expected to see.

I've been at this for three days straight, how the hell does she produce such power with so little mana? he asked himself.

She never did manage to explain that part to me, only that I needed to figure it out for myself but... his thoughts trailed off as he noticed another elf leaning on the framed entrance to the training ground with a water resistant cloak sheltering her from most of the rain.

"There you are, Anwill. It's taken me much longer to find you than I'd hoped it would," the elf said. "Surely *her majesty* wouldn't come all this way in this terrible weather just to watch me struggle with *you-know-who*'s instructions... have you?" he asked in a playful tone, raising an eyebrow.

Her respondent laugh could have melted the heart of a frost troll in the dead of winter. Her silver, braided hair quickly shuffled across a sleek, green dress that fit her form perfectly, accented by golden details on the hems and collar. She opened her eyes again, revealing the mismatching of her left and right; one violet, and one red.

"I can assure you, my old friend, that I have not come to gloat at your progress, or the lack thereof by the looks of things. I know *she* can be a harsh taskmaster, especially after having surpassed even your abilities with mana," she said, glancing inquisitively at the mana construct, raindrops turning into steam as they touched it.

"So then, why are you here, Aurae? I would think your *royal duties* would keep you far too busy to visit your childhood friend, but it seems this is not the case," Anwill said, cocking his head to the side. She shook her head. "You're right to say that it's not the case. I bring news that Thoma and his brother will be arriving sooner than expected," she said, revealing a letter she'd kept tucked behind her slim body.

Anwill, wiping the sweat from his brow with a towel, reached for the letter, revealing its contents. His eyes widened in surprise, but his thoughts soon shifted to force a nervous grin onto his face. "That little *monster*," he said to himself. "Monster? What do you mean?" Aurae inquired.

"Just a term Master Pyle used to describe him that... well, you'll see how well it suits him when you meet him," Anwill replied. Aurae looked at him, confusion riddling her nearly perfect features. "Is he... *misshapen*?" she asked, genuinely concerned for Thoma's wellbeing. "What? No. N-nevermind," he said, waving his hand.

She has absolutely no idea *what I meant,* he thought.

Aurae shrugged, and decided to move on with the conversation. "In any case, how are your preparations going? Have you contacted their mother about their arrival?" she asked. "No, in all honesty, I think it would be a much wiser decision to *not* tell her about any of that while she's been away. I can't imagine it would be good for her to focus on anything other than her task at hand," Anwill said, rubbing a dry cloth on the back of his neck.

"I see," Aurae said, pondering his words. "In any case, *my* side of the preparations has gone smoothly, though I would like to have a few extra mana constructs available for training," he said suggestively. "You know how expensive they are," Aurae pleaded. "I know, I know. But please, believe me when I tell you that Thoma is no ordinary boy. He will need all the help he can get," Anwill said, his position and voice firmly stated.

Aurae could only sigh in response. "I'll go tell the artificers to work on more of them. This boy had better be worth the cost," she said, shooting him a knowing look. "He will be, I *promise*," he returned.

Later that evening, deep into the forests of Erebos that lay near the city of Soule and more than a few days' ride through the densely packed trees, a woman lay silently behind a fallen tree with one hand on the hilt of her curved sword. Her steel-colored hair was loosely gathered at the back of her head, tied with a single, leather strip, with strands of hair coated in specks of dried blood that wasn't her own. She watched, through her golden eyes, as a portal began to form in front of her, pouring a few, horrid looking creatures out.

Great, they have horns now? These daemons, or whatever these new creatures are, are evolving at a much more rapid rate than they have the past few years, she thought, watching them scour the local area for any potential targets, as the sounds of their uneven footsteps flowed into her pointed ears.

The orc-like, humanoid creature that stepped through the portal had glowing, red eyes peering through slits in their chitinous faces. The protruding underbites that housed short, twin tusks clicked and hammered against a skinless upper jaw. Asymmetrical horns grew from the sides of their skulls, like brambles along a hedge wall, with some being much larger than others.

She glanced to her right and left, nodding to her team. The strike team consisted of two sword-casters, three spear-casters, five bow-casters, and one spell-caster, with one all-caster to command them all. For missions like these, it was essential to have at least one all-caster to take up any role that was deemed necessary should one of the members fall.

The teams, while cross-trained in each other's most basic forms and attack patterns, were often very closely knit, as their efficiency relied heavily on their trust in one another. Without it, these teams, and the missions they conducted on the outskirts of Erberos forest, would suffer *far* more losses than would ever have been necessary. The success rate of their missions was second to none.

We all know our roles. Is everyone ready? the woman asked, sending a mental pulse out to her teammates. *Ready when you are,* one of the elves said. His dark green hair and gentle features belied the violence this elf was capable of. *At your command,* a female elf mentally sent, already eyeing her target, gripping her spear tightly.

Go, their commander pulsed with mana, acknowledging her team's readiness.

Without so much as disturbing a leaf on the ground, or an insect in a mossy pad, they disappeared and got into their respective positions. While they could have placed themselves in locations prematurely, there was no consistent way of telling which direction the creatures would come out of, only the time and location. Thus, it was easier to adjust positions according to the direction the creatures faced as they left the portal, while hiding behind a piece of natural concealment.

The bow-casters infused mana into their bodies and leapt upward, concealing themselves in the high canopy that overlooked the portal. The spear-casters, already having gotten into position half-mooned behind the creatures, stood perfectly still behind a set of nearby trees. The sword-casters, including the commander, waited behind their piece of concealment for the moment the portal would close.

I count twenty of them, one of the female bow-casters said, gently blowing a strand of blood-red hair away from her hazel eyes. *I confirm Eirene's count,* Vyra, her twin sister, chimed in with a mental note, gripping her spear tightly. *Thrice confirmed here,* Derion said, his raspy, gravel-like voice carried his murderous intent, even though mental transmission as he fiddled with his twin daggers.

The portal closed.

Without a word verbally spoken nor mentally transmitted, arrows infused with mana rained down from the canopy, striking a few, unwarned creatures; piercing their skulls and forcing their eyes to roll into the backs of their heads. Blood like molten tar dripped from their mouths, as the air inside the now unalive creatures' lungs escaped with a *croaking* sound, its muscles reactively twitching as subconscious nerves spasmed.

The remaining creatures had all of a second to react to this assault, screeching in surprise and challenge like a pig being slaughtered. Even while many of them screamed, more arrows and the tips of spears borne from behind the numerous, large trees struck out, forcing more of their numbers to plummet. Some of the creatures managed to escape the secondary assault, but a war cry resounded from the fallen tree behind their original direction of travel.

One of the creatures managed to look back, just in time to see a pair of glowing, yellow eyes flash in front of its field of view, then disappear as its vision faded. Like a bolt of lightning, the commander dashed between multiple different creatures, slashing their necks and severing limbs from their bodies, while her teammates picked off any stragglers.

The entire fight lasted all of twelve seconds, as their efficiency was unmatched, yet again.

"Fuck, these things are hideous," the commander said, sharply twisting her sword and bumping the small, circular guard with a balled fist to shake off the excess blood. "Still can't find a better word than *fuck* to use?" Haldir asked, pulling a strand of his dark, green hair away from his face as he bent down to pull an arrow from a creature's skull. "Would you rather I called out your mother's name, instead?" the commander shot back, eliciting a chortle from Haldir.

"We haven't seen these before," Derion said, his voice rougher than the texture of the horns on the creature he was examining. "What do you want to call them?" he asked, the scar on his eyebrow gently contorting beneath a lock of black hair. .

"You know I suck at giving names to *people*, let alone creatures," the commander said in jest. "True, though with that in mind, we should probably let you name these creatures anyway," Vyra chimed in, her scarlet eyes locking onto the commander's with playful intent. "*Mi-mi-mi-mi-mi.* Shut the fuck up," the commander mocked Vyra's tone in return, punching her lightly in the shoulder. "Hey, that's my throwing arm, watch it!" she chuckled.

"It will never cease to amaze me how fast you are," Eirene said. "It was like watching a bolt of lightning spread across them. I could hardly keep up, even looking down from where I was perched," she said, her eyes, like Vyra's, looking the commander up and down. "Reach the fifth stage, and I'll teach you how to do that," the commander said playfully.

You know damn well I can't, Eirene shot mentally. *You could if you tried. Your sister is almost there, after all,* the commander replied, a wry grin showing on her face. *Train me, then. I'm too scared to try it alone,* Eirene shot out desperately. *When this mission is over, I'll do what I can to help* all *of you break through from your current fourth stage to the fifth,* the commander said, trying to comfort her companion.

"If you two are done having your moment, we still need to decide what to call these things, and what our report will be when we return.

Today should be the last day until our replacements come," Derion said, his near-black eyes stared intently at the intricacies of one of the horn's structures.

"Did you just rip that one out of its head? Gods above, you creep me out sometimes," Vyra shot, noticing the creature beneath him missing a horn. "I need to analyze it, though a larger sample might be required," he said distantly, thinking of all the experiments he would do when they returned.

The commander, able to read his thoughts, walked over to the nearest felled creature and swiftly separated the head from the torso. She kicked it up and over to Derion with her foot. "That a big enough sample for you?" she asked. With a terse nod, Derion immediately turned to analyze the severed head. "*Aaaaaaand* he's gone. It'll be a week before anyone aside from the commander can hold a conversation with him," Vyra said, throwing her arms up in the air as she did.

The rest of the strike team chuckled at her comment, and finished plucking the arrows, not the horns, out of the deceased bodies. "*Hurrrok...* I think I'm gonna puke," Eirene said as she caught Derion stick his finger into the creature's mouth, feeling around for whatever he could find. "That's a good name, *Hurrok*. We'll call them that," he replied, unfazed by her demeanor.

"Hurrok it is, then," the commander said playfully. "Still, though, I have to wonder what the hell is happening in the Underworld to force them to become like this," she said pensively. "Does it really matter? Perhaps the Undergod is just angry that his minions aren't working as well as intended," Haldir said, wiping the blood from the tip of his spear. The commander paused, ruminating over his words for a moment before shaking her head.

"It's not like him to throw careless thought into his creations," she said, pinching the bridge of her nose. "Look at this," Derion said, his gloved hand soaked in black blood. "The plates are *growing* together, but where there were deformations, horns sprouted instead," he said.

A brief analysis won't really give us many answers right now, Derion, but I'll be sure to keep that in mind for whatever experiments you may need to perform, the commander transmitted. Again, with a terse nod, he continued inspecting his newfound toy.

"Well, well! It looks like all the work is done for us," a voice called out from behind a score of trees. "Velgar, it's good to see you again, my old friend," the commander said, clasping his forearm. He was a burly elf, a rare genetic occurrence, with a thick beard and braided, walnut hair. Some considered him to potentially be of dwarven descent, but there was no record of that anywhere.

"It's good to see you, too, commander, but I know you've been out here for far too long already. We'll catch up between another rotation," he said. "Of course. I'm long overdue for a long bath and some warm food," she chuckled. Cracking a small grin, he patted her shoulder, and got into position immediately.

The average time between portal openings is finicky, but on average it's about once an hour. It's just too bad I can't stay and catch up with the rest of them, the commander thought.

She ordered her team to gather their things, and within a few minutes, they were already making their way down the trail, as they had done so many times before. "Go home and get some rest, old friend. You've earned it," Velgar said without looking at her, eyes locked into the general position of the next portal. "Stay sa-..." she cut herself off, as the portal immediately opened, spawning three, armored and weapon-bearing creatures.

Without hesitation, she drew her sword, and performed the same dash maneuver she had earlier, though this time, her sword found no purchase in the creature's skin. With scales like plate armor, standing approximately a head taller than her, and with a piercing, violet gaze, the lanky creature held its own, as the commander tried to push her blade into its gullet.

"What are you?" she asked, briefly looking him up and down. The creature grunted, furrowing its brow, and launched her backwards into a nearby tree. "Commander!" Eirene shouted out. "Don't you fucking *dare* come closer. None of you," she shot back. *Go back to Myrdin and report what you're seeing here to Anwill,* she mentally sent to the rest of her strike team.

Go, she commanded.

Hesitating ever so slightly, her strike team trusted her judgment, and proceeded to support their bodies with mana, speeding them along the well-worn trail that led through the forest of Erberos. The commander, no longer sensing their presence, stood back up.

Do not interfere, no matter what happens. I'm going to go all-out on these fuckers to see what they're made of, and you would all just get in the way, she transmitted to Velgar.

Her razor sharp focus must have told him all he needed to know, because he didn't, rather *couldn't*, respond. "You there, in the middle," she pointed her gently-curved sword at the one who had sent her flying. The creature heard her speak, and turned to face her.

Are they intelligent? she asked herself.

"Do you understand speech, or are you just some hyper-strong creature I've never seen before?" she asked, a slight tinge of worry that it actually *did* understand her seeped into her mind. "*I* do, though I cannot speak for the others," a voice like rocks tumbling down a mountain emanated from the creature.

There was no movement of its mouth. Mental transmission, maybe? the commander thought.

"How do you know our tongue?" she asked. "That is for me to know, and for you to not survive long enough to ever find out," the creature said. Immediately as it finished its sentence, it appeared in front of the commander, nearly catching her by surprise.

If I hadn't reached the fifth stage of mana manipulation, I might never have reacted to the fluctuation of mana in time, she thought, feeling her sword bite into her opponent's.

Again, she was sent flying backwards through a tree or two before finally crashing into the ground. *How the actual fuck is it so strong?* she asked herself, gritting her teeth through the pain that resonated through her entire being. "Ah, I'm going to take an extra long bath after this bullshit," she said, cracking her neck as she regained her posture.

Her eyes glowed more intensely *as she drew an exuberant amount of mana from the Ethereal. Even though she didn't necessarily need to draw additional mana from the realm, she did so anyway; bringing her body to the upper limits, though careful to not risk collapse.*

With a deep breath, she lurched forward, the world turning into naught but a green and brown blur around her as she approached her target.

Even being at the fifth stage, I'll never get used to this feeling, she thought as she sped towards her target.

Bringing her blade up to strike, a cone of displaced air began to form around it due to its speed, aiming for the creature beside the one who had sent her flying. Her blade, moving at the intense speed that it was, severed multiple, suspended raindrops along the way.

Not as smart as the big bad, huh? she thought as her sword found the gap between its heavy scales, separating its head from its body.

Before the blood could even spurt out, her sword was already decapitating the second of the trio, with just enough space between the folds of the scales for her sword to spread and slice into. As her sword sang, both headless bodies were shaken by the sounds of the sonic booms it had left behind.

She dashed toward the third, the one who had sent her flying earlier, who somehow managed to get its jagged blade up in time to block at least one of the strikes. Its parry was successful, though it failed to even notice the other fifteen cuts she had already unleashed upon his body.

Such precision, it thought, feeling the commander's blade slice between the scales, reaching skin, flesh, and sinew in every location at the same time.

My body won't move. Has she already cut me off from my basic motor functions? it thought, feeling pain finally begin to register in its brain, as streaks of crackling mana followed the commander's movements.

She reappeared behind him, her face darkened, revealing only her glowing eyes and hair reflecting minimal light. "You're not going to like this next part," she said as if she were already looking down at him.

"Kneel," she commanded, kicking the back of its leg down into the ground.

The creature's body hadn't yet registered that it was unable to move, even though its brain was slowly becoming aware of that fact, as well as the pain that followed it. The world lurched back into motion, as the commander reduced her mana output, appearing in front of the creature with her sword at a gap in the scales on its throat, the blood from the other two creatures finally catching up to the rest of reality as the creature slammed into the same tree it had sent the commander into earlier.

"I judged you too leniently," the creature coughed, all of the intricate, disabling cuts finally registering all at once. "Who is your master? Who created you? Why are you here?" the commander asked, wasting no time, knowing this creature's life was ebbing away.

"More... will come. You will... *pay*," it gurgled, succumbing to its wounds as its sharp chin dug into its own chest.

Shit, I killed it too fast, she thought, swinging her blade swiftly to flick the black blood off.

"Commander!" Velgar shouted, stepping out of his hiding spot. The commander inhaled deeply, a sense of relief coming over her that no one appeared to be hurt. "I'm fine, Velgar," she said, lifting a hand up to halt his approach. She watched as the blood dripped from the creature out of every possible crack she could see.

"You're coming with me, *upgrade,*" she said darkly, looking down at the space in the scales near its nape. Within a second of her decapitating the creature, a dark explosion of mana rang out, almost like a signal. "What the fuck did you do?" she asked the lifeless creature, obviously not expecting an answer.

Far above her in the canopy, however, a featherless, winged creature watched.

CHAPTER 33
SUNDERED

A few weeks had gone by since Meliss' reveal as being half-dwarf. While much hadn't changed in our daily lives, she *did* end up spending a lot of time with Thorn and Ren, learning about dwarven culture as much as she could. I would've joined in, but between Pyle's, Bernar's, and Taegin's individual lessons, my time and energy were stretched thin.

My assimilation into the second stage of mana was nearing its end, and I could summon it at will, even if it did draw a lot out of me. Still, that was mostly attributed to my physical fitness, rather than my ability to manipulate mana. "Don't worry about feeling like you're about to puke," Pyle said, chuckling at my pale face.

"I would if I'd had time to eat anything this morning. The sun won't be up for another few hours, and yet, here we are," I shot back. "Night training is important, and training on an empty stomach allows for a much clearer head. Not to mention it prevents you from feeling lazy while you digest your food," he replied. I sighed and nodded my head. "I know, I know..." I said, lifting my hand to stop him from going any further. "Come on, then, you'll never keep up with Anwill at this rate," he said, patting my back.

I stood up, and looked around for a brief second as I caught my breath. Knowing I could recover more quickly with the second stage,

I infused mana into my muscles and bones once more, the mana seeping out from my eyes like steam from a kettle. "Ready?" he asked. I nodded my reply, as words would have only distracted me from what I was going to try to do next in hopes of catching him off guard.

Will it even work? I thought, observing his footwork and weight distribution in his stance. His, now lowered, center of gravity made it hard to catch him off balance. *But if I could just...*

Pwang.

I gritted my teeth, just barely able to react to his attack. I consciously breathed in deeply, allowing both ambient mana and air to flood my body, reinforcing my arms. "Not bad, little monster," Pyle smiled, pushing away from me and preparing another attack. This time, however, I pushed in. Sensing how the earth and air were moving around my body, I had a much better handle on my movements than I'd ever had before.

Pyle must have noticed what I was working up, because he immediately side-stepped, changing his body position to prepare for a slash. I pushed off the dirt, kicking up a cloud as my mana infused muscles propelled me forward at a ridiculous rate. Just as his slash began its arc, I took one extra step, pushing into the attack before the apex of his blade could reach its maximum velocity.

Gotcha, I thought, wrapping my arm around his hands and using his elbows as a fulcrum to try and disarm him. Unfortunately for me, a toothy grin had been on his face the whole time, as I noticed an intense build up of mana emanating from him. "Shit," I hissed, realizing I had fallen for his trap.

I pushed away from him as fast as I could, but he expelled his mana like it was overflowing from him. I *drew mana from the time-*

less realm, and infused it into my sword, hoping to counteract the explosion somehow. I swung down as hard as I could, expelling as much of my own mana as I could to cut through the blast.

The resulting power struggle between mine and Pyle's mana was intense. So intense, in fact, that the pressure it gave off knocked a few of the younger synners off their feet and caused more than a few less-affected heads to turn our way to observe the power struggle.

A visible coating of mana on my sword against the half-sphere arcing out from Pyle. It was a sight to behold, for sure, as the combination of the mana began to shoot mana-sparks all across the training field. I struggled to maintain my grip on my sword, using every ounce of strength and concentration I had as I was suspended in the air.

Gods above and below, he's too fucking strong, I thought, feeling my strength begin to falter.

I pushed more and more mana into my body and sword, causing small fissures to begin appearing on it as I grit my teeth. *More*, I thought. *I need more mana. No, wait, I need* sharper *mana, not* more. *I need it to be more precise.* I struggled to maintain focus, feeling my body begin to fail. *Irun always used to call you* Lanky, *so why not turn your mana into something that suits that as well*, I thought, closing my eyes for a brief second.

I could sense Pyle's curiosity, as he maintained his steady output of mana. The aura around my blade began to condense further, supporting both the spine and the edge simultaneously. I opened my eyes, giving Pyle a smirk.

"*Sunder*," I commanded, my voice altered by the mana reverberated through the air. As if following my exact intent, the mana along the edge spiked, cleaving Pyle's spell in twine, exploding the mana between us. I, for one, was sent flying in the opposite direction from the explosive mana, but Pyle remained standing, covering his face and neck with his arms.

Still in my second stage, I forced a kick out in front of me to help me rotate enough to not slam the ground flat on my ass. I landed deftly, skidding backwards a little ways before finally coming to a halt. I held my blade out away from me to avoid accidentally cutting myself if I needed to roll further, and noticed it suddenly becoming very *light*.

The steel had turned into a glass-like structure from the intense heat provided by the mana, and the rapid cooling from its decompression. It wasn't as quick as a bladesmith's quenching of a blade, but it was enough for martensite to form along the cracks that had riddled the blade like lightning. They had apparently formed so deeply that as soon as enough heat had dissipated from the blade, it dismantled under its own weight.

"Damn it, that was my favorite training sword, too," I thought solemnly. Pyle, on the other hand, had already rushed over to me. "Thoma, are you alright? What the fuck *was* that?" he asked, extending a hand out for me to use as support.

"I realized I couldn't win in a contest of strength with you, so I had to improvise," I replied, a slight grin showing on my face. "And what was that thing you said? *Sunder*, I thought I heard you say? Was that a new spell you've come up with?" he asked excitedly.

I shook my head. "I wouldn't call it a spell, so much as it was more of a *command*, I suppose," I said, not exactly knowing how to explain the feeling. Meliss ran over to us, having paused her training with Thorn momentarily. "Thoma, are you alright?" she asked from a short distance away. Pyle, on the other hand, regarded me curiously, like he couldn't quite put his finger on me.

"I'm alright, Meliss," I said, ignoring the exhaustion I was beginning to feel. "By the gods, what a fight that was! You were like *pwaaah*, and Pyle was like *bwoooom*," she said excitedly, miming our battle as she made her sound effects. "It was incredible," she said, finally settling down after a few more vocalized onomatopoeias of our battle.

"Thanks, but I don't exactly know what I did," I replied, unsure of how else to process what had just happened. "You do, actually," Thorn said, injecting himself in the conversation. "I *do*?" I asked, more confused than I think Pyle was. "You actually hit the nail on the head, but your insight into what you said isn't exactly present," he continued.

"What do you mean my *insight* isn't exactly *present*?" I asked, wondering what that could possibly mean. "Where Ren and I are from, we call our understanding of mana manipulation *insight*. You said you *commanded* the mana, and you weren't entirely wrong, but you're still not sure what you did to get there," he explained.

"So, what you're saying is I subconsciously used some sort of mental image that allowed me to do that?" I asked, thinking back on what I did during the clash. "That's a *part* of the whole, but not quite it. Having a mental image drastically improves your command, or *intent*, but the strength of your *will* alongside your *control* play a much larger role than you might think," Thorn said, trying to figure out how to explain it better. "You'll find out more when you train with Anwill, as I'll leave that part to his expertise," he continued.

Like what I do with my Whip of Doom, I thought, remembering the first time I'd ever cast it.

I could hear myself and Meliss sighing simultaneously. On one hand, I couldn't wait to break through to the next stage and get stronger, but I also didn't want to leave her just yet. I'd gotten used to having her around, and it was a bit of a pain to think about leaving the following day.

She must have noticed what was going through my head, and wrapped her arm around my waist. "I can't wait to see what you'll be able to do when you get back," she said, kissing me on the cheek. Pyle raised his eyebrows in surprise, while Thorn merely held a single eyebrow raised in confusion at the gesture. "Thank you, darling," I said, kissing her forehead. Even coated in a light sheen of sweat, she still smelled *clean.*

Don't be a fucking creep, Thoma, I thought, feeling my face flush slightly.

Pyle cleared his throat. "Speaking of being able to see what the fruits of our training are, how about a little sparring match for you, Meliss?" he asked. "I'd love that. It'd be a great way to close out the day," she said cheerfully. "I'll be rooting for you," I said, giving her a warm smile.

"Thank you," she said, returning the smile. "But who's going to be my opponent?" she asked, looking around. Most everyone else already had training partners, and she had been working closely with Rosie and Roburn, so those two weren't going to be good choices, as they *literally* taught her most of what she knew.

I hadn't totally ignored her while she was training. Most nights after dinner, or even after our bed times, I'd help her by correcting some of her forms more... intimately than I knew Roburn or Rosie would dare. We'd grown much closer during those moments, and I knew our connection was something special, perhaps not the *puppy love* as some had initially thought. I didn't know what that meant, but I was just glad to have someone I could share my innermost thoughts with outside of my brother.

Breaking away from those memories, I continued to scan the training area for a worthy opponent. My eyes locked onto her opponent, and I figured now would be as good a time as ever to see at least some of what he could do.

"Thorn," I said, gesturing with a bow, extending my arm out in invitation for him to fight Meliss. Understanding immediately, he nodded in response. "Thoma, you can't be serious," she said, nervousness scouring her fine features. "Rot in complacency, or rise through adversity," I said, keeping my tone as encouraging as the words would allow.

"Thoma is right, Meliss," Thorn began. "It would be a pleasure to instruct you further," his eyes flared as his now-honeyed voice rang out. A spear made of pure, golden mana instantly conjured in his hand, thudding the ground by his feet astonished many of the bystanders.

A spear-caster? I could almost hear Meliss' say through the expression she wore on her face. "I thought you were a sword-caster," she said, drawing her own weapon. The rest of us backed away, giving the two adequate space for their mock duel. "I'm an all-caster, but because you've only been training with swords the past few weeks, I want to see how you handle something you *haven't* gotten used to," he said, getting into a stance that would have threatened even the most seasoned of veterans.

His air-tight stance held a palpable aura, with the haft of his spear tucked at his side and the tip floating above the ground in front of him by his right knee. Even knowing she was still a beginner, I could tell Thorn didn't want to make her think he was going easy on her, even if he was. It would have destroyed her self-confidence to know that he went *too* easy on her.

I could see Meliss swallowing dryly, as she got into one of the defensive stances she'd trained over the past few months. "Ready when you are," Thorn's eyes held a kind of calculated coldness I never knew he could have.

It's like he's already planned exactly how much speed and force he's going to use, I thought, feeling his intent through the mana that radiated from him. *That's got to be intentional, like what Taegin was doing to me during our sparring session but this is much more dense,* I thought.

Meliss dashed forward with surprising speed. Her conditioning and training visibly paid dividends, as she reached him in a matter of a few seconds. A quick move, even for someone without mana. Thorn, however, held his posture, his eyes level with her center of mass. I watched him closely to see if I could pick up anything from his fighting style.

With calculated speed, he raised the tip of his spear just fast enough to allow Meliss time to react. She ducked under the tip of his spear, which already began to whip around for another thrust, and aimed a thrust at his chest. With little wasted movement, he side-stepped the blow, the air around her sword grazing his clothes, sending a gentle ripple across them.

Not bad, I thought. She thrust again and again, while dodging his strikes. After finding no purchase in her strikes, she tried a few slashing attacks. Her form was good, a clear handle on the basics of swordsmanship showing, but nothing out of the ordinary.

"Why are you holding back and sticking to the basics?" Thorn asked, almost as if he read my thoughts, parrying another strike in the process. Meliss gritted her teeth in concentration rather than *frustration*, like she understood he was way out of her league.

"I didn't expect the tricks you taught me to work on you, so I'm trying to figure out how to respond to your movements while keeping the pace of the battle steady," she said like she was reading it out of a textbook. "That's good, but you should be more vigilant," he retorted, a nondescript look on his face.

Since his expression alone wasn't warning enough, in conjunction with his words, he jolted a feint, forcing her to shift her direction of travel instinctually toward her off foot. Just before she stabilized, Thorn's heel swept underneath her, knocking her off her feet.

The resounding *thud* of her, and the wheeze that followed marked the end of the mock battle. "Are you alright?" he asked, his warm smile returning to his face. I could see Meliss blushing a little, as she took his hand to help herself back onto her feet. "About as alright as I can be after getting knocked on my ass," she retorted, dusting herself off.

"Was that really your first time fighting against a spear? That initial dodge of yours would suggest otherwise," I said, walking over toward the pair. "It really was my first time, but I don't feel like I did well at all," she said, her tone dropping a semitone near the end. "How did you know to duck under the initial thrust?" I asked, genuinely curious where she had learned a move like that.

"It just *felt* like the right thing to do, I guess? I thought that if I could bring the tip of the spear up, the only thing I'd have to worry about, for at least a second, anyway, was the heel of the haft," she said matter-of-factly. I smiled, feeling a sense of pride in her words that I never thought I would. "You did well, I promise," I said, patting her head. "Thank you, darling," she smiled warmly.

"*Awww*, you two sound like an old couple already," Bernar said, his bitterness due to Leona's absence seeping through his facial expression. "You're just jealous," I shot back with a grin. "I'm not saying shit about that, but I won't give you the satisfaction of rubbing it in my face," he said, jutting his chin into the air in an act of defiance. "Yeah, he's jealous," I nudged Meliss.

Before I even realized his eyes had flared, I was on my back, the air in my lungs leaving so quickly I thought my soul had finally abandoned me, too.

"I don't think I deserved that one," I grunted, rolling over to my side. Meliss had only noticed me at that point, as she couldn't follow Bernar's movements from where he was to where I once stood. The only reason I knew that was because of the look of shock plastered on her face like a mask after feeling the displaced air he'd left in his wake.

"You didn't. But, as your older brother, I have to keep you in check since the gods ruined a perfectly good asshole when they put teeth in your mouth," he said, towering over me. Pyle and Thorn, who had never actually heard us exchange insults before, stifled a unified chuckle.

"Yeah, yeah. I get it," I said, taking my brother's outstretched hand to help myself up. "So, Thorn, what do you think? Is she ready to learn mana manipulation?" Pyle asked, hinging on the elf's answer. His hand lifted to his chin, as he thought of the correct answer.

"To me, she's ready. Since being under our instruction, I can see that she has much greater control over her own body than she did before. However, knowing how much this will change her life, and because she is not yet an *official* synner, the final say is hers," he concluded, looking at her. "What's your answer, then?" Pyle asked, patience mildly escaping his tone in excitement.

She gave me a searching look, like I was the one who actually had the answers instead of her. "Like Thorn said: It's your choice," I said comfortingly. "I've never really gotten the chance to make my own decisions. Gods, even to come here was a long-winded debate with Leona. This is the first *real* decision I get to make on my own, and I can only *hope* it's the right one: I want to learn mana manipulation," she said, her fine features scrunching with determination.

I'm so proud of you, I thought, holding back a tear of joy.

"A wise decision," Taegin said from behind the two of us. We turned to look at him just as the scar on his left cheek scrunched with the proud smile he wore on his face. "Thorn and I will handle the processing of the Gwynnleaf, while Thoma," he paused, looking at me. "You will be there, too. I have a gift for you before your journey to Caegwen," he continued.

"Of course, Master," I replied, bowing my head lightly.

Moments later, we left the training area, and made our way down to what we called the *Awakening Chamber*. While it wasn't anything grandiose, it did house the equipment required for refining the Gwynnleaf, as well as a large, runic circle traced along the floor. "What's that for?" Meliss asked, pointing down at the runes on the floor. "Those runes are to help guide your consciousness through initial contact with the Ethereal," Pyle explained as Thorn and Taegin worked the gwynnleaf.

"*Guide my consciousness*? Is there anywhere else *for* it to go?" she asked. "As I'm sure you might have guessed, there are two primary types of mana: Light and Dark. Cliche, I know, but to help us keep consistent naming conventions, these simplistic sounding names were put in place," he began. "These two are different from elemental and environmental mana, which, with enough training, can *also* be controlled, but today, we will simply work on your initial contact," he concluded.

"So what will you need me to do to make *initial contact*?" she asked, curiosity clawing at her more voraciously than before. "The best way that I can explain it is that you're going to have to quiet your mind, dispelling all thoughts, both negative and positive, away from your goal. Once that has happened, the Gwynnleaf tincture will guide you through the rest, and prevent you from getting *trapped*," Pyle said.

"What do you mean it will *guide me*? Like, it will tell me what to do? And what do you mean by *trapped*?" she asked. "Not verbally, but you'll feel it pulling you, in a sense. Oh, and by *trapped* he means that your consciousness, without the use of the Gwynnleaf, is at risk of being stuck between the realms. If you didn't have the tincture, and something distracted you, the odds of you getting *trapped* are far higher," I chimed in, feeling relevant for once.

It'd been so long since I was in her shoes, I'd almost forgotten what that initial contact felt like. "I-I see," she said, trying to find a memory she could use to relate to his words.

While Taegin and Thorn were working on the tincture, Pyle and I helped her meditate. We both pushed mana around her, enveloping her in the warmth she would feel when she first drew it from the realm. This was a process carefully tailored to each person, as depending on the amount of mana they could handle during this pre-process could help determine how much of an aptitude they would have.

Pyle and I glanced at each other when we realized she was handling about as much as a junior would after two years of training. "Are you sure you've never used mana before?" Pyle asked. "I'm sure. This is about the same feeling I had when I still wore the earrings, so if anything, this is my *normal*," she said, her eyes still closed.

"Are we about to have another monster?" Pyle asked under his breath, shaking his head. "Pyle, Thoma. It's time," Taegin said, handing a small, glowing vial to Meliss, while Thorn handed me a pair of cerulean flasks "What's this?" I asked, eyeing them curiously. Their structure was crystalline, wrapped in small, leather bands with runes inscribed along the length of the leather. The metal lids and mouth of the flask barely protruded out of the structures that were each a little larger than my palm.

"A gift from Ren to both you and Bernar. I don't know how or why he does many of the things he does, but after he told me *what it is*, I had to take it up with the Master," he began. I looked at him curiously, wondering what Ren could possibly have given him. "I know Ren has powers that few can begin to comprehend, but why would he give *us* a gift?" I asked

"He said you'd understand, but you're both not to drink it until you get to Caegwen. And, after having discussed a few things with the Master, I've come to realize that there was much more in you than just *potential*. I just wish I could see the look on your face when you find out what I mean," he said, patting me on the shoulder, and giving me a warm smile.

Confused. As. Fuck, I thought, but returned the smile just the same.

"Diolch, Thorn," I said, putting one hand across my chest and bowing lightly. He smiled even more brightly, and patted my shoulder twice before stepping away. Meliss also eyed her vial carefully. The glowing tincture inside had about the same consistency as oil as it gently sloshed around inside.

"There's still time to back down, you know. If you choose to go through with this, you will also become a synner," Taegin said, his piercing gaze searching Meliss' eyes. "I'll do it, Master," she said, nodding her head. "Like I said to Master Pyle before we even left Coltend: I never want to feel like I cannot fight back again," she said, her conviction much stronger this time. "So be it," he replied with a nod, stepping out of the runic circle.

"Drink," he gestured to her. She put the vial to her lips, and stared down its neck, watching the golden liquid flow towards her. Her eyes opened wide as she drank every last drop. "It tastes like a warm, summer day feels," she said, handing the empty vial back to me. "Indeed it does. Now, go sit in the middle, just like we practiced,"

Pyle said. With a terse nod of understanding, she sat in the center of the runic ring, crossing her legs as she descended to the floor.

"Remember, clear your mind, and let the tincture guide you. I will be here to pour mana into the circle," Taegin said, his voice soothed by some extra mana he exuded to help calm her nerves. She nodded once more, closed her eyes, and followed along with the breathing pattern we had taught her just an hour prior.

And now, we wait, I thought.

I could tell the sun was beginning to come up at this point, because I could see small rays of sunlight seeping through the crags of the thatched roof, casting gentle light around the room. Taegin's mana infusion into the circle had provided us with most of the light we needed prior to this, but now, the gentle blend of azure and golden light bathed us all in soothing visuals.

The only sounds being made inside the room were that of Meliss' breathing pattern, supplanted by the soft hum of the circle's mana. Thorn, Pyle, and I sat on the bench nearby, patiently awaiting the results of her first contact.

Come on, Meliss. You can do it, I thought, knowing this process, even with the Gwynnleaf tincture, could take hours upon hours, if not *days*. Knowing there wasn't anything I could do to help her, I merely rested my head on my folded hands. Thorn had apparently decided to meditate as well, though I'm not sure entirely why. His powers, like Ren's, were still very much a mystery to me.

This went on for approximately ten hours, or at least that's what it felt like, as we had no way of keeping time inside the room for that explicit purpose. I had to hand it to her, as I knew it wasn't easy to sit in the same position for even two hours, let alone ten.

You can do it, I thought, closing my eyes, and picturing her sitting in front of me, with the Ethereal realm spinning its globe of bright mana above the empty space.

Suddenly, through my eyelids, I noticed a glow. It was faint at first, but it began to grow in intensity. I opened my eyes, feeling the warmth of mana brush against my skin.

She did it! I nearly shouted, getting up from my seat. Thorn, who had already sensed her drawing mana well before I did, held up a hand to stop me, softly shaking his head. I tore my eyes away from him, only to notice Meliss' once phthalo green eyes had turned into obsidian. Mana floated gently across her skin, like an artist's brush floating on a canvas.

I stood in awe, as I hadn't ever seen the awakening process myself, though Taegin's razor sharp focus didn't waiver at all. The mana suddenly began to coalesce and condense into her left hand, forming a small, swirling globe of pale blue and green light. Red streaks began to chase after them, followed closely by dark orange.

The Ethereal has responded to her call, I thought, thinking back on my first time. Obviously, I had seen something similar during my time, but that's because what I could see *was* in the Ethereal realm. Seeing it manifest here in the Real, however, was a beautiful sight in and of itself.

Once the trailing tendrils of mana finished coalescing, Meliss's eyes returned to their normal phthalo green. Without anyone saying a word, we allowed her to understand what she was experiencing, as she gazed at the palm of her left hand where the sphere had coalesced just moments prior.

"I... I did that?" she asked, as if unsure of what she was looking at. "It's beautiful... I can't even begin to describe it," she said, a tear forming in her eye. Taegin, releasing his hold on the runic circle, let out a gentle sigh of relief. "I'm proud of you, young Meliss," he said, a tired smile grew on his face. "Welcome to the Synners of Codrean," he said warmly.

She giggled lightly, still holding the globe in her hand, as she tried to sit up. "I... oh my. How long have I been here?" she asked, plopping right back down on her ass. "The sun has just set, and dinner is about to be served," Pyle said just as her stomach rumbled. "Do you want me to help you up? If so, you might want to do something with that mana first," I said, gesturing to the sphere.

"*Oh*, this thing. Right. Uhmm... one second," she said, closing her eyes again. The sphere began to undo itself, gently unraveling in the palm of her hand, seeping into her skin as if it was a part of her. Taegin, uncharacteristically, chuckled. "I've seen maybe twenty others able to do that in my time as the Master, each with exemplary talent for mana. I'm looking forward to watching you grow," he said encouragingly.

"No pressure," I added, a grin smeared on my face.

We all left the Awakening Chamber together, Pyle, Thorn, and Taegin were all talking amongst one another, while I helped Meliss back up the stairs. Her legs hadn't yet gotten used to moving again, so what little support I could give her, I did. "How do you feel?" I asked after clearing the stairway. "Hungry. Need food." she said, turning nearly primal at the smell of the meal just a few score meters away.

Never get between a woman and her food, I noted.

The rest of the night was rather uneventful. Meliss was too exhausted after the meal to really stay up and talk much, so I led her back to the female dorms and dropped her off at the door. I, on the other hand, had already spent much of my day focusing both on her and the twin flasks Thorn gave me. I couldn't, for the life of me, figure out what they were for, so I ended up falling asleep more quickly than I anticipated.

The following morning I woke up, and packed my gear. Ren, who was already awake by the time I got out of bed, silently helped me gather and pack my things. He never really said much, but I could tell he had a good heart underneath his cold exterior. I thanked him silently, as Bernar and I were going to leave before dawn broke to make it as far as we could the first day.

Knowing him, he'll probably want to stop by Coltend Castle to visit Leona. I wouldn't mind seeing her again, either, I thought.

I carried my bag, sword, and rations I had prepared after dinner the night before, and headed toward the stables. Bernar was already there, though it seemed he hadn't been there long. "There you are. Do you have all your shit you're going to need?" he asked. "Yeah, I've got my stuff. Oh, right, almost forgot," I said, pulling out one of the twin cerulean flasks.

He eyed it carefully, and perhaps saw something I couldn't. "Who gave this to you?" he asked, gingerly taking it from my hand. "It was a gift from Ren, Thorn and Taegin, though we're not supposed to drink them until we get to Caegwen," I said. "Really? Huh, can't imagine why, but if Thorn said so, I'll take his word for it," he said, wrapping it in a piece of cloth and sticking it into one of his saddlebags.

"Did you think you were going to leave without saying goodbye?" Ed's voice called out, Meliss, Thorn, Ren, Taegin and Pyle following close behind. "Not a chance," I chuckled. "You'd hunt me down, and she would kill me if I did," I said, pointing to Meliss as well. She was still sleepy from the day prior, and rubbed her eyes gently.

"Why did it have to be today?" she asked. I realized, then, that it wasn't that she was tired, but *crying*. "I-It's just time, Meliss. The Master said it, and I'm ready to face my next challenge," I said, trying to sound a little more positive than how I was feeling after seeing her in that state. "I don't want you to go," she sobbed lightly. "Darling, you have a whole world of training ahead of you. By the time I get back, you probably won't even notice I left in the first place," I said, cupping my hands around her jaw.

"Of course I will, dummy!" she said, lightly punching my shoulder. I kissed her forehead, and turned to face Taegin, my grandfather. No words needed to be exchanged, save for a silent nod of understanding between us. "When you get back, I'll reach the second stage, I promise," Ed said, holding out his fist toward me. "I'm sure you will," I replied, bumping his fist with my own.

Thon and Ren now approached with Pyle, as if they had waited their turn to speak. "I will ask the gods to watch over you and your brother in your travels. *Oh*, I forgot, Ren had one last thing for the two of you," Thorn said, motioning his friend forward. Ren's dark hair and scarlet eyes seemed to float against the still-darkened background not lit by torches as he approached us.

"Please, stand together," he said in his soft voice, motioning for us to stand side by side. Bernar and I followed his orders, and closed our eyes. With his hands placed just where our cores lay, he *pushed mana into them, as if searching for something. I can feel him digging around in there like a mole in the ground*, I thought, flinching slightly at the strange feeling in my chest.

After about a minute, Ren pulled his hand away, and what I could have sworn was a smile appeared on the corners of his mouth. "I anxiously await your return, cou- ... " he said, cutting himself off. "Thoma, Bernar. I'm sorry I don't speak much, but I will say this: you will *both* need to speak to Queen Aurae when you arrive. Keep those flasks on you, and I will speak to you when you return," he said.

I didn't even know he could *talk that much*, I thought.

My brother and I thanked him for the flasks once more, and stepped away from the group. "Don't cross into the fourth stage without me getting to spar with you in the third, little monster," Pyle said, crossing his arms like some stubborn child. "I'll keep that in mind," I returned with a warm smile.

Meliss and I shared one last glance, her tear-filled eyes glazed in torchlight. I tried to give her an encouraging look, but knowing I would be away for as long as I would be, I couldn't muster anything other than a thin-lipped smile. I turned my horse and glanced over at my brother.

"So... ready to see mom again?" Bernar asked.

CHAPTER 34
CLIPPED WINGS

Athar slumped against the wall, exhausted from the last sparring session of the day with Irun. Sweat poured from his head as he caught his breath, leaning against the edge of the training room. "Gods above and below, Irun, you're incredibly fast," he said between gasps. "Thanks, but you're actually getting better at sword-casting. I'm impressed with your progress the past few months," Irun replied, a few beads of sweat falling off his chin.

"Yeah, but there's still a limit on how much mana I can pull, it seems," Athar said, feeling a little down. "Don't worry about how much mana you can pull, it's about what you do with it," Irun replied. "I know, I know. It's just... *frustrating*. Like I'm about to learn to fly, but get my wings clipped by something I can't, or don't know how to, control," he said, mentally kicking himself.

That's kind of how I felt, Irun thought, recognizing these emotions as if they had been his own.

"Well, what if we asked *him*? To... uh, you know... help?" Irun asked, trying to offer a solution to his adopted older brother's plight. "I don't know if he would help, but we can at least try," he said, pondering the offer briefly. "I mean, he's helped me a lot the past few months after having done something to my core. It's like he's holding me back on purpose," he said, not realizing the weight of his words.

"What do you mean holding you back? Not even my old master would do that if the student were gifted enough. Can you explain why you think that?" Irun asked, his curiosity peaked.

"I don't know how to explain it, exactly. It was like he dug around in both my brain and my core at the same time, like he was looking for something," Athar replied, his long, dark hair being swept back, flicking a few specks of sweat onto the wall behind him. "That's a weird way of putting it, but I'll trust you on it," Irun replied, his face twisted with confusion.

The Masked One can do that? Shit, this might be worse than I thought. I wonder if he looked into mine at some point and I just didn't know it, Irun thought, thinking back on his past encounters with his new master.

"So, do you want to give it a try, or are we just going to sit here and wallow in self-pity?" Irun asked after a few beats of silence had passed. "Yeah, I just hope he's not busy," Athar said noncommittally. After gathering their gear, they made their way down the many halls of Valdis searching for the Masked One. However, after about thirty minutes, there was no sight of him.

"Only one place he could be, and I'm not sure I want to fuck around and find out if he's in there," Athar said, caution ruling his voice. "Where would that be?" Irun asked. "In the summoning chamber where he communes with the Undergod," Athar said, a chill running up his spine as he recalled the last time he was in Volzuk's presence.

The pair made their way down to the chamber quickly and quietly, just in case he really *was* in a meeting. Without any warning, they were both stopped in their tracks as if they had hit a wall. In truth they had, but not a physical wall, rather one of pure mana. "Holy shit, do you feel that?" Irun asked, pressing his hand against the air. "How could I not? I never realized mana could *become* this dense," Athar replied, poking the translucent wall in front of him.

Come, the Masked One sent to their minds.

The pair lurched forward, and were met with the sight of the Volzuk, the Undergod. Athar, who had already seen him before, wasn't quite as taken aback this time around, though still stunned by the smell of rotting flesh and sulfuric gas. Irun, on the other hand, nearly pissed himself. The loose flaps of skin and exposed bones hither and thither didn't help Irun realize that he was in the presence of a god.

"You have a new slave, I see," Volzuk's voice boomed inside the summoning chamber, the runes on the floor flickering slightly as he spoke. *Shit, he's not moving*, Athar thought. He grabbed the motionless body of Irun by the nape, kicked his foot out from under him, and forced him to kneel.

"My apologies, Lord of the Underworld. He has not yet been accustomed to your presence," Athar said, trying to keep himself from releasing his bowels as well. "That much is evident, but who is he? Why is he not speaking? I don't even hear any of his thoughts," Volzuk said, peering curiously at Irun. "Great one, he is known as Irun Mothac, once a synner of Codrean, he has since betrayed them and joined our cause," Athar continued.

"I see," Volzuk said unceremoniously. "He's the one who brought you information on the Gwynnleaf's location, mage? Sad that you needed to resort to such tactics, as I'm sure your power would've been more than sufficient to destroy their fortress in the first place," the

Undergod continued. The Masked One sucked in a sharp breath, as if he were about to say something, but kept his composure.

"Was that a hint of defiance I felt just now? Mind your thoughts, mage, lest I tear out your core," Volzuk said, not even bothering to acknowledge the situation further.

Tear out his fucking what? Irun finally thought, snapping out of his daze.

"Ah, I was beginning to wonder whether you were just some mindless, reanimated corpse," Volzuk said, hearing his thoughts. "It surprises me to know that your former master did not cut out your tongue with that sort of language, though I'm sure he had his reasons," the Undergod said, giving Irun a questioning glance. "It would seem you think I've made a mistake in choosing this boy," Ardrin finally spoke up, his tone calm and composed.

Athar, knowing *both* of these two, powerful overlords could hear his thoughts, tried his best to not think, breathe, or say anything at all. "Oh? And what do you suppose would have happened if another *had* been chosen? Would you still have him under your control after having done so *many* horrible things towards his former comrades?" Volzuk asked, bending down a little to peer into the Masked One's eye-slits.

The Masked One said nothing in return, merely flicking his head to the side. "Not likely. You needed someone subservient and innocuous, exempting them from any sort of suspicion," the Undergod continued. "You *know* why I chose him. His proximity to Thoma Fayren was just sufficient enough to not rouse too much suspicion. Thoma, being *so close* with Irun's former master, was a well of information I couldn't ignore," Ardrin replied.

Irun's thoughts swam with all of this information, trying to process it all at once, but failing miserably. "Regardless of your reasons, we got the information and resources we needed to begin the next phase of our plan," Volzuk said, his brows furrowing in mild frustration. "In any case, we will continue our conversation at a later time. Return to the Underworld when you are done with your... underlings," Volzuk commanded, releasing the summoning spell and leaving a cloud of death and sulfur-smelling smoke in his wake.

Ardrin turned in a fury. "Nothing? You couldn't even say your own name? You made me look like a fool for choosing you, *little shit*," he said, not even bothering to hide his anger by flaring his mana around him. The palpable aura knocked Irun face first into the ground, breaking his nose.

It's like a royal ochelon is sitting on my back, Irun thought, struggling to breathe under the sudden change in his weight.

"My lord, I... wasn't prepared to..." Irun struggled, trying to get both words and air out of his lungs. "Prepared to *what*? Interrupt me? It seems you have some lessons to learn, and I *know* coming here was ultimately *your* idea," Ardrin said, increasing the pressure even further.

He's going to crush me flat, Irun thought, his eyes wide as he coughed up blood.

"I still could," the Masked One said, reading his thoughts. "You would have been dead a long time ago if I didn't need you to do one more thing for me," he continued. "I... will do... your bidding," Irun managed to say, his voice wheezing. "You say that as if you have a choice in the matter," Ardrin said, releasing the pressure on Irun. The boy coughed more blood, spitting it out onto the floor as soon as the pressure released. Athar rushed over to him, making sure he was alright.

"I will not ask if you thought that was necessary, my lord, though I do not have any means of healing him," Athar said in an attempt to coerce his master. "It *was* necessary, Athar," the Masked One replied. "The tenuous balance of power and necessity between myself and the Undergod is now more strained than it had been when *you* first met him," he continued.

"I *did* sense something was off, but I didn't know it was *that* tenuous," Athar replied, pouring a small vial of deathmold into Irun's mouth. The Masked One sighed, shaking his head. "It has gotten worse since I delivered the Gwynnleaf to him, though, for now, it's nothing I can't handle," he said solemnly.

I know he will deem me obsolete once the final part of his plan comes to fruition. Who's to say what he will have in mind when that time comes? Ardrin thought, staring off toward the summoning circle.

"My lord, I understand that now might not be the best time to ask, but I have a request to make," Athar began, looking up at him from his kneeling position. "What is it, then?" the Masked One asked, not bothering to look down at him.

"During my training with Irun, I've begun to notice there is some sort of *limiter* on the amount of mana I can draw. Is there a way to fix that, and if so, can you help me?" Athar asked, his voice more confident than he anticipated. "*Hooo?* A request for more power?" Ardrin asked, finally turning to look at him.

"Indeed, my lord. I recall you once said that you *also* constantly search for more power, and so I figured you would be the authoritative figure to help me break through my limiter," Athar said, hoping to appeal to his better nature.

"I did say that, didn't I?" Ardrin asked, directing the question to no one in particular.

"Very well, but first, I need to verify something," he said, approaching the young man. "Do what you must, my lord," Athar said, knowing what was coming and bracing for the sickening feeling about to rise. He towered over Athar, who was kneeling over Irun's now unconscious body, and placed his hand on his head.

The Masked One *drew in dark mana once more* and condensed it in his hand, pouring it into Athar's body as he searched through his core. Within a few seconds, the Masked One removed his hand, flicked his head to the side like a bug had just flown in front of it. "I can't bring you up much further, it will be too risky," he sighed and shook his head. "What? Why, my lord? Am I not worthy of power? Have I not proven my dedication to obtaining it?" Athar asked, his tone pleading rather than angry.

"You have, and therein lies the problem," Ardrin replied solemnly. "W-wh-what do you mean, my lord?" Athar asked, his voice shaking in confusion and fear. "You have... *potential*, Athar. More so than I ever did at your age, by any means. However, there is a problem with your core that not even *I* can repair," Ardrin said, removing his hand and turning away. "A *problem not even you can fix*? How is that even possible?" the young man asked, his face contorting in confusion.

"I cannot say everything right now, as that tenuous balance I spoke of earlier would be completely obliterated if *he* were to find out about this issue. Nevertheless, bringing you up any further than I am about to would pose too great a risk, one that neither you *nor* I can afford to face," Ardrin said, his tone serious but gentler than Athar had expected.

"I... I see, my lord," he said, his eyes darting back and forth trying to piece information together. "But, I will still help you reach your next limit, anyway. I believe you have enough control over your mana to not lose yourself entirely because of it," Ardrin said. "Really? You'll help me, my lord?" Athar asked, his eyes regaining some of their lost life.

"I will, but you must understand something before I do this," Ardrin began. "What is it, my lord?" the man asked, sensing his master's tone of caution. "You may begin to hear voices, but do not fret, they will *not* harm you so long as you keep full control over your mana," Ardrin explained. "*Voices*? What kind of voices?" Athar asked.

"I would be lying if I said I knew what they would say or try to coerce you to do," the Masked One replied. "Basically, you want me to ignore them and suppress them with mana, my lord?" the man asked. "If you can manage it for the next few months, perhaps I might consider helping you along even further. That would only be if you can prove yourself a capable mage," Ardrin replied.

Athar nodded his agreement. "I understand, my lord. I will do whatever it takes to make this worth your while," he said, bowing from his kneeling position. "I look forward to seeing your progress," Ardrin said, *drawing more mana from the Underworld, forcing the quick, dark tendrils to do his bidding. As he stood beneath the dark, lifeless sphere while molding his spell, he noticed a figure off in the distance.*

What is that? Can it see me? Ardrin thought, trying to focus mana into his eyes to be able to see more clearly. Just as he did so, the figure, who might have been grinning with malicious intent, vanished.

Damn it, I couldn't get a good look at it, but I think it was... grinning, *he thought, shaking his head.*

He continued to draw a bit more mana to finish shaping his spell and returned to the Real moments later. Observing the swirling globe of mana in his hand, he spread it out into a complex, geometric pattern, twisting and molding it as it rotated. His spell, now completed, resulted in a strange, hexagonal shape, with multiple offshoots of mana branching off into something akin to a large crack in a frozen pond.

"Stand," he commanded Athar, who responded accordingly. He closed his eyes, and took a deep breath. "Once I give this to you, you will need to immediately wrangle your mana back under your control," he said, now staring intently at Athar who swallowed dryly. "I'm ready, my lord," he replied with conviction.

To potentially alter the course of history with one, single spell, Ardrin thought, nearly chuckling at the ridiculousness of it all.

He pushed the geometric spell into Athar's chest. Immediately, dark tendrils of mana began to whip around the summoning chamber, causing the very air to begin to ripple in response. "Control it!" Ardrin shouted over the cacophony of tens of whip-like sounds cracking through the air. Athar's body convulsed and wriggled as it fought against the mana. The lashing of mana tendrils began to subside, when a voice that wasn't Athar's spoke.

"Accretion," the voice said, its tone *sounded* human, but was far from it. Immediately, the mana ceased to lash out, as Athar stood, with his eyes closed and face plain. "Athar? Are you alright?" Ardrin asked, taking one step closer.

Just as he did, Athar's features contorted into the same, strange grin. His chin was pointed inwardly, as his eyes peered straight ahead with an unnerving smile growing instantly on his face. "Who are you, and what have you done with Athar?" the Masked One asked.

That's the same grin I just saw in the Underworld, he thought.

Athar, or what at least *looked* like Athar, didn't reply. Instead, only lifted a finger and shook it, never once changing its strange countenance. It had a sort of anxious *hunger* to its eyes, like it was just waiting for a chance to devour whatever was in front of it. "You son of a..." Ardrin began, but before he could finish his sentence, Athar's face contorted into one of sheer, unadulterated panic as he collapsed unconscious onto the cold, stone floor.

"What, and I couldn't in a thousand years stress this enough, the *fuck*?" he asked aloud. "Perhaps I can help explain, my lord," Karak's nauseating voice chimed in from the doorway. "In addition, to the explanation, I bring news of Athar and Irun's progress, as well as news from Caegwen," the daemon continued, slowly moving towards the Masked One.

"*What* news from Caegwen?" Ardrin asked, his curiosity peaked.

CHAPTER 35
CAST DIE

As the sun crested over the distant Rhydian Mountains, Leona was standing in front of the large window that looked out over the eastern portion of the city. The beams of sunlight piercing through the morning clouds of the incoming storm made this view infinitely more beautiful.

After a few moments of taking in the sight, she turned to her bedside table, and realized that there was no breakfast waiting for her there.

I miss Meliss. She would always bring me a morning snack, even knowing I would rarely ever eat it. I hope she's alright over there with Thoma, the Master, and... Bernar. By the Graces, I miss them all. I want to see them again, but I don't think it would be good for me to do that right now. Not with the country being in the state it's in, and the work we still have to do to fix what happened just a few months ago, she thought.

After letting out a mildly frustrated sigh, she turned away from the bedside table, and put on the dress she had laid out for herself the previous night. *Just to avoid Clare's morning breath,* she thought, chuckling slightly at the memory of her and Meliss sharing whispered words that one morning.

The day dragged on, as multiple meetings with local leaders and market managers began to bore her to death. This, however, wasn't enough to stop her from going out to the training yard to briefly observe Neko and Marte's training with Thorsen.

I can't quite make out what they're saying, but the way they speak to each other kind of reminds me of Bernar and his little brother. The sheer amount of back-talk is incredible. I wonder where they got that from, she pondered, placing the tip of her finger on her chin, as she tried to imagine what their parents must look like.

I'd wager it was the father that taught them that, she concluded. *There's just no way their mother is anything like them.*

"Your Majesty," a familiar voice sounded off from behind her. "Fulco, my dear!" she said excitedly as she turned to meet her attendant who was accompanied by two guardsmen. "*Oh,* like you two don't know who this is," she jested at the guardsmen. They both looked at each other, shrugged, and bowed their own dismissal.

"How have you been, my old friend? It is good to see you again," she said, nearly embracing him. His features had been roughened, and a closely kept beard grew on his face. The bags under his eyes were tell-tale signs that sleep had been absent in recent days or weeks, but otherwise, he held a smile, with both arms clasped behind his back.

"I have fared well enough, considering the circumstances, Your Majesty," Fulco said, tears welling in his eyes. "The escape must have been difficult for you," she realized, recalling hers and Meliss' own flight.

"I-it was," he stammered, holding back tears. "But, that doesn't matter now. All that matters is that you're here, safe and sound!"

he forced a weak smile. Leona returned the smile, but only partially. "What are you not telling me? What *actually* happened, Fulco?" she asked. The words, though meant in consolation, stabbed like a flaming hot iron.

"M-my lover, he... he didn't make it out," Fulco said, a single tear racing down his tense expression, as the memories began flooding in. "I only just escaped with my life and a missing arm because of his self-sacrifice. He was c-caught by one of those *traitorous* bastards," he said, the tear catching in his short beard as he let go of the empty sleeve he'd been holding behind his back, lowering his head.

Leona's eyes widened as a lump grew in her throat. "I-I'm so sorry, Fulco," she said, feeling her own emotions begin to well up. "It's alright, Your Majesty," he said, sniffling back some snot that threatened to run out of his nose. "It has been a few months now, but I still cannot get those images out of my head," he said, wiping away another set of tears.

"Enough about me and my fear of things that go bump in the night, Your Majesty. I'm glad to see you safe and sound! How did you manage it? There were so many of them that I... I thought you'd been taken, or worse," he said, trying to shake off the wave of emotions that ran over him. "And I would have been were it not for Meliss and Thorsen," she replied. "Meliss? The young girl from the Gramm Isles? I always did like her," Fulco said, reminiscing a little about their time together.

"Yes, she was instrumental in my success. She saved me from creatures and men alike, as well as helped me become more acquainted with some of the synners that came to our aid," she briefly explained. Fulco's eyes widened in surprise. "You mean to tell me that those...

brutes helped save you? By the gods, where have *I* been?" he asked in shock.

"You'd be surprised to find they can be gentle, warm, and kind, though more than capable of doing whatever is necessary to rid this world of evil," she said, furrowing her brow a little. "Besides, you'd be even more surprised to find how good some of them are in bed, what with being so isolated and all," she immediately turned her thoughts to Bernar.

Fulco, on the other hand, nearly fainted with her words. "Your Majesty! You have to be careful that those around you won't use it against you," he said, putting his hand over his mouth and looking around frantically to see if anyone had heard what she said. "But since I am no such person: Spill it," he said, a wry smile showing on his face. "Gladly," she returned the grin.

The setting sun cast darkened shadows along the Rhydian Pass. Gwili Gwynn, leader of the bandits along the pass, patiently waited to give his other members the command to pounce on an unsuspecting caravan. While there were plenty of merchants who had come through that day, this one was special in that it carried a lot of precious materials and gold to help rebuild Coltend castle. While it wasn't uncommon for kingdoms to send wealth to one another in support or solidarity, this caravan was *late* to the endeavor.

I wonder if that tip I got from those odd-looking Harutians was right, he said, recalling their strange garb. *They certainly didn't look like normal travelers, what with their odd-looking knives. That wasn't normal Harutian garb, and I knew, for the first time since that fateful duel on this pass, that I was in over my head with them,* he thought.

He could see his followers already in position to strike their respective targets. He looked to his second in command, and gave him a nod to begin the raid. Arrows soared and met their targets, as the elves expertly picked off each cart's driver, bringing the caravan to a halt.

The horses became frightened by the sound of the whizzing arrows and screams of their felled drivers. The guardsmen quickly drew their swords, but by the time they could react, there was little that could be done to defend themselves nor the cargo they were meant to.

Gwili and his group's efficiency was astounding.

"Well, that worked out well. For a moment there, I thought we'd actually have to draw our swords," he said, coming down from his infamous rocky high-point. "I thought the same, though I didn't realize they'd have that many guards with them. They must've been bringing something important," Gwili's second in command said, his voice gruff and tattered by years of living roughly on the mountainside.

"Indeed, Wyrran, there were far too many this time around. Come on, let's find out what their *real* purpose was," Gwili replied. Wyrran's sharp eyebrows furrowed in response as he gave a curt nod. His walnut, braided hair was tied sharply behind his head, not making any movement. Gwili and Wyrran led the others from carriage to carriage, opening each and every chest along the way.

About halfway through scouring the convoy, Wyrran spotted a note in one of the driver's pockets which, upon closer inspection, held a royal seal. "Gwili, c'mere. You're gonna want to see this," he said, pulling the note off the dead body. "This doesn't look to be the size of a ledger," Gwili noted the blood-spattered letter as he took it from Wyrran's hand.

Cracking the royal seal on it, he opened the letter, reading the contents. His eyes widened as he reached the last sentence. "... this will be the first act of my revenge," he read aloud. "Revenge? Who wants revenge, and for fuckin' what?" Wyrran asked, snatching the letter, as Gwili looked off into the distance.

"Do you remember, before the massive horde rolled through, how those Harutian and Coltendian commanders were dueling?" Gwili asked. "I could've given two fewer shits about where they were from, but yeah, I remember them. Why?" Wyrran asked. "It would appear something more has happened than we originally thought, and we *might* have just spoiled a part of the remaining ruler's plan by raiding this caravan," Gwili replied, a nervous smile growing on his face.

"You're telling me that we just fucked with something we weren't supposed to? How in all the realms were we supposed to know that?" Wyrran asked, spreading his arms wide. "It would seem fate has a funny way of doing things, and thus, the die is cast," Gwili replied, shrugging. "In any case, so long as we pull our arrows and leave no trace, we should be *fine* and no harm will come to any of us," he continued, plucking an arrow out of a dead guardsman's head.

"You've got a real care-free attitude for someone who might get targeted next, you know?" Wyrran said, pulling another arrow out of the driver's chest. Suddenly, off somewhere down the caravan, a voice was cut out by the sound of gurgled blood. "The fuck was that?" Wyrran asked, turning in the direction of the sound.

The two didn't have time to investigate further before another voice was cut out by the same, gurgling sound. "We're under atta-..." the voice was silenced. "No one could take us by surprise like that,"

Gwili said quietly. "We should go. Now!" he urged. Wyrran shook his head in frustration, and drew his sword.

By the time they had made it to where the sound of the initial gurgle was, blood had already seeped through the ground and made a small stream that flowed under the wheels of the carriage in front of him. "Not idly does the blood of my comrades return to the earth. Find it!" Gwili hissed, growing frustrated.

Whatever the hell this thing is, it's fast. If my own members cannot react to it, this will be a repeat of that nightmare to remember, he thought as his eyes darted around.

"There!" Wyrran said, spotting a dark figure dashing by. "It's going from cart to cart, looking for something," he whispered, realizing the strange behavior. *It's just killing witnesses along the way*, Gwili thought. "Don't let it see you. If it does, assume it will try to get behind you and slit your throat like it did the others," he whispered to his second in command. "How do you know that?" Wyrran asked, visible confusion strewn across his gruff features.

"Because it's what I was trained to do when I was a synner," Gwili replied solemnly. Wyrran nodded, and kept his focus razor sharp toward every little detail around him. Gwili closed his eyes for a brief moment, trying to feel the air around him through mana.

It's been too long since I last used this, but I have to try and at least hone in on elemental mana to figure out where it is, he thought, taking a deep breath.

As he closed his eyes, he briefly *drew mana from the Ethereal* and coated himself in a thin sheen of it. Thin enough to where others couldn't detect it, but more than plenty to amplify his senses tenfold. The air's elemental mana flowed and swayed with the wind, but there were a few distinct disturbances in it. Most, unfortunately, were others who fell victim to the mysterious creature.

It's fucking fast. I can hardly keep up with it even like this, he thought, watching its movements through the displaced air like a hand waving through steam.

"It's coming this way," he realized almost too late. Just as the words left his mouth, Wyrran managed to duck under an elongated claw that came for his throat. *Was that actually a claw?* Gwili thought as he got a decent look at the creature. Its chitinous hide was thick like armored plating, while its features held little definition save for two slits on what would be its face; where a pair of glowing, red eyes stared back at him.

Shit, he thought.

He dodged an incoming blow, realizing quickly that it wasn't an elongated claw, but a dagger of some sort. *I couldn't identify that even if I tried. I've never seen a creature like this. Is it some kind of mutated glick or a new breed entirely?* He thought, dodging a sequence of quick attacks. He parried a few with a pair of daggers he withdrew from their sheaths, resulting in a loud *clanging* sound, reverberating along the pass' rocky walls.

"Hello there," he said coyly, holding his own against the pressure against his daggers. The creature didn't respond with words but with an extreme amount of force, sending him flying into a pile of stones. Gwili slammed against the rock, coughing up a bit of bile as he did so.

"That wasn't very nice. Here I was, trying to be polite and you just had to be *rude*," he accented the last word, by pumping his body full of mana. His eyes leaked with the excess, but it wasn't enough to be alarming. He dashed forward, his daggers prepared to strike, when he met his target's hard shell. "No joy, eh?" he jested, striking repeatedly at any soft-spot he thought he could see.

The creature, while non-verbal, *had* intelligence, and understood what he was trying to do. Wyrran, however, was a factor the creature hadn't accounted for, as he managed to observe the creature long enough to find a weak spot just behind its knee. He cut deeply, but was unable to sever whatever sinew helped this creature move.

Realizing it wasn't going in its favor, the creature darted out, far surpassing Gwili's speed and raced down one of the many roads of the Pass. "Wyrran, you're in charge. I'm going after it," he said without a moment's hesitation. "Drop that son of a bitch," Wyrran said. Gwili pumped more mana into his body, and gave chase, following the blood trail provided by its recent wound, as the blackened blood stood out against the dirt road.

After what felt like an hour of mindlessly tracking the creature, Gwili spotted it just off the path by an incredibly large tree. *Is it tending its wound?* he thought, staring at its strange behavior from behind the cover of a fallen tree. Almost as if it had heard his thoughts, the creature looked in his direction, and dashed further into the woods.

Gods above and below, does this thing have infinite strength? he thought, pushing more mana into his already exhausted body. *It's been forever since I've done this, and I'm surprised I've even gotten this far,* he thought, feeling the fatigue beginning to settle in.

Just as the string of words had finished in his head, he came to an abrupt stop. Off to his right, he noticed one of the protective charms used by the elves to help keep excessively strong creatures out of Caegwen's borders. "Ah, well, those are working well, aren't they?" he thought, staring at the charm of what was once his homeland.

"Either this one is broken, or this creature has an innate ability to hide its presence, even from protective charms of that sort," he said quietly to himself, looking around for any clues that might help him determine the correct answer.

I would go further, but as an outcast, if I'm caught... he thought of the repercussions.

shook his head in an attempt to knock the idea from it. *It's no use. I cannot go any further,* he thought, glaring at the path in front of him. *I just wish I could go* home *again,* he sighed tiredly, exhaustion, frustration, and sadness evident in his eye.

Home, he thought.

CHAPTER 36
A CAEGWENI WELCOME

Bernar and I finally began our journey to Caegwen. The cool breeze in the air, I thought, would make the trip a little more enjoyable. As we rode down the same path we had taken on that fateful morning, where Ed got injured by my spell, I glanced around at the trees around us.

Gods above, it feels like forever since then, I thought, recalling seeing Jehn Boone's cart being stuck in the mud.

"What's on your mind?" my brother asked, noticing my lack of mental presence. "*Oh,* I was just remembering my first fight here," I said, shaking my head to snap me out of my short-lived daze. "*Ah,* yeah. I remember that day," he said, not finishing his thoughts. There was really nothing more to be said about it, so we just left the conversation hanging in the air.

"In any case, I'm glad we all made it out of there alive," he said, steering the conversation in a different direction. "Yeah," I agreed, my eyes shifting to the back of Celer's dark nape. "*Oh,* I've been meaning to ask you about something," I said. "What about?" he returned. "It's uh... it's about Leona," I said, trying not to appear as nosey as I was.

"*Oh*? What do you want to know?" he asked, giving me a wry, knowing smile. "*Ha*? No, nothing like that, you fucking weirdo," I said, chuckling as I shook my head. "I want to know what your plan is with her. Are you planning on getting *married* or something?" I asked, emphasizing the last bit of my sentence to really make him think about his answer. In all honesty, I didn't really care, but I knew Meliss would be happy to know her former master would be in good hands.

"I... I've thought about it," he pursed his lips, turning away from me. "*Ohohoooo*, was that a bit of blushing I saw there?" I teased, reaching my arm out and poking his shoulder. "Shut up," he snapped, though not out of anger, more embarrassment than anything else. "I said I've *thought* about it, but whether she would take me up on that offer is another story entirely," he said furrowing his brow in what I thought was frustration.

"*Ah*, I... I see," I said, understanding the weight of the decision that wasn't his alone to make. "What would that make you if it *did* work out?" I asked. "Well, I'm not of royal blood, so probably just a consort or something along those lines," Bernar said, rubbing the back of his neck with a nervous grin on his face. "Consort Bernar Fayren," I mused, letting the words stir in my mouth and thoughts. "*Deadman* Thoma Fayren," Bernar said, shooting me a glance that could have skewered a wild boar.

Hehehe, I should probably stop pushing my luck, I thought.

The hours went on as we finally made our way to Coltend Castle. There had been a few renovations since we were last there, and it was good to see the city bustling with people again. "Hello there," a voice called out. I knew from the accent that it wasn't Thorsen, making me a *little* disappointed.

The setting sun to our left as we neared the southern gate reflected its rays off the pommels of our riding swords. "*Ooh*? Synners, are we?" he asked, after a closer look at our armor. "Indeed, we are, my good sir. May we pass?" Bernar asked.

"Of course, we've been expecting you, though *I wasn't expecting* one so young as you," the guardsman said, pointing to me. "There are younger ones, you know," I muttered under my breath. It was evident that the man either hadn't heard me, or simply chose to ignore my comment. "But how did you know we were coming today?" I asked, recalling the fact we hadn't seen any ravens fly overhead.

"*Ah*, yes. Well, some of the elves that were with you, before you all left a few months ago, left us with these strange-looking devices. Once a bit of mana is infused, they create a link with another one just like it, allowing us to see threats far beyond our normal capabilities. So far, there are only a few that surround the castle, but our mages are working on making more of these *things*. There's actually one between here and your fortress at Codrean," the guardsman explained, combing his thick, dark mustache protruding from the front of his open-face helm.

"Didn't know we had those," I said, half to Bernar as to myself. "Well, I think I've kept you here long enough. Her majesty, like I said, has been expecting you," the guardsman said with a warm, welcoming smile.

We flowed through the city, mostly on horseback, passing through the streets, dodging a few pots of shit and piss thrown out the windows along the way. "*Heh*, reminds me of the first time we were here," I said, chuckling lightly. "It's good to see everyone getting back on their feet, though I'm sure there are those here that couldn't make it out," Bernar said, his tone growing a little more heavy near the end.

"But, we did what we could, and I'm sure Leona understands that," he stated, a resolute tone coming through. "I'm sure she does," I replied, feeling the weight of the battle resting on my shoulders like an old wound had reopened. After hearing what Edryd had told me, I was more than appalled at what Irun helped Ardrin conjure up for their assault. I knew, however, that there was little left that I could do or say about the matter, other than just move on as best I could.

"Thoma? Bernar?" a voice suddenly called out, knocking me out of my thoughts. I hadn't realized it, but we had ridden all the way from the beginning of the poorer district to the front of the main palace without my noticing.

I wonder if anyone else does that from time to time, too, I thought, wondering if this lack of mental acuity was just something that happened to me alone whenever I thought too much about something.

"By the Graces, it really *is* you!" the familiar voice spoke out again. "It's good to see you, too, Fulco," my brother said, whom I followed in dismounting my own horse. "Welcome back to Coltend Castle, you two! It's good to see you well, healthy, and uh... *not* covered in bloodied grime this time," he said as cordially as he could.

I remembered his face turning a pale shade of green when he noticed the blood from the battle still relatively fresh on our jerkins the first time I came here.

"Luckily for us, we didn't run into any trouble this time around. However, you don't need to worry about us too much this time around, as we won't be staying long," Bernar said politely, though I could hear the longing to stay evident in his tone. "I see," Fulco replied, almost as if reading his mind.

"Well, it is of little importance to me whether you stay a day or a month, especially after all you synners have done for us. I would be honored to better serve Leona by helping you two with whatever it is you need," he continued.

Do not *abuse that,* I shot my brother with a mild glare, to which he merely chuckled and scratched the back of his head.

"We would be the honored ones to have the great Fulco attend to us," I chimed in with a bow. "My, my! It would seem Meliss' departure has affected *your* behavior as well," Leona's voice rang out from behind her servant. Bernar's mouth widened into a cheerful grin at the sound of it, while I could hardly keep myself from wriggling my eyebrows at him mockingly.

"Queen Leona," I bowed, pulling my brother downward with me, forcing him out of his daze. "Get that shit-eating grin off your face in public, you numbskull," I whispered. "You're right," he whispered back, hardly audible to anyone who wasn't within a meter's range of us. "It is an honor to see you again, Your Majesty," Bernar said, lifting his head just enough to look at her beneath the fallen strands of black hair.

"Come now, is this any way for two of the saviors of Coltend to be reacting to my presence?" she asked loudly enough as if to make sure the rest of the guards in the vicinity knew we wouldn't have to treat her so formally.

"Rise, synners of Codrean," she commanded, her voice demanding respect, though regal and warm. "Come now, tell me about how these past few months have been, and I will fill you in as well. I'm quite anxious to hear how Meliss has been doing from your perspective, even though she writes as often as she can," Leona said, her voice teeming with excitement.

I could only chuckle shyly, but knowing her, Leona wouldn't stand for anything other than a top-notch analysis of her former servant's progress.

We spared no details regarding Meliss' progress, though we *did* keep the fact that she was a half-dwarf a secret, lest some unwanted ears still within the palace get a hold of that information. By nightfall, we had consumed a fanciful, yet small, feast Leona had prepared for us, drinking and telling more stories of our lives while we were away.

I could feel we had grown a lot closer, but there was always this gap between myself and Leona that I, for my brother's sake, decided to keep well maintained.

"So, how about it?" Leona's voice, I quickly realized, was directed at me. "How about *what*?" I asked, confused at her question. "Well, if I'm reading the situation correctly after what you've told me, it almost sounds like you would want to *marry* my former servant," she said coyly.

I nearly spat my ale, taken aback at her words.

Return to sender, my once inhibited thoughts now let loose with the infusion of alcohol in my system.

"Fine, but only if you marry Bernar," I said, sipping down the last bit of ale in my mug after I said it. "You little..." I could hear Bernar seethe, but he didn't continue after he noticed Leona seriously considering it. "Well, you *have* talked about it before, and now that things have calmed down quite a bit, I see no harm in taking him in as my official consort," she said, one extended finger rubbing the base of her chin.

As she pondered the ramifications, muttering to no one in particular, Bernar leaned in next to me. "How you get away with saying some of the shit you do will never cease to astound me, but thank you," he whispered.

"*Heh*, I wish I knew as well," I retorted, the grin I was trying to hide escaping and showing itself bare. Leona, finally snapping out of her thoughts, turned to face me. "So, when do you think this should be done? Should I have you and Fulco work together to arrange our marriage?" she asked.

"Your Majesty, while I may be intelligent in certain aspects, wedding planning is *not* my field of expertise," I began. "*Oh*, please, at least give me a timeline to work with. How long do you think you'll be in Caegwen for?" she asked, inching closer to me until her face was mere centimeters away from my own.

"I *uh*... I'm not sure. A few months? Maybe a year, at most? However, I don't suspect Bernar will need to be present for my entire training. With that in mind, you could, theoretically, do it even before then," I said, lacking confidence in my own words. I would be lying if I said I could even focus with her being so close, as her hypnotizing eyes peered into my soul. "Well, I would rather you be present for that day. After all, you *were* an instrumental piece of the puzzle in getting us this far," she said coyly.

"I... *what*?" I asked, shocked at her words.

"Let's just keep it simple and say I was a little *jealous* of you and Meliss, but I digress," she said, leaning back into her chair, sipping her mug of ale. While I couldn't exactly read what was going on in Bernar's head, his face was an odd mixture of surprise and shock to hear her admit that. "I must say, it would be nice to have you *and* your brother stay with us here at the palace, don't you think?" she asked my brother who was obviously still in shock. "Y-yeah, of course," he answered almost automatically.

He has no idea what he just agreed to, does he? I thought, a wry grin showing on my face.

We spent the rest of the following two days discussing and planning loosely, allowing room for any discrepancies that might arise. When that was all said and done, we said our farewells, and continued on our way to Caegwen.

Riding towards the Rhydian Pass made me realize just how large the once-distant mountain range actually was. Towering well into the clouds, the peaks of the perpetually snow-capped mountains loomed so far above me that it hurt my neck just to find the peaks.

"Sometimes I forget how sheltered you were," Bernar said, watching me look straight up the steep face of the mountain before the path began. "It's just incredible to me that something so beautiful exists," I said, chuckling softly, still in awe of the grandiose mountain in front of me.

"*Eh*, just wait until we get to Caegwen," he said with a shrug. "What do you mean?" I asked, wondering what could possibly leave me more awestruck than the size of the mountains. "Just wait," he replied with a smirk.

Going over the well-worn pass, I could tell that there was a lot of untold history strewn about it. From broken carriage wheels, to carvings in the rocks that lined the path, I could tell that, over centuries, each generation had left *some kind* of mark.

"If you look closely, you might even find some scribbles left behind by synners from long ago," Bernar said, interrupting my thoughts.

"Really? I thought it might be a possibility, but..." I trailed off, looking around at the carvings more closely.

"You *do* realize that the synners were once all very closely knit with each other, right?" Bernar asked. "I do," I lied. Until that point, I hadn't really put two and two together, but after that brief history reminder, I started to realize that the world was actually much *smaller* than I had anticipated.

Well, at least as far as cross-country societal interaction went, anyway.

"I know it's because of the long-standing tensions between the countries, but are there any other reasons we don't interact with other synner schools anymore?" I asked.

Bernar paused as if choosing his words carefully. "I can't exactly say for sure, but I *do* know that only Codrean and Caegwen still have good relations with each other. As for Harut and Hjalfar, their cultures are far too different for them to maintain peaceful contact with one another," he said, turning right at a fork in the path, following the direction of a signpost.

"But *why* do they have such difficulties with each others' cultures? As far as I understand it, elves and humans are vastly different from each other, but we still manage to maintain good relations with them," I said, rubbing my chin as I considered the possibilities. "I wish I knew," Bernar replied, leaving me to ruminate over the little knowledge I had of the Continent's socio-political situation.

We were nearing the top of the Pass, and I noticed it was becoming eerily quiet. "Something's off," I whispered to my brother. "I don't know what, exactly, but I can *feel* a change in the air," I continued.

Bernar didn't verbally reply, but signaled for us to dismount, as if he already knew *what* I felt.

We moved forward slowly, hands on the hilts of our blades, when suddenly, we heard a rustling from a nearby bush. I drew my blade as swiftly as I could, and immediately pushed into the second stage. I could feel the mana leakage wisp from the corners of my eyes, licking at my temples like a warmed feather, as my senses became enhanced. Feeling every fiber of my muscles tensed around the hilt of my blade, I furrowed my brow in concentration.

But for whatever reason, my brother hadn't moved an inch.

"*A-ta-ta-ta*, calm down, now," a man's voice resounded from behind a nearby bush. He came out with his bare hands exposed and lifted near his head in an attempt to show us he meant no harm. "Who are you?" I asked, my voice rumbling due to the mana enhancement.

"*Ooh*, now *that's* a tone I haven't heard in a long time," the man said, raising his thin, dark eyebrows in surprise, widening his sky-blue eyes. I could see, just behind his hands, a faint movement of what appeared to be his ears raising in conjunction with his brows.

"You're an elf, I see," I said, my grip still taught around my hilt. "And *I see* your powers of observation are astute," the elf replied in jest, lowering his hands. His tunic was well kept for a bandit, with bits of leather armor and bracers offered succinct but sufficient protection for anything he might face along the Pass. They looked new, almost *too* new for someone who appeared to reside in the mountains.

But why the fuck isn't Bernar reacting? I thought momentarily, not taking my eyes off the bandit just in case.

"I see you're wary of me, and were you a part of a caravan, you'd be right to be so," the elf said, maintaining a non-threatening stance. "However, as you are but a pair of travelers, we have no need to rob you of your possessions or other such things we might find value in. Rather, we would offer *protection* and *guidance* to the likes of you," he continued.

"Awfully convenient," I muttered, cocking my head slightly. "For both of us, yes. We only target larger caravans, though for some fucking reason, those idiot merchants haven't gotten smart to that, yet," the elf said with a shrug. I glanced at my brother, noticing a grin on his face. Whatever was going on in his head, I couldn't figure out, but he wasn't exactly saying anything, like he was waiting for *me* to figure out the best way to handle the situation.

"What is your name, boy?" the elf asked. "Technically, I asked you first," I shot back. "*Hmm*, fair enough. My name is Gwili Gwynn, and while I'm sure you've noticed the others surrounding us, I am the leader of this little group of mountain bandits," he said, putting a hand to his chest and extending his left out as he performed a mid-level bow. "Now that I've upheld my side of the pleasantries, it's time you've held up yours, isn't it?" the elf asked me.

Getting lessons on etiquette from a bandit is not *what I expected on this trip. Guess violence won't be the answer right now, but it* is *always an option*, I thought, noting his tone and poise.

"My name is Thoma Fayren, and I'm a synner of Codrean," I said, sheathing my sword. "And one capable of the second stage of mana manipulation at that," Gwili noted. "Most human synners tend to reach that at a much later age, don't they? Or am I so out of touch that the new generations are leaps and bounds ahead of their elders and I'm only just now finding out about it?" he asked.

I was surprised to find him so well informed, but then again, I had to consider the fact that he was *constantly* interacting with merchants. "Most reach it a few years later than I did, but I fail to see how that could matter to you," I replied, trying not to give too much information away. He chuckled at my reply, putting a few fingers to his forehead. "An angsty little fucker, ain't he? Bernar, how much longer are you going to let him do this?" he asked between breaths.

Wait, what? I thought, turning to look at my brother, whose grin had grown into a full-blown smile and hearty laugh.

I'm sorry, shit-head, I couldn't help it," Bernar said, patting me on the shoulder, laughing heartily as he walked over to the elf, clasping his arm in a greeting. "What the fuck just happened? Do you two know each other?" I asked, releasing my second stage. "Of course we do, Bernar was one of my best friends during his time in Caegwen, even though he's about a decade younger than I am," Gwili replied. "How am I just now hearing about this? How are *you* friends with an outcast?" I asked, not bothering to hide any expressions of confusion that grew on my face.

"He wasn't always an outcast," Bernar began, still chuckling at the situation. "He was one of my best friends *and training partners* during my time under Anwill," he said, gesturing towards the elf. "*Training par-...* You were a synner?" I asked, astonished at the revelation that this *bandit* and I had a lot more in common than I originally thought. "I was, yes, but I couldn't keep up with your brother *nor* the harsh training regimen that *monster* put us all through," Gwili explained.

That only explains half *the story*, I thought, furrowing my brow.

"But as for *why* I'm an outcast now... well, that's a story for another time alongside a warm meal and some booze," he said, as if reading my thoughts. "I see. In that case, I won't pry, but I would love to hear that tale sometime," I said, nodding my head in acknowledgement. He smiled, much more warmly than I had expected him to, but I could tell there was an unspoken pain behind his eyes that the smile couldn't hide. "Gladly," he responded.

"Bernar, are you taking him to Caegwen to train like you did?" the elf asked directly, shifting the somber mood of the conversation back to something a little more light-hearted. "Of course, the Master has deemed my little brother to be ready for the third stage," my brother replied, an air of pride evident in his voice. "*Third stage*? Gods above and below, how old are you, boy?" Gwili asked, genuinely astonished at my brother's answer. "I just turned eighteen a few months ago," I replied, discarding my previous desire to hide my age. There was no reason to do so anymore, I figured.

Gwili whistled critically. "At this rate, he might just beat you out of your record for reaching the fifth stage," he said to Bernar, a wry grin creeping onto his face. "We'll see about that," Bernar said, returning a knowing look to the elf. "Indeed we will, but we won't see shit if I keep you here any longer," Gwili said. "It was good to see you again, Bernar, and a pleasure to make your acquaintance, Thoma," he said to the both of us. "It was good to see you, too, old friend," my brother replied. I could only bow in response, as I was still trying to wrap my head around the situation.

"*Ah*, one last thing before you go," Gwili began. "There was a creature unlike one I've ever seen before that escaped into the forest near the border. I don't know where it was ultimately headed, but it was *fast*," he continued. My brother's eyes opened widely. "What did it look like?" he asked. "Dark, plated armor-like skin, and ugly as fuck," the elf said succinctly. Bernar contemplated the words carefully, but ultimately shook his head.

"I don't think I know of any creature that looks like that," he said. "Maybe it's a new breed of daemon?" I asked in hopes of sparking his thoughts. He pursed his lips and shook his head. "We'll keep an eye out for it when we're in Caegwen," he said. "Good. Just bear in mind it's sneaky and likes slitting throats from behind," Gwili said with a nod.

"We'd best be off, then. I'm not sure the leaders of Caegwen know this *thing* is running around their forests," Bernar concluded, clasping his forearm with Gwili's as they said their farewells. I extended my arm as well, mimicking my brother. The elf looked at me with a small amount of surprise, but ultimately returned the gesture with a firm clasp around the base of my forearm.

"Take care of yourself, and don't overestimate your abilities. Just because you're ahead of your time, doesn't instantly make you better than everyone else," he warned. "I'll keep that in mind. Thank you," I nodded, giving a final squeeze of his forearm before letting go. My brother and I mounted our horses, and waved goodbye to the elf as we rode down the path marked for Caegwen.

As we descended the path to the elven country, the stark change in flora was astonishing. From an arid, rocky terrain with naught but shrubberies and short trees to an increasingly dense forest with towering canopies was breathtaking. Caegwen, it seemed, was a country that grew *with* the forest, rather than around it.

Traversing through the forest, I could only just make out a few elven huts that lay scattered amidst the trees. The building materials used for such huts seemed to be made of all-natural materials, making them almost blend into their surroundings like a sort of camouflage.

"I've never seen anything quite like that," I noted, gazing at a massive sequoia tree. High within the branches lay a few, naturally formed structures that appeared to grow *from* the tree, rather than be built *onto* it. "And you won't anywhere else," my brother stated. "Elves have the capabilities to wield natural mana like no other species. Well, aside from the dwarves, that is, but they were nearly driven to extinction a few centuries ago," he continued.

"What do you mean they can *wield natural mana*? Do you mean to tell me that they can manipulate the growth of a tree to create these structures?" I asked. My brother chuckled at my words, almost as if he found it more of an amusing statement than an actual question. "I don't want to spoil that for you," he said, shaking his head. "Fine," I sighed. "You know, it would be handy if you could give me *some* answers from time to time," I said, punching his shoulder lightly.

Bernar raised an eyebrow at me in mock surprise. "Listen, little shit, I could give you a lot of answers and information that would push you through to reach new heights of knowledge. But what would be the point of spoon-feeding you that information without asking the *right* questions? If I tell or teach you *what* to think, not *how* to think, would you be any better than those followers of Mideia who just blindly accept everything put in front of them?" he asked, his tone growing sharper.

"N-no, I guess not," I replied, digesting his words. "Exactly. Because the Master and I have been trying to teach you to find answers for yourself, you've already surpassed many of the others your age. Your inquisitive nature is *not* to be frowned upon. Rather, I *encourage* you to find your *own* answers to things, and adjust your views or opinions based on new, factual information provided as opposed to blindly believing anything told to you. You've got a good head on your shoulders, so don't waste your intelligence. *Find* the right questions," he continued.

I've never seen him so adamant about something like this. Was it something I said? I thought.

I couldn't figure out *why* he felt so strongly about what he just said, but I knew he had a point. Being taught *how* to think rather than *what* to think was vital to my growth, though I had never really realized it until now.

"I'll do my best," I said after a few moments of quiet consideration. "I just don't ever know what the *right questions* are, or how I'm supposed to figure out *how* to find them," I said, a small amount of dejection seeping through my voice. Bernar sighed, perhaps realizing he had been a little too hard on me. "It's alright, I'll help you find them, but don't expect me to spoon-feed them to you, fuck knuckle," he said, giving me a light punch on the shoulder and a wry grin.

We continued down the path for the remainder of the day, observing all the different kinds of plants, trees, and animals I'd never come across before. Even the books we had learned most of our academics from couldn't lay a finger on seeing the real thing in front of me.

There is no way those books could ever do any of this justice, I thought, watching a giant plant with a broad head and fang-like spikes catch an unsuspecting rabbit who mistook the plant's lure for food.

I'm supposed to train in this environment? I thought, glancing around momentarily.

Approaching the palace, Vesryn merely gestured for the guards to open the gates without a word being spoken. I couldn't hear any gears turning to open the gate that was similar in shape, though smaller in size, to the one at the entrance of the capital. Behind it stood a magnificent palace with a general visage akin to gigantic tree roots that spread outward from the center toward the rest of the city.

The palace, like an enlarged and magnificent version of some of the houses I saw, towered over the rest of the city. The root-like structure that formed the core of it was, in reality, the base of an incredibly large tree; the canopy of which spread out like massive, circular awning. Nearing the top, I could make out a few smaller structures, though what purpose they served I could only imagine.

I learned, quickly, might I add, that I did *not* hide my amazement well, as my brother tapped the base of my chin, forcing me to close my mouth. "Careful, you don't want to accidentally eat a bug, do you?" he chuckled. Wordlessly, I grunted, but continued to follow both him and Vesryn towards the palace, where two figures stood at the top of the stairs with a pair of guards at each of their sides.

"Welcome, Bernar and Thoma Fayren, synners of Codrean, to Myrdin Palace," a soft voice said. From so far away, one might have thought that even shouting wouldn't have carried a voice so well, but elven mana manipulation was still something I struggled to wrap my head around. Following the captain and my brother's example, I got down onto one knee, placing my right hand across my chest.

"It is a pleasure to have you here again, Bernar. After so many years, we were beginning to think you *weren't* coming back," Aurae said, her voice flitted through the air like a feather. "It is both an honor and a pleasure to be in your presence once more, your majesties," Bernar said, his tone and enunciation unlike anything I'd ever heard him emit before.

Where the hell did that *come from?* I asked myself.

"Please, rise. I would like to get a better look at you both," Elhael said, leading his wife by the arm down the steps as we rose to our feet. Their presence was astounding, but not oppressive. It was, for lack of a better word, awe-inspiring.

The king and queen neared us, and I could see their fine faces up close. Aurae's silver hair and mismatched eyes coupled with her flawless, porcelain skin and fine bodily proportions would have made her stand out against a crowd of a million. Elhael, on the other hand, still looked the same as I had last seen him at Coltend during the meeting, but his silver hair was now tied into a braid, pulling his hair away from his lime-green eyes.

"As for you, I've seen you once before, though I can't quite recall where," Elhael finally spoke, his hand gesturing to me. "I'm astounded at Your Majesty's memory," I began, doing my best to mimic my brother's tone and intonation. "We've met once before, during the initial counsel at Coltend Castle, though I did not expect my face to be remembered, Your Majesty," I continued humbly.

I could have sworn I saw my brother giving me a look of approval, but I was too scared to turn my head to make sure that's what I saw.

"Indeed, I remember now. Although, at the time, I had no idea you were Bernar's brother. There was a bit of similarity, to be sure, but I hadn't had the time nor mental presence to confirm it back then," the elven king stated, his features scrunching a little as he pieced memories together.

"*Oh*, I see, Your Majesty," I said, feeling the weight of his words.

"In any case, welcome to Caegwen. Anwill, our retired Master Synner, spoke quite highly of you and your skills during his time with your people," Elhael continued, gesturing with one arm widely. "It is an honor to be here, Your Majesty. Thank you for allowing me to come here and train under Anwill," I said, continuing my humble tone.

"And what makes you think he'll be the only one training you?" an intense, female voice spawned just behind me, followed by a crushing amount of mana.

Who the hell is she? I didn't even sense her presence, much less hear her approach, I thought, frozen in place at the intense aura exuding from this person behind me.

"I-I-I... I meant nothing by it, my lady," I stammered, struggling to maintain my composure and not allow my knees to buckle under the weight of the pressure. While Elhael pinched the bridge of his nose, Aurae and Bernar's expressions, at least from what I could tell, were of expectant amusement.

"*My lady*? Is that any way to address your *mother*?" the voice scoffed, her tone turning a bit more playful as the pressure released. "M-mom?" I said weakly, turning around as I felt her presence backing away from me. "In the flesh," she said, giving me a warm smile.

Memories of my distant childhood flooded my mind, as I saw the familiar grin strewn across her fine features. Her steel-colored hair, braided on both sides and tied behind her head, accented her strong, yet feminine jaw-line. She was wearing a similar set of armor that

Vesryn was, though she hadn't put on her rerebraces and couters, only her gauntlets and pauldrons.

Her chestplate held different details than Vesryn's, with an insignia on the left side of her chestplate that signified her position as commander. She was tall, about as tall as I was, incredibly fit, and held her toned arms wide in an expectant embrace.

I dashed into her arms without a second thought, and I felt them tightly wrapping around me, matching my embrace.

"I can't believe it's you! Y-you're here! I-..." my words trailed off. I couldn't find anything to say, after all, it *had* been about fourteen years since I last saw her. The only thing I could do was try to hold the river's worth of tears back from spilling onto her armor. "I'm here, it's okay," she said, her once strong voice trembling with the words as she held me tightly.

In all honesty, I could've stayed like that for an eternity, but the reality of the touching family reunion was that it wasn't going to last that long in front of the *fucking* king and queen of Caegwen.

"Let me get a good look at you," she said, pushing me back, revealing her own bloodshot eyes staring straight into mine. She patted my shoulders and gave me a once over glance, at my black, leather jerkin. "What happened to your hair? And why are you so skinny? We need to put some more meat on these bones. How the *fuck* did you make it to second stage being this lanky?" she asked as bluntly as a smith's hammer.

"Hard work and dedication?" I answered with a shrug. She chuckled at my answer, and held my face in her hands. "Regardless, I'm proud of you, Thoma. I'm... sorry that I've been away for so long," she said dejectedly, turning her head away from me. That was when

I noticed it. "M-mom...?" I stammered, shocked at the sight before me.

Pointed ears, I thought, the two words hammering countless questions into my head.

Her ears, however, were not like Elhael or Aurae's ears, which protruded out a little more. Rather, hers were much more akin to Thorn and Ren's ears, which pointed sleekly towards the back of their heads, only protruding about as much as a normal human's. She must have seen my expression, because hers contorted into anger immediately.

"Wait, you don't...?" she asked, as if having heard my thoughts. Her angered expression turned even darker, as she cupped my face once more, turning my head to either side. "That son of a bitch. Gods, I married a real winner back then," she sighed. To say I was confused would've been the understatement of the year. "Who and *what* are you talking about?" I asked, my face still squished in her hands.

"Do you remember your father taking you to see an old man in a hut?" she asked. "I-I do. Father said it was for *my own good,* or so he made it seem," I replied, to which my mother seethed. "Siraye, what is this about?" Aurae asked.

It was the first time I'd heard my mother's name, her *real* name, that is, and it felt like a piece of my personal puzzle just fell into place.

"Your Majesty, you know I don't ask for much, but I would greatly appreciate your assistance here in just a moment. I've just figured out what happened to my son," she answered. Aurae, queen of Caegwen, nodded.

Never would I ever have thought that my mother would have such a strong influence, even over the royal family.

"Thoma, I need you to do something for me," she said, looking me in the eye with a mixture of anger and determination. "Of course. What do you need me to do?" I asked, matching her energy. She placed her hand on my chest, and immediately, I felt another placed on the top of my head. It took me a second to realize it, but it wasn't my mother's hand, it was the queen's.

"I need you to be as still as you can. *Oh*, and bite down on this. This is about to fucking *suck*," she said, pushing a leather glove up to my face. The fact that she spoke the same way Bernar and I speak with each other, immediately made me feel more at ease with the whole situation, prompting me to bite down on the glove.

"Ready, Your Majesty?" my mother asked, glancing over my shoulder. "At your command, Siraye," Aurae replied. With a final nod from me, my mothers eyes glowed more intensely *as she drew an immense amount of mana from the Ethereal.* The last time I felt anything even remotely similar was during Taegin and Ardrin's battle in the palace, but even that began to pale in comparison to what was happening here.

I could feel it begin to wrap around my core, flowing through and around it like a rapidly moving stream. That stream, however, soon turned into a raging waterfall as I began to feel something inside my core shattering like glass. I followed my mother's order of staying still, but a sharp pain began to resonate from my core out to my extremities in waves.

I bit down harder on the glove, and struggled to stay awake. While my entire body was going through a change I couldn't quite explain, there were two things I noticed through the pain. The first was that even through the pain I could feel something was happening to my head, but exactly what I couldn't quite tell. The second thing was that my brother, for whatever reason, was grinning widely as he fiddled with the small pendant he always wore pulled out from under his jerkin.

A final push of mana into my core flushed an insane amount of pain through my body, more than it was already going through, and I felt... warm. I could tell something had been *released*, but what exactly, I had no clue. "*Ohohoho* shit, look at him," my brother quipped excitedly. Both my mother and the queen moved away from me, my mother's eyes widening as she let out a sigh of relief.

"Gods above, I thought I'd *lost* you," she said, visibly relieved, though being a little more cryptic than I had expected. "*Lost me?*" I asked looking down to see if there were any major changes to my body. "How could you have lo-..." I cut myself off, noticing a lock of steel-colored hair falling in front of my eyes.

"What the...?" I said, reaching up to it to make sure that the lock of hair was my own. I had generally kept the sides of my hair short, with the top being a little longer so I could comb it over if I wanted to. My bangs had always been just long enough to reach down in front of my eyes, but this color wasn't my own.

Or, at least, I don't think *it's my own,* I thought.

After a moment of careful consideration, I recalled what I felt during my mother's push of mana. My head had changed, and, with my hair being a different color, I immediately reached for my face. That's when I felt it. "*Heh*, pointed ears. Who would've thought?" I asked no one in particular.

"Clearly I, as well as your brother, would've thought so. Perhaps even your *grandfather*, had he not been such a stingy bastard with all of his little secrets about us being members of the Arwydus clan," Siraye said, moving out from in front of me, revealing my brother. "*Oh*, what the actual *fuck*?!" I exclaimed as she moved out of my line of sight, revealing my brother.

He had the same, steel-colored hair as my own, and pointed ears just like my mothers. He was also holding a pendant that looked like a small grouping of vines wrapping around a sphere of mana dangling between his fingers. I'd only ever seen its chain around his neck once or twice, so I never thought much of it.

That is, until he swung it gently as if he were playing with a kitten or a toddler.

"Who the hell are you, and what have you done with my brother? *Oooh*, you-know-who's going to flip her shit when she sees you," I said, stifling a laugh. "She'll likely never see me like this, but I swear on all that you hold dear, if you tell her about this..." he trailed off. I quickly held up my hands in surrender. "Alright, alright. I get it. But what happened to me? What did you and her majesty do to me?" I asked, turning to my mother.

She looked at me with such endearment, I thought my heart was going to melt. "Thoma, when your father took you to that man in the hut, he sealed away my features that passed down to you and your brother. He *hated* the fact that the two of you looked so much like me, and so he had a pendant made that could suppress those features," she began.

That explains why he had tar-black hair while mine was brown, I guess, I thought.

"I already knew he didn't like the fact that Bernar shared my features, but when you were born, your features were too much for him to bear. When I heard what he had done to Bernar with the pendant, I tried to destroy it, but the sealing magic placed on it prevented me from destroying it without hurting him, which isn't usually how seals like this work," she continued, her brows furrowed in frustration.

"I warned him that if another pendant was made, that I would annihilate him *and* his side of the family. Realizing I meant what I said, he swore to never make another pendant. What *I* failed to realize, is that that same, suppressing enchantment could be placed on someone's core, which is what he did shortly after I left you two to come here," she continued.

So that's why everything *hurt so badly,* I thought.

"When your brother came here to train with me and your grandfather all those years ago, he and I performed numerous experiments on the pendant, eventually finding a way to break the seal. However, we reasoned that it would be too much of a shock and reveal some information about our family that shouldn't be public knowledge," she said, giving me a knowing look.

I'd understood what she meant. Having it known that the Master, Bernar, and I were related might have caused a bit of suspicion, especially given our family history of being Pelantyrs.

"And so, you *remade* the seal, but this time, you removed the part that would hurt him if he ever took it off," I surmised. She nodded her head in agreement. "*Heh*, it's like you read my mind," my mother said with a slight chuckle.

"There's one thing I don't understand, though," I began, turning to look at Aurae, who had been standing nearby silently, peering at me with her mismatched eyes. "How does Your Majesty come into play?" I asked, trying to be as respectful as I could, but I could feel the utter confusion reigning the tone of my voice.

"How do I explain this...?" she said, her thoughts trailing off as if caught off-guard by my question. "Let's just say that I'm a *deviant* in the realm of mana manipulation," she replied, letting her words hang.

She's not going to tell me everything is she? Is she like Ren, who has a different kind of control, or perhaps interpretation of mana? I thought, trying to piece it together in my head.

"Interesting line of thought you've got going on, but I'll let her tell you that herself, eventually," Siraye interrupted the cacophony of my thoughts. "Did you just...?" I trailed off. "Read your mind? *Meh*, it's not *that* hard to do to an unprotected and untrained mind. Also, who's Ren?" she cut me off, shrugging her shoulders as if what she had just said didn't just blow my mind.

"Rennyr Virie, one of the elves we summoned prior to our counter attack on Coltend Castle. He... *helped* my best friend with his core, but I'm not entirely sure what he did nor how he did it. I *do* know he used mana, however," I explained briefly. "Another deviant, you say? What color were his eyes?" Aurae asked, her interest peaking as she took a step closer to me, visibly excited.

For the first time, I actually *looked* into her stunning eyes. At this point, it felt difficult to tear my own away from hers.

"Red, though *both* of his are, unlike your beautifully mismatched ones, Your Majesty," I said, adding the flattery to the end of my sentence to not sound disrespectful. Her eyes opened wide in excitement. "I would very much like to meet him someday," she said, a pensive smile growing on her fine features.

Elhael cleared his throat from a few paces behind her. "Well, this has *truly* been an eventful day, what with the revelations and all, but I'm sure you two are exhausted from your journey," he stated. My mother wrapped her well-toned arm around my shoulder.

"Don't worry, Your Majesty, I'll make sure these two are well taken care of, just as I will handle the majority of Thoma's training while he's here," she said in a much more friendly tone than I had expected. After having seen her interaction with Aurae, however, I quickly realized that she held much more influence here than I could ever imagine.

"Very well. Join us for supper, you two. After you've washed up and had a change of clothes, which my servants will provide for you, I will send someone to fetch you," the king said with a curt nod. Bernar and I bowed, thanking him for the offer as we took our leave, escorted by our mother who rubbed her knuckles on my scalp as she tucked my head under her arm.

"When the hell were you going to tell me you knew about what that bastard of a father you two have had done to my sweet boy?" she asked Bernar as we walked down the naturally formed halls of the palace. "More specifically, when the fuck were you going to tell *me* I even *had* a seal on my core?" I chimed in.

"Hey, two versus one isn't exactly fair," he raised his hands placatingly. "Grandfather told me not to say anything to either of you until you two met. He said he would leave it up to your *best judgment*, mother," he continued explaining, the retort my mother gave in response was merely a curt scoff.

"That old bat should've gotten rid of it himself," she said frustratedly. "He could've done that?" I asked, raising an eyebrow. "Of course he fucking could've, but for whatever gods-forsaken reason, he chose not to, leaving it to me to find out the hard way that my son's core, appearance, and physical capabilities had been *tampered* with," she said, seething with the last few words.

I could tell she was exceedingly angry at my father. To be fair, both Bernar and I never really liked the fucker, but his blood still ran through our veins nevertheless.

"Well, now that the cat's out of the bag, what do you think of your *real* appearance?" she asked after letting out a sigh. "It's going to take some getting used to, but I can feel my entire body has *changed* somehow. Like there was a heavy ball and chain I'd been dragging around all of my life suddenly being detached from my body," I said, trying to explain the levity of how my body now felt after the seal had been broken.

Both Bernar and my mother grinned wryly. "You've made it to the second stage with that handicap on you; an impressive feat for *any* species, half-elf or otherwise. I can't *wait* to see what you'll be able to do when we start training you in earnest," my mother said, an eagerness in her voice letting me know I was in for a world of hurt.

I wonder how much different it will be to train without a restriction I didn't know I had, I thought.

You'll see just how much faster you'll grow without it, my mother sent to me mentally, catching me off-guard as her soothing voice resounded in my head. My expression certainly gave me away, as she was looking at me with mild amusement at this new development.

Without the handicap, you might even surpass me one day, but not anytime soon, my brother chimed in, transmitting his thoughts for the first time. *You could* also *read my thoughts the whole fucking time?* I asked, shooting him a blatantly pissed-off stare.

Surprise, asshole! he sent back with a shit-eating grin on his face.

CHAPTER 37
BUMP IN THE NIGHT

G wili was nearly asleep beneath the furs he called a blanket when he heard the sound of hooves barrelling down the pass at a break-neck speed.

What the hell is it now? What deranged merchant would travel in the night, let alone at a speed like this? He thought, groaning as he abandoned the warmth of the furs.

He grabbed his bow and short-sword that were stationed next to his bed, and strapped them quickly to his body, making his way out of the small, dug-out cove he used for shelter against the elements. He *felt* the rushing horses before he'd heard them, as vibrations travel faster through the ground than sound does through the air. This, in turn, gave him just enough time to see them.

What the...? he thought, as even his elven eyes struggled to see what was before him.

A group of horsemen clad in dark, cloth sashes that wrapped around their bodies like bandages rode through the Rhydian Pass beneath a full moon's gaze. There was little detail that could be made out as they rode, since their attire was specifically *designed* to throw off someone's eye should they end up spotting them.

"Wyrran," Gwili whispered over to his approaching second in command. "What the hell *are* they?" Wyrran asked in a similar whisper, still trying to keep his eyes on the blurred figures that passed by. "I'm not sure, but they're not like any monster I've ever seen," Gwili replied, his tone uncertain as his eyes tried to focus. "Do you think it's more of those... *things?*" Wyrran asked, recalling the creature that had passed through a few days prior.

"Unless those creepy-looking fucks learned to ride horses, I don't think its more of them. Look, see the way their clothes make them blend in with their surroundings as they move?" Gwili noted, making subtle use of a pointed finger to try and trace their movements. "I can hardly see them, and I'm even pumping mana into my eyes," Wyrran squinted, following the figures as best he could.

Gwili nodded in the silver light. "What doesn't make sense to me, though, is why these things are headed toward Coltend, unless..." he said, pensively, recalling the letter they had found. He got up from his position and raced over to where he kept the letter, stuffing it into a leather pouch.

"I'm going to investigate. Once again, you're in charge, Wyrran," he said, lightly tapping his friend on the shoulder as he got up. "At this point, *I* might as well be *running* the damned group myself," Wyrran scoffed, but nodded his acknowledgement.

Within a few moments, Gwili was mounted on one of the few horses they had. For the most part, these were used as supply carriers, not intended for travel, as many of the bandits didn't feel the *need* to travel.

This horse could never keep up with those riders, but if I can just follow their trail, Gwili thought, as he did a quick check on the saddle, tightening the girth and adjusting the stirrup lengths a little before mounting.

He set out after them, following what little trail he could see in the silver light. While not at break-neck speed, he managed to keep a decent pace, making his way down the pass and into the rebuilt town at the base of it.

The tracks have become a little more muddled, but at least no one has been through here as recently as they have, he thought as he observed the paths more carefully.

Through the towns that followed, and over the course of the next two days, he followed the tracks to the best of his ability. "Because *of course* they'd be going to the fucking palace," he said aloud as he concluded the last leg of his journey, the tracks becoming far too muddled to be made out anymore.

But how can I turn this in my favor? He thought, scratching the back of his head as he stopped a good distance from the gate.

I mean, it's not like they know *I'm an outcast, right? There's no way they could. But, how do I present this? I have no proof nor confirmation that they're here for malicious reasons, nor who or what their target might even be if they were. Aaaaagh, it's just too risky. I don't want blood on my hands for not having said anything, but I also don't want to get caught being somewhere I shouldn't,* he considered, rubbing his chin pensively.

"You there," a voice called out, having noticed him. *I've been had,* Gwili thought. "Yes? What is it I can help you with, guardsman?" he answered in as unassuming a tone as he could muster. "You can help me by stating your business," the burly guardsman answered. "O-of course," Gwili raised his hands placatingly.

Shit. What the fuck do I do now? Honesty is the best policy, right? He thought, unsure of his own question.

"I was just coming from Caegwen by way of the Rhydian Pass when I spotted a strange group of riders headed this way. Curious, I followed them for little over two days, and their tracks have led me here," Gwili answered, his tone unwavering and words far more unnerving as he spoke them aloud.

"So, you just decided to *follow* a group of people from the Rhydian Pass on a whim?" the guardsman asked. Gwili chuckled nervously. "I understand that it *sounds* bad, but I am a man of honor and integrity," he said.

Well, when it suits me, anyway, he thought.

"But would a man, or *elf*, by the looks of things, really have a reason to follow a random group of riders without a cause? No, of course not, what a ridiculous notion," he said, crossing his arms in front of his chest to form an *X,* shaking his head. "Why did you follow them, then? Out of the goodness of your heart?" the guardsman asked, unamused by the elf's antics.

"Because they moved like nothing I've ever seen," Gwili sighed. "What do you mean? I thought you said these were normal riders," the guardsman asked, now more guarded than before. "I called them *random*, but I don't think they really are. I get the feeling they're here *for* someone, and that someone needs to be warned," Gwili said, his tone growing a bit darker and more forceful with the last few words.

The guardsman shuddered with the way the elf had spoken, and nodded his head. "F-fine, but at least give me a name so I can have someone introduce you," the guardsman said. "Gwili Gwynn of Caegwen," the elf replied, the words tasting slightly bitter in his mouth. "Very well, Gwili Gwynn, I will have someone escort you to the palace. But know this: If you're found to be lying, you will pay for it with your life," the guardsman warned.

"I'm glad it's not the first time someone's threatened my life, otherwise, I might've taken offense to that," Gwili retorted with a wry smile, following the guardsman toward the large, Eastern gate. After having his name taken down in the entry log, Gwili was escorted to the front of the palace with haste.

I just wish we didn't have to move as quickly as we did. It's been ages since I've been inside a real city. Maybe I'll get the chance to do some exploring if all goes well, he thought.

The assigned escort led him through the city and all the way to the palace, passing through a few areas that were still being rebuilt after the assault. Once the elf and his escort had reached the palace, they were greeted by a host of guardsmen, with one towering head and shoulders above the rest, with straw blonde hair and full-plate armor.

"Hallo there," the giant man gestured, nodding to the escort to bring the paperwork he was holding. "Your name is Gwili Gwynn, correct?" he said, reading the name aloud for all those nearby to hear. "It is, ser knight," Gwili said, bowing his head awkwardly, sensing something odd about this group of guards. "It has been a long time since I've been in any sort of... civilization, however, I come with a message for whoever is in charge of the guards in this place," the elf said, looking around briefly. "That would be me," Thorsen said in his thick accent.

Oh. So it was the giant I sensed, Gwili thought.

"To avoid any further confusion," he began, swallowing dryly, "I would like to ask your name so I better know how to address you," the elf said. "Magnar Thorsen, commander of Queen Leona's royal guard," the giant gestured, placing a hand on his chest and giving a curt nod in greeting.

"Well, Ser Thorsen, I'll get straight to the point, though I think it would be best if I gave you my message away from this much exposure," Gwili said, a tone of worry ringing in his voice. Thorsen raised an eyebrow, but gave a confident wave for his guardsmen to allow the elf to pass. "It's alright, men. I'll take him from here," Thorsen said.

Either he's an idiot, or he's confident enough in his skills to where he knows he could take me down if he needed to, Gwili thought, remembering his training from long before he became an outcast.

The pair walked down a few halls, moving away from prying eyes and ears into a private meeting room adorned with a large wooden table, chairs, and a small chandelier that hung overhead, dimly lighting the room. A painting of the late King Truls adorned the wall, though it looked like it hadn't been cleaned in decades.

"So, what is this *message* you have for us?" Thorsen asked, getting straight to the point. He sat on the chair at the head of the table, and gestured for Gwili to sit at the side. "Ser Thorsen, I come bearing some rather strange news, though I hope that I have reached the right ears in time," the elf began. Thorsen's brow raised questioningly, but he gestured for the elf to continue.

"With absolute transparency, I am a bandit. Well, more specifically, I'm an *outcast*, but that's a story for another day. I can sense the mana within you, and know that you are *also* something of that ilk, so there is no point in either of us lying," Gwili said plainly, as if laying out cards on a gambler's table.

"A good observation, but get to the point," Thorsen said, drawing conclusions of his own, but not saying anything. "A few weeks ago, my bandit crew and I... *took care of* a large caravan that was moving through the Pass. When we were searching their belongings, we came across this note that didn't make much sense to me at the time," Gwili said, producing the note he and Wyrran had found in the cart and handing it to the commander. Thorsen's eyes scanned the words quickly, working their way down the page, as Gwili continued his explanation.

"I hadn't given it much thought, but then just the other night, a group of mysterious figures just crossed over the Rhydian Pass. I'm not sure where they came from, and I can all but confirm they *are* human," the elf began, eyeing the giant seriously.

"It was difficult to determine at first, but the way their bandage-like clothes forced their appearances to shimmer in the moonlight, I could tell that there was something different about them," he continued. Thorsen interlocked his fingers, and set his elbows on the table. "Please, continue," his thick accent grumbled.

"Over the last two days, I've followed their tracks through towns and other such places, and they have not stopped once. Which, from my experience, means one of two things: Either these figures are fueled by hatred, or the training they've been subjected to is harsher than anything either of *us* have been through," Gwili concluded, leaning forward and resting his forearms on the table.

Thorsen sat pensively for a few moments, as if considering the validity of his words. "You say these figures were *shimmering*, but I'm not sure what you mean by that," he said after a few moments. "It was like their clothes forcefully averted one's gaze, blending their forms into the background," Gwili said, a slight shiver running down his spine.

"I don't know what to make of it, at least nothing I can think of would be a certainty, anyway," Thorsen said gravely, furrowing his brow. "Damn it. Is there anything we can do to prepare?" Gwili asked, genuinely confused. "Nothing you need to concern yourself with, but I will see to it that you are properly compensated for the information," Thorsen said, getting up from his chair. Gwili, unsure of what else to do, followed the giant out the door.

I can't miss an opportunity like this, he thought.

"Ser Thorsen," he called out after him. "What is it, Gwili? Do you have more information you wish to share?" the giant asked. "Yes. W-well, no, but I can help you fight them," the elf said, nearly begging to be included. "We have plenty of guards who can handle such things. What makes you think you'll be useful?" Thorsen asked without trying to sound condescending, but more out of practicality and pragmatism than anything else.

"I know what they look like, and if their clothes were anything to go off of, I'd say I could potentially know their *tactics* as well," Gwili said, a smirk rolling across his face as he presented an old amulet, weathered and worn. Thorsen looked at it with mild surprise, but shook his head, deciding it might be best not to say anything.

"I acknowledge that I haven't seen them, at least not personally, and would be an idiot to throw away *that* kind of information and knowledge you hold," he said pensively. "Can I trust you? Not as an *outcast*, but as a former synner with the hopes of restoring his name?" he asked.

The bastard saw right through me, Gwili thought with a nervous smile growing at the corner of his mouth.

"You can. I have no reason to betray you, after all. Like you said: I want my life back, and I'm not about to fuck that up a second time," the elf replied, a determined look on his face. Thorsen nodded and gestured for him to follow behind him, turning away without a word.

Those... things. I wonder what they're actually *capable of. He seemed to know little about them, and I've never heard of them before, but since the countries have long been at war, techniques, interaction, and exposure with other such groups has been extremely limited. To be fair, I've never cared much for things, other than myself, that go bump in the night, but the look on his face when he said it...* Gwili thought, trying to draw any sort of conclusion he could.

"You said you *might* even know their tactics, correct?" Thorsen asked as they proceeded down halls Gwili noted the details of. "I'm sure they'll have shit I've never seen before, but what I *can* do is shed some light on what they *might* be capable of," the elf said, reaching out to touch a bust of a face he couldn't recognize.

"Would you help me, then?" Thorsen asked. "With what, exactly, Ser Thorsen?" Gwili asked without hiding his confusion. "With training them," the giant said, opening a door that led to a training ground where Marte, Neko, Leona and a few other soldiers were training.

I just came to deliver a warning, but this is turning out better than I ever could've expected, the elf thought.

"Thorsen!" Leona called out, beckoning him over to her. She was in a light leather jerkin, her midnight hair tied up in a close-fitting braid and brandishing a wooden short-sword. Neko and Marte were also in similar training attire, though theirs looked much worse for wear than the queens, naturally.

"Your Majesty, I apologize for interrupting your training," Thorsen said, bowing low. Gwili, who hadn't realized who the giant was talking to, quickly followed suit.

Did he just say Your Majesty? The elf thought as he stared at the ground by his feet.

"Arise, Commander," she beckoned him with a gesture. "And who might this be?" she asked, noticing the elf who, until now, had been dwarfed by the size of the commander. "Gwili Gwynn, Your Majesty. A humble elf of Caegwen," he said, not daring to look up at her.

"*Oh,* I didn't know King Phrys had sent an envoy! Are you here with a message about my lo-... I mean, Bernar and Thoma?" she asked, stammering her recovery.

How the fuck does she know Bernar? That... that handsome son of a bitch has done it again, hasn't he? Gwili thought.

"No, Your Majesty, though I did see them along the Pass as they crossed into Caegwen not even two weeks ago," he said, a wry grin he was unable to hide showing on his face. "*Oh*, I see," she said dejectedly. "In any case, what brings you here, Gwili?" she asked in a friendly tone.

"I wish I were the bearer of good news, but as I've discussed with Ser Thorsen here, Your Majesty: I think someone has snuck into the castle and is out for blood," the elf said in a grave tone as a serious expression began to darken his face.

Her eyes hardened, her knuckles turning white as gripped the sword tightly. "I'm no stranger to attempts on my life. It's why I'm currently out here training, in the event of a next one," she said, twirling her sword and ending it with a sharp swing, bringing it to a halt down at her right side.

"I suggested that, with him being the only one who has actually seen them, and since he has some experience in the matter, that he train those of you here in counter-stealth tactics," Thorsen said, noticing the air change throughout the course of their conversation. Leona eyed her commander curiously. "Do you trust him, commander?" she asked, her tone serious and expectant. "I do, Your Majesty," Thorsen replied with a nod.

"Well, then. No point in dallying around any longer, is there? Marte, Neko, come here," Leona said, calling the two others to join the group. The pair trotted over quickly, but as soon as Marte caught Gwili's gaze, she blushed, hoping he hadn't noticed.

It's been a long time since anyone has blushed looking at me, he thought, smiling warmly at her.

"Gwili, these two are Neko and Marte. They're here helping me train in some basic swordsmanship and self-defense after the attack we had here recently," Leona said, gesturing at the pair. "It's been a few months since I've started training in earnest, but I, like the others, will be looking forward to your instruction," she continued.

"I-I-I don't know what to say, Your Majesty," Gwili said with a bow. "I will do my best, but know that we likely do not have a lot of time to train," he continued. "W-well, we can start today if you're up for it. Th-there are a few hours until sunset," Marte said bashfully. Neko shot her a disgusted look, but was able to keep his verbal composure.

"No time like the present, right?" Gwili said warmly, suddenly ignoring the fatigue he'd felt from his journey. "I knew you'd be up for it!" she exclaimed. Leona and Thorsen looked at each other and communicated a mutual feeling of surprise with a simple shrug and upturned lips.

"Ready yourselves," Thorsen called out, tossing Gwili a wooden training sword. "I'll let you have the first attack," the elf said, snatching the blade out of the air, immediately pushing the tip towards his opponent. "That's probably *not* a good idea," Neko said warily. Gwili raised an eyebrow at him, but as soon as he had turned his gaze, Marte dashed forward, leaving a small crater in the ground behind her.

Taken aback by her speed, Gwili only just managed to get the wooden sword up in time to catch hers. "Your size betrays your speed, I see," he said, shoving her backwards with a heavy push. "And you're better trained than I thought," she said, preparing another attack as soon as she regained her balance. She swung from above aiming for his clavicle, but he expertly parried away the blow, and rammed the pommel of his training sword straight into her sternum.

Wincing with the pain, she swung a wide arc with her sword, forcing the elf to bend and twist his body just to get out of the way of it. Again, she cut aiming for his clavicle, but this time it was a feint, rotating the point of her blade downward into a thrust aimed for his gut. He parried the blow, and swung an attack of his own, forcing her to duck.

A swift knee strike stopped just centimeters away from her nose. "That's two," he said, stepping back. She huffed but could only grunt a response as she began a flurry of strikes and thrusts. Each strike began to generate small gusts of wind as the speed of the strikes ramped up.

Is she trying to force me to use mana? Oh, I get it, the elf thought, a wry smile growing on his face.

"Well, come on then, I know you can do better," he said as a taunt, but the tone he gave was more encouraging than anything else. "*Oh, I know I can,*" she grinned, as her pupils dilated, covering her irises and sclera entirely. "*Hoho!* A stage one? Here? This is your doing, isn't it, Ser Thorsen?" Gwili asked, unable to contain his amusement. "He's been teaching us how to use it the past few weeks," Neko chimed in, not bothering to hide his smug expression.

*Us? What does he...*his thoughts trailed off as he was forced to deflect a flurry of incoming strikes as Marte infused her sword with mana.

"Better not underestimate me," Marte jeered, a slice aiming at her opponent's head. He parried the blow, redirecting the blade away from him, but was forced to block another aimed at his liver. He rotated his blade and struck from above, but she was fast enough to block it, using both hands to support her blade. She pushed away from it, skidding backwards with the force, but quickly dashed forward again.

She's unrelenting, but she'll burn out quickly if she keeps this up. Time to teach the pup a lesson, he thought.

His eyes began to glow, though no mana leakage could be seen. The pupils, irises, and sclera of his eyes began to glow with golden *mana he drew from the Ethereal.*

It's been a long time, old friend, he thought, staring upwards.

The sphere of pure mana twirled with countless tendrils and streaks of mana crashing into each other, forming the familiar light-show high above him. He reached out with his hand, like he had for so many years, beckoning the mana to come to him.

Marte saw the change, and immediately backed off. "What the...?" she asked aloud, glancing over at Thorsen, who was watching their battle with pure excitement in his eyes. "You're a synner?" she asked, amazed at his mana control. When he didn't respond with anything other than a wry smile, she shook her head, trying to get rid of her surprise and refocus on the battle before her.

She dashed forward, screaming at the top of her lungs and generating enough force with her swing to crack a royal ochelon's skull in half. She hit her target, or at least what she thought was her target, anyway. The shimmering mana that held the image of the elven synner began to dissipate, and she could feel the cold grip of reality settling in.

However, aside from that sinking feeling in her gut, one thing she hadn't noticed was the blade that was now at her neck until a soft breath just behind her left ear presented itself. "What's *this*? A soldier caught off her guard?" he asked softly, sending gooseflesh barreling down her entire body. "W-what...?" she stammered, trying to figure out where the person in front of her had just gone, as well as what to do about what she was currently feeling.

Thorsen, who already knew this was likely to happen, chuckled in amusement, while the others remained wordlessly stunned.

"To answer your question from earlier, I *was* a synner, but as for what happened, that will be a story for another time with good food and better booze," he said, releasing her from his grasp. Her face was as red as an apple, and she could still feel the gooseflesh riddling her entire body.

He stepped away, releasing his mana that accidentally let out a small, concussive burst, making Marte stumble a little. "Oh, I apologize. It's been quite some time since I've used that," he said, raising a hand placatingly. "It's alright, I just... I wasn't expecting you to be able to use mana, let alone be a fourth stage," she said, rubbing the base of her neck as they walked back to the group.

"How did you do that move? It was like you were there and then *not* in an instant," Neko blurted out, still awestruck by Gwili's move. The elf chuckled lightly, and placed a hand on Neko's shoulder. "While I don't think we have the time to be able to get you to a mana manipulation stage high enough to do that, I *can* explain how it works," he said, giving Neko a warm smile.

Neko, who now had sparkles in his eyes, nodded excitedly. "Yes, please!" he said, jittering like he was 15 years younger than he was. Marte couldn't help but stare at the elf, even going so far as to ignore Neko's antics. Leona and Thorsen chuckled, but when things calmed down, the reality of the situation returned, sinking the mood.

"Well, it's best we begin an *actual* lesson. After all, I'm not sure how much time we'll really have before they make their move," Gwili said solemnly. "Everyone, please line up," Thorsen called out to the other guardsmen who had also stopped their training to observe the short duel.

"Let's begin," he said to the elf, glancing around at those who were gathering before him. The guardsmen seemed uncertain of who the elf was, or why he was in the palace in the first place, but their preconceptions were immediately shut down when the elf finally spoke.

"My name is Gwili Gwynn, former synner of Caegwen, and former trainer of stealth operations at Sionaer. I'll be blunt, I have traced a group of potentially nefarious individuals here to the castle," he said, his tone curt and flat as if reading from a script. The guardsmen looked at each other, concern strewn across their facial features. Marte and Neko, however, had their jaws agape after hearing him say the word *trainer*.

"That said, I have been inducted by your commander, Ser Thorsen, into this group to help teach you how to counteract their techniques. While I will not claim to know all of them, as techniques vary from country to country, there are certain principles that *all* stealth operations must adhere to," he continued, eyeing the ones before him carefully.

Each one had a determined look on their faces, as if to show that his words were *truly* reaching them, rather than falling on deaf, inattentive ears. "Lastly, we do not know how much time we have before they act, so I will teach you some of the essentials today so we can begin preparations immediately," he said firmly. Just as the final words left his mouth, however, Thorsen caught sight of something moving on the ramparts above them.

That better not be what I think it is, he thought, squinting his eyes to get a better look, but ultimately finding nothing.

CHAPTER 38

UNFORGIVEN

"**W**hat do you mean he's been *exposed*?" Ardrin asked, his question dark and foreboding as he checked Athar's pulse and breathing. Karak, who had just witnessed what happened, raised his hands placatingly. "My lord, I know what that sounds like, but it might not be as bad as we thought, provided this *human* can keep his wits under control," the daemon said, saliva still dripping onto the floor.

"I know what's in his core, Karak, but my question is about that *smile* he gave... I've never seen that before," Ardrin said, a mild concern raised in his tone. "*That* is what we daemons call the *alternate*," Karak said. "The *alternate*? I've never once heard of that before. What is that supposed to mean?" Ardrin asked, looking down at Athar.

Have I made a mistake? He asked himself.

"The alternate self. Monsters and daemons, such as myself, don't have them, but some humans *do*. Without adequate training or power, a human can easily be overcome by their alternate self, though for how long is dependent on their mastery over dark mana. Think of it as looking into a mirror, though your reflection is actually *you*, instead of what you're *seeing*," Karak tried to explain.

Ardrin tried to wrap his head around this concept, but after struggling with the thought for a few moments, he ultimately shook his head. "Why haven't *I* had that experience, then?" he finally asked, looking back at his second in command.

"Because your ability to manipulate dark mana was bestowed upon you by the Undergod himself, allowing you a sort of *protection*. Athar, for whatever reason, didn't have that. Or, at least, perhaps there was a sort of delayed activation?" Karak asked, more to himself than to the Masked One who eyed him carefully.

"That would partially explain the panicked look on his face before he passed out, at least," Ardrin said, glancing back down at the young man, who still lay unconscious on the floor. "You *know* why that happened, my lord," Karak began. "Though I think I do not need to explain *that* portion of it to you, correct?" the daemon asked, tilting his head to the side a little. The Masked One nodded his agreement, though there was a heavy air about him.

Damn it, I knew it was a bad idea. If that alternate *hadn't shown up...* Ardrin's thoughts trailed.

"If you're wondering whether he will live, the answer is yes, but it will be a few days before he wakes up, at least, my lord," Karak said, almost as if reading his master's thoughts. "I understand," Ardrin said, hiding his concern behind a flat tone.

"So, what news of Irun and his training?" he asked, changing the subject. "He's been progressing at a rapid rate, as Irun has trained him well. *So* well, in fact, that they've even formed a little *pact* with each other," the daemon sneered, almost as if disgusted to say the words.

"A brotherly pact?" Ardrin asked, almost as if he already knew the answer. "Precisely, my lord," Karak responded with a nod. "Well, at least he'll have someone he can *somewhat* relate to. In any case, tell me of the news from Caegwen," the Masked One said, not wanting to delve into that conversation any further.

"The hegraphenes have been deployed recently, though they were quickly dispatched by one of the elven synners, my lord," Karak began, recalling the events that took place. "*He's* already putting *them* to the test?" Ardrin asked pensively. "*He* thought they would be ready, but I suppose that female elf has surpassed his expectations," the daemon replied.

Female elf? A synner capable of taking down a hegraphene? Surely he can't mean... Ardrin's thoughts trailed once more.

"In any case, she was powerful enough to defeat them, though how many of them she can *actually* take on is another story, my lord," Karak said, his raspy voice filled with what sounded like excitement. "However, we have another problem that requires our attention, my lord," the daemon continued. "One of our... *experiments* got loose and..." the daemon trailed off, averting his gaze. "And *what*...?" the Masked One's impatience began to show.

"It's gone, though to where I don't know, my lord. I accept full responsibility for this accident," the daemon said, bowing his head low enough to nearly touch the floor. Ardrin sneered beneath his mask in frustration.

"You *lost* our experiment? How could you have let that happen, Karak? You *knew* its importance was *paramount* to the next stage of our plans," he shouted, dark mana flaring from his body, crushing the daemon to the floor with an imposing aura of mana. "Forgive me, my lord. I didn't realize it was capable of escaping the ward I'd put around its cage, much less hide its mana signature," the daemon sputtered, struggling to breathe.

Ardrin released the pressure, causing Karak to cough and gasp for air. "Go back to the observatory and find out where it is, and what it's doing. When you do, I want you to take Irun with you and retrieve it," he commanded, pointing a finger toward the door the daemon had come from.

"Do *not* for a fucking *second* think I've forgiven this mistake of yours, Karak. If you fail me now, you will pay for your transgression with your *life*," the Masked One threatened. "It will be done, my lord," the daemon responded, bowing its head, putting its disfigured hand across its chest before it walked away.

I feel that will be no meager setback, but it could also *work out in my favor. Let us see what happens*, Ardrin though, scooping Athar up with his mana claw, carrying the man behind him.

Meanwhile in Odensby, Wien made his rounds throughout the palace. The night was quiet, almost eerily so, with little to no movement in the palace whatsoever. He strode down a hall, observing a few of the paintings as he went, his greaves and armor the only things apparently making noise.

I've been here for months, and even though I've reported daily to Commander Lande, I haven't made any breakthroughs. At least these paintings are beautifully done, he thought, tracing his finger across one of the frames, picking some dust off of it.

He eventually made his way up the stairs, nearing the royal bedroom, when he saw a light coming from beneath one of the doors a little ways down the hall. Moving forward to investigate, as quietly as he could manage, he pressed an ear to the door.

Is someone... sobbing? He thought, pressing his ear more closely.

Suddenly, the sobbing stopped, and he could hear the latch on the door being undone, forcing him to awkwardly step back. "What the hell do *you* want?" Unni's bloodshot eyes angrily stabbed into the young sergeant's. The redness of her face and smeared tears were indicative enough that she had been crying for some time alongside an open bottle of wine that was still on the desk.

"I-I'm sorry, Your Majesty," Wien said urgently, bowing as he did. "I didn't mean to intrude. I was just doing my rounds and I saw the candlelight from beneath the door," he continued. Unni glared at him, but ultimately conceded her rage.

"It's alright," she sniffled, wiping away a string of snot. "I've not quite been myself lately. I thought that after coming here, that everything would be okay. Instead, all I'm met with are compounded memories, ones that eat their way into my dreams, and rid me of any restful sleep," she said, the exhaustion in her voice giving true meaning to her words.

Well, what the hell do I say to that? Wien thought.

Unni began to sob again, failing to keep her composure. Wien, reaching his hand out to comfort her, stopped short, reeling his hand back in. "Y-Your Majesty, this might be imposing and well out of my place to ask but, would you like me to sit with you awhile?" he asked, in as comforting a tone as he could muster.

She glanced at him briefly with her tear-filled eyes then tore them away, nodding subtly as she moved to open the door a little more for him to enter without a word. The study, which held an elongated chaise with velvet upholstery and books, tomes, and scrolls all strewn about the place, as if a madman had lived there, felt *smaller* than it really was. The soft candlelight revealed the open letter on the wooden desk, though its contents were illegible from the distance he was currently at.

She sat on the chaise, and after a few, awkward moments, motioned for him to sit next to her. Awkwardly and wordlessly, he moved over to the chaise and sat down next to her, keeping his hands flat atop his knees.

"You know, I've always wondered what it would be like if I ever got my life back," she began as Wien glanced around the room, trying to avert his gaze from Unni's nightgown that was a little more revealing at the top than he had originally noticed. "What do you mean by that, Your Majesty?" he asked, still averting his gaze as a drop of sweat ran down the side of his cheek.

"You needn't call me that right now. I don't think I look very *majestic* right now, given my state," she gestured to her face with a pointed finger, staring at him. He could only nod his response, though quickly realized that keeping eye contact with her was going to be nearly impossible.

"In any case, what I mean is that my life for the past twelve years has been... *difficult*. I've been in love, so *madly* in love with a man who sought only revenge for what had been done to his family, when I..." she trailed off, stifling a sob, prompting Wien to look at her again.

"Sorry, it's just been a while since I've had someone actually *listen* and not just try to *solve* my problems," she chuckled, realizing the ridiculousness of the situation. "In that case, I guess you're welcome," Wien said bashfully, an awkward smile on his face. Unni looked at him, and really *saw* him for the first time, admiring his walnut hair and blue eyes for the first time.

"I remember you from the gate when we first arrived," she said, finally putting a face to a place. "I was there with Commander Lande," Wien acknowledged. A thoughtful look grew on Unni's fine features, as her eyes squinted as if to try and piece something together. "*Commander Lande.* She was the one who was glaring at me, correct?" she asked, more to confirm her thought process than actually get an answer. "Y-yes, she was," he replied awkwardly. "I don't think she likes me," Unni chuckled half-heartedly.

"Th-there's nothing *wrong* with you, at least not as far as I can tell, anyway," Wien began, struggling to find the words as Unni glared at him. "I-it's just she's known King Anders for a long time, as have I, you see," he continued awkwardly. "He's never made mention of her before, so what gives?" she asked, raising an eyebrow.

"W-well, I think it has more to do with her being... *protective* of him, in a way," he replied, trying not to give away Trina's real intent. "*Protective*, you say? Could've fooled me with the way she was eyeing me like a hawk. I'd say she was out with a *vendetta* on me," she scoffed.

I should be a little more careful of what I reveal here, and take note of what she *does,* Wien thought as he saw her reaction.

"Why would she have a vendetta against you?" he asked cautiously. Unni stared at the floor, as if both reliving the memories and deciding whether to tell him her thoughts. "There was an incident a long time ago that involved Anders, ultimately leading to him becoming an outcast," she began, shying away from most of the details. "I'd be willing to bet she thinks that *I* have something to do with it," she said in a half scoff.

With the way you're talking, you just might, Wien thought.

"I-in any case, the only thing I can attest to their relationship is that they've known each other for a very long time," Wien said, as if trying to preemptively deflect the direction of Unni's hatred towards Trina. "You're right. I almost feel like an *imposter* around him, if that makes any sense to you," she said. "I don't think you're an imposter. Maybe you're in his life for a reason, or perhaps he's the one in *yours*," Wien said in a poor attempt to comfort her.

Unni, for the first time since the beginning of their conversation, felt a smile tug at the corner of her mouth.

"Thank you," she muttered almost inaudibly. "I've felt so lost lately. I know Anders takes good care of me and is always looking out for my mental health, but..." she trailed off, pausing momentarily. "But *what*?" Wien asked. "I... don't think I deserve him," she said with a heavy sigh. "I know it's not my place to ask, but *why*?" he asked tentatively.

If she doesn't want to answer that, it's okay, but I have to try, he thought.

"Because I was *there*," she said weakly, her voice was a thin whisper, like a breeze struggling through the crack in a doorway. "You were *where*?" Wien asked gently, hoping his tone sounded non-judgmental and unassuming. "I was there when... when his family was killed," she said in the same, wispy tone, contorting her mouth as she began to cry once more.

Holy. Fucking. Shit, Wien thought.

"The incident I was talking about got former King Mads' family killed due to my own fault. I knew they were going to ambush us from the North, *not* the South. When I was interrogated, I blamed his wife for the lack of intel. She was my commander in the recon unit we were attached to. She didn't have mana capabilities, but she was intelligent, beautiful, kind, and *damned* good at her job; everything I wasn't," Unni began sobbing uncontrollably.

So that's *why Commander Lande was suspicious,* Wien thought, swallowing the weight of her words, remaining quiet as he let her proceed.

"I was so *jealous.* Jealous of what she had with *my* Anders. Jealous of how fucking *happy* he looked with her. I wanted that, I wanted *him,* for myself, but I didn't know it would be taken that far," she continued, heaving dryly at the thought of the next words that came out of her mouth.

"When the attack on Mads' family happened, I was there *with* Anders on duty. I watched the royal family be slaughtered in front of us, as we fought off the rest of the outcasts who came for them," she began to explain through her sobbing.

"I didn't think about it at the time, but Mads would end up blaming our squad for what happened to his family since ours was the most experienced. When I was questioned, I lied about having bad intel, putting the blame on his wife in hopes of being able to separate him from her. However, what I didn't account for was how *badly* Mads would take that news, and what he would do next," she said, a chill running down her spine.

Wien sat in silence, anxiously awaiting whatever came next.

"I was *there,* you see, when... when his family was *made an example of.* I... *I* slit his child's throat, forcefully enough to the point of decapitation, while Mads defiled and killed his wife and unborn child in front of him," she said, her voice weak and trembling, as she collapsed into Wien's lap.

What the actual fuck did I just hear? Wien thought, shaken to his very core.

They sat there, Unni's head in his lap as she sobbed uncontrollably, while Wien stared blankly into the wall in front of him. "I... I've done horrible things, and all this happened because I just wanted to push him away from his wife... I just...-anted...-im for my... -self," she trailed off, choking on her own words. Wien, however, sat in shock, unsure of what to do or say at that moment.

"I-I won't tell anyone what I heard here tonight, and I want you to know that I will keep any and all secrets you reveal to me, now or in the future," he lied, feeling his heart pounding in his chest like a war drum as he listened to Unni's sobbing.

That's the best I can offer right now. I just hope it's enough, he thought.

"Thank you," she said between the breaths of her sobbing as spit was bubbling from her lips. "Do you think he could ever forgive me if he found out, or would I be as unforgiven as Mads was?" she asked. Stunned by her question, Wien's eyes opened wide as he pondered the correct way to answer.

"I... I don't know," he finally said after a few moments. "I can't speak for how Anders would react to that news, but you're probably going to have to tell him at *some* point. Otherwise this *will* eat away at you, more than it already has," he said in a calm, even tone.

"I know," she said, curling up even more tightly. A few moments of silence went by, as if both were digesting the information. "C-could you just sit with me for a little while longer? It's nice to have someone just *be* here and not have to *hide* anything," she asked weakly. He looked down into her questioning, bloodshot eyes.

She feels so small, he thought, truly noticing the weight of her body on his thighs for the first time.

"O-of course," he said, beginning to stroke her hair in hopes of calming her down. As he did so, her sobbing returned, though not as strongly as before. Every sob shook her curled frame but began to subside as time went on, falling into slow, even breaths.

What the fuck do I do now? He thought.

As the night went on, Wien's thoughts ran rampant, trying to figure out the best course of action.

Do I tell Commander Lande what I just heard? Do I hope she tells Anders, and that he judges her accordingly? Gods above and below, why the fuck did I get saddled with this? He thought, still stroking her hair, unsure of whether she was fully asleep.

Eventually, however, he decided he had to get up and continue his rounds, gently placing her on the chaise, and grabbing a blanket from one of the closets to wrap her in. She rustled gently, adjusting her body to better be wrapped in the blanket as Wien stepped away, closing the door behind him as he left the study. "Damn it," he whispered, sighing and pinching the bridge of his nose.

I don't want to tell the Commander about that, but I don't have any other choice, he thought as he pressed against the inner corners of his eyes.

He continued his rounds through the night, and ruminated on the correct course of action. Dawn came, as did his replacement, allowing him to go home, pour himself a drink, and lay down on his bed.

CHAPTER 39
HUMBLED

I stared at yet another ceiling of a room I couldn't recognize.

Waking up in the warm bath after having dozed off, supported by the same root-like structures that built the walls around me, filled me with a sense of refreshment I hadn't felt in ages. I knew I was somewhere in the palace, but *where*, exactly, I had no clue.

That's probably the best bath I'll ever get while I'm here, I suddenly thought, remembering why we had come here in the first place.

I looked in the mirror, and was taken aback at just how different I now looked. My silver hair held no traces of my former brown, though my green eyes stayed the same. I still had the same muscle mass, which was a little disappointing, but at least I looked how I was *meant to* now.

And that *is going to take some getting used to,* I thought, touching the tips of my pointed ears.

A black leather, at least what I thought was leather, tunic that looked not unlike the jerkin I normally wore, had been laid out for me. It wasn't the traditional jerkin I was used to wearing back in Codrean, but it *felt* lighter, that much I was certain of.

The accent of the clothing was that of a wine-colored undershirt and matching, dyed-leather sashes. After having fought with the sashes, buckles, and other such things required for tightening and adjustments, I let out an audible sigh of frustration.

I know how to put armor on, but what the actual fuck *do I do with this thing?* I thought as I played with a loose piece of leather that flopped around lazily.

"Do you require assistance?" a female voice said. It sounded young, probably somewhere around my age, though I knew whoever this was might actually be much older than I was. "*Uhhh*, yes, please. I'm a little lost with what to do with this...*strap*," I said, for lack of a better word. "Can I come in, then?" the female asked, her tone light and playful. "O-of course," I stammered.

Oh, no... my thoughts trailed.

The elf who walked in didn't look much older than I was. As far as I could tell, she didn't look any older than about twenty-five, though I knew she was likely *much* older than that. Her voice perfectly matched her fine, pale features, silver hair and a pair of violet eyes that felt like they were staring directly into my soul.

She wore a fine, dark olive dress, with silver inlaid into the seams that highlighted themselves against their dark background. She greeted me with a warm smile, one I felt I had seen a long time ago, but just couldn't place exactly *when*.

"It's a pleasure to meet you, Thoma," she said in a warm tone that matched her smile perfectly. "*Ah*, I'm assuming my brother gave you my name," I said nervously to which she nodded in agreement. "He did, indeed. Do you still need help with your gear?" she asked, giving my entire body a once over.

While much of my body was covered, I felt almost as if she could see *through* my armor, and I didn't even know her name.

I'd be lying if I said I didn't flinch on the inside.

That rat bastard didn't even bother to warn... I stopped, remembering that my brother actually *had* called me *sheltered* not too long ago.

"Yes, yes please. That would be wonderful. I couldn't figure out what to do with this strap, Miss...*uh*..." I trailed, hoping she would catch onto what I was getting at as she helped me re-tie the lash. "Ysevel. My name is Ysevel," She said, meeting my eyes. "Just *Ysevel*?" I asked, noting the lack of a last name. "*Just* Ysevel," she replied, glancing down at my waist momentarily.

Suddenly, she wrapped her arms around my waist, pulling me in fairly closely. I could feel a couple of strands of her silver hair brushing up against my cheek, as her warm breath battered my neck for just a moment.

No sooner had she done that, she pulled back, and finished adjusting the strap, tucking it into my belt neatly with a knotted finish. "There we are! Looking like a true Caegweni elf now," she said, patting my shoulders. "I thought most elves were awkward about physical touch," I said, almost in disbelief. "*Oh*, most are, but I find sharing physical touch to make connections much more intimate and personal," she shrugged.

"Since most of us live so long, we often grow... *distant* from each other. That kind of culture has, unfortunately, bled over into even the younger generations," she said, a slight frown pulling at her soft, pink lips.

No, no, no, motherfucker. No. I mentally slapped myself.

I cleared my throat. "You say that as if you were a hundred years old," I said playfully, to which she merely raised an eyebrow. "But,

I'm sorry to hear that," I said, my tone dropping a little as I tried to recover from whatever dumb shit I had just said. "In any case, thank you, Ysevel. I'll *uh*... try to remember how to do this myself, next time," I said awkwardly. "Of course! But if you ever need my help with something, don't hesitate to call on me," she said, smiling brightly once more.

She reminds me a bit of Leona, but who actually is *she?* I thought.

"Come, I'll guide you to the banquet hall," she said, extending her arm. "Are you sure this is alright?" I asked, taking her arm in mine. She put a hand on mine, and leaned her head on my shoulder as she glanced up at me with puppy-dog eyes. "Are you *embarrassed* of me?" she asked playfully, pulling herself away quickly and laughing heartily.

"N-no, I just... I wouldn't want people to get the wrong idea. Especially not my brother, since he knows I have a..." I paused. I hadn't really considered what Meliss and I were, since we'd never put any sort of label on it. We knew we liked each other and slept together a lot, but...

How much further would that go, realistically? I thought, considering what Leona and I had talked about as well.

"Meliss. You have a Meliss,," she said, finishing for me. "Bernar?" I asked, already knowing the answer. "Yep," she smiled, squeezing my hand a little more tightly. "It's okay. I won't try or *do* anything that will jeopardize that, whatever *that* may be," she continued in her playful tone.

Why do I feel like she knows more about my situation than I do? I asked myself, but decided to not say anything.

"Th-thank you," I managed to say, the cacophony of my own thoughts nearly bleeding through the filter I'd put on my tongue. We continued walking through the city, observing the intricate designs in the surrounding architecture that, I noted once again, all seemed to feed from the same root. "How does that work, exactly?" I accidentally said aloud. "How does *what* work?" she asked, glancing at me curiously as she searched my green eyes with her violet ones.

Ahhh, fuck, it's hard to look away, I thought.

"H-how do all the buildings seem to connect? Is there like a *central root* hub or something that all the buildings stem from?" I asked, a nervous smirk strewn across my face as I looked away. "Well, they come from the Hynafol Arboraneth," she said matter-of-factly. "The *what*, now?" I said, not realizing she had spoken actual words. "The Hynafol Arboraneth, also known as *the Ancient Tree*," she said, translating the words.

"Hynafol Arboraneth," I repeated softly. She must have either been surprised at my pronunciation, or laughing at how *badly* I'd probably fucked it up, but she never did explain the reason she chuckled. "So what does it do, exactly?" I asked, unsure of how else to word the question. "It's what helped the elves to learn elemental magic," she began without missing a beat.

"It did? How?" I asked, genuinely curious. "We're taught in our history lessons that the gods once came down to the Continent, though for what reasons, we do not exactly know. Like how the synners of Codrean were once gifted the Gwynnleaf, so, too, were the elves given the ability to manipulate natural mana more efficiently," she continued, pointing a finger at a large tree housing multiple hut-like structures embedded into it.

"So *that's* what Nenvalur meant when he said that the Gwynnleaf wasn't the only source of power, and how this city was built," I said, more to myself than anything else. "Correct. However, there are still so many mysteries from that time, as much knowledge was lost during the Battle of Nemoria," she said, her tone dropping quite a bit.

I was stunned, to say the least.

Until she'd told me, I would have never guessed this place had been the focal point of a battle, let alone that it was primarily created by ancient, elven mages who could manipulate elemental mana to this degree. Nevertheless, I was humbled at my lack of worldly knowledge, as I'd never heard of the *Battle of Nemoria* until now.

"Has anyone ever tried to reclaim some of that ancient knowledge?" I asked, not really expecting an answer. "There was *one* but..." she trailed off. "*Ah*, we're here!" she snapped up excitedly, looking up at the two massive doors in front of us. I hadn't realized it, but we'd walked from my room to the royal palace's banquet hall.

As one might expect, there was a massive, central table with intricately detailed carvings on it, flowing from one side of the table to the other like the movement of a river. Atop it was a feast laid out, with all sorts of meats and leafy greens I couldn't really identify. Above the table hung a pair of large chandeliers made of the same root-like structures as the rest of the building itself. In the off-shoots of the chandeliers, glass containers filled with a warm, yellow mana-flame lit the room softly.

"Ah, you've made it! And in *good company*, I see," my mother said, gesturing over to us from the far end of the table. She was wearing a black dress that folded multiple times across her chest, leaving the top of it and her neck exposed. Her hair was braided, and hung down over her left shoulder, embroidered with a few, silver trinkets.

I blushed, and not lightly at all.

"*Oh*, Commander Siraye, you play too much! Look at what you've done to your boy. He might actually stop breathing if you make another comment," Ysevel said jokingly, her laugh was light and warm, just like her smile. "She's right, mother. How could you do that to the poor turd?" Bernar chimed in from beside my mother, wearing roughly the same clothes I did. He'd taken off his pendant for the dinner, and actually looked like a respectable half-elf for once.

"Is this payback for what I did with you and Leona?" I asked, finally seeing what was happening here. My brother, saying nothing in return, merely shrugged. "In any case, we're so glad to see you've finally met our *daughter*," Elhael said with a heavier emphasis on the last word like a brightly colored frog in the forest that screamed *danger*.

"Y-your majesties," I started, making sure I addressed both the king and queen accordingly. They wore matching, olive colored tunics, with silver sashes not unlike Ysevel's. It was only *then* that I'd actually made the connection. "W-wait. You're..." I stammered. "Ysevel Phrys," she said warmly, tapping my hand as my arm was still interlocked with hers.

Shiiiiiiit, I thought, averting my gaze to allow myself the nervous grin that immediately spawned on my face.

We sat next to each other, as my mother and Bernar sat just opposite us, with both Elhael and Aurae sitting side by side at the head of the large table. "It has been a long time since we've had any visitors.

In truth, since the last time Bernar was here, I believe it was," Aurae said, breaking the silence with her voice floaty and ethereal.

"It is good to see you both again, your majesties," my brother said with a half-bow. "But now that we have Thoma here, we would like to ask him a few questions," Aurae said, glancing at me warmly. "O-of course! I'd be happy to answer whatever I can, Your Majesty," I said, mimicking the bow my brother had given earlier.

"What do you plan to do with our daughter?" Elhael asked sharply, to which Aurae shot him a frustrated scrunch of her fine features. "Now is *not* the time for questions like that, *dear*," she said. Her tone might not have seemed like a threat to any normal person, but having spent enough time with Meliss, I'd learned what a veiled threat sounded like when I heard one.

It seemed like the king had as well.

"My apologies. It's not every day we get visitors, let alone one that could be a potential *suitor* who would fit well with her maturation point," he said, subtly lowering his head. I thought I saw Ysevel blush, but she had turned her head away before I could confirm that.

Even a king bows to his queen, huh? I thought, a wry smirk threatening to show itself as I ignored his comment about me being a *potential suitor.*

"Why did it take you so long to come here?" Aurae finally asked, not in an aggressive tone or anything, but more out of sheer curiosity than anything else. I furrowed my brow, trying to piece together a coherent answer.

Uhhh... how the fuck do I answer that? Do I tell her that both my brother and, apparently, grandfather failed to tell me that my mother was here and that she could release a suppression spell placed on my core that I didn't know I even had? Sure, that makes sense, I thought derisively.

"Your Majesty, I would be lying if I said I knew. I think it had something to do with me finally reaching and becoming comfortable with the second stage of mana manipulation," I said, pulling whatever answer I could out of my ass. "I see," she replied, a pensive look growing on her face. "In any case, how was it that you came to reach the second stage with such a handicap on you? I know Siraye and I removed it together, but how did you manage?" she asked, her tone light and curious at the same time.

It was difficult to get a read on her. On one hand, I could feel she was assessing me and my abilities to answer her questions, but on the other hand, I felt a sort of... *playfulness* about her.

No, that can't be right. She's the quee-... my thoughts stopped. *So that's where Ysevel gets it from,* I concluded with a slight smirk on my face.

"To answer your question, Your Majesty, I think the best way to explain it would be to tell the story of my fight with the ochelon in the cave," I said, proceeding to explain the entire story. My mother, after hearing me give vivid details of searing the slash across my back shut with pure mana, sat in a mild state of shock.

"You didn't..." she said, a bit of her disbelief leaking through her tone. "*Oh,* he did. After he killed the *first* one, that is," Bernar chimed in. "The *first* one?" my mother asked, raising an eyebrow. "Yeah, there were two. The first one was a female, the second was a much larger, red-furred male. That fight was tough enough for me to unlock the second stage without meaning to," I said, scratching my cheek. I spent the next few minutes retelling the tale of the towering creature being torn limb from limb and how I felt during that moment.

Probably not the best idea to describe a drawn and quartered animal at dinner, my brother sent, cocking his head toward the royal family who were visibly shaken.

"Gods above and below, Siraye, is *anyone* in your family normal?" Elhael asked, breaking his silence after having listened intently. "No, I suppose not," she chuckled lightly, a slight bead of sweat trailing down the side of her cheek. While everyone else, including me, chuckled, Ysevel eyed me carefully, but allowed herself a small smile as she turned away once more.

"So, when do we begin training him?" Bernar asked. My mother put a hand on his shoulder, supported by a surprisingly toned, muscular arm. "Tomorrow morning at first light, we'll start the basics. Knowing what your brother is capable of now, or at least a little bit of it, I'd like to have a sparring session with him to see what he's made of," she said in a light tone.

Tomorrow morning, I thought, the weight of the words snowballing into my reality.

The remainder of the hour went on with us telling tales of Bernar's and my adventures in Codrean, Coltend, and up in the northern country of Hjalfar. I avoided saying the name of the synner school in Fangsdalr, as it wasn't my place to reveal that name to them, but told them the story of how master Pyle helped train me.

"He sounds like he would be fun to spar with," my mother said, a thoughtful look on her face. "Maybe not as fun, what with you being a fifth stage and all. You could probably easily kick his ass," I said, accidentally snapping her out of her thoughts as her features twisted from mild happiness to melancholic worry.

"Yes, but even being a fifth stage might not be enough for the upcoming battles," she said almost under her breath. "What do you mean?" I asked. She went on to tell us about her encounter with the creatures in the woods, and how the second wave was much more difficult than the first to defeat.

"So these... *hurroks*, they're like an incomplete version of the ones you faced only moments later?" I asked, mentally comparing the details of the two new creatures in my head. "Yes, but the latter has the potential for *intelligence*," she said almost dreamily. I couldn't quite place the tone she'd just used, but I knew it could mean something vital for the development of our enemies.

"Well, in any case, we've already spread out information on how to defeat them. Any fifth stage synner *should* be able to kill one just fine, but a fourth stage might have some trouble with them," she said matter-of-factly. "Have you seen any *other* creatures around lately?" I asked, suddenly remembering what Gwili had warned us of on the pass.

"What kind of creature?" Aurae asked. "I'm not entirely sure. Bernar's friend, Gwili Gwynn I believe his name was, told us of something he chased to the border of Caegwen before halting. He said it was fast... *too fast*," I explained. The elf's name must have struck a bad chord with the royal family, as all three of their faces, including my mother's, simultaneously scowled as soon as it left my mouth.

"That *rat* is still alive?" Elhael asked, his tone growing dark. "Y-yes, Your Majesty," I answered in a half-questioning tone, not wanting to give away too much information. "It is a damned good thing he didn't cross the border. If he had, he would have been punished with a fate worse than death," he said, his tone cold and unforgiving as his balled fists turned an even paler white.

That's an intense aura he's giving off. How badly did I just fuck up? I sent a glance to my mother, whose eyes widened and head shook in response to my question without a word.

"I-I see, Your Majesty. I apologize for mentioning his name, but he *was* the one that warned us after all," I said, bowing my head. "It's alright, Thoma. There's no way you could've known what he did, so all is forgiven," Aurae said in a level-headed tone.

I'll tell you what happened later, my mother said through her mental transmission. *Aaah! I'm still not used to you being able to hear my thoughts, much less send me some of your own,* I thought, trying to hide the surprise on my face, knowing she was still listening. *You will, eventually. Just know, for now, that it's not as bad as you think. He just... gets his dick in a knot over it,* she said, a grin tugging at the corner of her mouth.

I fought for my life to stifle both the snort and smirk at her last comment.

"In any case, that *creature* he mentioned, we haven't seen or heard anything about it until just now," Aurae said, taking over the conversation. "I will be sure to post guards to be on the lookout for this new development. For now, however, it is getting late, and we *all* have a big day tomorrow," she said, nudging the king to rise first. As he did, she removed her napkin from her lap, and straightened her dress as she stood up, nudging her daughter to do the same. Ysevel also rose, and moved identically to her mother as if they had rehearsed it for a competition.

"O-of course, your majesties," my mother said, bowing once the rest of us had stood up. "Thank you for the lovely meal, Your Majesty. I hope that our time here in your country will be fruitful," I said, bowing to Aurae as she led the king away. She nodded in response, and after a moment's pause, she looked at me, and then her daughter, then back to me.

"Ysevel, dearest, won't you escort Thoma back to his room? It's his first day, after all, and I don't want him getting *lost*," she said, a childish smile tugged voraciously on her fine features. Ysevel, blushed, but this time, we had *all* seen it happen. "O-of course, mother," she said, bowing her head. "Thank you, dear. I would also like it if you helped him tomorrow at first light by guiding him to the training area," Aurae continued.

"That's alright, Your Majesty. I'll be the one to wake this little shit-head up," Bernar said, punching my arm. "Language, son. You're in the presence of royalty," my mother said, punching *his* arm even harder than he had mine. Aurae chuckled softly. "It's quite alright. I've known Bernar long enough to have heard all *kinds* of interesting insults. After all, I did help train him, remember?" she smiled.

If my mother's face could've killed a person, Bernar would have disintegrated instantly.

Heh, nice going, fuck-ass, I thought. *Shut up,* he muttered through his thoughts.

As we took our leave, Ysevel took my arm once more. The once golden light of the forested city now shone with a blueish light of fireflies and mana-flame lanterns scattered throughout the city. I tried to strike up a conversation with her to try and break the ice,though this time she was a little *less* playful than before.

"Is something the matter, *princess*?" I asked, laying it on a little thicker than I had intended. "N-no. I'm fine," she said, looking away from me. "When were you going to tell me that you were royalty? Might have been nice to know before I nearly became a piece of skewered meat from your father's glare," I nudged, hoping to lighten the mood a little.

"I wasn't going to, but my mother all but forced me to when she asked me to attend the dinner," she said dejectedly. "Why weren't you going to tell me? Or is that one of those reasons I'll just have to guess until the day I die?" I asked, a hint of sarcasm in my tone. "I just... I didn't want to be treated differently because of my family's status," she said softly.

I paused.

I hadn't really considered what it must be like for her. Not having visitors, friends, or anyone even remotely *close* to her age, or *maturation point,* as the king had put it. I knew she was much older than me, but that factor could've played a role within the palace walls. It must have been difficult for her to develop socially, hence the childish behavior when she first met me.

Not so different from me after all, huh? I thought.

"I won't pretend I understand what you've been through growing up the way you did, but if it helps, I promise I won't treat you any differently than I would if you *weren't* royalty," I said. The light in her eyes returned, as she gleaned at me in surprise. "Really? You'll just mentally block the fact that my father could have you skinned alive at a moment's notice if you hurt my feelings?" she asked, pursing her lips to one side as she raised an eyebrow.

"I-I'll do my best," I allowed nervously, rubbing the back of my head. She smiled brightly, like a ray of sunshine had been borne into the blue-light night. "Promise?" she asked, turning to face me, her tone was still light, but serious nonetheless. "I promise," I said, mustering a warm smile.

She dropped me off at my room and bid me farewell with a turn and wave of her arm. I slipped out of the formal attire, and noticed there was a brand-new training jerkin set out for me on the table that lined the far wall. "How the...?" I asked softly to no one in particular. With no answer readily available, I brushed my teeth, and got under the covers of the moss-lined bed with a root-like frame once more.

Dawn came, and with it, the sound of my brother banging on my door. "Thoma, get the fuck up already!" he shouted from outside my door.

I'm sure his voice is ringing throughout the city. I should probably get up before he pisses off the neighbors. Wait, do I even have neighbors here? I thought, forcing myself out of the comfort of my bed.

"I'm up, I'm up," I said, hoping he would stop banging. A few minutes later, I managed to get into the training attire provided for me. It was lighter, *much* lighter, than my normal jerkin and I could tell that it would offer me much more protection from slashes than stabs. The leather armor padded my shoulders, chest, back, abdomen and legs. It had a lot more open spaces than I was used to, particularly allowing for much more movement between the joints, but at the sacrifice of more protection.

I guess that has to do with their fighting style, I thought, rotating my bent arm in a short circle, testing the fit.

Opening the door, I found my brother in the same kind of armor, though he had removed his pendant, and one leg raised as if to kick the door in. "I... wasn't... going to," he stammered, lowering his leg as he saw my face non-verbally questioning just what the hell he was doing. "Sure you weren't," I said sardonically.

"A-anyway, we'd better get going. We don't want to be late, as mom will *not* take lightly to that," Bernar said, starting to walk away. "Speaking from experience, *huh*?" I asked but got no reply.

We made our way through the remainder of the palace, greeting the guards as we went. Even though they promptly returned the greetings, I could tell there were more than a few confused looks. I just chalked it up to there rarely being visitors to the royal palace, and left it at that since it continued all the way to the palace gate, where Ysevel, clad in her own training attire, was waiting for us.

"Good morning, Ysevel," I said warmly. Even though I was still sleepy, I tried my best to feign being awake. "Good morning, Thoma," she returned just as warmly. My brother, however, stared at us questioningly. Pulling me aside, he pushed his face right next to mine. "What about Meliss, huh? If that's out the fucking window, at least let me know so I'll know who to blame for my feelings of solitude after I marry Leona," he hissed.

I could just see Ysevel craning her neck to try and overhear our conversation.

"Nothing happened," I hissed back quietly. His golden eyes narrowed as they peered into mine. Finding no lie, he shoved me back and huffed lightly. "Good," he said, clearing his throat and straightening his gear with a tug. "What was that all about?" Ysevel asked with a raised eyebrow. "Nothing," we replied in unison with bright grins on our faces. She looked at us curiously, but probably decided it was best to leave it be.

Finally, we made it to the training area just outside of Myrdin. I looked around at the facility, and tried my best to understand what everything did. While much of the training equipment was similar to that of Codrean's, there were plenty of artifacts that I didn't have even the slightest clue of what they did. Towering sequoia trees loomed overhead, breaking up the early rays of the sun into bright beams that pierced the canopy and scattered across the training ground.

The humanoid, and partially translucent, training dummies silently standing in formation were also expertly crafted, though I couldn't quite tell whether they were static or if they could move, as the bases of their feet appeared a little worn.

Maybe it's just from moving them around a lot, I surmised.

I very quickly realized that both Ysevel and Bernar had both backed away from me as I observed my surroundings. Feeling something was off, I activated the second stage.

Maybe it's that creature Gwili talked about? I thought, moving my hand to my sword. *Not quite,* my mother's voice rang in my head. Without much else in the way of a warning, I felt a tendril of mana from my right. Reactively, after having trained so much with Bernar, Pyle, and Taegin, I reactively drew my training sword, swinging it in one, fluid motion in the direction of the tendril, biting into something I couldn't see until a second later.

My mother's training sword.

Through my struggle, I could tell that the blade held a gentle curve, though a lot less significant than a scimitar. Its thin blade had a wave-like pattern that ran along its length near the edge of the twin-colored blade, and a small, rounded guard that was only a little larger than the handle. There was no pommel on this blade, at least not one that I could visually identify in the traditional sense of a pommel, but she held it with both hands as one would a normal sword; one choked up on the guard, the other down near the base of the handle.

"Well done, but you're late," she said, her golden eyes meeting mine as I struggled against her strength. For her slim, toned frame, she was extraordinarily powerful, but I could tell she was holding back. "Sorry. I had to learn how to wear an entirely new set of armor in a matter of minutes," I strained, even though it was amply clear she could overpower me at any given second.

"I knew you were good, having bested not one but *two* ochelons, but I didn't think you were *that* good," she said, a subtle hint of surprise in her tone. "I might be a little better than that, now," I said, pushing mana into my legs and arms to dash away.

To the naked, un-enhanced eye, it would have looked like a blur had just passed from one side of the training ground to the other. Unfortunately for me, however, Siraye followed my movements with absolutely *no* difficulty.

"Impressive," she said, cocking her head, her downturned lip pursed outwardly. "Let's see if you can keep up, then," she said, flaring a bit of her mana.

Taegin used to do the same thing when he was teaching me to read mana, I thought. *You might not want to let those kinds of thoughts distract you,* my mother said in my head again as she dashed forward with a speed I could hardly match.

It was like she could *see* exactly how fast I could react to something, a lot like how I saw the fear shooting down Irun's spine during our battle.

She swung from below in an uppercut motion, forcing me to side step and parry the blow away from me. As if unaffected, she swung again and again, aiming blows at my hips, legs, and stomach. I dashed away, hoping to get another angle on her, but she was faster than I ever could've imagined. Within an instant, she was right in front of me.

"Running away?" she asked coyly. "No, just looking for a better angle," I said, starting a combination of blows I'd trained so often at Codrean. Swing after swing, I felt her parrying and deflecting my blows away from her body like she was swatting at annoying flies. As a grin began to form on her face, I decided to surprise her.

During one of my swings, I cast my *Whip of Doom* from the tip of my sword as the tendril shot off to my left, wrapping it around one of the training dummies I'd spotted earlier and quickly pulled it towards us. The dummy, now soaring through the air, shot like an arrow towards my mother. A mild twitch of surprise hinted across her features, but without any form of hesitation, she reached her arm out and *pulsed her mana* like Nenvalur had when he held the portal open.

"*Oh,* shit," I allowed, seeing the grin on her face turn into a menacing sneer.

While parrying my sword with her own, she used her free hand to pick up and slam the dummy at me, shattering it right where I had been standing only a half-second prior. Noticing she'd pushed me back, she began pulling more and more items from the training area, in attempts to crush me to the ground, forcing me to roll and pirouette out of the way as they came.

A little savage, don't you think? I asked, knowing she was listening. "Savage?" she asked aloud, her once coy tone now engulfed in full-on rage. She began moving even faster, slamming training artifacts without even moving her arms, as she seemed to levitate them without even using something like my *Whip of Doom*. She swung and swung, forcing me to backpedal and parry as best I could as she pushed the limits of my ability.

"You're keeping up decently, but how will you manage this?" she asked, stomping her foot on the ground. The ground seemed to grow distant, as I began to realize what had just happened. With her stomp and perfect control of her mana, she managed to use it to cut out a perfect circle of earth around where I was standing, and lift it into the air.

I leapt off, thinking I would land back down on the ground, but quickly found that she had conjured another one just like it behind me. I repeated this process again and again, beginning to wonder just how many she could have up at one time.

I never discovered the limit.

With the malicious grin still on her face, she dashed towards me, using the floating platforms of earth she had just created to make her way towards me, as her sword was now alight with mana-flame. Jumping between platform after platform, we swung at each other and parried attacks left and right as we bounced along the platforms. Dashing towards her in a desperate attempt at an attack, I was met with a vicious, wet blow to my spine, slamming me to the ground beneath us.

Without much motion from her, she replaced the holes she'd made in the ground with their original components of earth and rock, and stood victoriously above me, pointing her sword at me. "Do you yield?" she asked, her breathing was slow and steady as if she'd been asleep the entire time.

Grunting with the pain I felt in my back, I got to my feet, standing as straight as I could in the newly-formed puddle beneath me. She eyed me curiously, but that curiosity quickly turned back into a chagrined smile. "*Nah*, I've got one more thing I wanna try," I said, pushing as much mana into my muscles, tendons and bones as I could physically manage.

"And what's that?" she asked, merely raising an eyebrow in response.

"A speed blitz," I grinned.

With a flash of mana, I dashed behind her, leaving a puff of mist behind me, preparing to strike at her from behind with the flat of my sword.

I've got you now! I thought, hoping it would distract her just enough to make her hesitate. *Know your place,* her voice beamed into my head alongside an intense glare that met my eyes just as my sword was coming down. Just as it did so, the figure, who I thought was my mom, shimmered and twirled as my blade passed through it.

What the fuck...? I thought, widening my eyes and trying to piece together what happened as a cold, dull piece of steel pressed against my neck.

"*Hahaha,* you thought!" she chuckled from behind me. "Not a bad move, but unrefined, for sure. Now, sit," she said, pulling her sword away from my neck, replacing it with the palm of her hand as she swept my feet out from under me and forcing an abrupt meeting of my ass cheeks with the dirt below. "*Ow*! The fuck was *that* for?" I asked, rubbing my backside. "*That* was for getting cocky. Didn't your brother ever warn you *not* to do that?" she asked, glancing over at him briefly.

"*Oh,* I've warned him alright," Bernar said, raising his hands placatingly, as if doing so would wash his hands of any guilt. My mother shrugged, and sat down with her legs crossed in front of me. "That was a decent fight. It seems your grandfather taught you well, after all. I just wish you'd been able to come earlier," she said, a tone of regret subtly floating in her voice. I watched as her expression flicked through a few emotions, but settled on a grin.

"What was that move you did earlier with the dummy?" she asked. "My best friend, Edryd, calls it the *Whip of Doom,*" I said, giving credit where it was due. "*Whip of Doom?*" she asked sardonically, raising an eyebrow. "Well, I suppose there are worse names for something like that, but it is what it is. It was a well executed move," she shrugged.

"How did you do that trick with the ground? All those platforms floating in the air? I've seen Bernar use mild earth-mana manipulation before, but never like that," I said, recalling him pulling the stone doors inside the cave apart like a curtain. "*Oh,* that? It's a common strategy my team and I developed to throw less-intelligent creatures off kilter," she said matter-of-factly.

"Team? What team?" I asked. "I'm sure you know from Taegin that I originally came here looking for the lost artifacts of the gods, correct?" she asked. I nodded. "Well, we found all of the ones in Caegwen, though there are still two that are missing," she said frustratedly.

My eyes widened as I processed what she said. "You *found* them? Do they still work?" I asked, though I had so many more questions lined up. "*Eh*, they do, but we've come to find out that unless you have a full, well-coordinated team capable of wielding the artifacts, they're not as useful as they were once thought to be," she said dejectedly.

"Unfortunately, the team that I had when we found them got split up due to increased invasions from the Underworld. We've been extraordinarily busy since just before the attack on Coltend Castle, monitoring and striking at the portals as soon as they opened across the country," she said, averting her gaze.

I could only nod in understanding. Things really hadn't been the same since then, and I supposed that whatever she was dealing with was far out of my league.

"In any case, that was a good first match, but since we have a lot of training to do, it's probably best if you met some of the people you'll be working with, first," she gestured behind me. Standing next to Ysevel and my brother were three more elves, only one of which wore similar training attire to that of my mother.

The tallest of them, standing at least a head taller than I was, had dark green hair and an unstrung bow in his hand, with his quiver tied to his waist like a sword's sheath. The second had blood-red hair, hazel eyes, and a toned body that suited a spear-caster nicely.

The third, however, was one I didn't expect, as his lanky frame and matted, black hair seemed to greatly contrast against the features of the other two, especially the twin daggers at his sides. "Thoma, meet Haldir, Vyra, and Derion," my mother said, pointing to the three in the exact same order I'd noted them in.

"It's a pleasure to meet you, and I look forward to your instruction," I said with a bow. "*Oh*? A sword caster? *Aaaand* of course he looks *just* like you, Commander. I wonder if he's got your attitude, as well," Vyra said, noting my features as soon as I lifted my head from the bow.

"It will be an honor to work with you, and I look forward to teaching you all that I can," Haldir said, putting a hand on his chest in a formal bow which I returned promptly.

"Commander, he really does look just like you. Would you mind if I ran a few experiments on him? I'd heard from Lady Ysevel that he'd had a seal on his core, after all," Derion said, his raspy voice and malicious half-grin sending chills down my spine.

"Yes, he does. Happy to hear it, and absolutely the fuck *not*," my mother said, addressing all three of her companion's quips and greetings quickly. "Thoma, you will be training with these three members of my team, alongside Ysevel whom you've already met," she paused, repeatedly raising her eyebrows suggestively.

I did my best to ignore both my mother's wry suggestivity, and Ysevel's tomato-red face.

I'm getting the feeling this is probably going to be a long day, I thought, not bothering to hide the grin on my face as I shook my head and chuckled.

CHAPTER 40
LOOMING SHADOWS

"It's been two months and *nothing* has happened. What the hell are they planning?" Thorsen asked, slamming his fist on the table of the meeting room. The afternoon sun shone through the large window, sending a few rays of sunlight to bounce off his armor and refract around the room.

"Commander, this is no time to begin freaking out. To be fair, we didn't even know if they were here for the queen herself," Gwili said, leaning his elbows on the table opposite Thorsen.

Thorsen scoffed. "You said they were human, and that you followed them to the castle. We've trained and waited, waited and trained. What the hell is going on? Why haven't they made their move, yet?" he asked, the concern obvious in his voice. Gwili rubbed his chin across his shiny Coltendian bracers, as he had been inducted into the Warrior's Guild under Thorsen's supervision.

"There are a few reasons they could be doing this," Gwili began with a sigh as he closed his eyes. "There's not much else to be done if they don't want to be found. Naturally, they won't expose themselves using the same clothes as they did when they traveled," he continued.

Thorsen looked at him curiously, lifting an eyebrow, as if suggesting he continue.

"If they're smart and well-trained, which they might actually be, they'll hide amongst the crowds for a while, scouting things out and making sure they know their infil and exfil plans, as well as how to handle any other obstacles they might encounter," Gwili said, glancing up at the giant. "So you think they're biding their time? Two months is a little long, wouldn't you say?" Thorsen asked simply.

"The problem is, if they're as well-trained as I think they are, two months isn't a blink of an eye for them. Honestly, if they've held out this long, I'd wager they have other intentions outside of simple, cold-blooded murder. They're waiting for something, or maybe they're just gathering information," the elf replied with a shrug.

Thorsen pinched the bridge of his nose and sighed heavily. "Why can't things be simple? Whatever happened to good, old fashioned fighting? Everything these days seems to be plans upon plans, and subterfuge beneath subterfuge," he said, his impatient nature bleeding through his tone.

"Not everything in war is just swinging swords and hoping you hit your target," Gwili said plaintively. "*War*? You think we're at *war* right now?" Thorsen asked, his tone growing a little darker, to which the elf merely shrugged again.

"I'm not saying we are, and I'm sure as shit not going to say we aren't. At the very least, not with anything, or *anyone* we know. The Masked One has up and fucked off to the North, and he's been pretty quiet, too. It's like the calm before a storm we can't see coming," he said, sighing heavily.

Thorsen thought about his words carefully, running his fingers through his blonde beard. "I don't suppose we have a way of setting a trap for them, do we?" he asked after a few moments of contemplation.

"Nothing *they* would fall for, I think," Gwili said defeatedly. "The best thing we can do, instead of having our thumbs up our collective asses, is train. Gods above and below, even *that* might not be enough," the elf continued with a scoff.

Neko and Marte, who had been sitting quietly on the far side of the table until now, glanced at each other. "Do you think we'll be okay?" Marte whispered, but Neko could only shake his stubbled head. "I'll be honest, I have no idea. We just have to keep training until something happens, I guess," he returned quietly.

Marte held a subtly fearful look on her face, and gripped Neko's hand tightly. He looked down at the oversized hand and then to the face that was on the verge of tears. Without a word, he simply turned his hand palm up to better hold hers. "Hey, we've been training a lot the last two months. It's not like we're as weak as back then," he said, trying to comfort her with an encouraging tone and warm smile.

"I know..." she nodded in short movements. "I guess I'm just... anxious," she said after having some difficulty admitting her emotions. Neko chuckled through his nose. "The *giantess* herself? *Anxious*? Never thought I would see the day," he jeered, shaking his head. She glared at him. "I'm only kidding. I'm anxious, too," he said, hoping she didn't feel as alone. She gave him a warm smile, and squeezed his hand a little harder before paying attention to the rest of the meeting.

After having discussed multiple possibilities, it became evident that the best course of action *really was* to wait, as no one present had any knowledge of their potential enemy's capabilities.

Still, they conducted whatever training Gwili conjured up for those following days. He taught them stealth tactics, how to read signs that most people would miss, how to conduct a strike on a building complex that was heavily fortified, and other such things from his time as a synner.

"You know, unconventional warfare like this makes me terrified for the capabilities we might have in the future," Thorsen said, just after Gwili had finished another lesson with him, Neko, Marte, and Leona, the latter being a surprisingly fast learner. "*Heh*, that's because you haven't heard even *half* of what we've already done with this kind of knowledge," the elf said, ever so slightly puffing out his chest as he turned away from the chalkboard to face them.

"I wish I would have learned at least *some* of this while I was receiving my lessons to be a queen. All I learned back then was how to properly hold utensils, bow, and laugh at jokes I found distasteful," Leona said, glancing at her notes to make sure she had everything that was written on the board. "Well, I'm flattered," Gwili said, a smile tugging at the corner of his mouth.

I'd never have expected a compliment from the queen herself, he thought.

"Nevertheless, there is one thing I don't understand," she began as she re-stacked her notes. "And what might that be, your majesty?" Gwili asked. All eyes turned to her. "Why don't they just attack? If direct action is the quickest and most efficient way of getting rid of someone, why haven't they attacked?" she asked.

Shit. I didn't want to be the one to have to tell her this, Gwili thought as everyone's gazes now shifted over to him.

"Because there's a difference between killing a person, and killing a *way of life*," he answered ominously. Leona's face paled, but she held her composure as best she could. "Please, continue," she urged after swallowing a dry ball of spit.

"When you're killing a person, you can physically see their life ebbing away, be it by your hand or another's. There is a definite *end*, so to speak, and with that comes an unspoken understanding that whatever this person did *could* happen again, if another were in similar circumstances. When you're killing a way of life, however, the slow shift in ideological morals and values can shift the way an entire *country* is ruled, for better or worse," he began to explain, never once breaking her gaze.

"So you're saying that these infiltrators have come into our country to destroy our way of life?" she asked, cutting straight to the point she thought he was trying to make. He breathed in deeply, and pondered how best to answer her question.

"You and Thorsen have both elaborated on the *coup d'etat* that the followers of Mideia conducted, and know the details of it far better than I ever could. With that said, why aren't there people still trying to overthrow your rule as we speak under the premise of that original *coup*?" he answered her question with one of his own.

Not fair, she thought.

"Because it was out of line with many of Mideia's ideals, so it didn't stick in the minds of the general populace," she surmised. "Precisely your majesty," he nodded his head. "Now, what if you had months, if not *years* to subtly influence the people of a country? What do you think would happen?" he asked.

She paused for a few moments, while the others held their breath to hear her response.

"You could, theoretically, overthrow the governing party using the masses. A democracy of defamation, of sorts, using propaganda disseminated through the masses to deem a ruler unfit to be in power; their ideologies, power structure, authority, and control over social order questioned and expelled from both the culture and country as a whole," she said, piecing her thoughts together.

"And what would be the aftermath?" the elf asked, raising an eyebrow. Leona swallowed dryly. "The country's ruling power would fall and potentially be replaced by an entirely foreign power, leaving little to no trace of its former self if done perfectly," she said dejectedly.

"Congratulations, your majesty," Gwili clapped his hands softly. "You have, just now, described subversion at its finest," he said, leaning both of his palms on the table. "But how do we prevent that? How do we stop them from doing *that* to *us*?" Neko asked as the worrisome tone he had in his voice was evident.

He wasn't the *only* one feeling that way, after all.

Gwili clicked his tongue, and turned to the chalkboard behind him. "The best way to do that is to look for it in daily life. Find out whether there *is* negative propaganda being said and who is promoting it. Where are their focal points for this propaganda and what sort of benefits are they promising for those who comply? How have they been spreading this information? And, ultimately, what actions are potentially being taken in regard to the aforementioned?" Gwili said, as he wrote down the bullet points.

He turned to find everyone copying them down and smiled. "So, how do we find these... *foreign entities*?" Leona asked. "In all honesty, the best way might just be to patrol the city," Gwili said. "It would be effective, but it would also draw too much attention, wouldn't it?" Marte asked.

"I'm not saying we pull the entire Warrior's Guild into it," the elf raised his hands. "If we have a few, select and trustworthy people who are keeping an ear out on the streets, we should be able to pick up on a lead here or there," he continued. Thorsen, bored by the idea, shook his head. "I will continue to do my duty to protect Leona with my life. I don't have the patience for doing such things," he said with a firm gaze.

"*Oh*, good! I'm glad you said something. I was afraid you'd stand out too much, anyway," the elf said playfully. Soon after formulating a list of those they deemed trustworthy enough to be in on the plan, they set it into motion. Undercover guards were posted at potential key locations that Gwili thought might pose the biggest threats. Unfortunately, those under Zari's command had different plans in mind, because in the weeks that followed, there was still no sign of any movement on their end.

Meanwhile in the Harutian palace of Escea, Fazel, her direct servant, searched the grounds for any sign of her majesty.

She couldn't have gotten too far. I hate *it when she does this,* he thought, scouring the palace garden in hopes of any sign of her.

The garden was incredibly large, however, and it would have taken any normal person the better part of an hour to search the entire place. Plants from all over the continent riddled the ground, pillars, and hung from arches constructed generations before her and Bashir's rule.

She's not in her usual spot by the gardenias. Where the hell else would she be? he thought, peering around yet another tall hedge-like structure.

Suddenly, he noticed a shadow looming overhead, followed closely by a falcon's cry far. He looked up, and saw that it was moving out towards the Eastern side of the palace itself.

That must be where she is. Eltam wouldn't fly far without her being somewhere ready for him to land, he thought after observing its flight pattern for a moment.

He followed it over to a clearing in the palace that looked more like a training ground than anything else. Zari stood in the center of a square courtyard with a leather pouch attached to a long string that she twirled overhead. She suddenly slowed the speed of its rotation, leading Eltam into an attacking swoop, always keeping whatever was in the pouch just out of the avian's clutches.

"A beautiful attack, wasn't it?" she asked as she put away the sling into the satchel that was hanging over her opposite shoulder. "It was, indeed, your majesty. But what are you doing out here? I've been looking everywhere for you," Fazel said, trying to hide his frustration. She didn't immediately respond, but instead pulled out a piece of raw meat from a pouch on her belt that held her white dress snugly against her skin.

"Do you know why I like falconry, Fazel?" she answered his question with one of her own. "I don't, your majesty, though I would love to hear about it," he answered after a moment's pause. "It's quite simple, really: To lure such an incredible predator into an attack, only to not let it catch its prey, is exhilarating to me. I *love* watching how it moves through the air; how it angles its body; how it folds its wings just right to gain the maximum amount of attack speed. It's fascinating, to say the least," she replied.

"I can't say I've paid much attention to it, your majesty," Fazel began. "Even when I was serving directly under your late husband, may Yarathea guide his soul, he never put on such a magnificent display," he said, glancing upward at Eltam as he flew overhead. Zari whistled and patted her arm twice, clearly displaying a piece of sliced meat in her gloved hand.

Eltam's mahogany wings and sharp talons gleamed in the afternoon sunlight as it swooped down onto her arm, tearing the meat she held to shreds. "They're incredibly smart animals. Trust with them is easily broken, but if you can maintain it, they are valuable hunting assets," she said, stroking its wing with the back of her hand. "Would you like to try it sometime?" she asked wryly.

"I don't think I'm quite cut out for falconry, your majesty," he said, flinching slightly as Eltam flapped his wings to regain his balance and eliciting a chortle out of Zari. "I suppose not. Though, I do hope that one day you see the value of it, and how the principles held within can be applied to our own situation," she said, rubbing her falcon's chest. "How so, your majesty?" Fazel asked as he reached his hand out to stroke its wing.

Eltam, however, thought he was being offered meat, and tried to nip at the bare hand that was coming to pet him.

Zari chuckled once more, pulling her bird away from her servant just in time for its sharp beak to barely miss Fazel's curled finger. "You see? If you approach something as dangerous as a bird of prey without prior knowledge of how best to get close to it, the chances of you being bit are high. However, with a little time and patience, one can gather enough knowledge to approach this creature without much hindrance," she said, gazing into its rounded eye.

"Are you referring to our hashishin over in Coltend, your majesty?" Fazel asked. "Of course! Why do you think we haven't heard news of their attack yet?" she asked almost playfully.

CHAPTER 41
AS ABOVE, SO BELOW

"Athar!" Irun called out, his voice resounding down the violet halls. He went from hall to hall, room to room but was met with nothing but silence and a set of watchful eyes he couldn't see.

Damn it, I haven't seen him in almost a week. What the hell happened? Did that thing *take over him again? What the hell do I do if it has? It's not like the Masked One is around to help me right now, and Karak has been gone for well over three months now doing only gods know what,* he thought, checking behind the crack in a doorway he found along one of the halls.

Unfortunately, Athar wasn't in that room, either.

Irun sighed and slammed the base of his fist into the nearby wall. "Damn you, Athar. Come out already," he muttered. "He's not here at the moment," a both familiar and unfamiliar voice said from above him. "A-Athar?" Irun asked, looking directly above him only to find a shape he thought he recognized, but seemed... *contorted.*

Without warning, the figure dropped to the ground, leaving a small crater with cracks in the floor of the hallway and forcing Irun to take two steps backward. "What the hell? Where the fuck have you been? It's been *days* since the last time I saw you," Irun said, his frustration evident in his voice.

Athar, or whatever was *inside* of him, that is, held a twisted, menacing smile that didn't reach his eyes. His hair was matted and greasy, and there was no small amount of grime on his hands and face. His tunic, once black and decently maintained, now had holes and slashes in it, almost like it had been dragged through the dirt.

"Like I said, he's not here at the moment. At least not *mentally*, anyway," the contorted version of Athar said in a hungry, raspy voice. It was evident that whatever or *whoever* was in control of Athar's body had a clear lack of basic hygiene skills, as bodily odor began to fill the air around the pair. "Then where the hell is he? What did you do to my friend?" Irun asked, furrowing his brows in both anger and disgust for the smell. "*Oh?* Is that *anger* I hear in your voice, *child?*" the figure asked.

"What if it is? What the hell do you *want* with him, anyway?" Irun asked, his tone remaining flat and even. The figure tilted Athar's head to the side. "It would seem you have grown attached to this *friend* of yours, but we *both* know how you end up treating your friends, don't we, Irun Mothac," the figure said, his voice seething with venom.

Irun clicked his tongue and looked away. "Just tell me what the hell you're doing to him. Is this going to be a permanent thing, or are you just waiting to see if a better host comes around?" he asked, turning his eyes back towards the figure.

"*Hmmm,* I haven't decided yet. I rather like this body. It suits me well. Better than I would have thought, if I'm being honest. However, it is... *incomplete,*" the figure said, putting a grimy finger to its chin pensively.

"*Incomplete?* What the hell is that supposed to mean?" Irun asked, taking a single step forward. The figure merely raised an eyebrow as it glared down at the prostrated leg. "Regardless, you are both about to be summoned to your master," the figure said, blatantly ignoring the question.

"How could you possibly know that?" Irun asked, almost under his breath. "Nevermind. I don't care. Answer my question about Athar, daemon," Irun said forcefully. "You're in absolutely *no* position to make any demands of me, nor am I forced to answer anything you want to ask me, though you will learn your place soon enough," the figure said, impatience weighing heavily in his tone of voice as it stepped back. "W-wait," Irun said, nearly outstretching his arm to grab him, but it was too late.

Shit, it's gone again, Irun thought.

"Wh-what the hell happened? How long was I out for this time?" Athar asked, his voice shaky, rubbing his throat as if a rope had been around it. "Gods above, when was the last time I *bathed*?" he asked, sniffing his own armpit and scowling in disgust. "It's been nearly a week since I last saw you, and even then, you were acting... *strange*. They're also getting more and more frequent," he said, not shying away from the concern in his voice. "I know, but it's not like I can really *control* that," Athar replied, rubbing his nape and looking away.

"How do you feel, now?" Irun asked. "Like I've just had my skull angrily fucked by an ochelon," Athar answered, rubbing his temples. "Still, it's better than the *alternate*, or whatever the fuck Karak had called it, taking over forever," he continued, sighing heavily.

"What does it feel like when it happens?" Irun asked, his concern was evident in his tone of voice. "It's hard to explain. I can kind of see what's happening on the outside, though my vision is like trying to see through a murky lake. My body, on the other hand, feels numb;

almost like I'm some grotesque marionette being tugged around on a whim," he said, stumbling over his words in an attempt to explain the otherworldly feeling. "I see," Irun said for lack of a better response, nodding his head in understanding.

"In any case, I'm glad you're back. You, rather, your *alternate* said that we would be summoned soon, so we should probably start making our way back upstairs. You *do* smell like shit, after all," Irun said, nudging his friend with his elbow. "Not entirely my fault, is it?" Athar retorted with a scoff, nudging him back.

After a long, and much needed bath, Athar looked at himself in the mirror that was coated in a fresh sheet of steam. The bathing room he was in was large enough to be considered fit for a royal family, though it had been at least a few hundred years since any such prestige had touched that corner of the citadel. There were plenty of cracks in the floor tiles, as well as a few scattered across the walls and bathing area. The faded paintings on the walls and cob-web riddled candelabras added to the unattended feeling present.

Couldn't quite get those knots out, this time, huh? He thought, grabbing a clump of knotted hair.

His eyes *darkened, as he drew tendrils of dark mana from the underworld. They moved quickly and deliberately towards his outstretched hand* as he condensed his mana in the real. Watching it carefully, he molded the dark, swirling globe of mana into a pair of shears, and pulled his hair taut with his free hand.

Snip.

Meanwhile, Ardrin was downstairs in the summoning hall, imbuing some crystals with dark mana. "Preparations are nearly complete, I should summon them here," he muttered to no one in particular in a self-satisfied tone, placing yet another imbued crystal into the small circle of them he created.

His eyes *pulsed with violet mana, pushing out through the halls of the citadel as he searched for his two underlings. He found Irun just finishing up a meal, while Athar, now having much shorter hair than normal, had just finished getting dressed.*

Ah, it seems my timing was perfect, he thought as he pulsed his mana out once more, dragging the two from their respective locations and into the summoning hall. Athar, having gotten used to the feeling, barely flinched as the world around him lurched. However, Irun's meal, freshly ingested as it was, threatened to depart his body as quickly as it had entered it.

"It's been quite some time since you arrived here, Irun. Get a hold of yourself," the Masked One said in a flat, even tone as he already expected this to happen. Irun's eyes grew wide, but he managed to hold back from puking all over the summoning hall's floor. "I'm alright, my lord," he said, regaining his composure as Athar stifled a chuckle.

"You two have grown close, from what I've heard. I see Karak's reports on your progress here were not unfounded," Ardrin said, barely turning his head to glance over his shoulder. Athar and Irun immediately froze, feeling the weight of his gaze looming over them. "I-indeed, my lord. We've even gone so far as to form a pact," Athar stammered, knowing he couldn't hide a single thought from his master. "Do you think it wise to have done that?" Ardrin asked, finally turning to face the pair.

While Athar's hair and general features had remained much the same, his muscles were also a lot more defined than they already were. Irun, on the other hand, had seemed to fully integrate with the daemon arm, so much so that even his features had developed into much more daemonic ones than he previously had. Short horns grew from his head, his eyes had gone from hazel to a dark orange and red mixture, while his once bright hair was now a darkened crimson that sank to his shoulders.

"Wise? Why wouldn't it be wise, my lord?" Athar asked, genuinely confused. The Masked One paused for a moment, but ultimately shook his head.

It's too soon to tell him, he thought.

"Nevermind. It doesn't matter right now. In any case, I see you're taking to your new arm and core enhancement quite well, Irun," he said, observing Irun's new features as he walked around him. "I have, my lord. It's been an interesting adjustment, but one I can already feel is well worth it," Irun said, bowing his horned head.

"Nevertheless, I know you two are confused by this pile of crystals behind me," Ardrin said, returning to his original position. "Are we doing another assault on Coltend, my lord? Do we require more Gwynnleaf?" Athar asked. "No. At least, not as far as I know at the moment," Ardrin replied, his tone dropping a little at the end.

"What do you mean, my lord? Didn't the Undergod fully explain his plan to you when he asked you to get it the first time around?" Irun asked. The Masked One sighed, and paused for a few moments, as if choosing his words carefully. "He did and... he *didn't*. Yes, we got the Gwynnleaf, but there is *something* he's hiding. I have an inkling as to what it is, but..." he trailed off.

No, I can't talk about that until I confirm it, he thought.

"In any case, we need to get going. We shouldn't keep him waiting any longer, as time works differently down there," the Masked One said after clearing his throat. "*Down there*? What do yo-..." Irun was cut off by his master's sudden movement, as he slammed his palm onto the ground.

The entire room began to pulse with violet mana, as the crystals in front of the trio began to lift off the ground. They swirled and went into a circular formation, as mana circulated from the edges of the formation toward the middle, letting off an intense glow as it swirled.

"It... it's a portal. Just like the ones that spawned just outside of Codrean," Irun said, recognizing the swirling pattern. "You're close, but not quite right, Irun. I can create two way portals, but I wanted to show you two how this one works before we go. Consider it a precaution in the event, however unlikely it may be, that we get split up," he said, as he deactivated the portal, putting the crystals into a satchel and handing it to Irun.

"Thank you, my lord," he said, taking the bag from the large, claw-like hand, realizing his own was much smaller in comparison. "I don't suspect we'll need them, but it's better to have it and not need it, than need it and not have it," Ardrin said, turning back toward the center of the summoning hall. He *drew an immense quantity of dark mana, and* condensed it into his palm, slamming it once more on the floor.

A new portal emerged, though this one was much larger, denser, and moving more quickly than the first one with the crystals. Athar gazed into the hypnotic swirl of dark mana, slowly moving his hand toward it as if he were being pulled by some unknown force. Irun noticed this, and grabbed his wrist, pulling it downward and jolting his friend out of his apparent trance.

"S-sorry. I don't know what that was," Athar apologized, blinking rapidly a few times. "Are we sure this is a good idea, my lord? Do we know if the *alternate* will act up while we're there?" Irun asked with no small amount of caution in his tone. "Only one way to find out," the Masked One said with determination. "Now, go through the portal one at a time," he commanded.

Hesitantly, Irun walked forward. "I'll go first, my lord. If anything, I'll be able to meet Athar on the other side and help restrain him until you arrive," he said, swallowing dryly in hopes of keeping his food where it belonged. Ardrin nodded his agreement, and gestured forward once more. As Irun approached, he could feel the mana resonating from the portal.

This mana feels... cold, distant even. At least, it does here in the Real. So much different from merely drawing *it from there using my consciousness. Although, I wonder if the Ethereal's is warm and welcoming. Too bad I can't use it anymore since having drunk the deathmold concoction,* he thought remorsefully.

He shook his head to clear his thoughts, and stepped into the swirling mana. His body lurched and contorted in a pool of mana as he lost all sense of direction, tumbling through the portal. Without warning, he was immediately spat out from the other side, landing on something dark, circular, and solid, as the air around him reeked of death.

He forced himself to move, as his body creaked and groaned in protest. He coughed once or twice, hoping to regain some of the lost air from his lungs, but was only met with a thick scent of death.

Oh, for fuck's sake, he thought as his stomach emptied itself onto the ground beside the portal.

Athar stepped through next, just in time to catch his friend vacating the remains of his supper. "That sucked," he managed to get out before falling to his knees, choking on the dense, sweet air. Ardrin, however, stepped through entirely unfazed by both the portal and the stench.

"Get a hold of yourselves. He's watching," he said, quickly and quietly like scolding a pair of toddlers. The two of them staggered to their feet, and observed their surroundings. Unlike when they drew mana from this realm, it was evident that there was much more going on than they normally perceived with just their consciousness. Creatures of all sorts meandered, lost in a daze they wouldn't wake from without stimulation. Others were predatory in nature, and slaughtered a few of them, dragging their corpses away, and feeding the wide river of blood and decaying bodies along the way.

The dark globe of mana hung well above them, though it looked much larger than they originally thought and swirled much more slowly in comparison. It also emanated a soft, dull light that coated the world around them like twilight on a rainy day. The trees and grass in front of them were withered into grotesque forms, some of which happened to look like screaming creatures. The terrain around them was highlighted by the fresh blood spilled by the creatures, presenting shades of red, green, and black like strokes of an oil brush.

"Gods above, and below," Irun trailed, his eyes widening and twitching as he observed his surroundings. "It's a little different than just bringing your consciousness here, isn't it?" Ardrin asked without looking at him. "Y-yes, my lord. I don't understand how anything can *live* here," he stammered, trying not to choke on what little air he breathed in. "I guarantee that it's not without difficulty, but come, we must move quickly. Technically, we're already late," the Masked One said in a low grumble.

"We're being watched, aren't we, my lord?" Athar asked in a hushed voice, noticing his master's tone. Without a word, Ardrin nodded, signaling for them to follow. They moved in silence, no one wanting to say a word lest they attract the attention of an unwanted guest.

Even in the Underworld, there is always a risk of these creatures becoming aggressive. They're surprisingly territorial if left to their own devices without someone to instill fear and order into their minds. Do not let your guards down, the Masked One sent to his two underlings mentally.

After what felt like an hour had passed, the trio paused up on one of the hills, overlooking a dismal plane with what looked like charred remains of vegetation strewn across it. While it still smelled of rot, there was little available to allow the trio to recognize even a single plant. Off in the distance, behind a veil of blood-red mist, was a natural construct that looked a lot like Valdis, though it was a lot more derelict than anything Athar or Irun had ever seen.

"Is that...?" Athar began, but halted, squinting his eyes to try and get a better look at it through the gloom. "It is, though not quite the same as *you two* know it to be," Ardrin answered simply. "Why were we so far from it when we first arrived, then?" Irun asked, genuinely curious. "I mean, it's basically the same thing as Valdis, why were we transported so far away from it?" he continued.

Ardrin stopped moving and turned on him like a snake to a mouse. "What part of *we are being watched* did you not understand?" he hissed, his eyes glowing violet far more than usual with the abundance of dark mana in the air. Irun was shaken to his core, as both him and Athar could feel the pressure his mana exuded drastically increase.

"Do not speak unless spoken to, especially not here. Do you understand what I'm trying to tell you, or is your family tree a fucking *stump*?" the Masked One spat, the anger seething through his tone. "I-I understand, my lord," Irun finally responded, after opening and closing his mouth a few times as if trying to find the words to say. Releasing the collar strap of his servant's armor, Ardrin turned and began moving towards the citadel once more.

"I will only say this to ease the questions I can feel worming around in that unremarkable brain of yours: the Undergod is *not* the only one in this place that has the ability to speak. There are entire populations with their own culture, civilization, and mannerisms that lurk about here," he said, gesturing around him briefly.

"If one of the clans' observers *just so happens* to be watching us, and you say something irresponsible, ignorant, or down-right offensive about them or their homeland, what do you think will happen?" the Masked One asked the pair trailing behind him. "Th-they'd be angry, and likely attack us, my lord," Irun stammered, feeling the weight of the words as they left his mouth.

"*Huh*, you're not as much of an idiot as I thought," Ardrin said sarcastically, turning around to keep moving towards the distant citadel. "As it currently stands, the balance of power between myself, the Undergod, and his subordinate clans here is tenuous at best. I'd rather not be forced to plough through my short list of allies with a bloodied claw," he continued.

As they moved across the field, Athar and Irun kept glancing around them to see if they could spot any of these so-called *observers*, but to no avail. They kept this up until they reached the gate, where they encountered a tall, daemonic figure.

It stood roughly two meters tall, with graphite-colored scales that looked like plate armor, burning red eyes, and three sharp horns spawning from the top of its forehead. At the crown of its head, a plume of long, black, scaly feathers was embedded into the thick plate. The blade it carried on its back was made of a similar material that the creature's scales were, gleaming softly in the sickly green light that adorned the citadel.

"You're late, mage," the creature spoke in a voice that sounded like crushed gravel. "My apologies, Gavar. There were some unforeseen complications that arose," the Masked One said, bowing his head just a little.

I've never seen you defer to anyone, or anything *for that matter. Who, or rather,* what *is this?* Athar asked, knowing his thoughts were being read.

"Lord Gavar Bacruh, leader of the Ironplume clan and Chief of all Hegraphenes, please allow me to introduce you to my two subordinates, Athar and Irun. The first, an abandoned bastard of King Truls Wishert, and the second a former synner of Codrean," he said the creature's name at length to explain everything subtly.

What the fuck is a hegraphene? Is this a new kind of monster that we've never even heard about at Codrean? Irun thought, his eyes wide and glued to the creature's visage.

Shut up, Ardrin sent back immediately.

"Addressing me by my full title to hopefully prevent your two subordinates from disrespecting me is a smart move," Gavar said, eyeing the pair behind the Masked One. "I see one of them even went so far as gaining a daemonic arm. That was *your* doing, I take it?" the creature asked, bending a scale above its eyebrow upward in curiosity.

"It was. He lost an arm during a fight with one of his former comrades, though I don't suspect he'll lose another," Ardrin replied, letting his words hang in the air. "I see," Gavar said with a tone that suggested little more than disappointment. "In any case, we should go. *He* has been expecting you for quite some time now, and it would be best to *not* keep him waiting any longer," the creature said, gesturing for the trio to follow him.

The large, metallic gate behind them creaked open, and the sound of heavy chains and gears could be heard turning behind the high walls. As it opened, the path before them was revealed to be a long, thin bridge, underlit by the same, green light as the rest of the citadel. While they were crossing, Athar noticed a few creatures on a distant, interior wall grinning down at him.

They don't look human, but they somehow feel familiar, he thought, quickly averting his gaze back toward the path ahead of him.

They're other alternates, *not unlike the one that resides within you, though these would sooner kill their hosts than settle for temporary possession. They must be sensing the one you have, that's why they're glaring at you, and not Irun or I,* Ardrin sent in an even tone, using the link he constantly maintained.

The doors to the citadel opened, and Athar immediately recognized the grand hall, its patterns and internal structure were incredibly similar to that of Valdis, though the ornaments differed slightly; the large skeletal skulls replaced with thousands of smaller, more grotesque ones. The pale, green aura still sulked throughout the citadel, though it was far less pronounced around the back of the throne room. Sitting atop a massive throne made of bones, sinew, and steel was Volzuk.

His eyes glowed an intense, blood-flame red, the tendrils thereof licking the base of his elongated horns. An elongated, clawed hand held his rested head that was titled to the side, while the other toyed mindlessly with a globe of pitch black mana.

"It's about time you arrived, *worm*," Volzuk said, his voice carrying down the length of the hall like a thunderclap. The intensity of his voice nearly knocked the trio from their kneeling position. "I apologize for my tardiness, my lord. There were some complications that arose, causing my delay," the Masked One said, bowing his head a little lower.

Volzuk lifted his head from his claw, a thin string of flesh and bodily fluid lingering as he pulled away. "*Complications*? You mean your failure of an experiment that escaped? The *alternate* that you also brought back with you during your last visit? Or was it, perhaps, the overall forgotten reason of why we kept sending creatures into Caegwen in the first place?" he asked, his tone level but threatening and full of disappointment.

"My lord, I have not forgotten about the artifacts in Caegwen. As unfortunate as it may be, the elves have already found and recovered four of them, according to the last report I received, and I'm sure they know I have the fifth," Ardrin replied. "So, the sixth is still missing?

It's unfortunate, but it at least allows me more time to develop my forces," Volzuk said.

"How much longer do you think it will be until the main force is ready, my lord?" Ardrin asked. "If the breeding goes as smoothly as I think it will, about two-thousand cycles," the Undergod replied after a moment's consideration.

Two thousand cycles? How long is that? Irun asked himself.

"Are you just ignorant, or have you already forgotten that I can hear everything you're thinking, worm?" Volzuk spoke up, his tone growing increasingly annoyed. "To answer your question, and it will be the last one of yours I ever answer, it is roughly *two years* in the Real; the equivalent of *two thousand* in this realm. Now, I've blocked out most of your thoughts since your arrival, incoherent babbling as it was, but I've had enough. Gavar, take him away, and far enough so that I cannot hear his thoughts during the remainder of their time here," the Undergod flicked a claw in a dismissive manner.

Irun was stunned with the pressure emitted over him, his mouth jolting as he tried to speak, but nothing more than an aerated whisper managed to leave his mouth. Without a word, he was picked up by his shoulder strap and dragged out of the large hall.

"Now, back to more important matters," he said, turning his gaze toward the remaining pair. "Athar, was it? I'm glad to see you've learned much and conditioned your body well since our last meeting," Volzuk said, leaning forward a little, resting his decrepit elbows on his knees.

"I-I have, great one. The Masked One has been kind enough to instruct me in the ways of mana, and Irun has helped me train since his defection," Athar said, bowing his head even lower. "*Oh?*

Interesting. Let me have a closer look at you," the Undergod said, sending a ruthless chill down Ardrin's spine.

Athar, for whatever reason, didn't feel the chill like Ardrin.

A low thrumming came from the end of the hall, and both Athar and the Masked One could feel mana being *pulled* from the atmosphere. Unlike when a consciousness pulled it, there was a palpable sensation, a sort of pressure, that exuded its will upon its surroundings. With a slight flinch, Athar held his own against the immense changes.

Just as suddenly as it came, however, the pressure halted, seemingly pausing the world around them. "You may rise," the Undergod's voice resounded from across the hall, though not quite as thunderous as before. Hesitantly, both Athar and Ardrin rose to their feet, and raised their heads to look at the owner of the voice.

His skinless and horned features were still present, though his form was much smaller. He still stood about a head taller than Ardrin, even after having absorbed the royal ochelon's core, but it was much less gigantic than his previous form. A soft and wet splattering could be heard resounding from the ground beneath his feet as he touched the ground. Within a single step, he appeared directly in front of the pair, not having made a sound.

"Welcome to Pydredd, the once-sister Citadel to Valdis, Athar," Volzuk said, moving his face mere centimeters away from the young man's. As the Undergod looked him up and down, settling on his core with an unnerving grin tugging at the corner of his mouth, Athar's eyes gazed into the blood-flame red ones in front of him, unflinchingly. "Thank you for welcoming us into your home, great one, though I'm not sure what *I* did to deserve the change of form," Athar said, his tone shaky and betraying his semi-stoic features.

A low rumble that resembled a chuckle came from the skinless figure in front of him. "I can tell you're doing your best to not show your fear, and hiding your thoughts; a beneficial piece of your training, I imagine," Volzuk said, mildly amused.

"I-I can't think of anything else to do in the presence of such power, great one," Athar said, bowing his head in subservience. "You've taught him well, worm," Volzuk said, shooting a look of both superiority and mild pride toward the Masked One. "I still have to apologize for Irun, as he's not as conditioned as Athar is, my lord," Ardrin said, meeting his gaze from underneath a furrowed brow.

"*Oh*, so *that's* the fool's name. No matter, he will learn his place in the world quickly, whether by my hand or another's," Volzuk said in a distant tone that carried an unspoken threat. "Regardless, I'd like to show you something that your master and I have been working on," he continued, wrapping a clawed hand over the young man's shoulder. Athar nearly shuddered, but managed to hold his own, merely squinting his eyes lightly at the cold, sharp touch.

"I'm sure you're wondering why your master attacked Coltend Castle, and I honestly doubt he ever had the intention of telling you," Volzuk began speaking and walking towards a hallway settled into the right wall of the large hall. "He told me he needed the Gwynnleaf, though for what reason, I never understood, great one," Athar said.

"In that case, allow me to educate you, in a way that your master clearly hasn't for his own reasons, I'm sure," Volzuk said demeaningly. "I taught him only what I thought was necessary, my lord," the Masked One said, a slight hint of frustration in his voice. "What *you thought* and *I know* are two, very different things, mage," the Under-god spat, forcing Ardrin to pause momentarily before continuing to follow the pair.

"Now, as you well know, if one is in the Real, one can draw from either the Ethereal or from here in the Underworld. However, what they don't tell you is that if one imbibes the Gwynnleaf solution, it allows them to draw from either realm without the risk of losing their consciousness to the realm, nor suffer any kind of major backlash," Volzuk began.

"Wait, so I've been drinking deathmold solution needlessly?" Athar asked, the shock evident on his face. "I wouldn't say *needlessly*, as without it you would have suffered a fate far worse than death only having drawn mana from this realm," Volzuk answered. "*O-oh,* I see. But, then, why didn't we have any of the solution the synners use, master?" he asked Ardrin.

"Because the attack I performed on Grundvollr about forty years ago didn't have much left for our experiments. The *one synner* placed in charge of making the solution was... *accidentally* killed and the information he held died with him, limiting our supply," the Masked One began to explain.

"That said, it was only a matter of time before we ran out of the solution, forcing our hand to find a larger source of the plant to be able to make it ourselves," he continued. "That's why you went to Codrean and Coltend with such a large force: To get as much of it as possible," Athar concluded.

Ardrin nodded his head. "However, this was not without its own set of problems, as now the entire realm knows of our, or at least *my*, existence. We simply didn't account for the Arwydus to be involved during our assault on Coltend, much less the potency of their strength. The assault on Coltend was more of an experiment of what could be done through mana-imbued crystals, and its success was quite impressive, even if it did take us well over three-hundred years to develop," he said.

"Three-hundred years," Athar said under his breath.

"That is why, once your master gathered as much of it as he could, we began developing our own experiments using members of Gavar's clan to help us push their power to their limits. It would also allow them to draw mana from this realm in the Real, as they solely rely on their own physical strength while deployed. We've just recently discovered this with the last batch that we sent to Caegwen. These experiments, in turn, help us lay the groundwork for... *future* endeavors," Volzuk chimed back in, taking the reins of the conversation once more.

There's still something I'm missing here, but I'm not sure if I want to ask it just yet, he thought as he digested the information, shielding his mind as best he could to avoid being heard.

Fuck it, he concluded.

"So, where do *I* come into all of this? What interest do you have in me, great one?" Athar asked, even more unsure if he wanted to know the answer as he turned to find Volzuk grinning malevolently. "You're quite observant, aren't you?" he asked, the intensity in his eyes deepening. "Unfortunately, now is *not* the right time for that discussion, as there is still much work left to be done," Volzuk answered, rubbing the base of his skinless chin.

"However, what I *can* promise is that the time will be coming, and it will be *much* sooner than those *fools* are ready for," he answered.

CHAPTER 42
FRAYED

The sound of spells being sent could be heard on the training field. It was a crisp, autumn morning, and the leaves were just beginning to turn all shades of gold, orange, and red. The cool air gently rustled the leaves that still clung to their branches, as the ones that couldn't gently floated toward the ground.

At least until the next burst of mana was felt.

Meliss wiped a bead of sweat from her brow, as *her eyes darkened once more. She stared up at the swirling globe of mana high above her, and extended her metaphysical hand out towards it, watching the tendrils of golden mana embrace her like rays of a morning sun. She felt it wrap around her, warming her* body in the Real through the cool breeze of the morning air.

She began to condense the mana into her off-hand, and ran it along the length of her training sword. The mana-flame coated the blade in a gentle, candle-like manner, casting some of its light on the sheen of sweat now coating her face.

Just like we practiced. Dash, pierce, and push, she thought, eyeing her target.

With one hand choked up on the guard, and the other gripping the pommel, she dashed forward with all the speed she could muster, feeling every fold of her jerkin and boots stretching out to accommodate her movements. The training dummy, approximately fifteen meters away from her, was being pulled left and right. Thorsen and Pyle had developed this kind of training together, and quickly found that it was a lot more difficult than it seemed to be.

As she approached her target, she let out a forceful grunt, exerting her energy once more to try to stab the target clean through. The tip of her sword sang through the air, as the mana-flame bent backwards with the force she generated. An almost whistling sound came from her sword, but stopped as soon as the tip pierced the target.

Instead of the target merely lighting on fire, Meliss pushed the entirety of her mana-flame into the target at once, forcing it to burst out into shards and splinters that covered the small corner of the training area. As they fell, she waved her hand in front of her face, trying to find a gap in the smoke to be able to breathe.

"*Aaaaaand* that makes twenty in a row! You're growing stronger, Meliss," Pyle said with genuine pride in his voice. Meliss, sheathing her sword, turned and walked towards him with a shrug. "I guess. *I* still don't think it's anywhere near enough, though," she said, her voice coming through more frustratedly than she would've liked to admit as she rubbed her ear.

She's still not used to her appearance, and is constantly comparing herself to the others around here, huh? Pyle thought, noticing her dejection.

"Meliss, I know how it seems, but there is something I would like to impart on you, if I may," he said in a gentle tone. "What might that be?" she asked, looking up at him. He chuckled softly, brushing a long strand of his white hair behind his ear as he bent to meet her eye. After a brief pause of the pair staring into each other's eyes, he flicked her forehead. "*Ow!* What was that for?" she asked. "Stop comparing your own progress to that of others," he said in a half scolding tone.

"What use is it to compare yourself to others, *huh*? The only thing that is going to do is give your brain more things to overthink about. *Oh, how am I ever going to keep up with so-and-so? Oh, no, this person is* so *much better than me at this or that!* No, child, this line of thinking is *not* the way you want to go about this," he began, putting a hand on her shoulder.

"There is knowledge *you* have that *they* don't, and there is knowledge *they* have that *you* don't. Experiences through life can and *will* vary greatly, this is true for all life on this continent. Regardless of your own inabilities and shortcomings, whatever they may be, you need to be patient and give yourself grace when you struggle to learn something many here took *years* to learn," he continued.

"It doesn't do you any good to worry about how far others have progressed. Be proud of what *you* have accomplished so far, and use others not as a tool for comparison, but as motivation to grow, instead; like they are a display of what *can* be achieved. Do you understand?" he asked in a tone full of patience and warmth.

He reminds me a bit of my mother, honestly, she thought, feeling her eyes beginning to water in frustration.

She nodded her agreement, sniffling and turning her head away for a moment. "Good, then how about we do a few more and move on to do something a little more exciting, yeah?" he asked, setting up another target before he had even gotten confirmation. As she continued her training, Pyle walked over to where the Master was observing a few of the senior synners conducting their training exercises alongside Roburn.

"Master," Pyle said from behind him. "*Ah*, Master Pyle. I was meaning to speak with you about something regarding Meliss," he said, wincing as he saw one of the seniors get tripped and slam into the ground harder than was originally intended. "Are you asking me for an update on her progress?" Pyle returned quickly.

Did the bastard read my thoughts? He wondered.

"No, but I've noticed you've been spending a lot of time with her since the removal of her earrings. Now, what seems to be the matter?" Taegin asked, turning to face his old friend. "Well, Master, she's been putting a lot of pressure on herself to catch up to the others," he said plaintively. "I see. It's only natural for someone like her to feel like that here. Comparison to others is a fickle thing, as we both know. But I do have to ask whether you're worried about her," Taegin said, lifting an eyebrow slightly.

Pyle shook his head. "I don't think there's much to worry about. If there is, there's nothing *I* or anyone else here can really do about it now that Thoma's up and fucked off, I mean," he answered with a shrug. The Master, now lifting the eyebrow even higher, scoffed and chuckled lightly. "*Oh*, to be young again," he sighed.

"In any case, I think we should have someone who at least knows Thoma well enough to help her through whatever it is she's struggling with," Pyle suggested. "I think you're right. Actually, I have just the person in mind," Taegin said thoughtfully, a wry grin showing on his face. "However, I'd like to speak with her first. Perhaps a second set of eyes will unveil something we otherwise might have missed," he continued. "Of course, Master. I look forward to your insight," Pyle said, dismissing himself and moving on towards Roburn's group.

After the day's training was completed, Taegin pulled Meliss into his study, and had her sit in the carved, wooden chair across from him. His hands were loosely on his lap, and his straight posture made him look a little taller than his usual, hunched over position. Meliss, kneading her hands out of nervousness, bounced her leg on the ball of her left foot.

"It's good to see you, Meliss. Thank you for accepting my invitation to talk," Taegin said warmly. "O-of course, Master. I'm just a little confused as to why I'm here," she replied nervously. "You have nothing to worry about, Meliss. I just have a few questions I'd like to ask you away from prying eyes and ears," he said nonchalantly.

By the Graces, is he trying *to give me more anxiety?* She thought.

"I understand that you're having some *difficulty* adjusting to your unsealed appearance, as well as during your training. I was wondering if you would like to shed some light on that with me. If not, I will respect your privacy, and will not push the subject any further," he said calmly. "Of course, Master. Might I speak freely, then?" she asked, using the conversational skills she'd picked up on in the Palace to their utmost advantage. "Naturally," he said without trying to show much emotion.

His tone suggests otherwise, she thought.

"I appreciate your candor, Master, but I know there's more to what you're saying and also what you're worried about than you're letting off," she said plaintively. "Picked up on that from Thoma, did we?" Taegin chuckled lightly, rubbing the back of his neck.

He even looks like him when he does that, too. Strange... her thoughts trailed off.

"Well, given what happened with Irun a few months back, we're just trying to take as many precautions as we can to prevent something similar from happening again," he said, interrupting her already distant thoughts of Thoma. "I see. In that case, I can put your mind at ease quickly. The pain and struggles we *all* have faced because of his actions will *not* be repeated by my hand," she said, furrowing her brows in determination.

She's grown a lot, Taegin smiled.

"Good, I'm both glad and relieved to hear that. However, Pyle has told me he's noticed, on more than one occasion I might add, that you still rub your ears as if they were foreign to you. Does being half-dwarf affect you that greatly still?" he said, trying not to sound impolite.

She mulled over the words for a moment before answering, and shook her head. "No, but I *do* feel a little bit like an outcast here," she said, her tone dropping a little. "What do you mean an *outcast*? Has anyone not been welcoming to you here?" he asked, genuine concern in his voice. "No, no. Not like that. I mean, we have Nenvalur's people here as well as some of Master Pyle's," she began, glancing off to the side and down as she said it.

"But even with all the diversity in this place, I'm the only half-dwarf. No one here can really relate to being so different from everyone else by that much. The others all have things they can relate to, but I was all but born into slavery and servitude, and have been through a lot as a result," she sniffled, wiping away a stray tear. Taegin just listened quietly, and leaned his elbows on the table, folding his fingers together.

"I just don't *feel* like anyone here can really understand what it is I'm going through. Being the only different one in such a far-off place from my homeland, and training to become something I was likely never meant to be is *not* easy. I just wanted to be stronger, and less afraid. Now? Now, I have all these questions about my past; ones I'll likely never get answers for, that is," she said, tears running freely down her face.

Taegin pulled a handkerchief from the corner of the desk, and handed it to her. She wiped her tears away, and made sure her nose wasn't dripping anymore. "Keep it. You have more use for it now than I ever have," Taegin said warmly. "Thank you, Master," she said in a stuffy voice.

"If it is of any consolation, I would like you to know that you're *not* alone when it comes to being *different*, as you so put it," Taegin began. "There are those here who have housed secrets for decades, ones they will likely take to the grave. Others have intricate pasts of their own. Irun, as shitty of an example as it is, was half-Harutian by blood and nationality," he continued.

I would've never guessed that. He didn't look even remotely Harutian to me, she thought.

"However, that didn't stop him from integrating fairly well with everyone around him. Yes, he was a hot-headed junior, but whether he admitted it or not, I could tell he cared deeply for his comrades, and they for him," he said. "But then why did Irun betray us all? It makes no sense if he was as *integrated* as you say he was," Meliss asked.

Taegin paused for a few moments. "Evil is a strange thing," he began after a few breaths. "It can lead some to embrace it as their own to fulfill a need one thinks they have, or force others into hiding forever behind a veil few get to see behind; frayed and scarred for the rest of their lives," he said, reaching into his jerkin, and pulling out a pendant similar to Bernar's.

Meliss looked at it carefully, noticing the intricate pattern like a metallic vine wrapped around a golden sphere that swirled at its center. Then, without another word, he took the chain off from around his neck, and placed the pendant on the table.

Wait, what the...? She thought, looking up from the table.

"Surprising, isn't it? What a little *evil* will push someone to do," Taegin said with a warm smile, his voice no longer raspy. His voice wasn't the only thing that had changed, however, as the wrinkles of his skin had disappeared, making him look more like he was in his thirties than his actual age. His ears, now pointed like Siraye's, helped to smooth back his steel-colored hair. Nevertheless, the pendant couldn't hide everything, as the scar on the left side of his face remained.

By the Graces, he's handsome. Waaaait, no. No. NO! She thought as her intrusive thoughts began to whirr.

"Y-you're an elf?" she said, trying her best to keep her tone hushed and calm. He chuckled, and nodded his head. "I am, and full-blooded at that. However, that is not important right now. What *is* important is that you understand that we're all outcasts in our own ways, some of us are just better at hiding it than others. Still, that should be no reason for you to feel left out in any way," he said, putting the pendant back on and reverting his features back to normal.

"Why did you do it? Why hide who you are?" she asked, after shaking her head clear of racing thoughts. "*Why*? Why does anyone do *anything*, I wonder?" he asked, putting a finger to his chin. "My reason was to protect my family, though that is not a story for today, let alone one I'm allowed to say at this current point in time," he said, conclusively.

The Master has a family? Gods above and below, how much do I not know about this man? Actually, how much does anyone know about him? She thought, rubbing the back of her neck.

"In any case, I just want you to know that what you're feeling in regards to *that* is normal. Pyle, I heard, already told you what you needed to know about training, so I won't say it again here," he said, leaning back in his chair.

"Is that why you brought me here? To show me *this*?" she gestured to the imaginary pendant on her own body. "A little trust and a change of perspective can go a long way, don't you think?" he asked with a wry smile on his face.

A change of perspective, huh? Oh, Thoma, she thought, immediately seeing his smiling face in her mind's eye, bringing up feelings she'd ignored for some time.

"Thank you, Master, for trusting me with that secret. I'll keep it safe, so don't worry about that," she said, getting up from her chair and bowing in respect. "I'd hope so, for both our sakes," he said, that same warm smile from before across his face again.

But why does it look... pained, or forced this time? she thought.

"*Oh*, Meliss?" Taegin called out from behind his desk, just before she opened the door. "Yes, Master?" she turned to face him once more. "I'd recommend talking to Edryd. I feel that conversation might prove... *helpful*, if nothing else," he said, the same, pained smile on his face again. Meliss nodded her agreement, feeling another small shift in her emotions. "I will. Good evening to you, Master," she said, closing the door behind her.

That's going to hurt. I'm so sorry, Thoma, Taegin thought, looking up at the ceiling and pushing a heavy sigh through his cheeks.

As Meliss walked down the cool, stone halls, she went over everything she had seen. Tagin's reveal as an elf had certainly shaken her, forming a small bubble of anxiety where the secret lay.

Gods above and below, my mind is absolutely full *of questions. Why did he entrust me with a secret of that level, anyway?* She thought, scratching the back of her head.

She continued down the halls, and out into the courtyard that separated the male from the female dormitories. As she stepped outside, she noticed that there was still some time before the sun was fully down, the golden light shining on the distant, titanic mountains. "Beautiful, isn't it?" a familiar voice snapped her out of wherever her mind had taken her.

She turned to see Edryd who was seemingly about to go for an evening walk alone, dressed in a loose-fitting linen shirt with drawstrings near the base of the neck, and trousers that didn't resemble pajamas nor formal attire.

"Yes, it's quite beautiful. I don't think I'd ever get tired of seeing a good sunset," she said, looking off towards the mountain range. "Well, I know a spot where we can see it better, and the best part is that it's not that far from here. Wanna go?" he asked in an unassuming tone.

Helpful conversation, right? She thought, recalling the Master's words.

"Of course. By all means, lead the way," she said, taking the extended arm held out before her. They made idle conversation about mundane and benign things like the weather as they walked a little ways toward the cave where Thoma had slain the ochelons, taking the path that shot off to the right. The path bent and weaved between countless gold and orange-leaved trees, accenting the light of the afternoon sun. "It's just over here," Ed pointed just ahead of them to a massive, lonely rock.

"How did *this thing* get here?" she asked, staring up at the massive boulder that seemingly surpassed the height of the trees. "No one but the Master knows that, and he won't tell us how or why this thing is here," he said, shrugging his shoulders. "He did show us these, though," he pointed to what looked like hand-holds and steps carved into the stone face with mana.

"Come on, we've gotta get up there," he said, pointing upwards. "Up there? Are you sure?" she asked, glancing at him with a raised eyebrow. "Would I lie to my best friend's girlfriend?" he said, mimicking her expression.

"Tell you what, since I've done this a lot, I'll go first. If you don't want to climb it, you don't have to, but at least shout your decision up to me, okay? That way, I'm not going to be sitting up there alone *and* confused as fuck," he said playfully, patting her forearm that was still linked around his. "Don't worry, I'll let you know," she chuckled heartily.

I haven't laughed like that in months, she thought.

He dug his hands and feet into the holes provided and began to climb with expert agility. "See you at the top," he said, turning as much as he could to show her a toothy grin. When he was out of sight above the canopy, she began her own ascent. "I'm coming up!" she shouted, almost forgetting to do so before making the climb.

The moss that had grown in the handholds of the rock was both a blessing and a curse, as her hands weren't getting cut up but her feet felt like they could slip at any moment. Reaching the top, she saw his hand extended out to her and took it. The pair grunted as they pulled on each other to reach the top, but he forgot to lessen their force when she reached the ledge, causing her to fall on top of him. "S-s-so sorry! I sh-should've... *uh*..." he stammered, realizing her chest was now pressed against his bare stomach.

Glick mouths, dead babies, grandma's wooden leg! Just think of something gross, please! Wait, grandma's fake leg did *look a little like a pe...* his thought's trailed and his face contorted into one of shock and disgust.

She chuckled and brushed a lock of hair from her face. "What's with the face? Am I too *heavy* for you?" she asked playfully. "Y-you know d-damn well that's n-not it," Edryd said, fighting for his life. "I know, dummy. I'm just teasing you," she chuckled, pushing herself off of him and out of the awkward position as her hand passed over his pelvis.

Thoma, please don't kill me and ignore this transgression of brother-hood, Ed thought, sweat pouring down his cheek as he imagined his best friend finding out about their situation.

Getting into a seated position, she looked at the colorful, leafy ocean before her, accented by the golden rays that bore through the distant clouds. "Alright, I've got to hand it to you, Ed. This really *is* beautiful," she said, pursing her lip and nodding her head slowly as she looked around. "Y-yeah. It really is, isn't it? I feel like this is something the Master must have used back in the day to *woo* the ladies," he said awkwardly, shifting into a similar seated position.

"*Woo*? You mean, courting?" she asked. "Y-yes. Courting. *Uh-huh!*" he nodded sharply a few times. "I guess I wouldn't know much about that. All I've known, since before Thoma anyway, was just one noble or other ordering me to do things I didn't want to. I learned more about being physical than emotional back then, so it's always been difficult for me to deal with things like that," she said matter-of-factly.

Edryd's face soured. "Those *bastards* would do that to you? It's a good thing you met Thoma, then! Well, about as good as it *could* be, given the circumstances back then and all," he said, scrunching the corner of his mouth into his cheek.

"That's just it, though, Ed," she began, but paused for a breath. "I... I'm grateful for him, and everything he's done. Truly, I am. He's shown me so much love, care, and attention that I don't know if I deserve, much less whether I could ever repay it. By the Graces, I'm not sure I'd even know where to start," she said, shaking her head and looking away.

"But..." he said, looking at her distant expression. "How did you know there was a *but*? Are you reading my mind?" she asked, finally turning to face him. "No, but your teary eyes are telling me much more than you realize," he began.

"Thoma, believe it or not, is a totally useless fucking crybaby when he's distraught. I know a dejected, hopeless look when I see one, and yours, right now, is no different than his," he continued, thinning his lips and tilting his head a little to the side.

Cheeky little shit, she thought, allowing herself a half-chuckle.

"Fine. There is a *but*, but I don't know how I can even say this without sounding like a worthless worm," she said. "Just get it out of your system, then. It's what we do all the time, but we've resorted to the extreme, unbridled use of profanity to ease the release of those pent up feelings," he said, chuckling lightly while she wiped away a stray tear. "Second time today," she said under her breath, while Ed watched her closely.

She took a moment to gather her thoughts, breathing deeply before she began to speak. "I-I almost feel that mine and Thoma's relationship was more out of convenience than anything *genuinely* romantic. The longer he's away, and the more knowledge I gain about myself, and the world around me, the less I feel attached to him," she said, tears rolling down her face.

Ed whistled critically, and took in a deep breath through his nose. "Now *that* was *not* what I was expecting," he said, running his fingers through the side of his hair. "I know, okay? I know how that sounds, but I swear, it doesn't have anything to do with him," she said, her tone far more laced with anger than anything else.

"I didn't say anything. I was actually gonna let you explain that one. This *is* my best friend we're talking about, after all," he said calmly. "Thank you. I mean it. It's just, ever since that first day in Coltend Castle, I knew he was different. The way he looked at me was genuine, kind, and cute as hell," she said, recalling his face as they left the castle.

"But when I saw him again up in the North on our way to Fangsdalr, and sat behind him on the horse, it just *felt* right. I couldn't explain it, but it was like there was a light at the end of the tunnel of shit I had been through in my life," she paused, plucking a stray leaf from her hair. "What happened, then? What has changed since he's gone to Caegwen?" Ed asked.

"It's difficult to explain. Maybe during this time away from each other, I realized that my past would always be there and that being with me wouldn't be worth his time, or love, for that matter. I know he says he loves and misses me in his letters, and that he can't wait to come home but... I just don't feel it's right for me to do that to him. He's pure, kind-hearted, and strong-willed like no other, but I can't do that to him. I can't ruin his life like that. My past is too damaged for that to work out well in the long run," she said, tears flowing down her cheeks and onto her lap.

What the fuck did I just get saddled with? This isn't just going to hurt him; it's going to break *him,* Ed thought, putting a hand on her shuddering back to help ease her sobbing.

"Listen, I know Thoma better than most. If he says that he wants to be with you, he does. There isn't much that could change his mind. I know that, and he knows that," he began, gazing off into the distance. "Then what the hell do I do?" Meliss asked between a pair of sobs.

"I don't know much about love, or anything romantic for that matter, but I do know this: Fighting a one-sided battle isn't going to be fair for anyone. If you *truly* don't feel the same way you did before and you don't see a way back or out other than ending things, then so be it. But, whatever you decide to do and however you decide to do it, the only thing I will ask of you is that you let him down easily," Edryd said with a heavy heart.

Meliss paused for a few moments, taking it all in and letting her emotions run freely for a little while. The sun began to creep behind the peaks of the mountains, casting their final, dying rays upon the golden countryside.

"I have to let him go, Ed," she finally said with a single, firm nod as if hardening her emotions. "I have to make sure he lives a life that he deserves, even though I don't think I'm a part of it anymore," she said, wiping away a stray tear with the back of her sleeve. Edryd shook his head. "You're an idiot if you think you're not going to be a part of his life anymore," he said, letting the words hang in the silence between them.

"You think he'll try to keep me in his life?" she asked, a half-scoff leaking through her teeth. "If you explain what's going on in full, I'm sure he'll be understanding, even if it breaks his heart. That, however, doesn't mean that he'll just expel you from his life, no. If I know Thoma as well as I think I do, he'll *find* a way to be your friend, even knowing he'll never be with you romantically," Edryd explained, giving her a warm smile and shaking her shoulder.

Meliss sighed heavily, and shook her head. "By the Graces, this is about to hurt, isn't it?" she asked. "Yeah. Yeah, it is," he replied, giving her a thin lipped smile. "Will you help me write it, then? You know him best, and I think it would be helpful to have it written properly, rather than having me word-vomit all over a piece of parchment," she said, a tinge of resignation in her voice, as if she had already succumbed to the numb feeling she once used so often.

"Of course I will," he replied with a heavy nod.

CHAPTER 43
AUTARCHICA PRIMARIA

Since we arrived in Caegwen, the days blurred into weeks, and weeks into months. I found out, very quickly I might add, that no matter how much time had passed, I found myself staring up at the canopy of golden leaves that surrounded the training ground just outside of Myrdin more often than not.

Anwill had often told me that it was considered *character development*, as he put it, and that honing in on the fundamentals was essential. My mother, Vyra, Haldir, and Derion, however, had a different approach which was *beating it into me* by way of mock battles. My mother believed that learning to both defend and attack against multiple assailants would hone my skills exponentially. To my credit, it was her and her whole team versus me today.

Of course, she might also be trying to break me, I thought.

I almost got caught out by being distracted with my thoughts, as I dodged one swing aimed for the back of my head and deflected another aimed for my ribs. Vyra, using her spear like an extension of her arm, redirected her deflected strike to try and trip me while I recovered from dodging another blunted arrow.

Derion, with his twin daggers, dashed in front of me with his fourth stage fully activated and slicing in a cross-attack, forcing me to parry it and use the momentum to carry me backwards. My mother dashed behind me, forcing me to deflect the incoming arrow while making sure the trajectory of my blade would also meet her own in time.

If she had been using her full strength, I don't think I would have made it, but my speed was just enough to meet her mid-swing. "You're getting faster, but you're still thinking too much," she said, sending me flying backward and towards the other three. Their barrage was unending, as swings, stabs, and arrows all flew in my direction. I parried what I couldn't dodge, and dodged what I couldn't hope to deflect. It was brutal, to say the least, as my use of second stage mana manipulation was being tested to its absolute limits, and I wasn't sure how much longer I could keep up.

Three of them are fourth stages, and my mom is a fifth stage mana manipulator. Granted, they're not going all out, but holy fuck *I need a breather,* I thought, parrying another stab from Vyra's spear.

Derion spotted an opening and caught the back of my leg with the back of his blade, not wanting to sever any tendons and ligaments I had, causing me to flip. Sensing the disturbed mana from Haldir's arrow, I instinctively pulled my blade up and placed the flat of it to my nape, blocking the arrow. As I spotted the ground to time my landing, I could just barely make out my mother's blurred figure drawing near.

This is about to hurt, isn't it? I thought in half a heartbeat, feeling my mother's hand grasping the base of my neck to continue my rotation. *Yep. Get good, fucker,* I heard her say in my mind.

I slammed into the ground, forming a large shockwave and dust cloud around me, forcing her teammates to shield their faces from the dirt being spewed like a volcanic eruption. I could feel the air leaving my body, and I struggled to maintain consciousness. Through the dust cloud, I could just make out my mother's figure towering over me, her glowing eyes piercing through the dust with a wide, toothy grin on her face.

"You could ease up a little when slamming the back of my head into the ground, though," I wheezed, reaching for the extended hand promptly appearing in front of my face. "Sorry, not *sorry*," my mother chuckled as she pulled me to my feet.

"Anwill thinks honing the fundamentals is what will make you grow, and to some extent, he *is* right. However, I've found that we learn at different paces," Vyra crossed her arms as she watched me dust myself off. "Apparently I'm not *that* quick to learn, as I keep getting my ass slammed into the ground," I chuckled, rubbing the top of my shoulder and rotating it to make sure it hadn't come out of place.

That's gonna leave a bruise, I thought.

"Well, from what Anwill has told me about your training with Master Pyle, I'd say we're similar in the ways that we learn," my mother said cheerfully. She hadn't even broken a sweat in our twenty-minute-long head-to-head battle.

"Maybe, but there's no way even with my decent proficiency at using the second stage could I hope to keep up with you," I retorted. "We'll see about that tomorrow," she said, patting me on the back. Anwill and Ysevel, who had been watching our duel, smiled as we walked over to them. "You've gotten stronger, Thoma," Anwill said, giving me a slow nod. "I'd hope so after having the shit kicked out of me the past few months," I chuckled, rubbing the back of my neck.

"He's right, you know. When you first arrived, I was worried *some-one* might break you if they squeezed you too much when giving you a hug," she said, tilting her head not-so subtly in my mother's direction. There was a slight chuckle that rippled through the group, and even I caught myself joining in.

"Well, it's not like I've really noticed much progress," I began. "How so?" Ysevel asked. "Well, I've been in armor all day, everyday for the past few months. By the time I bathe and get to bed, I'm so exhausted that I don't even have *time* to notice anything," I said plaintively.

"*Ah*, but you *have* grown, in more ways than one. You've matured a lot, both in and out of combat. I'm sure your mother and brother are just as proud, if not more so, than I am of you as well," Anwill chimed in. "You've also gotten a little more meat on those bones," my mother said, squeezing and poking my arm like a curious tod-dler. "*Oh*, and your hair has grown out nicely," Ysevel said, blushing slightly.

I'd be lying if I said I didn't appreciate the comment.

"Th-thank you. All of you," I managed to eek out, feeling my cheeks flushed with color as I turned my head, scratching my cheek. Unfortunately for me, I'd turned my head in the direction of my mother, who was lifting both of her eyebrows in rapid succession.

Mom, you know I couldn't even if I wanted to. Meliss is still waiting for me back in Codrean, I sent to her mentally. *I know, but I can secretly hope for a few elven grandchildren, can't I? What's the matter with that?* She asked, her tone riddled with expectant sarcasm. I chuckled mentally, and decided it was probably best to not answer that question.

"In any case, tomorrow's the big day. You should probably meditate with Ysevel again to make sure that you're prepared for tomorrow, because you'll be training with me," Anwill said, to which my mother nodded excitedly.

Subtle, I thought, watching that same, shit-eating grin Bernar normally had on his face growing on hers.

"I'd be more than happy to help you again, Thoma. If it helps you break into the third stage tomorrow, I'll stay as long as you need me to," she said, a small amount of her mother's regality leaking through her tone. "I'd appreciate the help," I replied with a warm smile. While I couldn't see them, I swore I felt Vyra and Haldir give each other knowing looks, while Derion's mind drifted elsewhere.

"Well, I'd better go clean up. It's been a long day already, and I'm sure that with the meditation session it will be even longer. I'd better get a head start before dinner, you know," I said, trying to bleed the conversation gently as I stretched my arm over my head. "Of course, dear. We'll see you at dinner, then?" my mother asked. "Your *growing boy* needs to eat, right?" I said sarcastically, which earned me another punch to the shoulder.

Within the hour, I was bathed, and standing in front of the polished silver mirror. For the first time in months, I actually noticed how much I had grown. My muscles were much larger than before, and incredibly defined. While I had noticed my diet consisted mostly of meats, greens, and sweet potatoes here, I'd never thought that it would help me grow as much as it did. I also may or may not have flexed once or twice in the mirror for good measure.

That seal must have also been doing a number on me. I wonder what Meliss will think when I get to see her again. I haven't told her about the changes I've gone through in any of the letters I've sent, but gods, I'm excited! I thought, feeling the butterflies in my stomach doing somersaults.

I got dressed in another green and silver tunic. At this point, I'd already gotten used to how their clothes worked, working the folds into each other and making sure nothing was loose. I had to learn quickly to avoid another similar situation to that of my first encounter with Ysevel. It always brought an awkward smile to my face to think about how the princess of Caegwen wrapped her arms around me to unfuck my training gear within the first minute of meeting me.

I shrugged off the thought, as I slipped my feet into the closed-toe shoes that color matched the rest of my outfit, and combed my hair over to where most of it was to one side, leaving a nice, straight part down the middle-left side of my head. I stepped out of the room, and began making my way to the meditation room, where Ysevel and I often met.

After what was about a fifteen minute walk, down the palace corridors and far away from any overly active areas, I made it to the meditation chamber. I pulled the latch on the door, and swung open the masterfully carved oaken door. Inside the room were two flat pillows and a mana crystal situated in the center of a large, runic ring. There were similar mana crystals along the walls placed inside glass housings that glowed a pale blue when infused with mana.

As far as I could tell, that was their only purpose. Beneath these glowing crystals were bookshelves about twice my height that lined the circular room, wrapping from one side of the door to the other.

"*Oh*, you beat me to it," Ysevel's voice came from behind me. She was wearing a similar tunic to mine, though she also wore fur draped along the width of her shoulders. "I've only just opened the door," I replied. "Well, I'm sure you've learned, during your cultural lessons with Anwill, that you're supposed to hold the door open for a lady," she said playfully.

"He did teach me that, though I can't say my mother had anything to do with *that* portion of my lessons," I said, returning the playful tone. She chuckled at that, knowing *exactly* what I meant.

Over the months that I'd been in Caegwen, she was always very much the *swing first or be swung upon* kind of person, though I never understood *where* she got those kinds of comments from.

"Well, far be it from me to teach *her* anything. When you've lived over two hundred years like I have, you quickly realize that no matter how hard you try, there are some people who will simply never change. I've known your mother since I was born, and she's never once faltered in her attitude," she said with a chuckle, taking off her fur and setting it on the ground beside her pillow.

She sat cross-legged in front of me, and I mirrored her position so that our hands and arms formed another circle around the mana crystal. We'd been doing this almost daily since the first week of my arrival. The temporary mental connection we had allowed us to not have to speak when doing this.

Apparently, as I found out through our mental connection, Ysevel was a lot like her mother in the realm of mana manipulation. I knew she was a fourth stage, though she never told me *what* her specialty was or why she'd never tried to break into the fifth.

Keeping it secret as usual, I see, I thought, feeling her warm, soft fingers gently wrapped around my palms.

"Shall we begin?" she said, already closing her violet eyes slowly, as she had so many times before. "Lead the way," I said, immediately feeling her mana pulsate through my body. The meditation we performed was simple in premise, but difficult to execute. It involved pulsing mana through each other's bodies until we achieved an equilibrium.

Once that was established, she would have me perform some exercises on the crystal in front of me; making me manipulate the mana inside the crystal and mold the crystal itself into whatever I wanted without breaking the equilibrium.

In the event that the equilibrium was broken, she would guide my mana back into balance, helping me to remember the sensation of being one with the internal mana-reinforcement of my body from the second stage, as well as external and environmental mana all at the same time.

Up until this point, however, I'd never been able to mold the crystal into anything even remotely recognizable. I tried to do something simple, like a rock or a cool stick I once found in the training area, but it always came out *wrong*, as if there were something I was missing.

You're doing it again, she sent through our connection, her mild frustration at my inattentiveness seeping through. *Sorry, I'll try to focus a bit more,* I replied, mentally chastising myself.

I focused on the rock again, this time *really looking into the mana that flowed into and around it. Mine and Ysevel's connected arms helped re-channel the mana towards the crystal, in the event that any more leakage than what came from my eyes was present.*

I remembered the first time I'd actually seen and felt mana that I hadn't drawn myself. It was a beautiful display of power that the Master had shown us during a training session. Memories of my time with Pyle up in Fangsdalr also resurfaced, seeing the ambient mana for the first time, even though it was a little blurry back then.

Since then, however, I continually honed my second stage to the utmost.

Why don't we try something simple today. How about a simple geometric shape? She asked. *You mean like a cube? I've done plenty of cubes and spheres, those aren't a problem,* I began, my frustration also evident in my voice. *True, but you've never tried* combining *them before, have you?* She prodded, knowing the answer already. *I'll give it a try,* I replied as I began to push mana into the crystal once more.

The first thing I made was a cube, to which the crystal responded easily enough. Then, *splitting my consciousness even further than it already was,* I produced a cone. Try as I might, I couldn't quite find a way to combine the two, regardless of how many different ways I spun the pair of objects.

It's not working, I sent over along with a bit more of my self-deprecating thoughts than I would have liked. *It's fine, but you sure picked some odd shapes to combine. Why don't you try a sphere and a cube? See if you can find a way to make those fit together a little better,* she said, guiding my mana from the cone back into the crystal.

I *pulled more mana* and pushed it back into the crystal and pulled out a sphere and brought it over to the cube. As I began to try to fit the two together, I noticed that they were extremely different, but there *had* to be something I could do with them.

Why would you suggest it otherwise, I thought, knowing she would hear my undertone.

As I meshed the two together, sinking the sphere into the cube, then expanding it repeatedly, or folding one into the other, I came out with a number of odd looking shapes. Most were uneven and strange, but there was one that stood out to me. A cube with perfectly rounded faces that were bulging outward as the edges and vertices of the cube sliced into the sphere.

Curiously, I pulled it apart, and tried to replicate what I had done, only this time, I felt a small pulse of mana respond to my command as the cube and sphere took their final shapes. I stared at it for a moment, and then realized what the exercise was about.

It has nothing to do with whether they fit together perfectly, it's about taking the two different pieces and creating something new. Like a bladesmith forge welding two different pieces of steel together to create a sword with a soft spine and a hard edge, I thought as I transmitted my findings to her. While our eyes had been closed the whole time, I could *feel* her smiling and nodding her head in agreement.

Good, now try other combinations, only this time, compound your new knowledge with other *shapes and forms,* she said. I could sense a feeling of pride emanating from her, but I refused to acknowledge it in case my concentration failed.

Slowly but surely, I crafted new shapes with the crystalline material between us. Eventually, I came to the realization that almost everything I had tried before had failed because I didn't understand the fundamentals of form. Basic shapes, like cubes, spheres, and cones made up most of the objects I knew, it was just a matter of figuring out which ones formed what objects.

Then how was I able to mold mana into my Whip of Doom? *I* asked, trying to figure it out. *Probably because you'd seen that form so many times when drawing from the Ethereal,* she answered readily and in an amused tone. *It was already familiar to you, and so it was much more easily crafted than what you're doing now,* she continued her explanation which made perfect sense to me.

I continued the exercise for a few more iterations and only stopped when I heard both of our stomachs growling. "*Oops,* we've been here way too long," I said, finally noticing just how hungry the exercise had made me. "It's a good thing dinner should be soon, if it hasn't started already," she retorted. "I'm fucking *starving*," she said. I sat there, frozen in time and space with my mouth agape. "D-did you just swear?" I asked, one foot in disbelief, the other in astonishment.

"I've spent a *lot* of time with you, Siraye, *and* Bernar. You really thought I wasn't going to pick up on your habits? *Pfffft,* please," she scoffed, blowing a raspberry with her mouth. I chuckled, but raised my hands placatingly. "Alright, alright! I didn't know you had it in you, is all. Only took you all of these months to open up like that," I said in response.

"In truth, it only took me about forty-five seconds to be comfortable enough with you to correct your armor that first day, remember?" she said, her tone both playful and...*demeaning*? I didn't know and I *definitely* couldn't tell what was going through her mind.

Except, obviously, making me the ass-end of her jokes.

"Y-yeah. I remember that," I said, scratching my cheek as I looked away. She giggled, covering her hand with her mouth, opening the door leading outside the meditation room. "Come along, Thoma.

We should get some food and good rest tonight. Tomorrow's a big day for you," she said, offering her hand to lead me out.

"I thought holding doors open and offering hands was for me to do for you, at least that's according to what Anwill taught me, anyway," I said, lifting an eyebrow and taking her hand. "*Meh*, a little role reversal here or there never hurt anyone, right? It costs nothing to be kind, after all," she said with a smile that could have melted a glacier. "No, I suppose it doesn't," I said, feeling the smile tugging on my own face.

We made our way to the banquet hall, and laid out before us was a lovely meal of roast boar, salads and other root-like plants that had been cooked until it was a perfect, golden brown. Sitting in their usual seats, Elhael, Aurae, Bernar and my mother were already seated at the table waiting for us.

"Glad you could find the time to join us for dinner, *Thoma*," Elhael said, noting that I, once again, had taken Ysevel's hand. "I suspect you weren't lost on your way here, so I don't see why your ha -..." he stopped and grunted, gritting his teeth as Aurae's thin-lipped smile cut through the sudden silence like a knife.

I was just glad he hadn't caught my mother and brother snickering like children as they stifled their laughs.

"I apologize for both our tardiness and any disrespect toward you and the queen, your majesty. Ysevel and I made a breakthrough in the meditation chamber today," I said with a bow. As soon as the words left my mouth, I realized I'd made some kind of mistake because my brother and mother stifled yet *another* laugh as Elhael grunted once more.

Was it something I said? I sent my brother and mother the question. *Not so much what you said, just the situation of it all. You two, alone in a chamber... making a* breakthrough *or two. You know, normal shit,* Bernar said, that shit-eating grin plastered on his face again.

Ah, yeah. That does *sound pretty bad, doesn't it?* I asked with mild dejection.

Does this mean I get grandchildren now? My mother asked, also wearing a shit-eating grin. *Fuck you both, I'm trying to focus,* I said through a mental chuckle. "Hey," my mother said, eyeing me dangerously. Her tone was light on the surface, but I could tell there was a seriousness to her words. The king, queen, and consequently, Ysevel all raised an eyebrow at her. "Sorry, we were just having a family discussion," Siraye said, rubbing her nape.

Aurae cleared her throat, taking the reins of the conversation. "So, Thoma, tell us of this *breakthrough*. I hope it has prepared you for tomorrow?" she asked, her regal voice reverberating like warmed butter. I proceeded to explain what I'd learned, and after seeing the confused looks on everyone's faces except for Aurae's, I started to learn a little bit about hers and Ysevel's potential abilities.

My mother, however, looked a little concerned.

"Shit, I never learned to do *that*. Why didn't you just fuse them together where the faces of the objects met like I did?" Bernar asked, his mouth full of food. "Funny thing is: I tried, but the way I did it ended up making more sense to me than merely fusing them together like you explained," I said, shrugging my shoulders after taking another bite of my boar meat.

After we finished dinner, Ysevel followed her parents up toward where the royal bedrooms were, as I followed my mother's signal out into the palace garden. Robust bushes, covered with flowers of all sorts of vibrant reds, yellows, and blues were strewn about the well-maintained area. Along the moonlit pathway, there were grapevines that hung over the path on their respective frames, their leaves turning orange as the weather began to cool.

"You know, I'd always hoped I'd get the chance to spend a lot of time with you. Watch you grow into a fine, young man. It's all a mother could want, really," she began, kicking a twig off the pathway. "I'm sorry, Thoma. I really am," she said after a few moments' pause I'd given her. "For what, mom? You've done nothing wrong," I said, putting an arm around her shoulder.

"Not like that, Thoma. I mean for disappearing without a trace. Not just for a year or two, but for most of your life. I was so caught up in my quest to restore our family's heritage with the artifacts that I ended up losing track of time," she said, her tone dropping a little near the end. "Mom, it's okay. I'm okay. Bernar, well, he might be a few marbles short of a full bag, but he's okay. We understand *why* you did what you did, so please, don't beat yourself up over it, okay?" I said, trying to be as understanding as I could.

"Thank you, son. It's... It's good to hear that from you," she said, a thoughtful smile grew on her face. Seemingly out of nowhere, she let out a chortle. "I know I told you that the artifacts don't really work without a fully-trained team, but I actually am the sole owner of the *Dreambinder Jerkin*," she said in a hushed voice.

My eyes struggled to stay in their sockets.

"Y-you have it? What the fuck? Why didn't you tell me?" I rapidly shot the questions. "*Shhh,* quiet down," she hushed. "I didn't tell you because I wanted to see if you were going to figure it out. Well, that and because I feel like we were being watched the whole time we were out there training," she said, putting a finger to her chin as she looked upward.

"Never really could find the right time to tell you that, because if anyone outside of Myrdin found out I had that, let alone that we have Pelantyr heritage, it'd be an absolute *nightmare*," she said, her tone growing a little more serious now. "I... I can't believe it," I stammered, struggling to keep my hundreds of questions at bay.

"Is that how you're able to move the way you do?" I asked after picking the one I wanted to know the most. "*Pffft*, no. That's all me," she scoffed. I whistled critically in response. "Well, Ardrin is still alive and in hiding somewhere," I said, letting the words hang. "I suppose it's only a matter of time before he figures out *I'm* still alive. We need to be ready for when he does," she said, sighing lightly.

"I can't wait to reach the fifth stage, mom. I want to know what it's like to be on-par with you and everyone else in our family. Well, except dad. *Fuck* that guy," I spat. "I *did*, but it gave me you and your brother, so I guess it wasn't a total waste. And to think I *almost* swallowed you," she chuckled, tousling my hair. "Un-fucking-called for," I said my thought aloud, disgust evidently showing on my face as I held back dinner.

We walked for a few more minutes and eventually found a marble bench to sit down on. She asked me a lot of questions about my time in Codrean after she'd left. She was visibly angered to see how much I'd suffered unwittingly, but ultimately decided it had made me a better person in the long run. I'd also told her how Bernar had been more like a father figure to me, to which she was more surprised than anything else.

"I know it's getting a little late, but why was everyone surprised when I told them about the cube and the sphere from the meditation chamber," I finally asked, filling the short lull in the conversation. My mother bit the knuckle on her index finger, obviously deciding whether to tell me the reason behind their surprise.

"Autarchica Primaria," she said after a long pause. The two words could not have been more foreign to me. "*Autarchica Primaria*? That doesn't sound elven at all," I said, trying to figure out whether I even recognized the language it was in. "It *is* elven," she said, hushedly. "And strictly so, but it's ancient. Far older than the country of Caegwen itself, and *well* before its language was developed into what we know it as today," she continued.

"What does it mean, though? I'm lost as fuck," I said, feeling my face scrunch in confusion. "That's just it; no one really knows," she began. "It has only ever appeared twice in any elven lineage. The first time was during the creation of the Caegwen, the second being in you. No one knows the full extent of its power, or what that power *really* is, but it's said in some of the ancient texts that it's a part of something bigger. *Much* bigger than any of us," she explained, furrowing her brow in the process.

"And I just so happen to have this obscure and rare power? Sounds awfully convenient," I said, raising an eyebrow. My mother looked at me with eyes that could have pierced through dragon scales. "Son, I don't know how else to explain it to you, but this is serious. No one currently living knows what that power can actually do. The only reference we have to it is the written legend of the creation of Caegwen, and even *that* can't fully be trusted," she said, her tone carrying the weight of her words.

"What the hell do I do with it, then?" I asked, spreading my arms. She turned away from me, and glanced up at the silver streaks of moonlight cutting through the treetops. "Hone it. Push it to its limit. If you've already discovered it while only being able to manage the second stage, I don't see it taking you too long before you catch up to your brother and I," she said encouragingly. "Honestly, with the Autarchica Primaria, you're more likely to surpass us," she scoffed.

I took in her words, considering them carefully. I didn't know what the extent of this power was, nor how to fully utilize it, but I knew from the gravity of her tone that it was *vital.* Vital enough to the point where, outside of those who already knew, I would have to keep it a secret.

"Well, it's getting late," she said with a sigh as she stood back up. "You've got a big day tomorrow, and I can't *wait* to see you crush it," she said, her warm, motherly smile shining brightly on her face. "Thanks mom. I'll do my best," I said, returning the smile. Just as I did so, I heard Ysevel's voice calling out my name from the entrance of the garden.

I wonder what she wants, I sent to my mother. *Maybe now I'll get grandchildren?* She replied in jest. I chuckled and shook my head. *No, mom, she's holding something like a letter. Oh! It might be from Meliss,* I thought excitedly.

My mother's face contorted into that of pure, unadulterated, and clearly visible disappointment.

"I'll be right there!" I called out before giving my mom a kiss on the cheek. "Love you, mom. I'll see you tomorrow!" I said, waving curtly as I set off at a jog. As I did, her disappointed face turned into a mixture of both shock and joy.

"What is it? Who's it from?" I asked, slowing down enough to not accidentally trample my impromptu messenger. "It's from Meliss," she said, handing me the letter. "It's been what, about *a month* since you last heard from her?" she asked. "Y-yeah, something like that. Sometimes the ravenry isn't available, so it can take a little while," I replied, noticing her usual signature was written a little shakier than normal.

That's odd. Her signature is normally so elegant when she writes. Eh, she was probably in a hurry, I thought indifferently.

"Well, what are you waiting for? Go on! Read it," she said encouragingly. Breaking the seal and unfolding the parchment with an excited smile on my face, I turned half-way away from her and leaned forward into the light from the long hallway behind her. As my eyes scanned the page, I felt a cold, icy claw gripping my stomach. My heart began to pound fiercely, as dinner threatened to present itself once more to the outside world.

"Thoma, are you alright? You're as pale as a cloud. What happened?" she asked. I couldn't pay attention to anything else she said after that, as my hands began to tremble, and my knees grew weaker by the second. Everything around me turned into a blur, as tears welled in my eyes halfway through the letter.

"Hey, what's going on?" she asked again, her tone soft and breathy as she placed a hand on my shoulder. I lifted my head, and stared down the hallway. My eyes, now leaking both tears and mana from the second stage, pulsed. "I have to go," I managed to croak, not wanting her to see me in the state I somehow knew I was about to be in.

I pushed an ample amount of mana into my legs, and bolted off as quickly as I could, creating a small crater in the ground where my feet were. "Thoma!" I heard her call out by the time I was at the end of the hallway. I turned down the path to the right, and I was gone like a lightning bolt in a storm, as I knew I would only have a few moments before whatever composure I had left failed.

I made it to my room just in time to puke out my dinner into the mana-controlled sink. The gut wrenching feeling of what was said in the letter came in waves, and those waves forced me to buckle and fold onto the ground into a ball in the corner of the bathroom, using my hands to pull my knees tightly to my chest and sobbing uncontrollably as tears streamed down my cheeks.

I could feel my breathing hiccup and stutter from time to time. There were a few moments, even, where I had to swallow a large amount of stringy, gummy saliva, otherwise I might have choked on it. My stomach cramped without anything left inside it to heave up and out as I buried my head into my forearms and screamed silently; feeling the blood rush to my face and eyes as they became increasingly more bloodshot.

Dealing with death, I found, was much easier than dealing with whatever *this* was. Death, to me, was a much simpler thing in the fact that once it occurred, it was an *immutable fact*. The irreversible action of passing on from this mortal plane to the next was something we *all* had to go through at some point, making it easier to understand.

This, however, wasn't *quite* that. It was the pain of loss, but not a loss that couldn't have, somehow, been prevented. Whether that prevention could've been through my own doing or some extraneous circumstance, I didn't know.

I searched and searched through my mind, reviewing all of the letters I'd sent and everything she and I had talked about over the course of our time together. Nothing I had seen, heard, or read had ever given me any indication that this absolute kick to the dick was coming. There was no sign of it. Nothing. I clenched the letter tightly in my fist, crumpling the midsection, as I allowed myself another silent scream.

With the few moments of clarity that I *did* have, I forced myself to get the taste of vomit out of my mouth using the charcoal and mineral paste the Caegweni's used as a cleansing toothpaste. After rinsing my mouth out, I sat down against the wall of the bathroom again, the emotions flooding back to me as soon as I did. Time around me seemed to come to a halt, as my thoughts began to rush once more. A few moments later, I thought I'd heard a soft knock on the door.

I can't answer that. Not in this state, I thought, burrowing my head deeper into my knees.

"Thoma, are you there?" Ysevel's voice came from the other side, muffled ever so slightly by both the door and the copious amount of blood in my head. "Please, son, open the door. You left in such a rush, and with that look on Ysevel's face, I was worried something horrible had happened," my mother's voice chimed in, concern evident in her tone.

I can't, mom. I just... can't, I sent.

The emotional distress I was feeling must have carried through, because as soon as the last word was transmitted, my door was blasted wide open with an Exar spell powerful enough to turn the solid, oaken door to little more than chunky dust. "Alright, who do I have to *kill*?" she asked, her tone seething with both anger and concern as she stormed into the room like a bear protecting her cubs.

I didn't bother to look up. Gods above, I *couldn't* look up. I couldn't let her see my face.

"Is *this* the cause of the state you're in? Let me see that," she said, forcefully grabbing the letter from my hand. I could hear her uncrumpling and reading through it, as I could also hear Ysevel's steps moving in closely behind my mother. At this point, there was nothing more I could do except hold back more tears and sobs, as the snippets of the letter were read aloud.

"*Dear Thoma... can't burden you with my past... this was out of convenience... need to laugh wholeheartedly... explore life... without you... move on... I'm sorry,*" my mother finished reading and handed it off to Ysevel so she could read it, too.

"*Oh*, what the *fuck*? That's absolute *bullshit* and was *beyond* fucked up of her to do. And for *what*? The fuck was even the *point* of that? She could've just said she wanted to *slog down* someone else's prick and be done with it. Gods above and below, I could've easily mistaken that letter for some kind of *anal suppository* with how much *bullshit* was in it! Her genetics ruined a perfectly good *asshole* when she began to grow *teeth* in her mouth," my mother raged in complete and utter disregard for my emotional state.

As bad as I felt at that moment, I didn't think anything could've prepared me for that last sentence.

My mother huffed and moved over to squat down in front of me, placing her hands on my forearms. "I'm sorry, son. I really am," she said in a polar opposite tone than what she had just used. "I've also been through my fair share of heartbreaks, having lived as long as I have, and I understand what you're going through," she said, gently rubbing her thumb across my forearm.

She must have noticed my shuddering, because she pulled me in close, burying my face in her shoulder and stroking the back of my hair momentarily as she hushed me. I broke down even further, feeling the full weight of my emotions flooding out of me. After a few minutes of allowing me to sob uncontrollably, she slowly pushed me back, and cupped my face in her calloused hands, using her thumbs to wipe away the tears streaming down my swollen face.

"It's alright. These things happen, okay? Just because something is *over*, doesn't mean that it's the *end*," she said comfortingly. "It sure as fuck feels like it, though," I croaked before sniffling again, and using the back of my wrist to wipe my nose.

"Yes, yes it does. But it's *not*, and *that's* what is important right now, okay? What *is* important, however, is that you learn to pick yourself back up, dust yourself off, and take a step forward; no matter how small. Got it?" she said, her golden eyes gazing into my bloodshot ones as she looked for my response.

I could only nod my head curtly, trying my best to heed her words. "Good. I'm glad you understand that," she gave me a thin lipped smile. "Try to get some decent rest tonight, okay?" she said as she stood back up, placing her hand on Ysevel's shoulder as she left. I leaned my head on the wall behind me, feeling the tears rushing from my eyes to the tops of my ears as I felt the sobs returning.

Seemingly out of nowhere, and without having made a sound, I felt something brush up against my shoulder. I looked over to find

Ysevel sitting next to me, her eyes staring straight toward the wall opposite us.

"You don't have to be here, you know," I said weakly. "I know, but I'm going to be," she replied, nudging my shoulder with her own. "Was it something I did? Could I have done anything differently? Is... is this *my* fault?" I asked, feeling the strain on my voice.

I didn't receive a reply; not a grunt, not a nod, not a word. Instead, I felt her hand reach to the furthest side of my head, and gently pull downward, placing my head on the shoulder that had just nudged me. We sat in silence, but for how long, I didn't know. There were no words that needed to be said, no emotions or other physical contact was shared. We simply sat there, in silence, together.

At some point, I must have fallen asleep, because I woke up and felt an unusual weight on my head. I struggled to peel my eyes open, as the dried tears had forced my eyelids to stick together. I saw a lock of silver hair out of the corner of my eye and noticed the soft sound of someone breathing. I made the association quickly, and the resulting answer forced my heart to skip a single beat.

How long have we been like this? My ass is numb, and I think that's the sun coming up, I thought as I looked out of the window above my bed.

Ysevel must have felt my movement because she shuffled ever so slightly, and, luckily, lifted her head from mine. I stood up, shaking some of the blood back into my legs, and looked at the sleeping figure. Her face was far more peaceful than it should have been for someone to be sleeping in a seated position, so I decided to pick her up and move her to my bed.

She's surprisingly light, I thought as I picked her up, feeling her head roll and lean into my shoulder.

I gently placed her on my bed, and pulled the covers up to the base of her neck. Thankfully, the naturally formed door had already grown back, so it wasn't as cold in my room as it would have been had it not. She shuffled again, pulling the blanket up a little higher as her lips smacked together as a peaceful grin grew on her face. I looked down at her, allowing myself a weak smile to see someone so blissfully unaware of her surroundings, and then proceeded to get ready for the trial ahead.

I did what I could to clear my head before making it to the training area, but that emotional wound was still *far* too fresh for me to suppress it entirely as the sickly feeling from the night before threatened to leer its ugly head. As the sun began to peek through the trees, I saw my mother and Bernar having a conversation with Anwill and Aurae. Vyra, Derion, and Haldir were also present, but I couldn't make out what any of them were saying.

I have to focus on this. Get your head out of your ass, I thought , giving myself a slap on both my cheeks.

Everyone, aside from my mother, looked at me curiously. "There's the shit-head," Bernar said sardonically. "Sorry I'm late," I said, rubbing the back of my neck as a weak smile awkwardly showed itself. "It's alright, son," my mother said, wrapping her arm around my shoulders. "Are you rested enough, Thoma? Your eyes look a little puffy," Aurae asked, concern evident in her tone.

"No, but I'll be alright, your majesty. I'm quite used to doing stuff sleep deprived," I replied with a bow, trying to keep my tone from betraying my *actual* state.

"Are you sure you want to do this today? We can always push it to tomorrow, if you want," Anwill said, having *obviously* seen through whatever it was I was trying to do. "Yeah, I'm fine," I said, giving him a weak smile.

Fucked-up, insecure, needy, and emotional? my brother asked, knowing exactly what my version of *fine* meant. *I'll tell you later. I just want to focus on the test right now,* I retorted, my tone carrying much more emotion than I wanted it to.

"Very well, then. Let us begin the trial," Anwill said, stepping aside. My mother and Aurae gave me reassuring nods, while Vyra and the others gave me thumbs up in support. My brother, on the other hand, slapped my back, nearly sending me tumbling forward. "You've come a long way already, you *little shit*. Time to go *beyond* that," he said with a wry grin. I allowed myself a small, genuine smile as I recalled the horse-casting test we did when he gave me Celer for my birthday.

It's been almost a year since then, but so much has happened, it feels like ten, I thought, stepping into the training ring.

Around the packed dirt area, multiple semi-translucent training dummies began to float around the arena, pushing out to various ranges. There were also a few troughs filled with three of the four basic elements. I closed my eyes, taking in a deep breath through my nose, and out through my mouth, as I did my best to calm my nerves.

"Thoma, as you well know, the third stage of mana manipulation involves the direct control over environmental elemental mana being supplemented by your own. To help guide you through this trial, you must maintain your second stage and control your emotions as you reach for the mana," he began.

"I know you can already cast some basic elemental spells, but this takes it to an entirely different level of mastery. This trial will consist of how well you can manage the elemental mana, by using it to shape projectiles and strike down the training dummies with enough force to turn them red," he continued. I nodded my acknowledgement, and loosened my shoulders as I activated my second stage. "Begin," he commanded.

Until this point in time, I had only ever commanded a little bit of elemental mana as we were trained to do so in the first stage. While most had a specific element they felt more comfortable with using when reaching the third stage, I'd dabbled in all sorts of spells, giving me a blanket understanding of all of them, though it was at the sacrifice of my control.

However, now that I could use the second stage as easily as the first, my conscious effort was now focused on pulling the tendrils of elemental mana from the troughs and molding them like I would a Kyr spell; the same one I'd used during my horse-caster certification. However, instead of *only* drawing from the Ethereal, I had to pull from there *and* whatever element's mana I wanted to use in the Between.

I began to use the mana I'd pulled and infused into my body from the Ethereal to call out to the fire mana in the trough before me. *Reaching through both the Ethereal and the Between, I tugged at the violent and sporadic movements of the flame's mana, feeling it race towards my hand,* and seeing it coalesce into a sphere not much bigger than my fist.

As I stared at the sphere floating just above the ring I still wore to cast normal spells, *I could see the mana from both realms at the same time, reminding me vaguely of the cube and the sphere. Curiously, I tried to mold the spell into something a little more aerodynamic in hopes that it would reach the target faster.*

Using what I had learned with Ysevel, I formed a cone-like structure with the fire's elemental mana, and began to swirl it in front of me. I built up as much power as I could, *pushing and compressing a vast amount of mana behind it* , and sent it flying with a swing of my arm. It took every ounce of concentration I had, but it worked well. Almost *too* well, I noticed, because the flame shot out like a spear being thrust through water, puncturing the target about fifty meters away from me.

I think I'll call that one Flamebolt, I thought in the split second of my halted concentration.

Before I began gathering mana for the next spell, I could've sworn I heard someone's jaw hit the floor, but I refused to break my concentration to look back. Moving onto the next training dummy, I shot another *Flamebolt* with similar effects. Ten dummies later, and Anwill signaled for me to move on to the next trough; the one filled with water.

I extended my hand once more, *feeling the water mana swirl, flow, and ebb gently towards my hand. It felt* easier *to manipulate the water mana, as it reminded me a lot more of regular mana than the flame's did.*

I probably should've started with the water. Maybe that's why someone gasped behind me, I thought.

I molded the water into a highly compressed sphere, and sent it soaring through the air, turning the target's color into a vibrant red. I repeated this process two or three more times, but noticed that water didn't really like being sent flying like that. Instead, I decided to use what I'd learned with my *Whip of Doom* technique, and put it into practice. While it wasn't nearly as effective as my *Flamebolt* or even a Kyr spell, it still landed me the remaining targets designated for the water trial.

Air mana worked much the same way, as I wanted to save the earth mana for last, though it was a little bit harder to gather since it wasn't as dense as water mana. Still, I had to figure out how to *make air fly* in the direction and shape I wanted it to. After a little bit of trial and error, I found out that if I manipulated the air mana around an imaginary shape, it would respond much more easily than if I had tried to condense it directly.

There's a lot of potential stuff I could do with that, I thought briefly, already growing more accustomed to using it by the ninth dummy.

Finally came the earth mana. The light brown motes flicked and floated like the others, but *unlike* the others, they were *far* more densely packed together. *I reached between the Ethereal and Between once more, and felt the earthen mana's coarse embrace. Like reaching my hand into a barrel of sand and rocks, the mana felt sharp and a little difficult to focus with. It was stable and strong, sure, but it also had a unique property in that it actually* felt *like I was handling something* physical *rather than solely Ethereal mana.*

As I observed the way the earth mana moved, I'd noticed that in the barrel, there was a bit of dark moss along with it. For whatever reason, the phthalo-colored moss took on the shape of Meliss' eyes, glaring at me hatefully. My emotions began to spiral, as the memory of last night's turmoil began to play in my mind. Unfortunately, it wasn't enough to sever my concentration with the second stage, but the resulting lack of emotional control caused the dirt around me to respond accordingly.

Like my mother had done with the platforms during our training session, though not to the same level, my body was lifted a few meters into the air on a platform of solid earth, as vast amounts of dust and rocks kicked up around me in a torrent. "Thoma, control your emotions!" I could hear Anwill calling out, but it was no use.

Hey, fuck-nugget, you might want to calm down, my brother mentally transmitted, but I ignored it.

I was struggling too much emotionally, and I knew it. My control was decent, at best, but through the forceful pushing of my emotions, it began to grow far beyond what I'd imagined. I could feel the earth's mana responding to my emotions, swirling and spiraling into various small tornadoes, as the air's mana began to respond as well, followed closely behind by the water and fire's. Torrents of all four elements began swirling in front of and around me, growing larger and larger in size as I felt my emotional control slip away.

Son, you need to calm down! Please, you're losing control. Focus on the task at hand, my mother shouted in my mind. *I'm trying, but I... I need help. I feel so alone. Lost. Worthless,* I sent back, feeling the tears begin to stream down my face once more. *It's okay,* she began calmly, transmitting the warm, maternal smile through our mental connection.

We're right here. Bernar, me, your friends and training partners. We're all right here, Thoma. You're not alone; never were, and never will be. Your worth isn't determined by other people's treatment or opinions of you, it's how you feel about yourself and how you treat those around you. I know it doesn't feel like it, especially not with the clouds of sadness and loss looming overhead, or the pain you feel in your heart and core, she continued, her soothing voice flowing through my mind like warmed honey.

But, regardless of whatever you have believed until this point in time, know that you are worthy, you are loved, and most importantly, you are capable of overcoming any and all adversity. Regardless of your own perceived inabilities, or feelings of desperation and sadness, you must *push through,* she said, her voice becoming a little more firm as she began to sense a change in my mental state.

Be as strong as the earth, as malleable as the water, as transparent as the air, and as voracious as the flames. The world does not wait for you, nor is it kind to any and all who venture into it. It is cruel, callous, and dangerous, but instead of letting it control us, we can always control how we respond to it. Now, heed my words, hone your emotions, and focus. Call out to the elements and control them, she commanded in a soothing, yet forceful voice.

Her words struck me like a bucket of cold water on a winter's morning. Suddenly, I realized just how far I had let this drag on, deciding then and there that I would have to apologize once this was over. Feeling the four elements' mana surrounding me, I *reached through the Ethereal once more, grabbing every tendril I could and* lifted the swirling torrents up to where their bases were at the same height I was.

I held it for a few moments, but struggled to keep my focus like my mother had told me to do. There was something I was missing, and when I echoed her words in my mind one last time, I recalled her telling me to *call out* to the elements, almost like it were a test of my mental fortitude. I could feel them; the same feelings I'd felt during my fight with the pair of ochelons. They resurfaced, only this time, my will became words resounding in my head.

Hear me, heed me, and seethe with my rage. Bend to my will and become my blade. Make me sharp and keen of mind, sundering all, leave naught behind, I thought, tipping my head forward and glaring at my remaining targets from beneath a furrowed brow.

Tipping the swirling elemental tendrils upward, and using the same technique I'd used for my *Flamebolt,* I kept rotating and coalescing the multi-sourced mana around me. With my clenched jaw loosening and releasing a slow, guttural scream of a pure and unadulterated rage; leaning into the scorching feeling as heavily as I could while my eyes leaked copious amounts of mana.

I launched everything around me toward the remaining targets, obliterating not only them, but circular sections of the titanic trees behind them as well. The leaves from those trees fell loosely to the ground, as the blackened holes I left in the trees sizzled and smoked.

As the mana dissipated from my eyes, the earthen platform I stood upon began to descend back into its original position. I allowed myself a moment and took a deep breath, feeling the mana around me once more. Reminding myself of my mother's words, I tugged and pulled at each individual tendril of mana one last time like flexing a muscle I'd just found out I had. I could hear the crushing of rock, the flowing of wind and air, and the crackling of the flames in its trough.

I finally mustered the courage to turn around and look at those who had witnessed the whole thing. My mother was looking at me proudly, but the rest of them, my brother included, were standing there with their eyes wide open and mouths agape.

"I-I told you he was a *monster*," Anwill mouthed quietly to Aurae, who could only nod her head in shocked agreement. "Didn't think you were going to pull out of that one, little brother," Bernar said, crossing his arms and giving me a wry smile. "*Oh*, so *now* you doubt me?" I replied, raising an eyebrow as I wiped the remainder of a tear from my cheek. "That was... *incredible*, Thoma. I knew you were good with a sword but *that* was something else entirely," Vyra said, as Haldir and Derion nodded in agreement beside her.

"Welcome back," my mother said, wrapping me in a tight hug. I felt her squeeze her arms once, and then took a step back, holding me by my shoulders. "Who knew a breakup would be the catalyst for you to control not one, two or *three* elements simultaneously, but *four?* Not to mention at such a high intensity," she said sardonically. I allowed myself a short chuckle not because I had to, but because her words truly resonated with me, and I wanted to try to stick to that new perspective, even if it meant forcing a chuckle or two in that moment. "Thanks, mom. You saved my ass back there. I... I don't know what I would've done without you here," I said earnestly.

"Well, if I hadn't, I'm sure Aurae would've found a way to shut you down," she shrugged, stepping aside for the queen herself to approach me. "I think I speak for everyone here, including my husband, who's been in meetings since before you even woke up, that we're all very proud of you and your progress," Aurae stated with a warm smile. "Too bad my *daughter* wasn't here to see it," she said suggestively.

"Your daughter was instrumental in my success, your majesty. Without her instructions during our meditation sessions, I would never have been able to reach the third stage, let alone control them as I did," I said, giving her a low and respectful bow. "I see. Well, then, where *is* the instrument of your success?" she asked coyly. "Right here, and I *did* manage to catch the end of it, no thanks to him for not *waking me up*," Ysevel said from the entrance to the training area as she emphasized the last few words. Aurae and my mother's faces held the same expressions at varying levels of intensity, though one was far less subtle than the other, which I took in stride.

"W-well, you needed to rest," I said, scratching my cheek and looking away with a nervous smile on my face. "I can always nap during the day, and as frustrated as I am with you, I *do* have to admit that I'm *very* proud of you. Welcome to the third stage," she said with a wry smile. "Thanks for *everything*, Ysevel," I said warmly. "It's nothing, really," she said, averting her gaze from both of our mothers.

"So, are we just going to stand around here, or are we going to train? I've got a few things I would like to teach him," Vyra said, plunging the base of her spear into the packed earth. "Hey, I want in on it, too!" my brother added. "Just because he can cast a few fancy looking spells means his head is going to be a little bigger than it already is. Besides, it's kind of my *duty* as his older brother to kick his ass and make sure that doesn't happen," he said with a malicious smile.

I knew they were just trying to distract me from the previous night's events, so I just let it happen, heeding my mother's words once more. Still, it was a good feeling to know that I truly wasn't as alone as I thought.

"A four-on-one sparring session? How is *that* fair? I only *just* attained the third stage, and already you want to pit me against people who have been in the fourth and above for decades longer?" I asked, spreading my arms widely. "How about all five of you, including Anwill, against me?" my mother asked. "Nope, you'd kill us," we responded in unison as if we shared the same brain. My mother chuckled and raised her hands placatingly.

"Alright, alright. Just thought I would offer," she chuckled.

CHAPTER 44
A KNIFE IN THE DARK

As the sun was setting behind the distant hills that led towards Codrean, Leona strode through the royal gardens. Her long, white dress flowed gently behind her, catching the evening breeze as she walked. The last few rays of sunlight cast golden light on the dense clouds that coated the far-off Rhydian Mountains, making them glow like a dwarven mine.

"A beautiful evening, is it not?" she asked the two who accompanied her. Thorsen, and consequently Gwili, both accompanied her on her walk as her personal bodyguards. "Of course, your majesty. Though it may rain later this evening, as the incoming clouds from the Rhydian will be drawn this way as they follow the breeze," he noted. "For as educated as you are, Gwili, I occasionally find myself forgetting you were a bandit up there until a few, short months ago," she said, giving him a warm smile over her shoulder.

"Well, if you spend enough time anywhere, you learn to read the signs, your majesty. The Pass was always flooding, so my men and I used to position ourselves strategically on the rocks to avoid the dangerous flash floods," he said, shrugging his shoulders. "Have any of your men ever been caught out by those floods before?" Thorsen asked, genuinely curious.

"Once, yes," Gwili replied distantly. "But it wasn't entirely his fault. If anything, it was *mine*," he continued. "How could that be?" Leona asked, genuinely curious. "We had been tracking some merchants for about three days. We figured out the route they were going to take, and the time that they were going to take it," he began to explain. "So you were just waiting for them to come by?" Thorsen asked.

"Yes and no. We'd set a trap for what was supposed to be a small caravan, but was, in reality, a twenty-cart caravan; nearly doubling its originally projected size," Gwili continued. "By the Graces, that *is* a large one. I've only ever heard of them getting as large as twelve before," Leona chimed in. "So had we, your majesty. But, for whatever fucking reason, there was another, smaller caravan that asked to tag along to the original that we were already tracking," he said, his tone growing a little darker.

"That smaller caravan had sent two of their carts to the front, as they assisted the scouts in searching for potential dangers and ended up springing the trap too early. The rain began to pour on top of us, and I decided we could adapt it and make it look like these caravans were merely stuck, not disabled. As we tried to adapt the already sprung trap, with our numbers already being spread so thinly, we didn't have anyone on overwatch for rockslides. The rest, as they say, is history," Gwili concluded with another, much heavier shrug.

"I-I'm sorry, Gwili. Were you close to this person?" Leona asked. "He was my cousin. Younger by about fifty years. He was outcast along with me and the others after a misunderstanding back in Caegwen, your majesty," he replied solemnly. "*Oh*, I'm so sorry. I don't really know what it's like to lose a family member," Leona said, trying her best to sound empathetic.

"I do," Thorsen chimed in, putting a large hand on Gwili's shoulder. "I lost my wife during the attack on Grundsvollr. She died in my arms. I'm not saying it's the same as losing a blood relative, but I understand your pain, even if only a little," Thorsen said, not giving any further details. "Thanks, big guy. I'm sorry to hear about your wife, though," Gwili said, putting his hand on Thorsen's gauntlet.

"It's been over forty years since she passed on, so I've grown accustomed to it. I know she's in a better place, and I'm sure that I will see her again eventually," he said plaintively. "Have you never sought to remarry, or at least have another partner?" Gwili asked. "I have, but it's a little difficult to maintain that while in the position I'm in," Thorsen shrugged. "Well, I'm sure *Claire* would be lucky to have you," Leona said teasingly. Thorsen's face was as white as a marble pillar. "I-I... *uh*... I'm satisfied just doing my duty," Thorsen chuckled nervously, scratching his cheek. "Rude," Leona said, snorting thickly as she was stifling a laugh.

"I haven't heard anyone snort like that since I was last in Caegwen, your majesty," Gwili said with a light-hearted chuckle. "You know what? I take back my earlier comment of you being educated. You *clearly* don't understand when you're *not supposed to* identify a woman's flaws," she said, lifting her chin and huffing through her nostrils. "Do all elves treat people like this? I've always wanted to visit Caegwen, mostly because Truls never let me, but now, I'm not so sure," she teased.

"N-no, your majesty," Gwili raised his hands placatingly. "I was merely making an observation I thought would be humorous.

Please accept my humblest apology," he quickly replied with a bow. "Well, at least you're honest about it," she chuckled in response, knife-handing the top of his head gently.

I wonder how Bernar and Thoma are doing over there. It's been so long since they came through here that winter has nearly arrived. It would be nice to see them again, and see how much they've grown, she thought, smiling at the thought of Bernar's golden eyes.

A sharp, ice-cold breeze cut through the garden, as the three of them braced against the much colder air. "By the Graces, that wind is freezing," Leona said, crossing her arms against her body and hunching over to stay warm. Without wasting a second, Thorsen pulled off his bright red cape, and threw it around her, patting her lightly on the shoulders to make sure it was snugly secured.

"Th-thank you, Thorsen. Won't you be cold, though?" she asked, already feeling the warming effects of the cape. "I grew up with much harsher winters in Hjalfar. I'll be fine, your majesty," he said with a big, toothy smile across his bearded face. "However, I realize that you were not raised in such conditions, so it's probably best we go back inside," he suggested. "Y-yes, you're quite right," she said, immediately turning toward the entrance.

As the sun finished setting behind the distant hills, the clouds had also made their way to Coltend, laying down a thin sheet of snow that coated the stone walkways and streets like confectionary sugar on a cake. Smoke could be seen rising from numerous chimneys across the city that glowed a soft orange in the night, as fireplaces were being lit to keep the residents warm.

Down one of the many, empty torchlit streets, a pair of hooded figures walked abreast. Their figures, distorted by their attire, blended in nearly perfectly with their surroundings. A drunken man with a thick, scraggly beard and a bottle of some unidentifiable liquor stumbled out of a tavern and into the street. His clothes, while still in decent shape for a commoner, were soaked around the neck with the smell of alcohol.

"H-hey, watch where y-your walking," he said, stumbling into the pair. Some of the fluid from his dark, glass bottle leaked out, and landed on one of their blackened boots. "Am I th-that drunk, or are you made of liquor?" the drunken man said, trying to focus his eyes on the dropped liquid. He could see it on the ground, but it was distorted by the imagery that passed *through* the boots.

"We have no quarrel with you, drunkard, but if you wish to live, you *will* step aside," the first hooded figure spoke, his baritone voice inlaid with a thick, unidentifiable accent. The drunkard looked up, only to find a pair of sanguine eyes glaring back at him. The snow on the cloak just barely outlined the stranger's figure, forcing the drunkard to focus intensely.

"W-well, if you say so. I'd r-recommend you to go to the apothe... *apugh...*" the drunkard tried to respond, but ended up vomiting on the floor, lightly splashing the stranger's boots. "N-now look at w-what you made me do, *pink-eyes*! Those damned cloaks of y-yours keep *fucking* with my vision," he slurred, wiping the sick off his mouth with the back of his sleeve.

"Step aside, *now*," the voice commanded. As soon as the command was given, the drunkard stood straight up, eyes locked straight ahead, and took two, wooden steps to the right, letting the figures pass.

"We should have just taken the rooftops like I'd suggested," the second, unsoiled figure said quietly in a thin, raspy voice. "I told you we can't, Jesra. They're not solid enough to hold our weight, and they're going to be looking in places they'd expect assassins to come from," the baritone voice replied.

"Fine, Nizaam, but don't blame me if they spot us from too far out," Jesra replied in a hiss. "They won't notice anything's wrong until we're *very* close, and by that time, we'll make sure they saw *nothing*," Nizaam said, pushing past the drunkard.

As the pair approached the gate, they noticed the guardsmen near the front entrance weren't quite paying attention, spending most of their focus on keeping warm.

"It's colder than a Hjalfarian tit out here," the taller of the pair said, his teeth chattering rapidly. "I just wish we could've grabbed our cloaks. Wasn't expecting the weather to get this bad this quickly," the shorter one said, his pale, blue lips barely able to move.

The taller guard tore his cape from his shoulders. While it wasn't as grandiose as Thorsen's, it still signified that his rank was above that of a regular foot-soldier. He wrapped the smaller one in it, and made sure to cover his head. "Here, Deme, you take this," he said, patting the shorter guard's head. Just behind him, Deme noticed a shimmer moving past them. "Sergeant, there's something here," Deme said quietly. The sergeant looked around him curiously.

"I don't see anything, Deme," he replied with a shrug. "I swear, Sergeant, I'm not lying, look!" Deme lurched, grabbing his superior by the shoulders and turning him in the direction of what he saw. "Footprints?" the sergeant said quietly, noting the fresh imprints in the snow. "Deme, what did you s...." his voice cut short as blood began to spurt from his mouth. "Sergeant!" Deme called out, his eyes opening wide. Even though his body was nearly frozen, he mustered the strength to hold up the larger man.

"Somebody, hel-..." Deme's voice cut out similarly to his superior's as he looked down to his bloodied hands. Out of the shuddering, dim light, Nizaam stepped toward the pair, making sure that no further sounds would be made, his scarlet eyes burrowing into the sergeant's.

"You took too long, Jesra," he said, pushing his blade deeper into the sergeant's neck before ripping it out. "You were in my way," Jesra responded, her raspy voice nearly lost in the wind as she did the same to Deme.

"That still doesn't excuse your tardiness. Zari will not be pleased if this mission fails and *you're* the one to blame. Now, *focus*," Nizaam said, his voice low but carrying a heavy aura as he verified the life had left the pair's eyes. Jesra hissed, but fell in closely behind Nizaam as they made their way into the palace.

Meanwhile, Claire was drawing a steaming hot bath for Leona. The deep, blue bath with its golden rim emitted a cloud of steam that greatly reduced the visibility within the bathroom. "Your majesty, the bath is prepared!" Claire called out, dropping in a few rose petals. "I'll be right there," Leona responded from the other room.

I wonder if Thorsen will be available tonight. Ooh, I can almost taste the wine he'd gently pour for me as he whispers sweet nothings into my ears, Claire thought, bringing a grin to her puffy, rosy-cheeked face as she giggled with excitement.

Leona entered the steaming bathroom, and undid the lace holding the bath robe loosely around her slim figure. "By the Graces, Claire, are you trying to boil me like a lobster?" she asked in a playful tone. "I'd hoped it would warm you up after your little walk outside, your majesty," Claire responded, moving behind Leona and pulling the loosened robe from her shoulders. "*Ah*, of course. You're always so *thoughtful*, Claire. I don't know what I would do without you," Leona said, giving her servant a warm smile.

Claire blushed, and bowed deeply. "Th-thank you, your majesty," she said humbly, feeling the blood rushing to her face. As she left the bathroom, closing the door behind her, she immediately used her fingers to comb back the few strands of hair that had fallen in front of her face. With a brief shake of her head, she grabbed the empty bottle and tray of food, proceeding out of the royal chamber.

That's strange. Normally, there's a guard or two posted around here doing his rounds, she thought, glancing around the main hall as she proceeded toward the kitchen.

What uneasy feeling is this? Are the followers of Mideia back? She thought, noting the unease in her gut.

Cautiously, she stepped into the kitchen, which had already closed down for the night. Setting the tray down quietly, and picking up a large chef's knife, she held it closely to her as she moved back toward the hall. She heard a soft rustling noise followed by light, quick footsteps behind her. With a skill none would have assumed she had, she spun on her heel and pointed the knife in the direction of the sounds with a panicked screech.

"*Oh*, fuck off!" she said, tilting her head and lowering the blade at the sight of the mouse coming out of the open bag of flour. "Gods above and below! Nearly gave me a heart attack, you did!" she said, picking the miniscule creature in her thick hands, dwarfing it entirely. She popped open the window above the kitchen sink, and let the mouse go outside.

This bag of flour is ruined now. I need to throw that out lest her majesty get sick from some corrupted toast, she thought as she tied the fresh hole in the bag shut.

She carried the bag through the back door and toward the dumpster where she knew it would be picked up in the morning. Off in the distance, she could just see the front gate of the palace. Squinting her eyes through the snowflakes that now fell in much larger quantities, she could just barely make out the lifeless bodies of the two guardsmen with a light coating of snow.

What the...? How the...? The-... they're dead? I need to warn someone! If this is anything like that night with those freaks *from the Church, I need to keep quiet. Thorsen. I need to find Thorsen. He'll know what to do,* she thought in her panic, trying her best to keep from screaming.

Quietly moving back inside, the weight of her predicament closed in around her.

There are no guardsmen around. At least none that are still alive. Whoever is doing this has likely silenced all possible alarms and is likely on the lookout for anything that could pose a threat. With my figure, I don't think I pose much of one, but I have to be careful. I won't get a second chance at running away. Not this time, she thought, putting her finger to her chin.

I don't have a lot of time. If the last time something like this happened was any indication, they'd be going for Leona. Shit! Leona! She panicked, grabbing the knife on her way back into the main hall.

Just as she opened the door, she saw Gwili ripping his sword out of something that confused her eyes. The impaled figure shimmered, though the blood spurt made it evident that this was, in fact, a *person*.

Putting a hand to her mouth to stifle a scream, she nearly dropped the knife in the process.

Gwili, noticing her, put one finger to his lips in a *shushing* movement, shaking his head slowly. Nodding her compliance, Gwili motioned for her to follow him toward the stairway leading up to the royal bedchamber.

As quietly as she could, she moved over to him, tiptoeing her way across the vast, stone hall. "What are you doing here?" he whispered. "I was just bringing down her majesty's food tray when I noticed something was amiss," she whispered back. "Fuck. We need to get up there, now! Where the fuck is Thorsen?" he hissed as they moved up the stairs.

Claire shook her head. "I don't know either, I was about to go look for him and tell him about the two guards who died at the front gate," she whispered. Gwili's eyes widened briefly, then narrowed. "These sons of pig-fucking *whores*," he muttered. "No time. Catch up when you can, and if you see Thorsen, send him to the royal chamber," he said, his eyes solidified with mana as he dashed up the stairs at break-neck speed.

Fuck, fuck, fuck! Don't be late. Not this time, Gwili thought, leaning his head forward and picking up as much speed as he could in the tight corridors.

He turned down the final hall that led to the royal bedroom, and noticed the door was ever so slightly ajar. He heard a blood-curdling scream come from the bedroom, his stomach both churning and sinking in response.

No! Not again, he thought, giving himself a final burst of speed aimed at the crack in the door.

Bursting through the bedchamber, he reached the bathroom door, only to find a completely nude Leona struggling against a figure that was difficult to see, but not impossible with the steam that swirled around it. Without hesitation whatsoever, he dashed in behind the queen, slashing at the only portion he *could* see.

His sword cut multiple, clean slices through flesh and the cloak that seemed to distort the very air around it. Both Leona and whoever was holding her fell to the ground at the same time, only one was gasping for air, while the second now lay in a pile of twitching chunks of flesh.

"G-Gwili!" Leona coughed, not bothering to hide her nakedness as she pointed beside him. He lifted his sword up just in time to catch a curved blade barely visible through the steam. "You're both fast and extremely skilled if you could kill Jesra in what looked like a single blow," the baritone voice said, aiming another rapid sequence of strikes at the disgraced elf.

Shit, not only is he fast, but he's extremely hard to react to, even with the steam giving away his posi-... ow! Gwili's thoughts were cut off as multiple slashes suddenly appeared on his forearms.

"Who the *fuck* are you?" Gwili asked, grunting through the pain, blocking another incoming blow and getting in close enough to peer into Nizaam's eyes. "Why should I tell *you* who *I* am, Gwili Gwynn? I do find it quite ironic to ask a masked, nearly invisible person *who they are*," Nizaam taunted before landing another blow to Gwili's leg, forcing him to kneel before catching another slash aimed for his neck on his sword.

The elf allowed the slash to flow off the edge of his sword, and used his pommel to strike the figure in the groin. Doubling over momentarily, Nizaam sent his knee straight into Gwili's nose, breaking it and forcing his eyes to water. He caught himself before falling to the bathroom floor, and used what little momentum he had to swipe at the figure's midsection, forcing him back momentarily.

Gwili got into a guard on his knees, as he glanced over at where Leona had been just a few moments ago, only finding a slight shimmer in the mist instead. A smile dared to tug at the corner of his mouth, but it was quickly wiped away as yet another flurry of incoming blows sought his life. With their movements being as fast as they were, the steam began to dissipate.

Shit, I can hardly follow him even while having my senses enhanced with mana, he thought as he cut downward, hoping to strike his opponent.

Having cut nothing but air, he *did* get a chance to reposition himself between where he thought Leona was and her attacker. "You're going to lose this fight, elf. You don't have the might to stand against us," Nizaam said, now just barely visible. Gwili chuckled in response, eliciting a tilted head from the shimmering figure. "You *laugh* in the face of death? Perhaps I *was* wrong about you. You're not as cowardly as your history suggests," Nizam said, lifting his nose.

Gwili laughed even more defiantly as he felt a distant pulse of familiar mana. "*Oh*, no, no, no. I'm not *that* brave. I'm laughing because I didn't know death was nearly three meters tall with a thick beard and glowing eyes," he said, grinning maliciously. Within the confused heartbeat that followed, Nizam was flung out of the bathroom at a speed that could've rivaled the lightning god's and flew straight into the fireplace opposite the massive bed with an explosive crash.

"Thanks for holding him off. I'll take it from here," Thorsen said, tossing the torn cloak aside. "Not fair! I was just warming up! How the hell did you get here so fast? Did Claire find you?" the elf spat a mouthful of blood onto the tile floor and rolled his shoulder. "She did, but where's her majesty?" Thorsen asked. "I'm right here," she said, reappearing from behind the bathtub with blackened irises and sclera replacing her former blue ones.

Thorsen raised an eyebrow in response to her stealthiness. "A trick I learned from Gwili with this cloak, and by the Graces am I glad I did," she said, releasing her connection to the Ethereal as she was now wrapped in a cloak and armed with a small dagger she'd left just beside the tub.

"I couldn't react in time while I was in the bath, but thanks to *him*, I'll live to fight another day," she said, giving Gwili a grateful smile. Thorsen, however, was taken aback momentarily. "Is that the...? No, never mind, we'll talk later. For now, I'm glad you're alive," Thorsen said, returning his full focus onto the enemy before him.

"What a quaint little trick for a quaint little girl," Nizam said, pulling himself out of the wreckage. He quickly realized that his concealing cloak was no longer on him, exposing his dark, olive skin now covered in dust and ash from the fireplace.

His black and violet robes flowed about him with a strange aura, like he was under water but standing on dry land. They wrapped and wreathed around him in true Harutian fashion, but the now-exposed robes emanated a subtle and diffused mana from them.

"You know, I had once longed for the title of *Kingslayer*, though I suppose I'll have to make do with *Queenslayer* instead," he spat, raising his hand toward the window, summoning three others dressed in similar attire. These, however, had masks grotesquely modeled after their former victims.

No, those are *their former victims*, Gwili thought, noticing the treated, human skin stitched tightly across a metal plate.

"Get them, but leave Leona alive!" Nizaam commanded. "I'll cover you, go!" Thorsen said, readying a one-handed sword in his right hand while backhanding a seax in his left, both of which could have easily been two-handed weapons for a normal man. Gwili picked Leona up and bolted out of the room using his mana-enhanced speed.

"Bravado seldom favors the *foolish*. Kill this one, then meet me near the exit as planned," Nizaam said tiredly, beginning to chase after the pair, but was immediately cut off by the giant who abruptly appeared before him. "Do you really think this is fair?" Thorsen asked, his head tilting in curiosity.

His tone carries no fear? With his unpredictable speed, perhaps that is merely overconfidence in his voice, Nizaam thought momentarily.

"*Fair*? In my line of work, you don't *win* by fighting *fairly*," Nizaam scoffed, pausing to observe the giant's demeanor. "You thought I meant fair for *me*? I meant for your *men*," Thorsen said, his brows twisted to match his wry grin.

"I have you surrounded and outnumbered four to one. Do you really think you can win when your elven *coward* could barely stand against *me* in single combat?" Nizaam asked, spreading his arms.

"The only things around me are the *corpses* and *entrails* of your men that are about to hit the stones beneath my feet in the name of *my queen*," Thorsen said, his eyes flaring with mana as he dashed forward.

Using his backhanded seax to swat away one of the figures' dual blades, he brought his sword down arcing behind it to cleave his opponent in half. The second figure attacked with a short sword from the side, but the giant, moving absurdly fast for his size, twisted around and caught the blade aimed for his liver with the seax.

Twirling his own sword around his hip, he quickly skewered the second attacker, using the seax together with his sword to rip his enemy's torso apart, and sending the peeled halves flying while simultaneously making a clear path to his next target. As he dashed through the blood still hanging in the air, he deflected the next attack aimed for his throat with his seax, sliding it along the length of his opponent's blade, and burying the point deep into his skull.

Thorsen used his sword to sever the limp corpse in half, letting the skewered remains hang limply off his seax as the blood-soaked giant menacingly stepped towards Nizaam. The entrails that now fell to the floor squelched and twisted as the giant stepped forward, dragging them loosely behind him. "Still think that was a fair fight?" Thorsen said, towering over Nizaam and glaring downwardly at him.

"You gave my *hashishin* quick enough deaths to pique my interest. Fine. I will fight you in solo-combat, but if *I* win, I'll earn the *Queenslayer* namesake after all," Nizaam said, readying his blade. Thorsen merely grunted in response, using one blade to scrape the impaled body off the other, dropping the hunk of flesh onto the blood-soaked floor.

Nizaam sidestepped the fresh puddle of his men's blood to ensure stable footing, while Thorsen merely observed with his brows furrowed. Without much warning, Nizaam dashed forward, swinging his curved, black sword, creating arcs of sharp wind behind it, making each attack more like two.

Damn it, even though he only has the one sword, it's like his sword has a delayed attack, Thorsen noticed as he was being forced to use his now-mana-infused seax to counteract the slashing wind.

Again and again, Nizaam swung his sword, eventually pushing the giant back with both his speed and frequency of attacks, putting Thorsen quickly on the backfoot as small cuts began to appear through the linen shirt he was wearing.

He's trying to push me towards the window, isn't he? Fine, then, the giant noted, an idea sprouting in his mind.

Deflecting a series of attacks aimed for his torso, Thorsen willingly moved backwards towards the window, hoping his plan would work. "I thought you'd be more entertaining than this, but I suppose a quick death is all you'll earn today," Nizaam said, his confidence beginning to shine through his scarlet eyes as he unleashed another barrage of slices and cutting wind.

Stepping through the entrails of his former comrades, even the blood on the floor began to be pushed away from the amount of force he was putting behind his swings.

Just a little more, Thorsen thought, gauging the remaining distance to the window without answering his assailant.

"*Oh,* come now, surely this isn't *all* you can do. There's no way you're already burned out from slaughtering my men. I might earn the titles of *Queenslayer* and *Giant-killer* tonight," the hashishin said, now grinning wildly. "I'm not, but what was it you said earlier? *Bravado seldom favors the foolish?*" Thorsen asked, a wry grin now on his face eliciting a questioning look from Nizaam.

Schlick.

Suddenly feeling abnormally warm around his neck, he paused his attacks, stumbling a step or two backwards in pure, unadulterated shock.

What? Who could've possibly...? Nizaam thought, putting a hand to his wound and turning around to find none other than Leona, his original target, holding a bloodied dagger.

"Bitch," he gurgled, his eyes opening widely. "I've been called worse by lesser men than you. Now, *die,*" she said darkly, kicking his stomach with the ball of her foot and launching him into the giant who stood waiting behind the hashishin. Using both of his blades, Thorsen impaled Nizaam, bringing him along as he jumped out of the window.

His eyes glowed intensely, as he *pushed an immense amount of mana* into his legs to kick off the top of the gigantic windowsill, generating enough speed in the process to look like a meteor striking the cobblestones several stories below.

Leona, now being followed closely behind by Gwili, moved towards the broken window and peered below. She found Thorsen in a deep crater coated in a sheen of blood and entrails. "He's dead, your majesty," the giant called up with a raised thumb from below, dripping with chunks of brain matter and other unidentifiable pieces of the splattered corpse.

Wha-ha-haaat the fuck... Gwili thought, gazing at the giant as he whistled critically.

Leona slumped into a chair that sat in the corner of the bedroom, and put her hands to her forehead, her eyes widened and face paled as she took in the sight around her. "I did my best to ignore it on the way in, but this is ridiculous," she thought, staring at the disemboweled corpses strewn about her room.

It wasn't the visuals that triggered her, however. Instead, it was the sudden waft of opened intestines flowing straight into her nostrils because of the open window that forced her to puke.

Gwili stifled a chuckle as he held her hair. "First time? I was surprised you weren't shitting through your teeth earlier, your majesty," he said in a sardonic, yet light-hearted tone. "N-no. Sh-shut up," she heaved, once more, drawing a chagrined smile from the elf as he nodded his acknowledgement.

The bloodsoaked giant reappeared in the doorway a few moments later only to find Leona sitting pale faced in the chair. "I apologize for the mess, your majesty," he said humbly, one hand still on the hilt of his sword. "It's f-fine. I'm fine," she struggled, paused, then raised her index finger before hurling once more. "Let's get her somewhere a little *less* covered in blood, no?" the giant asked.

A few moments later, and after having grabbed Thorsen a set of towels to wipe the blood off his face, the three were gathered in one of the guest rooms. "So, what now? It took them months upon months to attack us, and we still don't know a fucking thing about them," Gwili asked openly, leaning his elbows on his knees.

"They knew our habits, guard rotations, backgrounds. Everything. The most we got out of them was what the color of their insides looked like," he continued, eliciting a stifled heave from Leona, still reeling in shock. "We know *one* thing for sure," Thorsen began, using a third, moistened towel. "What might that be?" the elf asked, lifting his head.

"We know they were Harutian, without a doubt. Which means one of two things: That whoever sent these *hashishin* are either in that country, or have contacts *in* that country who knew how to employ them," Thorsen said, his serious tone weighing heavily in the air.

"But who would send fighters such as those to kill our queen? What *reason* would they have to do that? They spent *months* here without making a fucking sound, and they chose *now*? Something isn't adding up," he said, the frustration evident in his voice.

"Because of Bashir," Leona said, her hair covering most of her face. "The *manwhore prince*? What the fuck would *he* have to do with it?" Gwili asked, spreading his arms widely. "Not *what*, but more like *who*," she replied, letting her words hang. "What do you mea-... *O-oh*... I-I see. Well, that *does* explain a lot," he replied, wanting to move on quickly after recalling the entire situation on the Rhydian pass with Gorm, Commander Ari, and Bashaa.

"If that's the case, then there's only one person who *could've* sent them," Gwili began, eliciting raised eyebrows from both of his counterparts. "Zari Ibn'Escya? Bashaa's widow? *Oh*, come now, you *don't* know who she is?" he asked, more confused than they were. "No, but I'm about to find out," Leona pushed her palms off her knees as she stood up. "Wh-what do you mean, your majesty? Surely, you can't mean..." he began, but was halted by a raised palm.

"I *do*. Send a message to Bernar so that he knows what transpired here. As for the three of us, well... We're going to pay *her* a visit," Leona said sternly.

CHAPTER 45

INADEQUATE

A rdrin grabbed a vial from the nearby table and swirled the dully glowing contents within.

Deep inside the alteration chamber in the underbelly of Pydredd, a score of hegraphenes were strapped to inclined tables, patiently awaiting for him to come around to them. The dungeon that was the alteration chamber had all sorts of bindings along the walls, some were constructed of pure mana, while others were made of some unknown, but likely *unbreakable,* material.

As Ardrin swirled the contents of the vial, he eyed the concoction closely, the dull-colored liquid came to a sludge-like halt when he stopped. Without too much movement of his head, he peered over his left shoulder briefly, then his right before pulling out a small, glass container filled with a violet and golden liquid. A curious mixture that glowed faintly, as it was only a small quantity.

Let this be enough, he said in his own mind, shielding his thoughts from any who might be listening.

He poured the golden and violet concoction into the larger vial, and swirled it once more. The entire room began to hum with energy, as the mixture began to glow intensely, emitting beams of light across the room. As the beams faded, so, too did the humming that resonated from the strange liquid.

As the hegraphenes tilted their heads curiously, Ardrin held the vial out in front of him in presentation. "Pay attention because I will only say this once," he began, his voice rolling like thunder throughout the dungeon. "Lord Volzuk and I have toiled long and hard to reach this point. If any of you wish to back down, say so now and we will find adequate replacements for you. If you decide to go through with this procedure, which may very well mean the deaths of you and your comrades if this goes poorly," he said, his tone carrying the weight of his words flawlessly.

Each of the hegraphenes glanced at each other for a few moments, but all nodded in unison once all their decisions had been solidified. "Excellent. Now, let us begin," Ardrin said, grinning beneath his mask. As he walked from creature to creature administering the concoction to each of them, he kept a close eye out for any signs of rejection, but found nothing out of the ordinary.

I'm relieved it's working this well with them, but it has only added more to a long list of questions than it has provided answers, he thought, pouring the concoction into the mouth of the final hegraphene.

He waited a few minutes after the final administration, ensuring there were no visible side-effects that were immediately present in any of them, especially the ones that had taken it first. "I apologize for the inconvenience, but I will need to keep you here for the night under close observation," he said with a dip of his head.

"However, when I feel comfortable enough to send you back out on your own, you will be briefed and sent out on a test mission to Caegwen with Irun. Do any of you have any questions regarding what I just said?" he asked, clasping his hands behind his back. When no answer came, he nodded curtly and excused himself from the room.

Meanwhile, in another, open-air courtyard of Pyrdredd, Athar and Volzuk walked together under the gloomy sky. The skinless figure walked a few steps ahead of the young man, with his hands loosely clasped behind his decrepit back. Until this point, the two had walked mostly in silence, save a few morsels of small-talk.

"Athar," the Undergod's voice rang out suddenly after a long moment of nondescript, yet awkward silence. "Y-yes, great one?" he asked, his tone exuding his surprise. "Now that we are far enough away from prying eyes and ears, am I correct in assuming your master must have told you that there was something with your core that he wasn't willing to expose?" Volzuk asked, keeping his tone almost explanatory rather than questioning. "Yes, he has, great one. Although to what end, I do not know," Athar replied, lifting his brows and looking off to the side as he shook his head.

"I see. Then what do *you* think it could be?" the Undergod asked, almost as if he already knew the answer. Athar paused, even going so far as to stop walking for a few moments as he considered his answer. "I think it could be something that could easily destroy who I am, and he, for reasons known only to him, is trying to prevent that," he finally replied, scuttling up a few steps behind Volzuk's left.

"*Destroy*, you say? Have you ever considered the fact that he might think you'd outgrow him in power? Or, perhaps, that it could potentially *break* the controlling hand that has pulled the strings of your life?" the Undergod asked, glancing over his shoulder.

"N-no, great one. In fact, I think he has always been looking out for me, in his own, admittedly *fucked up*, way," Athar said, scratching his cheek nervously. "What do you mean?" Volzuk asked, finally turning to fully face the young man, and halting his steps.

The young man froze, but regained his composure as he cleared his throat. "I don't think the Masked One is entirely a bad person, great one," he began, rubbing his chin with his index finger. "And what do *you* define as being a *bad* person?" Volzuk asked, his tone holding a subdued intrigue he was clearly struggling to contain.

"Like anything else, something, or someone, being *bad* is just a matter of perspective. What one may consider to be good, another may consider to be entirely evil," Athar said after a moment of consideration. "The way I see it, he was just a victim of unfortunate and sequential circumstances that eventually led him to where he is today. However, that is not to say that *all* of those circumstances *made* him a *bad* person. He was just responding to them as best he could, with the knowledge he had at the time, great one," Athar explained.

"So, you're suggesting that the *circumstances*, in accordance with a given perspective, are what determine whether someone is good, and *not* whether that person has caused physical, mental, or emotional harm to someone else?" Volzuk asked, lifting the muscles that would have been his eyebrow.

I need to get away from this topic before I say something I'm going to regret, Athar thought as he struggled to keep his words from leaking out.

Athar paused again, choosing his words once more. "I'm only trying to say that the circumstances of one's environment shouldn't delineate whether someone is a bad person, rather how they handled them in accordance with their own beliefs and morals, great one," he said, shrugging his shoulders.

Volzuk's skinless brows furrowed slightly in response. "But if the *beliefs and morals* of a person don't match your own, can you *then* make the determination that this person is, in fact, *bad*? What, or rather *who*, gave you the authority to be my judge and executioner because I exerted my free will or think differently? How does that make you any different from..." Volzuk paused, cutting himself off and turning away rapidly.

Oh shit. Too late for that, Athar thought, trying to hide his panicked expression.

Volzuk disguised a heavy sigh with a roll of his shoulders, the tendons of the fetid body clearly tensed as they pulled at the once-muscular frame. "Do not share any portion of what was said here with anyone else, Athar," Volzuk said, not bothering to look at him now. "You're smarter than you appear, but unfortunately, you still have a lot to learn about life; no thanks to your master," he said, glancing back over his shoulder, as a menacing, violet gaze stared angrily back at the young man.

"O-of course, great one!" Athar quickly bowed in reply, feeling the nervous sweat beading off the tip of his nose. "Lord Volzuk," Gavar called out from one of the many entrances to the courtyard. "What is it, Gavar?" Volzuk asked, turning to face the lord of the Ironplume clan with his hands still clasped behind his back. "The Masked One requests your presence in the alteration chamber, my lord," Gavar said with a bow.

I'm saved! Athar cheered internally

"Very well, then. Athar, go and fetch Irun, as I sense he will also be needed, but do not forget what I said earlier," Volzuk said, his tone hiding the malice he had just shown. "Great one, I do not know where to find him here," Athar replied with a slight skittishness in his tone. Volzuk paused for a moment, then flicked his eyes back to the young man. "He's in the training room practicing a new move, I see," the Undergod said with little interest. "I will find him, and heed your words, great one," Athar said, bowing even lower than the hegraphene as he left the courtyard.

I wonder what kind of new move he's working on, he thought has e proceeded down one of the gloomy halls.

While nearly identical to Valdis in structure, the color of the light that filled the large, metallic halls was much the same as the outsides; with its sickly green seeping through numerous cracks and seams in the walls. Athar could hear the sounds of clashing swords and grunts of exertion resounding from where he figured must be his final destination. Peering through the crack in the door to the vast training room, he saw Irun conducting a set of slashes and thrusts against what he saw to be a hegraphene.

Irun dashed under a slash aimed for his throat as the blade cut through the few strands of hair that lingered behind. With a forceful grunt, he swung the training sword at the creature's waist who, in turn, was forced to leap over it. Adeptly landing on its feet, it dashed directly backwards, turning to face its opponent in mid air and using the rotation of its swing to increase the power of its blow.

Irun was barely able to get his sword up in time to block it, and as a result, was sent skidding across the floor across the room. "It would seem we're almost evenly matched now, Irun, but we must stop here," the hegraphene glanced in the direction of where Athar had been hiding. Her glowing, violet eyes peered across the training hall like a hawk's as she was sheathing a sword made of the same material her scales were onto the back of her slim, yet athletic figure.

It looks a lot like Gavar, just without the horns and a much smaller plume, Athar noted now that the fight had calmed down.

"You're still so fast, I can hardly keep up, but having trained here for... gods, how many cycles has it been?" Irun began, but paused to try and find an answer to his question. "Nearly one-thousand cycles," the hegraphene answered, her voice far more melodic than it should have been. "I know that's almost a year in the Between, but how long do you think it *actually* has been down here? Ten years? Twenty? Hard to tell, what with the lack of aging and all," Irun noted, observing both his human and daemonic arms.

"I wouldn't know, but I'd imagine it doesn't really matter right now. We've been summoned," Athar interjected, coming out from behind the door he was using as concealment to watch them. "Athar! It feels like it's been *forever* since I've seen you!" Irun said in a much more cheery tone than even Athar expected.

"I... yeah, it's good to see you too, Irun, but we don't have time to exchange stories right now. We're supposed to meet with Lord Volzuk and the Masked One," he replied, gesturing towards the door.

"*Ah,* I see. Well, thank you for the training session, Commander Kaila," Irun said with a bow, which Kaila returned promptly. "Of course. It has been my pleasure to instruct you. May your blade purge your enemies, and cast down those who mean you harm," she said, a hint of a smile cracking the chitinous exterior of her face.

"Any ideas what this is all about?" Irun asked, still wiping the sweat from his brow. Athar shook his head in response. "I think they might try for another expedition, but that's my best guess, and arguably not my best," he replied. "What makes you think that?" Irun asked.

"It's just the way things have been lately. The Masked One and Lord Volzuk hardly speak to one another, while Lord Gavar has been training those augmentees non-stop since he got the *all-clear* from the Masked One. Since then, I've found myself often being put into challenging conversations with the Undergod, but for what reason, I do not know," Athar replied, his tone carried an air of both curiosity and mental exhaustion.

"Well, if it's of any consolation, I've been getting my ass kicked by Lady Kaila unendingly for however long it's been since we got here. Ever since that first meeting with Lord Volzuk, she's taken me under her wing to annoying lengths after my dismissal from the great hall," Irun said, rubbing his shoulder.

"You said *ten or twenty years*, right? Odd how it only feels like it's been a few *months* for me," Athar noted, as Irun shrugged in response. "I think it has to do with whatever *you're* doing while you're here. Maybe each kind of action has a certain time-law that the Underworld abides by?" Irun asked.

Athar could neither agree nor disagree with the statement, as the proof was already in front of them. "Gods, that explains why they count everything in *cycles* here, but cycles of *what* exactly?" he asked.

This line of thinking is going to hurt my head, isn't it? He asked himself, sighing deeply.

"Fucked if I know, but isn't *that* where we're going?" Irun asked, pointing up to the glowing room just ahead of them. Behind the swung-open doors was a massive portal, with a group of twenty fully-equipped hegraphenes, their eyes glowing a deep violet similar to that of Ardrin himself.

They snapped to the direction of Athar and Irun's footsteps from down the hall, immediately drawing attention to them. "Irun, Athar, come." Ardrin said, pulling them using the same technique he had back in Valdis.

Couldn't you have done that before? This place is much *larger than Valdis could ever be,* Athar sent to his master. *I could have, but for reasons I will not explain here, I just didn't* want *to,* Ardrin replied, lightly cocking his head towards the group.

"It's about time you arrived, *Irun,*" Volzuk said with a gravelly voice. "M-my apologies, great one. I was not entirely aware of how time functioned in this place. I beg you to overlook and forgive my stupidity," Irun kneeled, replying in a tone that almost seemed... *practiced.*

The Undergod was clearly pleased with this newfound display of humility. "I see Kaila has taught you your place well, as per my instructions," he glowered momentarily. "She has indeed, great one," Irun responded, keeping his head low. "Good, then I will get started right away without standing on ceremony," Volzuk retorted quickly.

"You're to command these twenty that you see before you. As I'm sure a former synner would know of the legendary artifacts given by the gods before Codrean became what it is today, you will find this mission most intriguing," the Undergod said, letting the words hang a little. "I am at your command, great one," Irun said, doing his best to hide the shock in his voice. "Lead them to Caegwen to begin your search for both the Dreambinder Jerkin and the Benevolent

Ring. My sources have told me that those two will be the most easily found," Volzuk stated.

The jerkin and the ring? What the hell could he need those for? Irun shielded his thoughts as best he could, desperately trying to remember Kaila's training.

"It will be done, great one. I will *not* fail you," Irun said confidently. "Good. You know what will happen if you do. Prepare to depart. I will open the portal. Do *not* underestimate the elves," the Undergod said menacingly. He turned to face the portal, and outstretched his hand. The umbral mana of the portal swirled and grew more intense, as dark tendrils of mana poured into it.

"Lord Gavar," Volzuk called out. Within a heartbeat, the leader of the Ironplume clan was before him, kneeling next to Irun. "Go with them, as I will need a second pair of eyes to make sure everything goes according to plan. Kaila will tend to the training of the others in your stead," he continued.

"It will be done, my lord," Gavar said, his subservient tone carried throughout the room. The Undergod dismissed the pair before him without a glance, letting them make their preparations accordingly.

Athar sheepishly walked over to Irun, whose face was contorted into one of both worry and anger. "Are you alright, little brother?" Athar asked, putting a hand on his friend's shoulder. "I'll live, thanks. Just a bit nervous, you know?" he said without a hint of a lie in his tone. "I'd be too if I were on such an important mission," Athar said as he nodded his head and lifting his eyebrows almost in disbelief.

"Do... do you think that there's a chance I'll see them again?" Irun asked quietly. Athar turned to face his friend again after having looked away momentarily. "What?" he asked. "Do you think I'll see them again if I go?" Irun asked again, more quietly this time. Athar was stunned but quickly glanced around to make sure no one had heard him. "I don't know if I can ever face them again. Not after what I did, not after the things I've caused to happen to them, or what happened with Isla... I just don't know if I could," Irun said, keeping his tone quiet and monotone to hide his true feelings.

What the hell do I say to that? Athar asked himself.

"Listen, I think that redemption is only something that is given to those who have earned it. Perhaps you, too, will get your chance at it, but I'd be lying if I said I thought it was right now," Athar spoke quietly, still making sure no one heard the two of them. Irun said nothing, but merely nodded his head in understanding.

"Now, chin up, you've got a mission to finish. Not as you once were, but as a commander of a strike force for the Undergod himself. I salute you, commander," Athar said with a crooked salute. Irun smirked and shook his head. "First of all, I'm not at the rank where I'm supposed to be saluted. And secondly, you know we don't *really* do it *that* way, right?" he said, correcting Athar's hand and finger position into a nice, crisp salute.

"There, much better," he said, sarcastically returning the salute, and walking off to join the group of hegraphenes. "Good luck, *little brother*," Athar said, pumping his fist. Irun glanced over his shoulders, and waved curtly with a pair of fingers held up, then reduced to just the middle one as a wry smirk grew on his face.

"Let's go," Irun said, motioning for the others to follow him as he stepped into the swirling portal. The realms lurched and bled into each other, though the color change was reversed this time around, going from the gloomy, violet and sickly green to a mist-filled, snowy forest. The tall canopy tore and scratched at the gray sky even as the snowflakes that clung to the leaves tried to drag them down. The ground was covered in a decently thick layer of snow, reaching up to Irun's mid-calf.

He lost his focus once more, although, this time, he was able to keep his last meal where it belonged. The dizzying feeling, however, remained the same. Gavar, who had followed him closely through the portal, was slightly taken aback at the feeling of snow beneath his armored feet. "What is this? Did we go too far?" he asked. Irun managed a soft chuckle as he recovered from the dizziness.

"It's called *snow*, Lord Gavar. When winter comes in this realm, the air is cold enough to keep the moisture from the clouds far above us frozen until it reaches the ground," he explained briefly and quietly, as he observed their surroundings. "But, to answer your other questions, I have no idea. I've never been to Caegwen, so I'm just as lost as you are. The only instructions I have are to go North until we hit a city of some sort, then move North-East from there and try to avoid being noticed along the way, which, in this weather and terrain, might prove to be a little difficult," he continued.

Gavar let off a low, chest-borne rumble, but clicked his tongue and turned to make sure the others made it through the portal. Within a few minutes, all had joined them in the dense forest, and Irun's heart began to beat more quickly.

"How does one find North in weather like this?" Gavar turned to ask Irun after a quick head-count. Irun, however, was already one step ahead of him, having stabbed a stick into the ground. "This stick will tell us where North is," he replied. "Elaborate," Gavar commanded.

I'm going to have to give him an entire lifetime's worth of knowledge, aren't I? Irun sighed.

"Keeping it as simple as possible, the stick's shadow will move after a fifteen minute period. You take the difference in direction of those two marked points, and you can figure out where the North is since the sun always rises in the East and sets in the West," he explained. Gavar scrunched a chitinous plate that could be viewed as an eyebrow, and thought about the information carefully.

"What about during the night?" he finally asked. "Find the brightest one in the sky and follow it, at least that's the easy way to remember it," Irun said plainly. "I would have you teach me these ways in greater detail during our journey. There is, surprisingly, much to learn from you about this realm," Gavar said, looking ahead. "O-of course, Lord Gavar," Irun said, bowing slightly before proceeding to explain some of the survival techniques he'd learned during his time at Codrean.

Moving cautiously through the snowy forest was easier said than done since the hegraphenes, no matter how good of warriors they were, were still unaccustomed to the realm's attributes. Even with the help of the Gwynnleaf concoction made by Ardrin himself, there were still some limits to their abilities that hindered their progress.

Even though I've taught them a lot of what I know, they're still leaving too many tracks behind and they're struggling to adapt to this realm. At this rate, we're going to get spotted before we even get close to Myrdin, Irun thought, noticing the long trail of footprints they'd left behind that were still noticeable even after their efforts to cover them.

Far above them amidst snow-capped branches, a scout who maintained a small outpost stirred beneath his thick cloak.

I fucking hate *the snow. Every damned time I'm put up here, I can never seem to get warm,* the scout thought, curling into a tighter ball as he hugged his knees.

His stomach growled quietly, which, to him, was a signal that it was time to eat. As he reached for the bag of rations, however, the wide, snow-covered branch shifted a little when it began to support his weight, sending his rations plummeting below. His eyes opened wide as he lurched forward to try and grab them, but the leather strap slipped through his gloved hand. The reality of going hungry that night sunk in like an anchor in water. Luckily for him, they caught on the stump of a branch just a few meters below.

That was too close for comfort, he let out a sigh of relief. *I'd hate to have to... what the fuck is that? Are those* tracks? *How the hell did I not see them before? Wait, those are...* the scout paused, having spotted the group below making an effort to cover their tracks.

Shit, I need to notify the Commander. She'll *know what to do with them,* he thought, leaving his rations and making his way back to the city.

As he moved, the snow that was once atop the branch holding his rations, finally fell to the floor below, drawing the attention of Irun's party. "Enemy?" Gavar asked simply. Irun scanned the surrounding area, but saw nothing immediately identifiable as a threat. "It's not unlikely, but we need to be *extra* cautious from now on. That means moving quickly and quietly, do you understand?" Irun asked, to which the group nodded their agreement.

We can't get discovered now. I will not be viewed as an inadequate subordinate anymore. This will not end well if we're found out before we're ready, he thought, looking ahead as far as he could given the density of the trees.

CHAPTER 46
SPLIT DECISIONS

A few days had passed since the events of my reaching the third stage of mana manipulation.

I tried my best to smile and be as cordial as I could with the emotional turmoil I was still in, but since having heard my mother's words during the trial, as well as the ones I said to *myself*, I forcibly repeated them in my mind. It became a personal litany, and I quickly realized that if I caught myself falling into a mental rut, I could use it to dig myself out.

At least, in theory, anyway.

Nevertheless, I tried my best to hone my skills and maintain full control over the third stage. It wasn't easy, by any means, even being a bearer of the so-called *Autarchica Primaria*; a power, I surmised, that I had no idea where to even begin exploring it. However, even with that in mind, Vyra, Ysevel, Haldir, and Derion, of all people, took great care in training me in the days that passed, while my mother, Bernar, and Anwill observed my movements closely.

I began to grow into my lanky body a little more since my seal had been broken, and I could definitely feel the difference. Now, having packed on a decent amount of lean muscle to at least be considered athletic, I was faster, stronger, and much more capable but still nowhere near my older brother's strength; even without him being a fifth stage. Still, it was sufficient for the training I was conducting, and I could feel myself getting stronger by the day.

And more sore, I thought of the welt on my buttcheek left from the day prior when my brother slammed me onto the ground.

My distracted thoughts were quickly severed as Vyra, being as close to a master level spear-caster as one could be without taking the trial, made her move. While she mostly focused on forcing me to find openings in her *get-the-fuck-away-from-me* techniques this one seemed to be a coordinated attack.

Derion, with his twin daggers, made sure I didn't leave any such openings of my own, and had me heavily relying on airborne mana particles to tell where he was coming from. Haldir, however, forced me to broaden my reach with elemental mana as he consistently took pop-shots from behind trees that pushed me to rely on elemental spells to deflect or destroy his arrows.

All of this while maintaining the third stage, huh? Fuck me sideways, I'm exhausted, I realized, just as another arrow was consumed by my *Flamebolt,* and Derion's daggers bounced off a rock I made airborne.

"Enough!" Siraye's voice called out, stopping us all mid-swing. My mother certainly knew how to infuse her voice when she needed to, and by the gods above and below, it was *terrifying.* We lowered our weapons, and bowed to one another immediately since we knew the consequences well if we didn't. "Nice move with the rock," Derion's gravelly voice muttered. "Thanks, Derion. I appreciate the compliment. You're surprisingly hard to follow along with, you know?" I returned with a smile. His eyes widened in panic, and he turned his face away from me, eliciting a soft chuckle from the rest of the group.

"He doesn't do well with compliments, or *being spoken to* for that matter, Thoma. You should know that by now," Anwill said, striding towards us alongside my mother. "Yeah, that's true, but he complimented me first," I grinned, patting him on the shoulder. He was a little taller than I was, so I had to make sure I wasn't going to accidentally stick my arm into his pit.

"Regardless, I have a question for you," Siraye began, while Anwill pinched the bridge of his nose. "O-of course. What is it?" I asked, removing my arm away from the obviously uncomfortable Derion. "How long has it been since you last wet your sword?" she asked, to which my brother snorted.

"I meant killing something, you fucking *child*," she added with a glare. "*Oh*, he's slayed *something* alright," my brother chuckled, hardly trying to contain his laughter.

If I knew my brother as well as I thought I did, I knew *exactly* where his mind went, and stifled a laugh of my own.

"The last time was back in Coltend Castle, so it's been about a year at this point," I replied, subduing a chuckle. "I see," she said pensively, losing herself in thought. "W-why do you ask?" I asked, realizing something was amiss. "You've been sheltered for far too long. Even with your experiences in recent times, there is still much about a *true* battle for you to learn," she began, clasping her hands behind her back just like my grandfather.

"Bernar, why *hasn't* he gone on more expeditions? You'd think, with your grandfather there, that he would have pushed him harder," she asked. Bernar merely shrugged. "It wasn't for a lack of him pushing Thoma, there was just no need for us to go anywhere. It's one of the main reasons I came here to train in the first place, as well as why *he* was given the choice to fight the ochelons," he replied, gesturing to me. "*Ah*, I see. Well, this next part will *surely* pique your interest," she said, turning back to face me.

"As it just so happens, I've received a report from Soule, a city located South-West from here, regarding some strange tracks found by a scout. He claims that, to the best of his knowledge, he's never seen anything like them before, and has requested that we send a small force to investigate," she stated, lifting an eyebrow at me as if hoping I would read the situation correctly.

"You're already going, and want me to go with you, is that it?" I asked, a wry grin beginning to show on my face. Bernar, however, shuddered. "Is it smart to take him with you alone? What if it's just bait to get you away from here and Aurae?" he asked, his tone dropping slightly to avoid being heard at a distance. "We could guard her together, as I will not be going on this journey," Haldir said, trying to ease Bernar's mind.

"They'll be alright," he began. "Besides, as a bow-caster, I've seen the way your mother fights from afar. She's incredible, to say the least, and even if there *is* anything down there, she'll make quick work of it. Not to mention Anwill is more than capable of defending Aurae on his own if need be," he continued, gesturing toward Anwill who was a little ways away talking to a guard.

"It will be alright, Bernar. If you want, you can even go with your family to make sure it goes well," Haldir said, putting a reassuring hand on my brother's shoulder. Bernar sighed heavily, and nodded his head.

"Fine, but you'd better send a message at the first sign of trouble, *old man*," he said, lightly punching the elf in the shoulder. "As one of the other *old men* in this place, I would, but it seems you might actually have somewhere else to be," Anwill said, having stepped away from the guard he was talking to.

He held a parchment in his hand, clearly from one of the carrier ravens, still heavily creased from the journey. "Here, I think *you* of all people here need to read this the most," Anwill said, his tone growing dark. "What's this?" my brother asked. "It's a letter from Leona..." he said, reading the first few lines. "Wh-what? No... That can't be," he stammered. "What happened?" I asked, moving in closer to see the letter.

"There's been an assassination attempt on Queen Leona of Coltend. She... she's gathered enough information to determine that it was of Harutian order, so she's going there personally to investigate," he said, his tone dropping in frustration. "That's fucking suicide. If she knows where they came from, why the fuck is she going *straight to the source*?" I asked, feeling my brother's frustration at Leona's lack of tactical knowledge.

"I think there's more to it than that. She'd have Thorsen by her side and making sure she didn't do anything rash. I'm confident they didn't make this decision lightly, especially not with him being a former synner," Bernar said, rubbing his chin. "Well, you'd better keep making sure he does his job," I nudged, trying to loosen the very visible strain on his features. "W-what?" he asked, taken aback.

"Listen, *shit-head*, we *all* know about your situation with Leona, to include Aurae and Ysevel, might I add," I said, putting a hand on his shoulder. "But right now, she's going to need you more than ever, especially if she's going straight into the country where these supposed assassins came from. Mom and I will be fine, so go. She needs you, I know she does," I said, encouragingly.

Bernar looked at me with both confusion and admiration. He let his face fall a little, as he broke into a heavy-hearted smile. "You've grown up, you *little shit*," he said, tousling my hair. "Fine, I'll go, but I swear to the gods both above and below, if something happens to you *or* mom..." he let his words hang.

"You'll *kill me*, I know. Bold of you to assume I'm not opposed to that after that letter from she-who-shall-not-be-named," I said sarcastically, giving my best shrug. He tilted his head as a thin-lipped smile grew on his face. "Damn you," he chuckled.

"Go, Bernar. You might catch her in time to meet her on the Rhydian Pass," Vyra chimed in after approving nods from all of us. He nodded his head in return, gripped the hilt of his blade, and dashed off faster than I'd ever gone using my second stage.

Holy shit, I thought, feeling the resulting gust of wind smack my face.

"Son, we should be on our way, too. It normally takes about a day or so for a carrier raven to make it here, so we're probably already late for the fun," my mother said, putting a hand on my shoulder. "Give me a minute to grab my things, I'll meet you at the stables. Is anyone else coming with us?" I asked, looking at the others. "I will. There might be something these tracks hold that I can learn from," Derion said in an eerily excited voice. Both my mother and I nodded our understanding. "And I will be going as well," a familiar voice came from behind me. "Ysevel, why are you here?" I asked, turning to face her.

She was already dressed and prepared for the journey, with a single-strap satchel hanging across her chest. Her armor reminded me a lot of my mother's but something about it seemed *different*, and I couldn't place what for the life of me. "Since when do you have armor like that?" I asked, moving in to inspect it more closely.

Without realizing it, I had drawn a line with my eyes from her stomach, to her pauldrons, and then straight to her chest in quick succession. "*Oh*, I-I'm sorry," I said, realizing I had been staring at her chest for a lot longer than I had meant to. "The ladies are covered, nothing to apologize for. Though I will admit the detailing around them is *superb*," she said, tracing a pair of lines with her index fingers along the details of the armor.

"Nevermind that, it fits you like it was entirely made for you," I noted, seeing not a centimeter of fabric, leather, or chain-link out of place. The leather, covered in what I could only guess were some kind of warding runes, seemed to hum with mana, though I couldn't tell what sort of element it came from, or if it even was elemental at all.

"It does, doesn't it? Curious," she said in jest, giving my mother a knowing wink. "Did you have this made for her?" I asked, noticing the exchange. "Not exactly," my mother replied, childishly looking away. I could only chuckle, but reality kicked in soon after. "So why are you coming with us?" I asked. "Surely your mother doesn't approve of putting your life in potential danger," I said, trying to lean on the fact that she was fucking *royalty* and not some mere commoner like myself.

"Mother always encourages me to go if I have Siraye with me. Says I might learn a thing or two about fighting and battles for when it's my time to rule by the future king's side, and what I should do in them should the need ever arise. Scrolls and books will only take you so far, you know," she said, giving me a wink. I could only smile in return. I knew, deep down, that I had been no different from her in a sense; always wanting to prove myself or learn something new in the process for personal development reasons.

"Alright then, I won't argue with that," I conceded. "Also, our mothers thought that now would be a good time for you to have some company of someone closer to your age," she added, a soft rush of blood reaching her cheeks.

Really, mom? I asked. *I-I don't know what you're talking about,* she replied curtly. *Elhael has no idea she's coming with us, and neither does Aurae, do they?* I asked, mentally chagrined. *Elhael would likely age a thousand years if he heard she was coming with us. What she said about her mother, however, was entirely true,* she replied, doing her best not to show the same, shit-eating grin my brother would've had in moments like this.

"If you two are done doing... whatever the hell *that* just was, I'd recommend Thoma grab his bags and meet us at the stables. Celer is already being fitted with a new saddle and horseshoes as we speak," Ysevel said, pointing her thumb somewhere behind her. "You're right, we need to get going," I said, prying my eyes away from the armor one last time and channeling mana to dash to my room.

"*Oh*, and Thoma," my mother said, just before I was about to step off. "I've got a surprise for you when you get done," she smiled wryly. Not knowing what the hell that meant, I nodded, and within a few moments appeared in my doorway. I grabbed a satchel, stuffing some basic hygiene supplies and other such things in there, and donned my leather jerkin. The snug, yet flexible leather jerkin felt a little tighter than it normally did.

I wonder if this will impede my movement at all, I thought. I'd never filled in *any* clothing before, so I wasn't entirely sure how it worked. The training gear I got from Maikell, which, apparently, was the name of the royal blacksmith, as I came to find out, had often suited me perfectly well. However, after not having worn my own jerkin for quite some time, I quickly realized just how much I'd grown.

I should probably swing by Maikell's shop before I go, I thought, rolling my shoulders to see just how much tighter the leather had gotten since I arrived.

Leaving the jerkin open in the middle, revealing my linen shirt below, I infused my muscles and bones with mana, dashing through the streets, feeling the loose bits of clothing flap violently in the wind. Within a few moments, and nearly knocking down a person or two, I'd made it to Maikell's shop.

It was one of the only stone-built locations in the entirety of Caegwen. This was not without reason, however, as only the blacksmith shops were needed to be built by stone, mortar, and other such conventional means to prevent them from being set ablaze should an accident occur.

The smell of fresh charcoal placed on the open flames of the forge being fed from a perpendicular angle by the box bellows filled the shop with a light amount of smoke and the sounds of a roaring, hungry flame. The bright orange fire encased a piece of unknown metal, heating it to a near yellow. Pulling the long piece out of the fire, the blacksmith used a dog-face hammer to strike and mold the metal to his will, accomplishing what would've taken a human smith two or three heats to do in just a few hits.

I winced at the high-pitched ringing that resonated from the anvil, but had a hard time tearing my eyes away from the added mana manipulation he was using to help shape the metal. It was curious, almost used more as a guideline than actually changing the metal itself, like a handrail on an elongated stairwell.

After a few moments, the metal cooled to a cherry red, then the dull gray color that normal metal would be in this state. Eyeing down his work, he checked for any crookedness or misshapen bits that might need to be fixed, though he quickly came to a halt when he noticed me standing in the doorway to his shop.

"*Ah*, Thoma! Welcome, welcome. Give me just a moment, I've got to make sure I don't put this somewhere it doesn't belong," the black-haired elf said, glancing around his workplace to find a spot to place the still-hot metal. His voice was warm, but I could tell there was an age that was kept well hidden by his maturation point.

If I had to guess, it was clear he was well into his thousands, at least.

"Why not just put it back into the fire? I won't be here long," I asked nonchalantly. He raised an eyebrow with a look of either disbelief or disgust in his green eyes, I couldn't quite tell which, and sighed.

"Do you have any idea what that would do to the metal? All of its toughness would be wrought out by the fire, and there would be nothing I could do. Hells, if I were to let it sit in there too long, you might as well try attacking someone with a stick of butter at that point, since you might end up doing more damage that way," he said dismissively, finally setting the metal down on top of a steel support base.

"So, how can I help you? Did your mother send you here?" he asked, pulling off the single glove he wore. The skin beneath the glove was clean and pale, while the rest of him looked like he had rolled around in a pile of ash and soot. "N-no. Was she supposed to?" I asked, a little confused. "Shit. Well, there goes *that* surprise," he said, scratching the back of his head. "He hasn't seen it yet, has he?" my mother's voice came from behind me.

Needless to say, I was confused as she walked past me and stood next to Maikell.

"What do you mean? I was just here to see if I could do something about my jerkin not fitting me properly anymore," I said, pointing to the undone buttonhooks of my jerkin. My mother's eyes widened as a smile grew across her face. "See? I told you he was growing," my mother said, wrapping an arm around Maikell's shoulder. "*Argh*, off with you, you brute," he grunted, shoving her arm off his shoulder.

"*Brute*? I'm just trying to be nice!" my mother said in jest. "Yeah, well, your version of *nice* hurts more than you think it does. Anyway, are you giving him what I made for him or not? I already got interrupted by the boy and I promised Vesryn I'd finish it by tomorrow," he asked, gesturing to me.

"Yes. We're about to head out on an investigation, so I'd rather he get it sooner than later," she said, patting his shoulder heavy handedly. He didn't budge, but I could see the red hand mark my mother left on his skin. "Alright then, give me a second here," he said, turning to grab a leather parcel wrapped in a cross-tied string. "Here you are," he said, giving me as warm a smile as he could muster. "It's not much, but your mom has truly helped us all out here, so I felt like I owed her a favor," he said, putting his hands on his hips.

"Th-thank you. I don't know what to say," I stammered, grabbing the parcel with both hands. It was surprisingly light for its size, but I laid it out on a nearby table that only had a few tools on it. Untying and unfolding the parcel, I could hardly believe my eyes with what was beneath it. "Go on, then. Try it on," he said, his tone growing a little warmer after seeing my reaction. "R-right now?" I asked, looking around for a changing area. "*Ah*, one moment," he said, reaching for a lever that lowered a curtain hung off of a metallic ring.

"There, you can change inside of that. Most people do, especially if I have to make any adjustments for their armor," he said with a shrug. The armor was intuitive enough to put on, and light enough to where I could lift it over my head with absolutely no issues whatsoever.

The armor was primarily made of griffin leather dyed a dark green and silver like my mother's armor. There were a few pieces of that same, unidentifiable metal in the chest and shoulder pauldrons. The bracers, sabatons, greaves, cuisses, and spaulders fit incredibly snugly, as if they were molded specifically to my body. Each piece of armor held intricate linework that swirled and flowed like the vines of Myrdin across them.

The gorget was adorned with the symbol of houses Phrys and Fayren, with them being located on the left and right, respectively. The Phrys family emblem of a lynx caressed by a crescent moon beneath a chevron, supported by two green dragons, and backed by a dark green shield with the words *Power for Progress, Progress for Peace* written on an unfurled scroll that bent upwards from the bottom.

It was more elaborate than ours, which was a diving falcon over twin, crossed blades, and backed by a black shield. The emblem was wreathed in a laurel with the words *They All Will Fall* written in a similarly unfurled scroll draped atop the shield. "I never thought we even *had* a family crest," I said quietly to myself, looking down in disbelief as I stepped out of the changing room.

As soon as I did, my mother's face lit up in a mixture of both pride and happiness, with her eyes beginning to well up with tears. "Look at you all grown up," she said, wiping away a tear as she chuckled. "Thanks mom. Maikell, I couldn't thank you enough for this absolute masterpiece," I said, giving the elf a warm smile and a bow. "*Bah*, that's not all I made you," he said, surprising us both. "What? What do you mean? I only asked you for the armor," my mother asked, shocked to her core.

"Yeah, but what good is such *good looking armor* if he doesn't have a sword to match it?" Maikell asked wryly, pulling out a sheathed longsword from beneath the table between us. The sheath held similar patterns to my armor, with both emblems stitched into it and stacked on top of one another. The guard held a gentle, upward curve, with an eight-sided pommel at its base. The wire-wrapped hilt held a braided steel divider midway through its length, and was gently flattened to better my grip around it.

"It's fucking *beautiful*," I said, not bothering to try and keep my language polite as I picked it up. The balance of the satin-finished blade was perfect in every single way. No matter how I held it, it seemed to flow far better than any blade I'd ever wielded before. "I cannot thank you enough," I said, acknowledging the amount of work that must have gone into making such pieces.

"*Nah*, I owed your mom more than just a favor. She saved mine and my wife's lives once. No amount of work I could ever do would be enough, even if she says *no thanks are needed*," Maikell said, his tone both reminiscent and humbled. My mother smiled at him warmly, and gave him a hug regardless of how dirty he was. "Thank you," she said, her voice muffled slightly. He was taken aback, as most elves would be in this situation, but patted her lightly on the back after a moment's consideration.

"Well, you'd best be off. Got a long road ahead of you on the way to Soule. Wouldn't want to be late for that, would you?" Maikell asked after clearing his throat, giving us both knowing nods. I bowed before showing myself out of the workshop, and rolled my shoulders once or twice, hardly feeling the armor at all. "What did I do to deserve this?" I asked my mother, who was making sure all the pieces worked together without hindrance.

"You're my son, and as such you deserve the armor fitting of that title," she said with a huff. "Does Bernar have anything like this?" I asked with a chuckle. "He does, but for the same reasons he wears the pendant all the time, he doesn't wear the armor," she replied. "I see. When did we earn a family crest? I thought those were only given to royal or noble families," I asked, idly fiddling with the design on my gorget as we turned down the path that led to the stables.

"It was a few years before I had Bernar. Aurae and Elhael gave it to me so that when I eventually came back, all would know of my station," she began. "The addition of the quote was my idea, though," she chuckled. I looked at her curiously, since the words *They All Will Fall* didn't exactly explain a lot to me at that point in time. "But what does the crest mean?" I asked, knowing next to nothing of symbology.

My mother gazed off into the distance for a moment, then answered in a hushed tone. "The falcon signifies hope and chivalry, the crossed swords mean that we are always on guard, and the laurel signifies the triumphs over evil. The words in the unfurled scroll mean exactly what you think they mean; that *all* of our enemies, both physical and mental, will fall without exception. Do you understand?" she asked, looking at me sharply.

I nodded my understanding firmly. "I do. I'll do my best to uphold what you've worked so hard for all these years," I began. "Besides, it's not like our useless prick of a father would've done anything about it," I chuckled, shaking my head as I looked away. My mother, on the other hand, didn't laugh.

"*Useless prick* as he turned out to be, there was a point where I *did* love him. He gave me you and Bernar, after all, so I can't be *too* angry at him," she said with a raised eyebrow. "*I know*, I know. I'm not denying that. I just wish he hadn't turned out to be such a piece of shit," I replied, raising my hands placatingly.

Within the hour, we were loaded up and ready to make our way to Soule. It would be a decently long journey, and with Bernar having gone to meet Leona in the Rhydian Pass, it would just be my mother, Ysevel, Vyra, Derion and I going to investigate.

I wonder if the five of us will be enough for this. I know they're the core members of my mother's team, but shouldn't Eileen be here, too? I wondered, as I looked out of the stable toward the massive gate.

"We'll be fine. Eileen volunteered to stay behind with Anwill this time around since you were *technically* taking her place," my mother said warmly, noticing the slightly worried expression on my face after having read my thoughts.

"I know, but the only other times I've seen any kind of *real* action, it felt like everything just seemed to happen all at once. It was always to our benefit to have combat veterans at our side," I said with a shrug.

"You were also in some very difficult situations, and none of which afforded you any time to deal with properly," she said, acknowledging everything that had happened during Coltend's invasion. "I guess you're right," I said, recalling how rushed everything felt, and how quickly we were all forced to grow up and deal with everything that had happened.

If that bastard hadn't... I stopped myself, not wanting to flood my head with endless questions.

Within a few moments, we began to ride through the city. Onlookers on the sides of the road cheered us on. Not to the degree of a full-blown parade, but they knew that whenever my mother and her team went out, it was for something of vital importance. She waved and smiled brightly at those who cheered her on, and I think I even saw her blow a kiss at one point. She was damned-near *regal* in her handling of the crowd.

I, however, was not, and Ysevel could only chuckle at my discomfort.

As we left the city of Myrdin, we turned South-West and headed down the path that led to Soule. It was well traveled, for sure, reminding me of the path from Codrean to Coltend Castle with its numerous cart-marks and hoof prints embedded into the packed earth.

The magnificent trees that coated the country of Caegwen like a blanket seemed much taller now that there was nothing else to block their full glory. The golden rays of morning sunlight cut through what little gaps in the canopy existed as birds sang their morning mating calls and songs.

The path was long. *Much* longer than the pathway from Codrean to Coltend, spanning nearly halfway across the country itself. Over the three days it took us to arrive, the snowfall began to grow increasingly denser as we approached our destination.

Caegwen wasn't quite as mountainous or hilly as I'd thought it would be, but it still held its fair share of steep inclines that we had to go over. With the occasional break in the treeline present, it allowed me to look out over the countryside. A beautiful sea of white lay out before me as far as I could see, and all I could do was marvel at its beauty.

"It's beautiful, isn't it?" Ysevel said from beside me. My mother, who rode just ahead of me alongside Derion, who was our master tracker, turned an ear towards us almost unnoticeably. Even after having been on the road for the past three days, she still looked just as clean and stunning as the day we'd left. "Y-yes, it really is," I said, mentally kicking myself for sounding like an idiot.

"You're still not comfortable around me, are you?" she chuckled, asking a rhetorical question as she noticed my flushed cheeks. "W-well, yes and no," I said, rubbing the back of my head awkwardly. Her response was merely a lifted eyebrow and a wry smirk strewn across her fine features.

I sighed heavily, and brought my arm down. "You've seen me at my worst," I began after a moment's pause. "You've seen me balling my eyes out, wishing a glick would've chewed my heart out with its nasty rows of teeth. You've also done a lot for me that I don't think I could ever repay you for. There are... *layers* upon *layers* of things that run through my head when I try to talk to you now," I said, my tone dropping.

She chuckled softly and warmly, like a kiss from a golden ray of sunlight on a cold winter morning. "You almost make it sound like you're not *worthy of my presence* or something," she said in jest.

"I'm not. At the very least, I don't feel like it. You're incredible, Ysevel; head and shoulders above most of the people I know. To top it all off, you've helped me in ways I didn't even know were possible, so, thank you," I said in a lowered tone, not able to bring forth any words or jokes of my own.

Her expression softened, realizing she had hit the mark with her words and that she was right about how I felt. "Thoma, I..." she began.

"It's fine," I cut her off, not wanting to hear her patronize me *or* my feelings to prevent them from bubbling up further. "I just don't know what I did to deserve such kindness from someone I admire," I said, feeling a smile tug at the corner of my mouth as I shook my head. It was the first time I was able to voice any sort of feelings I had toward her, and I felt immediately lighter. It was *refreshing*, like a sip of cold water on a hot day.

"*Oh*, so you *just* admire me?" she asked playfully as her chagrined smile beamed at me. I blushed and my eyes widened, realizing the truth behind her words as I turned to look away. I quickly realized that the way I'd said what I did gave away everything, while saying very little at the same time.

But, then again, so did she, I thought, suddenly compiling her expression with her question to extract their meaning.

You idiot, I kicked myself mentally.

I finally managed to look into her violet eyes. They were just as beautiful as the first time I saw them, only this time, they seemed *different,* somehow. It felt like they were looking *into* me rather than *at* me, and I could feel the blood rushing to my face as the butterflies in my stomach turned into a tempest. Without realizing it, I had been blankly staring at her for a few seconds with what must have been a stupid looking grin on my face.

"W-well, I mean..." I stammered as I began to try explaining myself. "No, no! It's okay! I understand," she said, raising her hand placatingly. "It's still too fresh, I get it," she said, still holding the same expression. I paused, trying to think of how best to answer that. When nothing came to mind, I allowed myself a small chuckle, and shook my head. "Thank you, though," she said, her tone was a little different than her usually playful one. "For what?" I asked, looking over to her. She was...*blushing.* "For telling me," she said, giving me a heartfelt smile. I could see her eyes beginning to water a little, or at least I thought they were, but my attention immediately shifted to my mother's booming voice.

Stop, she commanded mentally to us all. When we all looked at her, Ysevel included, we noticed some tracks in the ground. *Siraye, what are those?* Ysevel asked, sharing her mental connection with the rest of us so we could all hear her words. *I don't recognize these tracks. Thoma, Derion, go check it out,* my mother replied.

Is this for me to learn from Derion on how to read tracks? I asked, already knowing the answer. *Yes, he has insight into such things that I could never give you,* she replied as she turned to look at me. I nodded my head and dismounted, feeling my ankle sink into the snow. I patted Celer's nape, and briskly walked up to where Derion was waiting for me.

As we approached the tracks, I noticed they bled off the side of the path, and went over a small hill in front of us. I moved forward to follow them, feeling the dark, hooded cloak I was wearing being tugged back. I turned to look at Derion who was holding up a hand, telling me to wait. With a smooth curling of his fingers, he pointed a long, skinny index finger forward, just off to the side of the deep footprints.

A hand mark? It's human, then? I asked, hoping he could hear me.

When he didn't mentally or verbally respond to my question, I thought he couldn't hear me after all. I assumed my expression gave away what I was thinking, because he nodded anyway and allowed a wolfish smile to come to his face. Letting go of my cloak, he motioned for me to take it slowly, and observe my surroundings.

My mother said he had greater insight into these things, and I'm beginning to think that wordless communication is a part *of this insight,* I thought, nodding my head understandingly.

I stepped forward, this time much more cautiously and observantly, as I took in every little detail that I could. I gestured to another set of much lighter prints in the snow, ones that no fauna I knew of could have left. He observed it carefully, his eyes widening at a realization I could only deign to imagine.

Commander, we have a problem, he said, transmitting his words to me as well.

CHAPTER 47

BEREFT

Trina Lande sat in her office, surrounded by papers strewn across an oaken desk. The morning sun was beaming through the small, square window, hardly large enough for anyone to fit through, but the rays cut through the once candle-lit room like a knife to butter. The bags under her eyes signified that she either hadn't slept, or did, just very poorly.

She had her elbows on the desk with her hands folded together, resting her chin on them with her eyes closed. She let out a deep sigh, furrowing her brow as she did. Before her, in the torrent of papers, reports and other such informational reports, was Wien's report of that fateful night's events.

It's been nearly three months since then, and I still haven't decided what to do. What can I do? I knew she wasn't trustworthy from the moment I met her, but to this degree is appalling. What troubles me most is that no matter where I look, I can't find a fucking thing in any of these records about it, she thought.

Just as she was about to continue that thought, a knock came from the door, and with it a familiar voice. "Commander," Wien said from the other side of the heavy, oaken door. "Come in, Sergeant," she replied wearily, the exhaustion evident in her voice. Wien entered the room cautiously. He could tell, from a single glance, that she was not well. Not ill, or anything, but unnerved to her very core. "You requested my presence, ma'am?" he asked, standing in a position of attention.

She sighed heavily once more, and gathered her thoughts for a moment. "Sit down, please," she said, gesturing to the only other chair in the office. It, too, was stacked with papers and unidentifiable reports. "There's a method to the madness, but just set them aside for now," she said tiredly, knowing the look he gave the chair without even setting eyes on him. Having set the papers aside, Wien sat down in front of her, and eyed his commander carefully.

She's exhausted. Almost like the news aged *her a good ten years,* he thought, noting the bags under her eyes in much more scrutinous detail than before.

"I'm sure you're probably thinking that I'm a madwoman for going through this many papers," Trina began, her green eyes finally opening to look at the young Sergeant. "I was wondering what was taking you so long to act on what I'd told you, Commander. I wasn't going to ask, but..." Wien said, trying to lighten the mood. Trina let out a tired chuckle, and a thin smile broke out on her face. "I haven't lost *all* the marbles in my bag. There are still one or two left in there that keep rattling around the same way, and I can't figure out why," she said, putting her fingertips to her tilted forehead as she stared at the paper beneath her.

Wien looked at the paper carefully, and surmised what she was looking for. "You're still looking for any sort of hard evidence that could convict Unni of being the one that got Anders' family killed, aren't you?" he asked, suddenly realizing why there were stacks of paper strewn about the office in little piles. Some were taller than others, but for the most part, they were all from the same part of the records room.

"There's nothing. Nothing here that shows she was ever formally tasked with more than half of what she was. There are no witnesses, no surviving teammates, no loose ends for me to pick up on," she said frustratedly. "What kind of report are you looking for?" Wien asked, picking up a small stack of the papers in front of him, idly sifting through them as he spoke. "Something. Anything I can use as cold, hard evidence against her. *Anything*," she scoffed, spreading her hands widely and glancing around the room.

Wien read through a few reports, when a word he saw triggered something in his mind.

"Diary," he said softly, almost to himself. "What?" Trina asked as if she hadn't heard him properly. "This paper here says she kept a diary. The night I found her in her office, she was writing something on a piece of parchment. I couldn't make out what it was at the time, but it could've been an addition to her diary," he said, a tinge of hope in his voice.

Lande's eyes widened, then grew dark like a wolf stalking its prey. "That dumb *bitch*. Gods above, there's no *way* she'd be *that* stupid, but you never know. Wien, you need to get those papers," she said, her tone was cold and heartless, like she was commanding the execution of a horrible criminal.

That's not the tone she normally uses for a request, he thought, knowing how pragmatic she was as a person, and the respect she held from everyone around her.

"It will be done, Commander," he replied with a nod before rising from his chair. He gave a sharp salute, turning on his heel as he proceeded towards the door. "*Oh*, and Wien," Trina called out before he closed the door behind him. "Yes, ma'am?" he asked, peeking his head back through the crack in the door. "Don't get caught," she said warningly.

Wien cautiously made his way up to Unni's office. He knew she wouldn't be there, since around this time of day, she was always in the Great Hall with Anders, dealing with some of the city's sectional leaders.

Those meetings usually go well into the afternoon, so I should be fine, he thought, still not wanting to get caught by one of her personal guardsmen.

He had impersonated them to infiltrate the castle, and get closer to Unni in the first place, but his mannerisms nearly gave him away on a number of occasions. He didn't need to give them another reason to put him on their shit-list.

As he made his way up the stairwell, he could see just a hair beneath the doorway that led to the office. It wasn't much, but it was just enough to let him know that there was no one in there. No guards were stationed outside of it, either, but there were always roaming patrols lurking about.

Just like Mads had when he was ruling, he thought, carefully looking around a corner.

Seeing and hearing nothing threatening, he worked his way into the office, undoing the latch to the door, and gently pushing the heavy door open. The large office was well organized, this time around, with new candles inserted into the candelabras and un-stained ink pots placed on top of the desk. As he looked around, he tried to find anything that would resemble her diary, but didn't immediately see anything. He left the door ajar as he moved over to the desk, noting the well-worn metallic knobs had a lock on them.

They've got to be in there. No other reason to lock a drawer like that, right? He asked himself as he began to search for a key to unlock the drawers.

He searched and searched, but only found cobwebs and some questionably shaped, wooden dowels that were latched underneath the desk. He scrunched his features when his face got too close to them, reeling backwards when he realized what they were.

I might just be better off breaking the lock. The chances of her coming back before we find what we're looking for are slim, but it won't matter at that point, he surmised, pulling his dagger from his side.

He bashed the lock a few times before looking up toward the door and listening for any potential commotion that might have stirred. When no sound came from the hallway, he bashed the lock one last time, undoing the latch that clasped the metal bar without breaking it.

There's a little bit of damage to it, but it's unnoticeable if you turn it a certain way, he thought as he examined the lock.

Setting it aside, he rummaged through the unorganized papers, quickly glancing at each title until he found the one he was looking for. Every few seconds, he would pause and listen for anyone coming up the stairs, but every time, no sound came from it. After a few minutes of searching, he found the one he was looking for. It still had tear stains that blotched the ink in certain places, but it was still legible.

It's the only one in that state out of all of these. This has to be the one she was writing that night, he thought as he began to read the contents.

There was no title, no enlarged lead-in letter like the rest of them, no fanciful calligraphy. This was about as raw as writing could be. The tear stains blotched only a few of the words, but it was otherwise still fairly legible, even with the shaky handwriting.

It's clear that she was freaking out when she wrote this, but it's exactly what I'm looking for. It's the only thing out of all of these papers that's written about that night; almost as if she needed to get it off her chest. Was that why she confided in me that night? Wien thought, rubbing his chin.

He rummaged through a few more papers to see if there were any more from that evening, but there was nothing. Nothing of note or that held any sort of evidence regarding those events, aside from that one piece which he had tucked away in his armor. He reorganized the papers, closed the drawer and used the lock to close it shut once more. He tried his best to leave things exactly as they had been, but there was only so much he could do.

I can't stay much longer. If I'm caught now, this will all be for naught. The Commander put months of work into this, I can't fai-... his thoughts cut out as he heard footsteps coming up the stairs.

A burst of adrenaline struck his gut like a horse's kick. Within a few seconds, he quickly left the study, putting his frogmouth bassinet on as quickly as he could, and making himself as nondescript as possible. He heard voices resounding from what sounded like the middle of the stairway, and began to march as he would if he had been doing his rounds on that floor. The words were familiar, yet indecipherable, as the resonant echo from the stairway made it difficult to overhear conversations.

He did, however, recognize the voices.

Anders and *Unni? Shit. I'm in for it now...* he thought, doing a final check on his gear to make sure it was all in order.

As the pair drew closer, Wien positioned himself to be turning the corner by the time they reached the top of the stairs. Timing his exit perfectly, he just barely managed to pass by them almost unnoticed, standing at attention as they walked by him. The pair acknowledged the helmeted soldier, as only the most trustworthy were allowed to guard the rulers of Odensby; a tradition Trina herself had installed into the castle.

That was way too close, he thought, breathing a soft sigh of relief.

As he turned to continue his rounds, making sure that his movements were flawless, a voice called out to him. "Guard," Unni called out, sending a chill up his spine. "Your majesty," he turned to face her, dropping to a knee with a hand across his chest. He could feel his heart beating through the leather of his gauntlet. "Was my study door open when you arrived?" she asked plainly. While her tone wasn't accusatory, he knew it was a loaded question.

"Your majesty, I have only just completed my first round, and I have yet to verify the security of your study," he said, keeping his tone as even as he could with his heart in his mouth. "I see. In that case, please secure it for me. His majesty and I still have much to discuss about the day's meetings," she said dismissively. "It will be done, your majesty," he said, lowering his head a little more.

"*Oh*, and Guardsman?" Anders called out, turning to face him. "Yes, your majesty?" Wien replied, sinking back into his kneeling position as quickly as he could. "I thought the guard change was supposed to only be this evening. Did Commander Lande send you here?" he asked, curiosity ringing in his voice.

How the fuck do I answer that? Wien thought, sweat beading down the side of his cheek.

"Your majesty, I was doing my primary rounds when one of my fellow guardsmen came and told me that his wife was due for their child today. I am here to cover for his absence while his wife brings their child into this world, your majesty," he answered in an even tone. "Does the Commander know of this?" Unni asked. "She does, your majesty. She knows every one of her soldier's personal lives quite well, and sent me here in his place," he replied, glaring at her through the slits in his helmet.

Anders whistled critically. "I've always been proud of her for keeping such close contact with the men and women under her command. I should probably take a page out of her book and get to know those closest to me a little better," he said with a light-hearted tone.

You should probably start with the bitch *to your right,* Wien thought but said nothing.

"In any case, I'm glad you're here, Guardsman. In fact, I would like to start right now: What is your name?" Anders asked, genuine curiosity in his voice prompted Wien to answer truthfully. "Sergeant Bjorn Wien, of the 1st Royal Battalion, your majesty," he replied in a crisp, yet humble tone. "*Aha!* Bjorn, Ulfric's son! My apologies, it is difficult to see your face beneath the helm. I remember your father introducing me to you when you were just a young boy! You're all grown up *and* a member of the 1st, *eh*? I'm glad to see such an upstanding soldier guarding us *and* making sure that his comrades are well taken care of," Anders said, no small amount of surprise in his voice.

Unni, however, eyed him curiously.

"Thank you, your majesty. It is both a privilege and an *honor* to serve under your banner," Wien said in his well-practiced tone. "The honor is *mine*, Sergeant. I was a member of the 1st myself before misfortune befell my family," Anders retorted with a small amount of both pride and pain in his voice, to which Unni shifted uncomfortably.

Wien, of course, noticed the shift and grinned with malicious intent beneath his helm.

"I didn't know you were a member of the 1st, your majesty, and I am sorry to hear about your family. It is... *good* to know that we have a capable leader who understands the difficulties of being in the service," Wien said, his tone as honest as it could be. "Of course! We must always take care of those who keep us safe from enemies both foreign and domestic, no? In any case, I will not keep you from your duties any longer. You are dismissed," Anders said with a warm smile. "Thank you, your majesties. I will fulfill them *and* those of my comrade to the best of my ability," Wien said, lowering his head.

Once the two had turned and walked away, Wien let out a deep breath that he didn't know he'd been holding.

Fuck. Me. Sideways, Wien thought, his eyes widening as he realized just how close he'd come to being found out.

He completed his rounds until the evening guardsman came to replace him. Luckily for him, no further encounters happened between him and the rulers of Odensby. After conducting his shift change, he made his way to Trina's office, where she sat with a plate of half-eaten food, and a tall mug of ale.

"What's the meaning of this feast, Commander?" he asked as he opened the door, seeing the genuinely confusing sight of Trina Lande, of all people, drinking an ale with dinner. She wasn't prone to doing so unless there was something to be celebrated, but he had no clue what that could be. "I heard you had an interesting run-in with Anders today," she said in a more cheerful tone than her tired appearance would've allowed her to have in normal conditions. "I-I did, ma'am, but what is the meaning of this feast?" he asked again, even more confused this time.

"I'll tell you in a bit, but first: Did you find what we were looking for?" she answered his question with one of her own. "I did, ma'am, but I was nearly found out by the *bitch* herself," Wien added, clicking his tongue. Trina chuckled, and took another bite of food. "You know, I'm a little mad you never told me about your father, Ulfric. He was a good man, truly," she began, pointing her drumstick at him as if she were pointing a finger. Wien gave a half-bow. "Thank you, Commander. It means a lot to me to hear that from you. I just wish I knew how he died, since there was never any record of it," he said solemnly.

"Funny you should mention that," Lande began, a malicious smile strewn across her face. "You, of course, know he was a member of the 1st as well, correct?" she asked. "Yes, but what does that have to do with anything?" Wien asked, moving to sit in the chair as per Lande's gesture. She pulled out another plate of food and a mug of ale, and set the two in front of him.

"You know that Anders suffered greatly at the hands of both the former king and Unni's machinations, right? What if I told you that our discoveries are twofold?" she asked, taking another bite of her drumstick, smudging a bit of grease along the corners of her mouth. Wien did the same, and washed the food down with a gulp of ale before asking his next question.

"*Twofold*? What are you talking about, ma'am?" he asked, finally swallowing the remnants of the food still stuck in his cheek. "Twofold as in both Anders *and* you will have your revenge," she said, a sudden, heavy air filled the room. "Wh-what?" Wien paused his chewing. "Remember how I said that *appearances can be deceiving*?" she asked, following her question up with another gulp of ale.

"Y-you're telling me that Unni, now-*Queen of Hjalfar*, got my father killed?" he said, his tone darkening as his heart began to race. "Drink up, friend. Tomorrow is a big day for all of us, because *I* have a plan," she nodded, clinking her mug to his.

Needless to say, Wien didn't sleep a wink that night, even with the added effects of the ale.

The following morning, Anders and Unni were both seated in the Great Hall for yet another round of meetings. Farmers, mayors, and tax collectors all gathered around and deliberated what rates should be implemented and other such boring topics that few are interested in.

This has been going on for a week now. Can't we move on? Anders thought tiredly, rubbing the bridge of his nose.

Unni noticed his expression and laid her hand across his forearm, gently rubbing it with her thumb as the others in the hall argued and bickered with each other. He glanced up at her, pausing for a moment before giving her a thin-lipped and pained smile. "My lords," Anders called out, his patience having reached its peak. The others in the hall immediately quieted down, and turned to look at him.

"These deliberations have gone on for too long. I will have my financial advisor take this matter into his office, as I trust him to do what is right by all of you. Now, if you'll excuse my candor, we have other business to attend to," he said forcefully. Each of the men before him glared at each other, but ultimately bowed and took their leave before the next group was ushered in.

"Last one of the day, love," Unni said quietly, mentally preparing herself as well. "It's nearly midday, and we've had all of two meetings today. Who knew ruling a country would be so... *boring*?" he asked in a half-joking tone. She chuckled and patted his forearm while he gestured for the next group to come in. Oddly enough, there was only one person standing between the great doors. Backed by the sunlight, the person took a few steps forward after being instructed to do so by the guard.

Anders shielded his eyes from the sunlight that now radiated off the stone floor and into the hall, making his eyes water a little in the process. "Your majesty, may I present Sergeant Bjorn Wien of the 1st Royal Battalion," the announcer called out.

Unni shot Anders a glance that could've pierced steel. "What is *he* doing here?" she hissed quietly. Anders shook his head. "He wasn't on the list for today, so I have no idea, either," he said hushedly.

"Welcome, Sergeant! It is good to see you again," Anders said, warmly feigning his lack of surprise. Wien knelt before the throne a good distance away. "Your majesties, I thank you for allowing me the honor to stand before you," he said humbly, keeping his eyes downcast. "O-of course, Sergeant. We would be remiss to not uphold the sanctity of these kinds of meetings. So, tell me, what brings you here today?" Anders asked.

What the hell is going on? He thought.

"Your majesties, I have come before you today after giving yesterday's conversation some thought," Wien began, keeping his tone as humble as he could manage it. "I was told by my superior officer, Commander Trina Lande, that while it was true that my father served with the 1st Royal Battalion, there was no record of his death anywhere," he said, letting his words hang a moment alongside the gasps of surprise from the witnesses of the Great Hall's meetings.

Anders cocked his head to the side, and raised an eyebrow in curiosity. "There are no records of his death?" he asked with genuine surprise. "None, your majesty. Which I thought was strange, since we have records dating all the way back to the Lyse War, but nothing within a few years prior or after his death," he stated, eyeing the scribes in the corner of the room.

Anders pursed his lips and squinted his eyes, watching the man carefully. "And you're certain of this? How did you even get that information?" Unni asked promptly, intrusively inserting herself into the conversation with no small amount of concern in her voice. "I'm certain, your majesty. Commander Lande has also given me the authority to conduct research of my own accord, as well as granted me unrestricted access to files from that time period," he said, nodding his head.

I knew she was going to be trouble, but this takes things to another level, Unni thought, feeling a weight in her stomach that wasn't there before.

"And where is Commander Lande now to corroborate your story? How do we know that you're not just saying things to disrupt today's proceedings?" Unni asked, trying her best to save face. "Because I'm going to confirm everything he just said *and more*. As for my whereabouts: I'm right here, your *Cuntestry*," Trina said, her voice resounding from behind one of the larger groups of witnesses. Her words drew startled gasps and *oohs* from the crowd as she spoke them.

Unni's face, now soured by the name she was being addressed by, grew increasingly pale, as she gazed upon the pure, unadulterated malice that was plastered across Trina's face in the form of a smile. "Hello, Unni. It's been a while," Lande said, standing next to Wien who now rose to his feet. "What is the meaning of this defiance?" Anders asked, clearly confused by the whole interaction.

"Your majesty, do you recall saying that you were thankful for the 1st Royal Battalion for *protecting us from enemies both foreign and domestic*?" Wien asked, putting one hand on the hilt of his sword.

Anders' eyes darted around in confusion. "Y-yes. But this? This is insanity! How *dare* you address her majesty by such a *crude* name, Commander Lande? Even if you've known me for most of your life, you *will* extend courtesy towards her!" he shouted as spit flew from his mouth.

"And you, Sergeant Wien, how *dare* you say something like that here? You've gone mad, and I *still* have no clue what this is even about!" he exclaimed, rising from his seat and pointing his fingers at both who stood in front of him.

"If you stopped your childish shouting and listened to us, Anders, perhaps you'd see why we're doing what we're doing. Now, shut the fuck up and sit back down, *boy*," Commander Lande said, pointing her finger downward at him as her tone of voice grew more serious than he'd ever seen. "You'd better have a *damned* good reason for this, Trina, or I'll have your head," he conceded, sitting back down on the throne behind him.

"Why not just take it now? I have done nothing to deserve such disrespect, especially not from one as low as this steel-clad whore," Unni nearly spat but stopped when she remembered where she was. The crowd inside the hall gasped, though did their best to keep their murmuring hushed.

"Alright. *Alright*," Trina began, pursing her lips and sucking in a massive amount of air through her nostrils as she nodded her head. Wien nearly chuckled when he saw the face Trina made as soon as she heard those final words reach her ears.

He knew what was about to happen.

"Listen up, you wrinkly ball-sack that's about as beautiful as a bag of smashed assholes: I've tried to be nice, but I guess you two have skulls thicker than the castle ramparts. So, as a result of your family tree being little more than a single branch, I'm going to say this as plainly as I can," Trina hissed as she seethed with rage.

Everyone, including Anders, was too stunned to speak.

"Unni, you lying, sniveling, shit-sucking, life-ruining, drippy-tip-spreading *fuck-toy*. I know what that leprous taint of yours did all those years ago. I know your past, and I know the pain you've wrought upon the man who now sits beside you," she continued, taking a step forward.

Wien tugged at the nook in her elbow, but she pulled away in a quick and abrupt motion.

I know there's little I can do to stop her now, especially if she tore away from someone who would only want her best interests at heart, but what is she getting at? Anders thought as he sat quietly, observing everything from Trina's facial expressions, to Unni's changed one.

"What the hell are you talking about, Trina?" Unni asked angrily, standing up in a burst of motion. "We're not on a first-name basis, *child-killer*, so watch your tone," Trina seethed. Anders finally blinked. "What do you mean *child-killer*? Is there more meaning to your words?" he asked, leaning forward in his throne and resting his elbows on his knees.

"Do you know how trauma works, Anders?" Trina asked. Anders nodded his head. "I've seen many warriors fall to their inability to keep their minds in check, yes," he replied. "Do you *also* know that it can misconstrue memories? Replace certain things with others? It's a defense mechanism of the brain, apparently," Trina said, choosing her words carefully.

Unni scoffed, and began to chuckle. "What does *that* have to do with anything? Guards, I sentence her to *death by hanging* for spreading heresy and blaspheming against the *rightful rulers* of Hjalfar," she said in a harsh tone as anger flared in her eyes. "You know, I'd *love* to see any of *my* soldiers follow that order," she said coldly, spreading her arms widely in invitation.

"No? Not one? Not a single one of you *dare* to follow her orders? *Hmm*, it's crazy what being a good and honest person will do for you, isn't it? It's almost like *you have no real power*, here," she grinned without bothering to hide the malice behind her eyes.

Unni shivered.

"You can't command my soldiers like you did the former Kings' all those years ago, Unni. You also can't feed them false information, or place them in a location you *knew* they would be most likely to die like Ulfric Wien. To top it all off, you can't even tell them that the enemy will be most likely coming from the South, when in truth, *you knew* they'd be coming from the North," Trina began.

"What did you just say?" Anders asked, lifting his head up and refocusing his eyes.

"Unni framed you, Anders. She knew where the attack would come from, and when it came down to the interrogation, she framed your wife, the former commander of the unit you were a part of. She was also directly responsible for slitting your child's throat to the point of decapitation," Trina said, letting her words marinate in the crowd's minds as well.

"Murderer!" one of the men called out from the crowd. "Traitor!" another shouted out. Eventually, the entirety of the Great Hall was in an uproar. Trina gave Unni a cold stare as she spread her arms like a mage summoning the powers of the world.

"Silence!" Anders shouted, releasing a burst of mana that created a shockwave around the room.

Within a heartbeat, the Great Hall was silenced, and all that could be heard was Anders' heavy breathing. "Anders, my love..." Unni began as she tried to put her hand on the side of his arm, but was met with a swift, back-handed slap across the face. "Keep your forked tongue behind your teeth before I saw it off like you did my child's head," Anders seethed, as he drooled with rageful sadness, glaring at her shocked expression.

Giving him a moment to recover, Trina produced the page that Wien had taken from the office. "Why do I not remember it being *her*? How could I have been so blind?" he asked no one in particular as he stepped away from Unni's shaking figure.

"The mind does strange things when it suffers trauma," Trina began, taking a few steps forward. "It tries to replace one thing with another in hopes that it will make more sense. It represses certain memories in hopes of never being discovered. If you don't believe me, here is the proof of my words," she said, handing him the paper.

Anders looked it over and immediately knew it was Unni's handwriting. He was beginning to tremble as his eyes neared the end of the page coated in a thin sheen of salty liquid. "Y-you..." his voice now drenched in malice, aiming a trembling finger at the one whom he'd shared a bed with just the night before.

"Anders, m-my love, I just..." she was cut off, feeling the hot sting of a mana-infused slap this time. "You *dare* call me that?" he asked, taking a step forward as she took three back. "You got my wife and unborn child molested and murdered, then went on to decapitate my only living child with your bare hands. You've destroyed everything I once held dear and every good emotion I've ever harbored for you. As a final courtesy, and to appease my own curiosity, you will have thirty seconds to explain yourself," he said angrily but still trying to keep up appearances for the crowd around him.

"Anders, how can you believe that they didn't just write that themselves? How can you take the word of these two, insubordinate shit-stains on your banner over mine?" she asked, gesturing to Trina and Wien, who didn't budge. "Twenty-nine..." he began counting as he slowed his pace towards her like a wolf stalking its prey.

I have to come clean or he'll kill me where I stand, Unni thought as she froze momentarily, but recognized the urgency.

"Twenty-eight," he continued.

"Anders, it's true. I was the one who framed your wife for the attack on Mads' family. I-I-I wanted to get you away from her, and just wanted to make you happier than she could. I thought that it would be a way for us to finally be together, and that you wanted me as much as I wanted you. I see that I was wrong in thinking that way. I-I'm sorry," she stammered.

"Ten... nine..." he continued, not missing a beat.

"*Please*, Anders! Please try to understand! Forgive me, please!" she pleaded as her desperation became clear in her voice.

"*One*," Anders said, taking a final step forward.

He's not listening to me. I have to get out of here right now or he's going to draw his sword, she thought.

Seeing as her words did nothing to appeal to his better nature, she began to *draw mana from the Ethereal, infusing it into her bones and muscles* as she turned to make a run for it. Trina noticed this, and did the same, preparing herself for what she knew was about to happen.

Unni dashed forward, trying to make it out of the Great Hall before anyone else noticed what she was doing. Wien was too slow to react to her speed, and failed to notice anything at all. Trina, however, was faster, and ended up leaving a swirling ring of air bursting out behind her, as she surpassed Unni's speed, catching up to her in a single step. Trina had drawn her sword, and slashed at the back of Unni's leg, forcing her to stumble and slide across the remaining half of the Great Hall's carpet.

"*Aah!* You bitch!" Unni screeched as she writhed on the floor, trying to stop the bleeding. She drew a seax from her hip, and pointed it at her. "Don't you dare come any closer! Guards!" Unni shouted over her shoulder, never taking her eyes off her assailant.

Trina, however, chuckled and swung the blood off her sword with malicious intent and stood her ground. "Ten years," Anders called out from a few meters behind the commander. "For ten *fucking* years you lied to me. All those years I spent aiming my hatred towards Mads for what he did, when in truth, it should have been aimed at you," he said darkly. Trina, having sensed his anger, stepped aside. Unni, seeing his expression, began to scurry backwards, still unable to stand.

"You destroyed my life, Unni, and you couldn't even give me a decent explanation as to *why*. I can't believe I was so stupid; believing you so blindly, when in fact, I was merely ignorant of the true source of my pain that lay in the same bed as me, and not with Mads," he said with evident disgust.

Unni kept scurrying backwards, her mouth soundlessly wording unintelligible sentences. A dark cloud began to shroud Anders as he continued towards her. "A-Anders, p-please…" Unni began to cry, feeling the weight of her emotions beginning to drown her. "*Tears?* Really? Did you shed any tears when you sliced off my child's head? Did you?" he shouted the question at her, drawing his sword and aiming it at her.

No one, not a single soul, moved in that moment.

"I thought not," Anders spoke after having allowed a few seconds of expectant silence to pass. "Death is too quick a punishment for you," he said to almost no one but himself as his eyes darted across the ground looking for an answer. "You will be banished forthwith from the country of Hjalfar," he began, finally looking up at her blue, bloodshot eyes.

"What?" Trina asked, surprised at the lack of a more severe punishment, but he held up a single finger to pause whatever she was about to say. "No aid will be given to you within these borders. You will be stripped of your title, clothes, and any rights provided to you being a synner. I will also deny you of your rights for being of Hjalfarian Blodt," he said, receiving a number of gasps from the crowd still within the halls.

"Y-your majesty, isn't that a little *too* much?" one of the merchant lords asked from the sidelines. Anders glowered at him. "It is not enough to have her simply be stripped of her title," he seethed. "No, I would deny her entrance to the great Blodthall itself, and have her families eternally *beg* me for mercy in the afterlife," he spat, turning back to face the focus of his anger once more.

Unni was in shock at his words, but just as she began to open her mouth, Trina materialized in front of her, knocking the seax from her hand and sticking the tip of her own in her open mouth. Trina put a single finger up to her own lips, and shook her head at the miserable wretch beneath her.

"Commander Trina Lande," he began. "What is it, your majesty?" she asked, never once turning to look at him. "While I am greatly disturbed at how this information came to light, I have to thank you for doing so. Your unquestionable loyalty to this country has been noted," he said, letting out a heavy sigh. "Thank you, your majesty. I was merely doing my duty, but Sergeant Wien was instrumental in this being revealed," she said, twisting the sword a little, grinding it against Unni's teeth.

"I see. Then, as a token of my gratitude, I will allow you to both mark and brand the traitor. Leave her bereft of any option to hide who she is," Anders said with angered grit in his voice. Trina, gazing into Unni's eyes, smiled with pure malice. "As you command, your majesty, but what of Sergeant Wien's vengeance? His father was killed in the same assault that caused all of this in the first place," she said not forgetting her subordinate's lack of revenge.

Anders, recalling what the Sergeant had said in the beginning of the whole ordeal, rubbed his chin. After a moment's consideration, he finally turned to face the young man. "I am truly sorry about Ulfric's death. He was a great man, and an even better friend. Had I known there were no records of his death, I would have made the appropriate amends immediately," he said with a light bow of his head. "Thank you, your majesty," Wien hardly managed with the lump in his throat.

"I know it's not going to bring your father back, but I would have *you* be the one to give her a Mark of the Unforgiven of your choosing," Anders said, trying his best to sweeten his words rather than bark them. Wien was speechless, but nodded his head in agreement.

"Commander Lande, pull the sword from her mouth and replace it with a gag," Anders said, receiving a small glance of relief from Unni, but it was short lived, as Wien raised his hand. "Your majesty, if I may," he began, walking towards the trio, halting Trina's movement. "I've made my choice of Mark to give her," he said, his tone was almost *light* even, like a weight had been lifted from his shoulders.

"*Oh?*" Anders asked. "Yes, your majesty, I have," Wien replied, walking up to Unni and kneeling next to her. He gently pulled the sword from her mouth, watching her every movement closely. "W-what do you want? Are you here to gloat? Spit in my face and call me names? Go ahead, I've been through worse than anything a *boy* like you could conjure," she said, turning her face away from him.

His hand reached out to the far side of her cheek, pulling her close and locking his lips with hers. Her surprise, and everyone else's in the room, was evident, but she wasn't exactly in a position to argue.

Going out as a traitor with a kiss? *Sounds like something out of a fairy-tale. Maybe I can use this as a final* fuck you *to this place and Anders for what he's going to put me through,* she thought within the heartbeat that followed.

She leaned in further, opening her mouth just enough for one of his lips to fit between her teeth, gently biting down and pulling him closer. He tilted his head to the side, reaching for her tongue with his as she sucked on what was already in her mouth. The sound of their kiss smacked across the dead-silent hall like an ill-mannered person eating a persimmon while shocked expressions riddled the crowd, especially those nearest to the unlikely lovers.

Wien pulled his saliva-soaked tongue from her mouth and pulled back, giving her just enough room to stick hers into his mouth. She searched for his tongue with hers, but was immediately stopped when she felt his teeth instead of his tongue wrapping around it. He kicked his head to the side and bit down hard, splitting her tongue down the middle in the process.

A muffled screech and a stream of blood came from her mouth, as Wien spat a wad of blood onto the floor. The crowd gasped when they realized what had happened, causing some to introduce their morning meals to the rest of the Great Hall's members.

"There, that takes care of that," he said, wiping his mouth with the back of his gauntlet. Anders was shaken to his core, but did his best to hide it. Trina, on the other hand, didn't bother to hide her own surprise. "What, and I cannot stress this enough, *the fuck*?" she asked with a disgusted look on her face.

"His majesty she had a *forked tongue*, but we all know she didn't *really* have one. I simply *made* it real," he said with a malicious grin on his face. A look of both surprise and horror rippled across Trina's face, but after listening to the victim's muffled moaning, she shrugged, and sheathed her own blade, as she walked over to one of her soldiers.

He was standing next to a wide-mouthed, glass jar of an unidentifiable chemical that was primarily used for branding cattle. As soon as Trina grabbed the jar, Unni began to unintelligibly scream through gargled blood. She began to hurriedly crawl towards the door, but slipped on the bloodied, stone floor. Trina began to chuckle as she moved towards her. "You really thought you were going to get away without *me* having a go at you?" she asked, crushing the back of Unni's ankle under her greave, pinning her to the ground.

Unni screeched and halted her movement, turning back to face her aggressor, only to find her dipping a glass rod into the jar. The snake-like shape at the end of it was cupped on the side that faced upward, since most were branded laying down. This allowed the rod to hold a small amount of acid that would drip down through tiny holes not much larger than a needle's head.

Unni began to shake her head, as she watched the fuming rod come towards her, understanding that her fate was all but sealed. "*Oh, now* you want me to stop? What did Anders' child say when she felt your knife to her throat, *eh*? What did she say, Forked One?" Trina asked, knowing full well Unni couldn't answer at that moment as that was her intent.

She didn't want to actually hear a verbal answer, but instead watched as Unni's mind tore itself apart with the memory of the last moments of Anders' headless child.

Tears and snot began to stream down, mixing in with the blood around her mouth as she tried to open it, but when no words came, she merely sat there and sobbed. "If you think for even a moment that I will feel remorse for you, know that what I'm doing now is less than a fraction of what I would do if I had my way," Trina began.

"Know this, Fork-Tongue, even the Undergod himself would find it difficult to forgive what I would do to you. Pray to whatever gods will accept you that I do not find you again in life, because if I do, you will welcome death like an old friend by the time I'm done," she said coldly, glaring at the woman beneath her.

With a resigned look in her eyes, Unni looked up at Trina, and spread her arms wide.

The acid bore into her skin, making it blacken and bubble wherever it touched. The chemically burned imprint of a snake was now present on both of her hands, and the entire left side of her face. Strangely enough, she hadn't screamed when pieces of her skin had turned to blackened, misshapen mush, but instead, she merely winced and grunted in silence.

Her clothes were removed shortly after, revealing a toned body and perky breasts to everyone present in the Great Hall. She was then placed inside of a barred cage, being paraded along the streets by an angry mob as she was led outside the walls of Odensby. Anders watched with tears beginning to well in his eyes, as a mix of emotions spurred within him.

"Are you alright?" Trina asked, appearing beside him like a ghost.

Probably best not to ask that right now, she mentally kicked herself as she noticed the tears streaming down his face and into his beard.

"Not really, but I'm sure that with time I will be," he said with a sigh, shaking his head and sniffling lightly. "It's... a lot to process," he said, wiping a pair of tears from his eyes. "She was my confidant for years, and I was hers. I just never would've thought that this is how it would end; that *this* is how I would find out the true culprit of my family's demise. I loved her, Trina, I did, but now? Now those feelings have curdled like old milk, soured by the condemning actions of her past," he said bitterly.

"I can't begin to imagine what you're feeling, Anders. Truly, I am sorry that things have come about this way," she began after watching his expressions change in rapid succession. "I won't pretend I know what you're going through, or anything like that, but I *do* know that your only option now is to look forward. Look beyond your anger and sadness toward a future where you can be happy again," she said, putting a hand on his shoulder. He patted her calloused hand gently.

She chuckled through her nose, shaking her head with a hint of a grin shining through. "It won't happen immediately, though. These kinds of things will take time, and everything will happen in the way that it's meant to happen," she said, gripping his shoulder and shaking him somewhat roughly. "Come on, I think I owe you a drink after that shitshow," she said, patting his shoulder twice and walking past him toward the nearest tavern.

Anders chuckled, wiped the remaining tears from his eyes, and began to follow her down the steps.

CHAPTER 48
LAST LINE

After Siraye, Thoma, and the others had left for their expedition to Soule, Anwill immediately took to researching the Autarchica Primaria that Siraye had mentioned to him in private just before they left. He was deep in the archives of the Royal Library, as Aurae had given him permission to do so.

This, however, was not to satisfy any desires for power on any of their parts, rather, they searched for ways to better help Thoma control his powers.

There is not a lot to go on here, Anwill thought, setting aside yet another stack of papers that cluttered his mahogany desk.

The only information provided in these texts are that it was originally discovered when the first Realmwalker appeared, but how many had come with him, or before him for that matter, isn't stated here. The only other bit of information on it is that the Realmwalker helped shape Myrdin into what it is today, though what other places he might have influenced are not mentioned, he thought as he compiled the information he now had.

With a heavy, exasperated sigh, he leaned back into his chair, feeling the wood creak a little beneath him. He stretched his arms above his head, and yawned deeply before looking at the hour-candle he'd lit when he first arrived.

Shit, it's almost completely out. Have I really been here that long? He thought, noticing it was on its last marking.

He chuckled lightly, and shook his head while stiffened joints creaked as he got up from his seat. "I really should pay more attention to the passage of time," he said aloud, feeling the blood rush back into the lower half of his body. "You should, indeed," Aurae's voice came from around one of the tall bookshelves filled to the top with scrolls, tomes, and other such records.

"Did you come to see whether I was dead? I can assure you that though I may look like it right now, I am very much alive," he said, his voice a little raspy from the lack of both sleep and sustenance. "No, no, I know you're an absolute bookworm. I don't blame you for that, I just wanted to see if you'd made any progress," she said, waving her hand dismissively.

Anwill was pensive for a moment, but ultimately shook his head. "There really isn't much information left," he said, gesturing to the desk of unraveled scrolls beside him. "The only thing I could *really* find was that there were once people, or elves... or gods even, I'm not sure which, were called *Realmwalkers*," he said with a shrug.

Aurae turned immediately pensive as Anwill said the final word, as if searching through her memories to find anything useful. After a few, quiet moments, she clicked her tongue in frustration, and exhaled through her nostrils. "If the Great Abstersion removed so much knowledge from our realm, then why was *that* left behind?" she asked, voicing her thoughts.

"Perhaps *they wanted* us to find it," Anwill suggested. "But why now? It makes no sense. None of it does," she countered frustratedly as she began to pace the room, playing with the ring on her left index finger idly. "Aurae, I've done what I could here, but none of our records here give us any insight into what truly happened back then, regardless of how hard we look," Anwill said tiredly.

"I know, I know. I just..." she trailed off, hearing footsteps coming from down the hall. Anwill also noticed the distinctive sound of armored footfall, turning to face in its direction. Vesryn came out of the dimly-lit hallway, and raised a hand in greeting. "Hello there, old friend!" he exclaimed in greeting.

"Vesryn! It's good to see you again," Anwill returned the greeting. Aurae stepped out from behind him, and the guardsman's facial expression paled. "Y-your majesty! My apologies, I didn't see you were here, too," he said, nearly snapping himself in half as he bowed. "It's quite alright, Captain. Now, tell us, what brings you to this darkened corner of Myrdin?" she asked, gesturing for him to raise his head.

"As you wish, your majesty. I've come here to notify you that over the past few days since Commander Siraye's departure, my scouts have noticed a strange figure lurking about the borders of Myrdin," he said flatly, though his features couldn't hide his unease.

"*A strange figure*? What did this *figure* look like?" Anwill asked. "According to some of the scouts, it somewhat matches the description of a creature Commander Siraye fought nearly a year ago," he said plaintively. "That can't be. She killed the one she fought as well as the others that came along with it. There was no other time where these creatures have been recorded here," Anwill said.

It's impossible. Or, rather, it should *be impossible for there to have been another event like that without us knowing. Did it come from another land?* He thought, scratching the side of his head.

"She did, and the reports have confirmed as much since that time. However, this one apparently has strange markings on it unlike its predecessors," Vesryn said. "What kind of markings?" Anwill asked, his curiosity peaked.

"Like those of the creatures that attacked Coltend Castle," Vesryn replied with finality. He knew all too well what those words would mean, especially to one who was there.

"By the gods above and below," Aurae said, cupping her hand over her mouth.

Siraye never mentioned they had markings, did she? This is becoming a war on two fronts with two different enemies. There's always the possibility that these different creatures are somehow working together, Anwill thought, digesting the information.

"Vesryn, I need you to lock down the palace as soon as possible. None may enter or leave, use any means necessary to keep this place safe," Anwill said. His voice was calm, but the commanding tone he used held centuries worth of experience defending and protecting the royal family.

"It will be done, Commander," Vesryn replied, rendering a quick salute of a fist placed across his chest. "Aurae, I will have to stay by your side. We cannot let this... *creature* get anywhere near you or Elhael," Anwill said hushedly.

"You have never led me astray before, old friend. We will trust you with our lives as we have since the start," she said, a pained smile growing on her face.

Vesryn made his way swiftly to the palace walls, where those under his command stood ready to hear his orders. "I want all available archers to be stationed at regular intervals toward the palace. This foe does not escape any of us, and will *not* reach the palace unscathed!" he shouted, ensuring none of his words fell on deaf ears.

"Yes, sir!" his soldiers replied in unison. The swordsmen moved swiftly and with a precision the likes of which Coltend could never achieve. Within mere moments, every guard, archer, and available synner was in a strategic location, as the rest of the city locked itself down.

The general populace shut their doors more out of precaution than anything else. Even with just the one creature on the loose, there was no point in losing elven lives without a good reason.

"Where are you?" Vesryn whispered to himself, gazing out into the tall trees far from the wall for any signs of movement. Minutes went by, and still no sign of the creature was present. "Captain, do you think...?" Miranda, his direct subordinate, asked. "There's nothing to think about," he replied curtly, still gazing intently into the woods.

That was rude of me, he thought.

"Sorry," he said after a few moments. "I just don't want this bastard getting in here, and putting this city and its people at risk," he said with a heavy sigh. "No need to apologize. I was just going to ask if you think the creature might have gone another path," she said, her voice carrying little to no nervousness whatsoever.

"Eileen should be guarding the Northern gate, so I am absolutely certain *that* area is covered. Do you think it's trying to find an entrance to the palace that is less-guarded?" he asked, realizing the merit in her words. "If it's avoided our detection for this long, I'm assuming it *has* intelligence to some degree," she said, reverting her gaze from her captain back to the trees.

"You might be ri-...." he flinched, stopping mid-sentence as a splash of a warm, viscous liquid dripped from his face, and the *squelching, thudding* sound of a head hitting the floor reached his eardrums.

That's not my blood, is it? Vesryn asked himself, smelling the thick scent of iron near his nostrils.

He turned to look in the direction the blood came from, only to be met by a pair of stark, violet eyes angrily staring back at him. For a moment, its face almost looked like a black, predatory cat's with a chitinous plate in front of its mouth in place of his subordinate's, but he quickly realized that her head was missing from her body entirely.

"M-Miranda?" he asked, almost too stunned to speak as he stared into the pair of eyes. A quick swipe came for his head, which he just barely managed to dodge, relying on pure instinct and subconscious reactions alone.

"It's here!" he shouted, side-stepping another swing coming from above. An arrow soared through the air, aimed at the dark creature, seeking purchase between the plates of its thick carapace. Finding none, the arrow fluttered to the ground, prompting an annoyed, over-the-shoulder stare and a low-toned *grrrr* from the creature.

As it turned to face its attacker, Vesryn noticed the markings on its back, trailing up and down like a bioluminescent cluster of runes and other such arcane symbols that began to glow a deep violet.

What the fuck is this thing? He thought, watching the symbols begin to glow more intensely.

It dashed toward the archer, killing him in a single blow as his armor did little to protect him from the strike. By the time the others had caught onto what just happened, another three had their throats slit or heads decapitated, as bodies began to slump to the floor like puppets freed from their strings.

"Fuck!" one of the guardsmen shouted just as the creature appeared in front of him. It approached him slowly, almost like it was observing the elf's mannerisms and facial expressions before taking his life. A flash of movement and the sound of blood gurgling reaching Vesryn's ears once more force him into action.

He *drew mana from the Ethereal and began to infuse it into his* muscles, lungs, and bones as he dashed towards the creature. Drawing his curved sword from its sheath and slashing in one, fluid motion was one of his preferred techniques. The blade sliced through the air, then more air, and more air, until the realization struck him like a boulder off a mountainside.

It dodged my attack? Vesryn thought, realizing the creature was nowhere to be seen.

Quickly turning around out of instinct, he barely caught the thick, hardened claw on the edge of his blade. Blow after blow, he was pushed back into the ramparts of the palace wall. Arrows soared in their direction, hoping to distract or kill the creature.

Nothing seemed to work.

Suddenly, its body seemed to turn into a distorted mist, making it hard to follow without mana-infused eyesight. It made a dash towards the palace, almost ignoring everything and everyone around it. It dropped off the wall but with his mana-enhanced eyes, Vesryn saw it land with the deftness of a cat, making little to no sound as it did so.

"Where do you think you're going?" he asked, dropping down and chasing it through the emptied streets of Myrdin as arrows rained down from above. He tried to strike it a few times, but his sword's edge found no purchase, not even any sort of tactile response from the creature.

Shit, nothing's working, he thought momentarily.

As he chased it through the streets, he began to send mana up to the length of the blade itself. As the particles of mana began to seep into the blade, he commanded the mana to ignite, causing it to burst into a tightly controlled mana-flame. He swung at the creature, which forced its hand to deflect the scorching blade.

For the first time since its arrival, it growled in pain.

It hurt him. Physical attacks don't do much, but when infused with mana, they can actually hurt this thing, he concluded.

"Infuse your arrows! Bring this fucker down, before it reaches the palace!" he shouted. The bow-casters in the canopy descended rapidly, jumping from branch to branch, and rooftop to rooftop. A multitude of glowing eyes of varying colors began to chase the creature down the street, as Vesryn continued to attack as often as he could while keeping pace.

Arrow after arrow the creature dodged, deflecting some and returning others to their senders, leaving a trail of corpses and broken arrows in its wake. "Do not let it reach the palace! We're the last line of defense, so make it count!" he shouted.

The guards near the main entrance to the palace heard him, and saw the commotion near the bottom of the stairs. " Use mana to bring it down!" Vesryn shouted out once more, sending the guardsmen flying into action. They wielded a mixture of polearms and curved swords as they approached the incoming enemy. They all *began to draw mana from the Ethereal and* infused their respective weapons. Without any visible hesitation, each one made their first attack on the creature in rapid, well-trained succession.

The creature reeled in pain, unable to dodge all the precise attacks at once, as its violet blood began to spue all over the stairs. Vesryn saw an opportunity to strike and thrust his sword forward, stabbing into one of the runes that lined its back.

The sudden shift in its demeanor was palpable, as the smoky visage it once held immediately solidified.

The runes give it certain powers? What kind of magic is this? Vesryn thought momentarily.

He aimed for another that marked its shoulder, hoping to disable whatever other hidden power it had, but the creature decided otherwise. Twisting its body just out of the way of his blade, it caught the flat of the blade with the back of its elbow and raised it well above its head. He was taken aback by the sudden move, since the creature even went so far as to sacrifice another two wounds to its legs as a result.

Shit it's gonna... his thoughts trailed.

The creature swung its free arm up into the undercut of his helmet, its elongated claws piercing through the base of his jaw, digging deeply into his skull. "Vesryn!" one of the guardsmen said, launching an attack on the creature. It prepared its defense a little *too* well, as it begun to use the captain's body as a meat shield for the slices originally meant for it.

"You bastard! How dare you use his corpse like that?" the guardsman asked. A low, malignant snicker resounded from the creature.

"Because I can," a rumbling voice replied just as it was ripping Vesryn's head off of his torso, pulling out parts of spine and entrails, spilling them everywhere.

The guards were all shaken with the inhuman horror that they'd just witnessed, but now that this thing had spoken, none dared to move on it. "I do not have time for this," it said, gauging the distance between each guard.

With a flash of violet, it went from guard to guard, decapitating or sundering their torsos in two, leaving nothing but bloodied stumps behind as it reached the entrance to the palace. It looked out behind it, and saw that many of those who had been chasing it slowed down once they noticed that even the royal guards couldn't kill it.

"Fear really is a beautiful thing," it rumbled as it went toward the great hall.

Anwill, however, was already inside waiting for it.

A precise spear of fire mana shot right past its temple, cutting into and searing its flesh and forcing it to shift its course. Another spear flew, this one of earth, and again it shifted its course. A third flew of water, forcing it to reel a little more, but continued to progress towards him.

Fine, have it your way, Anwill thought, his hands beginning to crackle with energy as his irises glowed an intense, pale blue.

He brought his arm downward, striking the creature with a bolt of lightning from a modified Kyr spell. This time, it stumbled and had to regain its footing.

It looks almost human, but the thick plates scales and deep violet eyes are all but screaming another story, Anwill thought as he noted its visage.

"I see you're not like the others," the creature began, wiping a thin line of blood from its mouth. "Neither are you if you have the capability of speech," Anwill replied.

"Having the ability to speak is something many in this realm, I've noticed, take for granted. They often use it to incite idiocracies and spread falsities, or anything bereft of any real value, to either make themselves feel better or control the masses. Whichever the case may be, it is, and always has been, astounding to me that some still have the *gall* to believe that everything they say is correct without challenge," it said in a harsh tone with extraordinary eloquence.

"Unfortunately for me, this... *form* is incomplete, making the need for verbal speech necessary in the first place," it said, gesturing to its own body.

Anwill's interest peaked.

"Why are you here, then? Why not just stay hidden until your *form is complete*?" he asked.

I have to buy time for Aurae to make it to safety, he thought, readying himself for any sort of surprise attack.

"Mincing words will not delay your death, elf. Since I know you're stalling for time, I would suggest you do better," the creature said, readying its claws. "You will not defeat me. Do you think you can?" Anwill asked, drawing his sword.

"I wouldn't have come here if I didn't think I could," the creature replied with malice dripping from his voice.

To a normal human, it would have appeared as though the two had vanished into thin air, leaving only shells of broken sound-barriers, air pockets, and dust clouds in their wake. The two moved so quickly, it would've been nearly impossible for anyone outside of a select handful to keep up with them.

Blow after blow, deflection after deflection; the two were interlocked in a dance of strikes, parries and slices that sent the sounds of battle resonating through Myrdin's halls. A blow came for Anwill's side which he deflected, retorting with a strike from the pommel of his blade that landed squarely between the creature's eyes. It backed away for a split second, before coming in for yet another barrage of strikes.

Its speed is no joke, but I can tell it's beginning to tire. I need to end this thing before it reaches Aurae. What would Thoma do? Anwill thought.

Having spent ample time with him, Siraye, and the others during their daily training, his own repertoire of moves had *also* expanded drastically. At that moment, he recalled a specific move that Thoma had tried once before.

Let's hope that little monster was onto something, Anwill thought.

He parried another few strikes, backing away as he deflected the last of them to get into a better position. His eyes glowed pale blue once more, only this time, something was different. The creature, having recognized the color of his eyes when they first began their encounter, started to dodge at a much faster rate.

Anwil, however, had planned for that, having sent out hair-thin tendrils of lightning mana into the air around him, *feeling* every movement his opponent was making.

With the creature darting around at an increased rate of speed, trying to disorient its prey, Anwill stood with his sword held above his head, leaving his torso greatly exposed. "Fool," the creature muttered just before making a final lunge at his target. The muscles in its arm flexed and swung the clawed hand at the elf, cutting through the air hissing between the fingers.

Suddenly, the sensation came to a halt, as an entirely different feeling began to creep into the creature's mind for the first time since it first left its confinement chamber in Valdis.

Fear.

Realizing its mistake far too late, it had fallen for Anwill's trap. As its claw was about to make contact with the elf, he suddenly vanished from its line of sight. The creature, now feeling a strange crackle of energy at its back, tried to turn to face it but realized that the other half of its torso was going in the opposite direction. A bubbling *hiss* resounded from where the other half of its throat should have been, as the second half of its face appeared some distance away; the only violet eye remaining faded into a dull, gray sphere.

"Sunder," Anwill said aloud, not bothering to look at the creature as he sheathed his sword. The creature's halves fell to the floor in a heap, creating a darkened pool of violet blood beneath it.

"You can come out now," he said over his shoulder. Aurae stepped out from behind one of the pillars, pulling aside her cloak that, until then, had made her invisible. In one of her palms, there were twin spheres of swirling mana ready to be launched as a quick spell in the event she had to protect herself.

"You had me worried for a moment there, old friend," she said, finally relaxing her stance a little as she noticed the still-twitching halves on the floor.

"I was a little worried myself, but it seems Thoma's *Sunder* technique has proved to be useful against this kind of enemy. Not to mention that the Night-kissed *Mantle* did true *wonders* at hiding your presence," Anwill replied, flicking the remaining blood from his blade and returning it to its sheath. "Strange, though, isn't it?" Aurae said, stepping in a little closer to the felled creature. She read the marks that riddled its back, arms, and whatever was left of its face.

Suddenly, her mismatched eyes widened.

With a whirl of her hand, she conjured twin vortexes of air to hold the two halves upright and conjoin them to get a better view of the runic writings. "It can't be," she said, holding a hand to her mouth in shock. "What is it? Do you recognize these markings?" Anwill asked, moving over beside her to see what she was seeing.

"It's... an *alternate*," she said almost breathlessly. "A *what*?" Anwill asked. "An alternate form of self. A mirrored edition of one's soul. The dark to the light, the Ethereal to the Underworld, the earth to the sky," Aurae said, barely even flinching her head to look at Anwill during her explanation. "But these markings..." she trailed off, running her finger along a runic pattern that wrapped around its torso.

Her face paled.

"What are they?" Anwill asked. "Something that ties them to this realm. They're not *supposed to be here*, not like this," she said, walking around to the other side to observe its nape. "Who do you belong to?" she asked almost to herself, squinting her eyes and trying to decipher the split runes that found themselves in the path of Anwills blade. Her mismatched eyes began to glow more intensely *as she drew mana from the Ethereal*, infusing it into the marking.

The mark itself didn't respond, but the flesh that once held it *did*, reverting back to its natural state and displaying its runes proudly.

"Anwill," Aurae said, her hair falling in front of her face, covering her eyes. "Did it have the ability to speak?" she asked, her tone
dropping darkly. Anwill was taken aback by her sudden change of
demeanor. "It did, but what does that have to do with anything?"
he asked cautiously. "Because this wasn't just any *alternate*, my old
friend," she began, turning her head to look him in the eyes. "Whose
was it, then?" Anwill asked, being almost fearful of the answer.

"It was the alternate of Liagon, original bearer of the Benevolent
ring. *This* ring," she said, holding up her right hand, putting the
golden ring inset with a glowing, blue stone on display.

CHAPTER 49
ECHOES IN THE SNOW

*W*e have a problem, Derion's words echoed in my mind.

It hadn't really occurred to me until that moment that something even *could* go wrong, especially with the team we had put together. I stared at the footprints embedded in the snow, taking in their size, shape, and the distance between each step.

It's human, or at least one *of them is. I can't speak for the others, and* that's *where the problem lies,* Derion transmitted to the rest of them. I saw Ysevel, Haldir, and Vyra immediately entering defensive poses, carefully watching the spaces between the snow-laden trees.

I did my best to be as observant as possible, but something was bothering me, and I couldn't quite put my finger on what. No matter how I looked at the tracks, it didn't make sense.

These creatures might have been following this person through the snow like a predator stalking its prey, but the spaces between the steps compared to the size of the feet don't indicate someone was running *in this area,* I sent to Derion.

He acknowledged my line of thinking with a terse nod. *Your thinking is aligned with my own. This is something we must tread carefully with, Commander,* he sent, keeping us all in the loop.

Fuuuuck. Okay. Here's what we're going to do, my mother began after a heavy sigh. *We're not going to rush this, but we can't afford to waste any more time. I will go with Thoma and Ysevel to investigate these footprints. Derion, Haldir, and Vyra will follow directly behind us and spread out as we work our way along these tracks,* she said, moving her arm in a sweeping motion.

If it turns out that there is a much larger group than anticipated, I will let you know as soon as I'm able, but remember that you will be the rear-guard, understood? She asked, receiving silent hand signals from each of them.

I began to follow the tracks as closely as I could, though they were a little difficult to see in certain areas, either due to the light shining through the canopy or fallen snow that filled them. Still, it wasn't impossible to track them, and I used much of what I'd learned from Derion during the next three hours of us doing so.

We moved slowly but methodically through the forest. Haldir and Vyra were spread out on our left and right, while Derion kept a good few paces behind my mother, Ysevel, and I to prevent any direct attacks from behind.

Siraye, I hear something up ahead, Ysevel sent, pointing a finger beyond a mound of snow where the tracks curved up and over. I followed them into a small clearing, the light shining through the snow-capped trees. It was only a single set of footprints, but I could tell that *these* were the human's.

Suddenly, my mother grabbed my shoulder, and pulled me close behind a tree and put a finger to my lips to silence me. We could hear the sound of indistinct chatter much more clearly now, realizing we were much closer than the densely packed trees allowed us to believe.

As we all peeked out from behind our respective locations, we noticed dark spots in the snow ahead of us that slightly resembled *people* sitting around a stick in the ground. She had already told the others, Ysevel included, to get to a place of concealment before even approaching me.

Is that what we've been following? I looked up and asked my mother whose eyes were affixed to her target's like a hawk's to its prey as she peeked out from behind the tree. *It is,* she returned curtly. If I hadn't gotten to know my mother as well as I had in such a short period of time, I would've thought she was angry; but it was quite the opposite.

It was pure, single-minded, and unadulterated *focus.*

I recalled her lessons on what she called *knuckling down,* which essentially was diverting as much attention to a particular task or situation as you possibly could, though I had never *truly* seen her use it in action. It was mostly used for when *shit went South,* as it basically stripped you of anything unnecessary in those moments.

I couldn't use that during my third-stage exam not because I didn't know how to, but because I simply *couldn't;* not with my emotions being so scrambled from the night before the exam. I knew, right then and there, that this was a *special kind* of focus, one reserved for moments like these where even a single misstep could mean *death* not just for me, but potentially those *around me* as well.

Surround them, she commanded tersely to the others. I almost asked what I should be doing, but realized it was likely that she had already made the calculation that we could defeat the small group before having made the order. The unquestionable trust the others had in her was astounding to me, because not a single one of them said anything regarding her command. No quips, no jokes, nothing.

It was like they'd all *knuckled down.*

Wait, Derion said there was a human with them, I thought, not actively trying to transmit it to anyone.

That will be your target, as it's not entirely human anymore by the looks of it, my mother said, her tone was cold and almost bloodthirsty. I realized that it had been over a year since she'd been out in the woods killing anything that came through the portals. I could tell she was itching for a good fight, and there was nothing subtle about it once I'd noticed her unwavering glare.

I turned to peek out one last time from just around the tree, and I felt my stomach begin to sink.

I know who the human is, I said plainly, trying to keep my emotions and tone as even as possible. I knew I had to take a deep breath; I couldn't afford to let a year's worth of destroying and rebuilding myself go to waste. *What? How?* Vyra asked just as she was finishing getting into position. *Where do you know them from? Have you seen this person before?* Haldir chimed in.

Irun Mothac, former synner of Codrean. Old friend. Fucking traitor, I replied curtly, feeling myself sink into that emotionless focus my mother had told me about.

He's definitely uglier than before, but that's him, alright, I thought, noticing the daemonic arm and other such features now embedded into him.

He looked...*older.* Like he had somehow gained about *ten years* in the span of *one.* He was taller, more toned, wielding a much bigger sword than he normally would have when he was still one of us. He and a few other dark, plated creatures I didn't recognize the species of were gathered around a stick.

He was *teaching* them, I noticed. Teaching them how to read cardinal directions using shadows to gauge their direction of travel. That was a trick all synners had learned from a very early age in the event we ever got lost during a training exercise.

I sunk deeper into the cold, single-minded focus.

Thoma, are you alright? Ysevel asked, clearly seeing the effects of my thoughts showing on my face. *I'm fine,* I nodded, sending her as much of a level-toned thought as I could. I couldn't *entirely* shake the rage I was feeling, but I did my best to hide it and not respond to my emotions like a child would.

Regardless of my attempts to hide it, my mother noticed and patted me firmly on the shoulder, reassuring me that it would be okay.

Remember to aim for the soft spots between each plate of their body. Is everyone ready? She asked the others whom she noticed were already in position for their respective strikes. *At your command,* everyone, including Ysevel, responded in unison. I could feel my heart begin to respond to the need for increased amounts of air as it began to race behind my ribcage. Perspiration, even in the cold, snowy weather, began to form on my brow, as I felt my grip tighten around the hilt of my blade.

The silence, the calm before the storm, was *deafening* as the sound of my heart pushing blood through my veins *boomed* in my ears..

Go, my mother commanded.

Just as she did, we all fell into a single, coordinated attack, absolutely blindsiding the group of about twenty creatures and one, traitorous shit-nugget. I launched myself off a stone platform I'd created, barrelling straight into one of the creatures.

After *infusing an ample amount of mana into my blade*, I cut between the plates just like my mother had directed us to. My sword bit into leathery skin, muscle, sinew and then bone; severing the limb from the creature I attacked.

Multiple limbs from the other's targets flew in a similar manner, spilling tar-black blood onto the snow beneath our feet. Another one fell to my blade in the span of time it took my mother to kill three of her own targets. While they were decently spread out, she moved like a bolt of lightning between them; a visual blur for any un-enhanced eyes.

The creature that stood next to Irun, however, was nothing like anything I'd ever seen. I saw its scarlet eyes staring at me inquisitively as it tilted its plumed head, but it still followed every movement I made with terrifying accuracy like it was learning my attacks. After striking down yet another one of the creatures, I noticed it turned its attention to my mother. The distorted, bigger version of Irun, however, took longer than I expected to recognize me.

But now matter how much he'd changed, he couldn't hide what I knew to be *fear* in his eyes when he looked at me.

I didn't issue any verbal challenge, I didn't even want to exchange words with him. My only duty, having sunk deeply into the *knuckle down* mindset, told me to keep killing the lesser creatures, as the final two would certainly pose more of a problem.

The only problem was that I had miscalculated just how powerful the rest these fuckers actually were.

When we began our attack, we had caught them off-guard and entirely unaware of our presence. By the time we'd reduced their numbers to a little more than half, they realized they were being attacked and immediately sprung into action; drawing curved, jagged swords from their backs and hips and launching attacks of their own.

While I was taken aback at the speed of their attacks, I was glad to see that Ysevel held her own quite well with a sword; deflecting, sidestepping, and dodging attacks while implementing some of her own mixed in with spells and advanced sword techniques. I had always thought she would be more of a long-range attacker, but her skills were remarkable to say the least.

I'm glad I don't have to worry about keeping her safe, I thought, shielding the comment from the others as I sliced into yet another creature's neck.

The Plumed One, or *Plume* for short, said something in a language that sounded like mud and rock mashing together; lifting his muscular arm and directing it at Haldir, Vyra, and Derion. Each one of these creatures could stand and fight toe-to-toe with each of my companions, but I didn't have the mental capacity to focus on their fights as well as my own.

Because *he* was coming right for me.

A jagged blade swung down from my right, and I did my best to deflect it and immediately riposte with a quick thrust aimed for his throat. He ducked under it, trying to sweep me off my feet as I could feel the presence of dark mana surrounding his limbs. It didn't feel like he had been able to infuse it into his muscles, but his kick was swift nevertheless.

I used minimal movement to avoid the blow, aiming another series of blows at him, which he expertly deflected and eventually countered with a swing aimed for my liver and spine in quick succession. I deflected the first and parried the second behind my back, then used the resulting momentum to redirect his blade away from me just before trying to get an uppercut beneath his armpit.

Snow kicked up in a trail behind my blade as I swung, creating a beautiful arc of ice. Even though he side stepped my attack flawlessly, I immediately aimed another swing at his clavicle in hopes of cutting the fucker's head off. Unfortunately, Irun pulled his head to the side just in time for it to miss, using his pauldron to redirect my attack and elbowing me in the ribs.

I'm so glad this armor is as strong as it is. That might have broken a rib or two if it hadn't been so well-crafted, I thought, feeling myself become airborne and moving away from him.

A pair of the dark things came sprinting towards me at an incredible speed, barely allowing me enough time to react. However, the training I had been subjected to with my mother, her team, and Anwill had made me more efficient at taking on multiple opponents at once.

No other choice, huh? *Guess it's time to try* that *out,* I thought, trying not to let my emotions seep through into my actions.

The first came with a thrust aimed at my gut, which I deflected away from me, causing it to stumble briefly. I used the momentum of my sword to parry the other attack aimed for my neck. I allowed my third-stage to show for only a brief moment, as I cast a *Flamebolt* beneath its chin, bursting its charred brain-matter out the other side.

The brainless corpse fell to the ground with a wet and sizzling *thud*, while the other turned and swung desperately to try to break my defenses. I *condensed an obscene amount of mana* to the edge of my sword and, with a single swing of my blade, sundering it in half with a calculated efficiency I'd learned from facing off against my mother and her teammates.

As a third creature moved in toward me, Irun held his hand up and shot a blast of dark mana at it, knocking it into a nearby tree. Snow fell from the shaken branches and covered the either unconscious or dead creature beneath it. I turned my head away from where the creature had fallen, and looked at Irun in earnest.

His red hair had become even darker, while his muscles and overall build had grown exponentially since the last time I saw him. His armor, too, was complimentary of his build, as it wasn't full-plate armor, but more akin to a berserker's; with a pair of heavy, rounded pauldrons and armored plates protecting most of his torso. His greaves had much lighter armor than the rest of his build, though I suspect that was to aid with mobility rather than offer protection.

It felt, strangely enough, that even with all of the changes he had undergone, it *still* felt like the *old* him was in there *somewhere*, though amply corrupted by whatever havoc the dark mana had wreaked on his core.

"You've gotten stronger," I said almost proudly. "I've always been stronger than you. Although, looking back, that was never very difficult to be, was it?" he asked with a hungry grin on his face. After looking at me, *really looking* at me, he noticed I had also changed.

"You didn't have white hair or pointy ears before. What gives?" he asked, his voice a much deeper baritone than before as he began to circle me. "Why should I tell you? So you can run back to your master with your other severed arm and tell him what you've discovered?" I answered his question with my own, albeit a sarcastic one, as I began to counteract his circling.

He raised his sword's point to eye level with one arm as his eyes filled with rage. "You have *no* idea what I'm capable of now, nor what I've been through to get to this point. I *will* kill you this time, Thoma, and believe me: I'll *make sure* you suffer before the end as payment for what you did to me," he seethed. "*What I did to you?* More like what you did to *yourself*," I said calmly.

As the words left my mouth, I saw something in his distorted face twitch, but I couldn't place exactly what had gone on in his head.

"Then let what I've done lead you to your end. Ready for round two?" he asked, getting into a different guard than I was used to seeing him use. "Time to find out," my eyes flared with mana-leakage as I answered with a cold, distorted voice resulting from entering my second stage.

With a loud shout, he rushed in, swinging in a combination of blows that, I admit, were a little challenging to keep up with, even in my second stage. He put me on my back foot, kicking up snow and frozen dirt as we dashed and weaved between the trees, keeping pace with each other's movements and sword-strikes.

I'm only on the defensive right now, but I'm not going to last long if he can keep this pace up, I quickly surmised, beginning to consider my options.

I decided to bring our battle back around toward the main fight to check in on everyone. My mother and *Plumed* were still locked in combat, which was more surprising than anything else. While she didn't seem to be stressed or under pressure from the creature, she *did* have a look on her face that suggested she was *intrigued* more than anything else.

Vyra, Derion, and Haldir were just cleaning up the last few of the weaker ones, while Ysevel was casting some kind of healing spell on them from a distance. She had a few scratches on her, but nothing too serious as far as I could tell.

I felt a surge of mana behind me, and knew immediately that Irun was about to cast something my way. I quickly *felt for the snow's embedded water mana*, and summoned a pillar of ice behind and beneath me to block his spell, but it was obliterated by the force of whatever it was he had cast.

Again I felt the surge, but this time I reached further, grabbing at the frozen earth's mana and lifted a wall behind me. The spell was stopped in its tracks, but Irun, having upgraded himself, quickly dashed around the small wall I'd created and aimed a swing at my gut.

"Stop using cheap tricks and fight me like a man!" Irun shouted angrily. He swung repeatedly and grew increasingly angrier with each deflection or dodge that I returned.

He had no idea what I was planning.

I'd learned to bide my time through months and months of getting my ass absolutely handed to me by my mother, brother, and colleagues in Myrdin. All of my dashing and dodging was to see what the extent of his abilities were. Sure, he was fast, and held a lot more power than I had originally anticipated, but something was off, and I wanted to exploit it.

After having seen that he could only either force his way through my barriers, or cast spells that were strong enough to burst them to pieces, I realized that I had something he lacked: *Perspective*. Being strong and brutish was never my style, and even after having my seal undone, and putting on a decent bit of muscle, I still relied on my ability to see things that others couldn't.

That moment had finally come.

I got close enough to my mother and the others to where they would be a threat to him if my mother finished off her opponent soon, and I noticed Irun still hadn't caught on to that fact. His single minded focus of killing me, like I had wanted to when we fought the first time, would be his downfall, just like it was almost mine.

"Fine! Have it your way!" I shouted, making a blatant display of my torso. I held my sword arm out to my side with the point toward him, bending slightly at the elbow, while my other hand began to work the earth and air mana around me, causing it to swirl. He charged at me in a response of pure, blind rage to my challenge, aiming a vertical blow to cut me in half.

Just before the blow landed, I *pushed against the earth mana*, launching me to the side faster than I ever could've stepped, and caught the air current that I had created to carry me up and over him, forcing me into a rapid spin.

Once more, I *infused a copious amount of mana into the edge of my sword and muscles*, feeling everything as if it were a single, unified structure. Just before I finished my swing, I saw him barely able to react to my movements as he began to rotate his sword.

"*Sunder*," I said, furrowing my brow and gritting my teeth as my eyes glowed intensely.

With a burst of snow, earth, air, and blood that sent a shockwave around the two of us, our duel came to a dramatic close. "Thoma!" I heard Ysevel shout from my right. She must have been shaken up by the sudden shockwave, but I quickly dispersed the cloud surrounding us with a burst of wind-mana. I could hear her running towards us, but I didn't understand why.

I loomed over Irun as he tried to crawl away now bereft of his remaining human arm and sword. The bloodied stump of his shoulder was severed at the joint, removing it entirely from his possession. "You f-fucking bastard!" he screamed through clenched teeth, his voice, baritone as it was, cracked as he said the words.

Even though he was facing away from me, trying to crawl on his belly to escape, I could hear the sound of both tears and spittle fluttering as he shouted. There was a certain, gurgling sound that I chalked up to being a mixture of the two, and I would be lying if I didn't forcefully hide the grin that threatened to show itself.

"I told you that I would kill you, Irun," I began coldly as I stared down at him, hearing Ysevel's footsteps drawing closer. "I purposefully aimed for something I knew wouldn't kill you, but let you know what would happen if you tried to fight again when I severed your forearm," I continued, now beginning to hear muffled words coming through.

"I let you live once because you were my *friend*, Irun. The others here, however, might not be so benevolent. I will let you live again if you swear to never raise your remaining hand against the Continent ever again," I said, adjusting the grip on the hilt of my sword.

Irun spat a wad of blood onto the floor. "You think I'd come back here without a plan?" he said mischievously, a mild, pained chuckle resounding from his mouth. "I didn't come here just to pick a fight, *Lanky*. Gods below, I didn't even know you were here. I came here to *cripple* this country, and take the one thing being used to keep it safe," he gurgled blood as he began to laugh.

What the fuck does he mean by that? Wait, what is Ysevel shouting? Damn it, I can't hear her. Wait, why can't I hear her? I thought, trying to process his words and the ones being shouted at me.

Suddenly, just beneath the two of us, a spiraling circle of runes opened up, leading to a swirling torrent of violet mana. I didn't fully understand what was going on, or why the floor beneath me seemed to feed into an insatiable void. I looked over to Ysevel, who was within arm's length of me at this point, and held my hand out to try to tell her to stay away, but it was no use.

She grabbed my hand tightly.

The three of us sank down into the swirling portal, as we watched the snow-filled world around us disappear; leaving nothing but blood-soaked echoes in the snow.

EPILOGUE
AFTERMATH

*G*o, Siraye commanded. Within less than the time it takes a heart to beat, they had each struck their first targets. Black blood and darkened body parts flew in accordance with their strikes.

It looks like Thoma's going to have his hands full, she thought, severing the heads of three hegraphenes simultaneously.

She pushed forward, making sure that each of her companions were able to handle the enemies that came for them. Within a few moments, everything had gone according to plan, as she was able to single out the largest creature with the plume that protruded from the back of its head.

"I recognize your kind, and know you have the capability for speech. Who are you and what do you want?" she asked plaintively "You know that I can speak, and yet you do not realize that I am far superior to any of the others you or your companions have slain? To say I'm disappointed would be an understatement," Gavar replied, spreading his thick arms widely.

"Before we begin, know that I am Gavar, Lord of the Iron Plume clan of Hegraphenes; the greatest clan in the entirety of the Underworld," he said with a wide gesture. "What I want, however, is nothing I am willing to share unless I deem you a worthy opponent. Give me your name so that I might give you a swift end in return," he said, unsheathing a jagged blade that was nearly the length of his body.

Siraye chuckled as her golden eyes flared. "The mighty *Lord of the Hegraphenes* has already found me worthy of his blade but not his purpose? Fine, then. I am Siraye Fayren, Commander of the Royal Guard and of those that have kept your kind at bay for the last few centuries," she said, drawing her own sword.

"Then you certainly have survived many battles. From one warrior to another, know that I will not judge you lightly, nor will I leave you any room for error," Gravar said, getting into his stance as the battle raged on around the two of them. "I would expect nothing less," Siraye said with an excited yet voracious grin on her face.

A cloud of snow kicked up as the two of them dashed in towards each other. The clash of their swords rang out through the forest, creating a shockwave that knocked a few of the lesser hegraphenes off their feet. "You're stronger than you look," Gravar said, putting enough pressure on her blade to hold it in place.

"After the last battle I had with your kind, I learned very quickly to not even bother conserving my strength," she said coyly. They pushed away from each other, meeting up somewhere else away from the larger group for another barrage of strikes, stabs and parries.

Vyra, Haldir, Ysevel, and Derion had their hands full dealing with the others that charged them. Ysevel's sword cut beautiful arcs of blackened blood through the air, while Vyra's spear quickly found itself embedded beneath the jaw of a creature. Haldir had to retreat a little to make sure he wasn't going to get swarmed while nocking another arrow.

Derion, however, was dancing a fine tune of slaughter and death, the likes of which even his comrades began to question whether he was entirely sane after all.

After having cut two of the creatures down, Ysevel looked for Thoma and Irun, knowing their battle was still ongoing. She *increased the amount of mana in her eyes* to be able to see their signatures between the trees.

He's had to reveal his third stage so quickly? Either he's planning something or Irun really has him on his back foot. His old friend is most certainly hiding something, but I can't quite figure out what it is, yet, she thought, lifting her sword up to block yet another incoming strike.

Meanwhile, Siraye was still battling Gravar, both of them having inflicted minor wounds on each other. The blood from her cuts began to seep through the open spaces in her armor. Another slice came down at an angle which she barely managed to parry. Unfortunately, she was unable to deflect it entirely, as the tip of the blade cut from the top of her eyebrow down to the base of her jaw.

That's going to leave a scar, she thought as she clicked her tongue, wincing through the pain.

Increasing the amount of mana in her body tenfold, she dashed behind Gravar; her eyes glowing intensely as her face was little more than a blurred shadow. Gravar turned just a little too late, as her sword had already found purchase between the thick, chitinous plates that lined his body. She sliced at those seams repeatedly, feeling the edge of her blade bite into sinew and flesh alike, forcing the dark creature to its knees.

She heard a quiet gurgling beneath the chitin that covered the lower half of his face, and allowed herself a heavy sigh. "You were better than the last one I fought. I'm just sad it had to end so quickly," she said, using the point of her blade to tilt the hegraphene's chin up towards her.

"Unfortunately, the last one I'd ended up killing much more quickly. Gods, I wasn't even able to ask it a question before it croaked. Now that you've been beaten, *and* holding out better than the last one, I've got to ask: Why the fuck are you here?" she asked, glaring down at the kneeling creature.

"You've beaten me fairly, and I accept my defeat," he began with a bit of a cough. "I will honor your wish, from one warrior to another, so long as you offer me a quicker death than bleeding out like this," he said, black blood still pouring from his mouth and down his neck. Siraye responded with a simple grunt and a nod.

"We were sent here to collect the *Benevolent Ring*, as there is something the Lord of the Underworld requires from its contents," he said plainly. She hadn't expected him to reveal such an important fact and felt her eyes go wide as she understood what the creature meant. "Gods above," she said, realizing the weight of his words.

"But why tell me that? What reason would you have to betray your master like that?" she asked. "I bend the knee in the presence of powers greater than my own, and the display of power I just felt coming from that young man behind you has shown me enough to know that there is a change in the wind," he said with a gurgle.

"You mean my *son*?" Siraye asked. "*Ah*, is that who it is? Honestly, I probably should have taken *him* on, instead. I would've loved to have seen his true power up close. He would do well among *my clan*," Gravar said, coughing up a little more blood.

"I won't last much longer, and I am no threat to you. Kill me now and return to your son, for our mission has failed here," he said, breathing heavily. "As you wish, Lord Gravar. Thank you for the fight," Siraye said with a curt bow.

In one swift movement, Gravar's head rolled onto the snow covered ground, spilling black blood as it went.

It's been a long time since anything was able to lay even a finger on me without my permission. He did say something about his clan, *though that makes me wonder if they're* all *as strong as him. If so, we're in some pretty deep trouble,* Siraye thought, reassessing her wounds.

"Thoma!" Ysevel shouted. The desperation in her voice gave Siraye a sinking feeling in her stomach. For the first time in over a decade, she felt a familiar sensation beginning to sink in.

That feeling was *grief*.

With a strong desire to be near her son just like on that rainy night nearly two decades prior, she turned to find him. After a few seconds of searching in earnest, she found him standing over a ring of violet runes over a one-armed, disfigured human a good distance away from her current position.

Her eyes widened in shock.

I recognise that mana signature. It's the Underworld's portal mana, she thought, seeing the swirling pattern on the floor with her enhanced eyes. After she calculated the distance between them, she knew her battle with Gravar had taken her a little too far.

Shit, he's going to get sucked into the portal, she thought, dashing towards the trio, a sense of urgency burrowing into her mind.

She saw them sinking deeper and deeper into the ground, just as Ysevel was grabbing Thoma's hand, tears streaming down her face. Siraye felt the entire world slow around her, as she saw the last portion of Ysevel's boot sink beneath the closing portal, leaving nothing but bloodied footprints in the snow.

She came to a sudden halt, the wind from her dash swaying the snow-covered trees in her wake. She looked for any sign of trace-mana to figure out what happened, but there was nothing left behind; almost like they had never even been there in the first place.

"*Fuuuuuuuuck*!" she shouted, kicking the remaining snow where they had just been, falling to her knees shortly after. Derion, Haldir, and Vyra approached her, noticing Ysevel and Thoma's absence. "Where did they go?" Derion asked. "I saw them sinking, but I couldn't figure out what the hell was going on," Haldir said, still coming in at a trot. Vyra kneeled, placing a hand on Siraye's shoulder.

"Where did they go?" Vyra asked cautiously, looking down at the floor where the three once were. Siraye didn't respond immediately, but allowed a single tear to fall from her cheek onto the ground beneath her. "They went to the Underworld," she said after a moment's pause.

Vyra noticed her expression had hardened into what could only be described as *Death* itself. The cold stare and furrowed brow told the spear-caster and her companions all they needed to know about what was going through her head. "We need to send a message from Soule," she said coldly.

Over on the snowy Rhydian Pass, Leona, Thorsen, Gwili, and a few others such as Neko and Marte, made their way down the fork in the road that led to Harut. Gwili, having already noticed a few of his former troupe of bandits shifting in the bushes, rode up to the front of the group.

"Let me take point from here, your majesty," he said cautiously. "Are there dangers up ahead?" Leona leaned in to ask through chattering teeth while Thorsen also paid close attention to what was being said. "Y-yes and no. My former... *associates* are lying in wait for us to cross their path. I'll diffuse the situation and we should get by unscathed, your majesty," he said with an awkward smile.

Thorsen nodded his agreement to Leona, who then gestured for him to ride ahead. With a nod, he spurred his horse to pick up the pace into a trot until he came across the rock he once greeted King Bashir from.

However, there was a hooded figure standing in the middle of the road ahead talking to Wyrran, his former second in command, whom he almost failed to recognize. "Bernar? Is that you?" Gwili called out from a good distance away.

"*Ah*, there you are! Finally!" Bernar exclaimed, turning around to greet them. "I've been waiting for you all for nearly a week, and was about to go looking for you myself," he said, spreading his arms widely.

The rest of the group caught up as he walked towards them, noticing Leona was giving him a warm smile.

Gods above, she's still just as stunning as ever. I'm glad I remembered to put my pendant back on, otherwise she might have mistaken me for someone else. Also, why isn't she talking? he thought, noticing her thick, fur coat wrapped tightly around her in a fruitless attempt to stave off the mountain air.

"What brings *you* out here, though? I know we sent a message to let you and your brother know as a courtesy, but none of us expected to actually *see you* here," Gwili said, dismounting his horse.

"What? You really thought I was just going to let Leona walk straight into a country whose queen is probably trying to kill her?" Bernar asked sardonically. "Not that I don't trust yours or Thorsen's abilities to protect her, but I'd rather not be sitting around with my thumb up my ass and waiting for news," he continued, raising his hands placatingly.

"Well, we didn't mean to interrupt your training with Thoma," Thorsen said with a heavy shrug of his fur cloak. He was speaking in place of Leona who was arguably too cold to even unclench her jaw, let alone speak.

"Thoma has been on an expedition to Soule with my..." he paused, unsure of whether he wanted to mention his mother. "With my good friends in the Caegweni Royal Guard. It's been a few weeks now, and they should be coming home soon with news," he said, adding in a hopefulness to his tone.

"I see," Gwili began. "In that case we should probably continue moving," he suggested. Wyrran, however, gave him an interesting look. "Actually, I have a proposition to make," he said, turning toward Leona and Thorsen. "What might that be?" the giant asked.

"We could add my old companions to our ranks. I trust them like how you trust me, and I know for a fact they won't do anything to betray anyone I deem worthy," Gwili replied, gesturing to those coming out of the bushes behind and around the group. Thorsen looked to Leona who, amidst her shivering, gave him a nod.

"Very well, then. You'll have to introduce us later, as we have to make it to the town at the base of the pass by nightfall," Thorsen's voice rang out throughout the pass. There were a few *whoops* and cheers of excitement in response. "It appears luck favors you, friend," Bernar said to Wyrran, patting him on the shoulder.

Just as the cheers reached their peak, however, Bernar noticed a rider off in the distance.

That's the path I *took to get here,* he thought, realizing it was one of the Caegweni guards.

"Bernar! Bernar Fayren!" the rider called out. "I'm here, guardsman!" he replied with a wave of his hand. The rider came up to the group, recently doubled in size, and dismounted swiftly, grabbing the parchment from his satchel. He ran over to where Bernar was and handed it to him, backing off a little just before he spoke.

"There has been a direct attack on Caegwen. Anwill has disclosed all available details in this report," the messenger spoke as Bernar scanned the parchment quickly. "Vesryn..." he said, reading the names of the fallen which were written at the bottom of the page. "Has any other country been notified of this? Has anyone at Codrean been notified, yet?" he asked urgently.

"They have, but there is another problem that we've just been notified of regarding your brother's expedition," the rider said. Leona, Thorsen, and Gwili immediately paid much closer attention to what was being said. "What *problem*? What happened?" Bernar asked, cocking his head a little to the side.

"Well, you see. There was a message directly from Vyra that was transmitted from Soule. She said that while the expedition was a success on all other fronts, your brother and Ysevel have been missing since the last battle they took part in," the rider said nervously.

"*Missing*? How could they possibly be *missing*?" Bernar asked incredulously. "According to the message, Irun Mothac, the former synner of Codrean cast a strange spell on the ground," the guardsman began carefully.

"Ysevel saw the spell being cast, and went to help him out of it, but she was just a little too late, and ended up getting caught in the spell with him. Vyra, Haldir, and Derion were also unable to help, as was the Commander due to her engaging in combat with a difficult enemy. Thoma and Ysevel; they're... they're gone," the messenger said dejectedly.

"What the fuck do you mean *they're gone*?" Bernar asked, feeling his stomach sink.

AUTHOR'S NOTES

Wellp, that happened.

It's been one hell of a ride to get to this point, and to be honest, I didn't know the book was going to turn out this way until I wrote the chapter summaries (I write those first, then edit the story as I feel it should *really* go along the way). That said, let's get into this.

I wanted to take a different route with this book, and focus more on the interpersonal connections at play with the characters already established in *Weavings of Fate*, while introducing fresh characters into the mix.

The story was originally going to end with Thoma and Siraye being dragged down into the Underworld by Ardrin, but I decided to take a different path towards that end because of how the interaction with Ysevel flowed. I also wanted to explore more of Irun's character in this book, since in *WOF* he was kind of a shithead. Now you know why.

Well, almost the whole reason why, anyway.

In truth, *Echoes in the Snow*, I felt, helped to deepen the connections Thoma has to the world, and add in new dynamics that I could use for later installations. Ysevel and Thoma's relationship is just as important as the Fayren family's. It's vital to his growth, but I wanted that to happen more naturally than how it did with Thoma and Meliss in *WOF*.

Now, I know that some people probably hate me for the way things played out between them, but Meliss was never meant to "last" in that sense. Yes, she played her part in helping Thoma through the challenges, but like the character said, it was a relationship based more out of convenience than anything else. This *situationship* was a key factor in helping Thoma come to terms with his emotional connections to both his friends and family, as allowing him to display that kind of weakness, especially in front of his long-lost mother and new friends, *forced* him to grow.

Does that mean he's fully healed from it? No, but no one ever really forgets their first breakup, do they?

Moving on from that section, I felt this book was an appropriate time to introduce more magic into the fight scenes. I'd heard from a friend that he wanted to see more magic, and I took that personally. That said, however, the magic system in this world isn't meant to be *Harry Potter* or *The Beginning After the End* levels of use, but it's meant to be a *part* or *supplement* to their combat prowess.

For now, at least, as Book 3 (*The Synner: Godfall)* will certainly showcase a lot more of that style.

Everything builds on itself in this world. It's taken me a long time to get here, yes, but trust me when I say that the payoff will be worth it. I know that a lot of you still have questions, or maybe you don't agree with the way things have played out, but there's a reason for everything I'm doing here, so just lemme cook!

I'm sure some of you have *also* noticed that there were hints about certain things *aaaaaaall* the way back in the Prologue of *WOF* that were displayed or talked about here (See *Autarchica Primaria*). To put it simply, and without spoiling anything, the AP isn't *just a power*. I'm not going to tell you exactly what it is, as you'll have to figure that out for yourself in later installations, but just know that, for now and in *Godfall*, this *will* be a factor that comes into play.

I really hope you've enjoyed the story so far, and I can't wait to hear from you about *Echoes in the Snow*, and what your thoughts are on *Godfall* (Book 3). There's a *lot* to talk about in there, but don't worry, it'll have *plenty* of action sequences that will make you realize just how far the story has really come from its humble beginnings.

That's all from me for now, but be sure to follow me on social media (@nooburai) for potential future updates. I suck at using social media in general, as I often lack the time to post much of anything, but I'll try to keep you guys updated as much as I can, provided there's a genuine interest in the updates.

Stay safe, be kind to one another, and remember that you're never alone. I love you all.

www.ingramcontent.com/pod-product-compliance
Lightning Source LLC
Chambersburg PA
CBHW020922020726
47495CB00002B/305